T0385353

GIVE
HIM
TO ME

Also by Dorothy Koomson

The Cupid Effect
The Chocolate Run
My Best Friend's Girl
Marshmallows for Breakfast
Goodnight, Beautiful
The Ice Cream Girls
The Woman He Loved Before
The Rose Petal Beach
That Day You Left
(*previously published as* The Flavours of Love)
That Girl From Nowhere
When I Was Invisible
The Friend
The Beach Wedding
The Brighton Mermaid
Tell Me Your Secret
All My Lies Are True
I Know What You've Done
My Other Husband
Every Smile You Fake

DOROTHY KOOMSON

GIVE HIM TO ME

REVIEW

First published in 2025 by Headline Review
An imprint of HEADLINE PUBLISHING GROUP LIMITED

2

Cataloguing in Publication Data is available from the British Library

Hardback ISBN 978 1 4722 9815 7
Trade paperback ISBN 978 1 4722 9817 1

Typeset in Times LT Std 10.25/15pt by Jouve (UK), Milton Keynes

Printed and bound in Great Britain by Clays Ltd, Elcograf S.p.A.

HEADLINE PUBLISHING GROUP LIMITED
An Hachette UK Company
Carmelite House
50 Victoria Embankment
London EC4Y 0DZ

The authorised representative in the EEA is Hachette Ireland, 8 Castlecourt
Centre, Dublin 15, D15 XTP3, Ireland (email: info@hbgi.ie)

www.headline.co.uk
www.hachette.co.uk

For you. And everything that makes it worth it.

This story contains a storyline some may find triggering.

Prologue
Robyn

28 February, Secret Location

'Hello, Mr Fikowsky,' I say when my former social worker finally prises his eyelids apart.

'Whaaaa—?' he mumbles, trying to remember how to speak.

'You scared me there. I thought I'd hit you too hard or in the wrong spot or something. You've been out for quite a few hours.'

He blinks his bleary eyes and then moans loudly because the pain in his skull has obviously just made contact with every single nerve in his pain centres and they are not playing nicely together. He moves his right hand to his head, trying to check the areas of particular tenderness even though all of it hurts. He realises quickly that he can't touch his head. He can't in fact move either of his hands because he is tied to a chair in the middle of the darkened space we are in.

I watch terror bolt across his face, pooling in his eyes – he's just discovered his feet are bound to the chair, too.

'Who are you?' he demands. 'What do you want from me? I don't have any money.'

'I don't want your money, Mr Fikowsky,' I reassure. 'I want something far more valuable.'

'What are you talking about? What do you want? I demand you let me go. Right now!'

I step into the light then. Allow him to see me, dressed all in black from my skin-tight jeggings to my black T-shirt to my black utility jacket, my hood up and my neck scarf in place over my nose and mouth.

He quivers, properly scared now. Now he feels what I felt every time I knew he was in the children's home. Now he knows what it feels like when someone cruelly exercises the power they have over you.

'Please, please don't hurt me,' he begs. 'Please.'

'That all rather depends on whether you answer my questions in the way I need you to or not.'

'Please, I haven't done anything.'

'We both know that's not true,' I say. 'But we're not here about that. I have some very specific questions. If you answer them, I'll let you go.'

'Please, I don't know anything about anything,' he begs.

'But that's just it – you do. You told me years and years ago that you do.'

I pull down my hood, take my hat off and shove it into my coat pocket, then I lower the black snood from round my face. 'Hello, Mr Fikowsky,' I say with a wide smile.

'You!' he says. 'I know you!'

'You sure do.'

'Untie me this instant! How dare you! Untie me!'

'Weren't you listening to me? I told you very clearly that I would let you go when you give me the answers I need.'

'Untie me, you silly little bitch!'

My shoulders sag. He used to call me that and other stuff when we were alone. He obviously hasn't changed his attitude towards me, so that means we're doing this the hard way. I move out of the circle of light and grab the silver trolley, wheel it into view. I stop it right in front of Mr Fikowsky. It has an array of dental tools as well as a hammer and a screwdriver, a wrench and pliers, and a few other D.I.Y. tools, including a blowtorch.

'I hoped it wouldn't come to this. But you tossing around the B word like that means this is clearly needed.'

I pick up the pliers, hold them right up as I examine them, moving them this way and that, making sure Mr Fikowsky sees them, *properly* sees them. I know the exact moment when he understands what he is seeing, the precise second when all the scenarios about what I might do with them click into place in his brain. I know because that's when he sits completely still, when he stops being angry and indignant, when he stops thinking he can bully me into being fourteen again so I'll comply with his every demand. It's when he becomes very, *very* afraid.

I finally have his full, focused attention.

'Now, Mr Fikowsky,' I say, approaching him with the pliers, 'where the fuck is my father?'

Part 1

Kez

18 March, Brighton

'So, which international agent of mystery will be spilling their guts on your therapy couch today?' my husband asks from the other side of the kitchen. 'James Bond? Whatshisname from *Spooks*? Or I know' – he clicks his fingers – 'is it Danger Mouse?'

I've been staring into space, I think, and haven't offered him even the smallest morsel of conversation since Zoey and Jonah went upstairs to get ready for school. Jeb is obviously trying again to lift me out of the fug I'm in and bring me into the present with him.

'Something like that,' I say with a smile before I take a sip of matcha green tea from the pitch-black mug our twelve-year-old made in DT class. 'Although Danger Mouse doesn't sit still long enough for me to get a proper read on him.'

Jeb smirks, throws down the white dishcloth that he's been wiping the sides down with and comes to the table, pulls over a chair to sit closer to me. 'No, seriously, what are you up to today?'

Without moving my slightly bowed head, I lift my eyes to meet his beautiful liquid brown eyes. We hold each other's gaze for a beat too long, a moment too tense before I lower my eye line to contemplate the pale green-brown liquid that's been rendered black by the colour of my cup. I don't want to say it because it feels like it's the only thing I say to him nowadays when he asks me about my work. But I have to.

'Let me guess: you can't tell me,' he states.

'I'm interviewing today,' I say, deciding to give him something. I hate having to keep things from him. It feels alien, wrong. Since we got together properly over fifteen years ago, he has known almost everything about me. I haven't hesitated to share everything with him. But when I accepted this job at Insight, a government-adjacent organisation of psychologists and profilers, I signed all sorts of documents that make it impossible to be as open with him as usual. And besides, with all the things I've been through as part of this job and my previous, related job, I know that it's better – *safer* – for him not to know. 'It's the final stage of the interviews. We've been talking to them for three months. And this is the residential bit. They're here for three days with all sorts of intense stuff to do.'

'Three months? Must be a big job.'

'Must be,' I mumble into the depths of my cup.

'Do you know who you want to get the job?' Jeb asks.

'As with most things I do, it's more a case of who I don't want to get the job. Or, rather, who shouldn't get the job but probably will because the other people will want that particular psychopath over another, despite what I say.'

'How many other people are there on the interview panel?'

I think about it for a moment. *I can tell him this*, I decide. *It won't make any difference if I tell him that*. 'Seven in total.'

'Seven? That's a lot of interviewers.'

'Well, it's a very high—' *Ah, nope, can't say any more about that*. I shrug in the place of words.

If it bothers him that I've suddenly stopped talking, he doesn't show it. 'What are the other interviewers like?'

'What are they like? Well . . . the lead interviewer is Ben Horson. He's . . . Well, he keeps calling me "Miss" and treats me like I'm only there to take the minutes and make the tea instead of, you know, psychologically profile the person in front of me to make sure they're not too much of a menace to be put into a position of power. And when I do make tea, he never says thank you. To be fair, virtually none of the other men do. They kind of assume either I or Sumaira, the other woman on the panel, will make the tea and they never say thank you.'

'You make tea?'

'Yes?'

'You. Make tea?' Jeb's divinely full lips twitch with amusement. 'I'd pay real money to see that in action.'

'What you implying? I can make tea!' I declare. 'I make tea all the time.'

'Oh, I know you can make tea. I'm just . . . *surprised* you make it for someone who demands it of you, doesn't say thank you and treats you like the help. I'm . . . *surprised* you don't just dash it on their laps and walk out.'

Not as surprised as I am, that's for sure. 'Yeah, well, needs must.'

'And what need is that?' he asks, pointedly.

Can't tell you that, either, I think, so I lower my head a little more closely to the cup I have my hands wrapped around. My morning brew is rapidly cooling, the bitter scent of green tea and matcha disappearing as its temperature drops. 'Sumaira is a funny one,' I say instead. I can talk about the people, just not the job or the interviewees for the job. Or what I've found out that has me sitting here fretting rather than going into the office. 'She's a literal enigma. She seems really demure

9

and gentle, lots of glossy black hair, nose ring, intricate henna tattoos on her hands, but she has some shady special-forces stuff going on in her background – I'm sure of it. And the fact they didn't say exactly which department she worked for, just mumbled something about security and moved on, tells me there is so much going on there.

'And then there's Ed Baxter. He's all right actually. Over the last three months he's actually made me tea.'

'Oh yeah?' Jeb asks innocently, even though his interest has been piqued.

'Yes, dear husband, he's made Sumaira *and* me tea. And has never asked us to make him one, unless we offered.' I side-eye my husband's moment of high alert that there might be another man on the scene. I mean, after being married to me all this time, you'd think he'd credit me with it taking more than a cup of posh Tetley and nice biscuits to turn my head. 'There are a couple of others. Andres Neimeyer is boring as all hell. And he speaks so slowly. I'm always wanting to speed him up. And then there's Lou Langley who never speaks unless it's to demand a cup of tea. That's literally all he says. Even in our post-interview debriefs he just sits there not saying a thing, just pulling faces.'

'They sound like a delightful group. And what about Dennis?'

My entire being – body and mind – becomes rigid, tense, at the mere mention of the man who runs Insight. The man who I'd been forced to make a deal with that saw me going back to work for him as his deputy late last year. I hate his name being in Jeb's mouth. I hate his name being spoken into the atmosphere of our house. I don't want him to infect my home like he has infected my working life. Few things push me right to the cliff edge of sanity, but talking about *him* is one of them.

'What about him?' I ask quietly.

'Is he in on these interviews?'

'He's always in these interviews. Even if he's not in the room for the earlier stages, he watches via a live feed from elsewhere in the building. But today he'll sit in.' Today he'll sit in the corner, not saying anything, just observing.

My tea is cold now and I've lost my taste for it because I'm thinking about and talking about that man. I've known Dennis pretty much as long as I've known Jeb, and how much I hate him is inversely proportional to how much I love Jeb. Dennis Chambers sours everything. *Everything.* I carefully place the cup on the table, return to staring into space. Unexpectedly, Jeb's long fingers cover my hand, a warm, gentle touch that startles me. Our hands – like our bodies and minds – have always fitted like they were created to be together. It sounds soft and a bit woo-woo to think like that, but ever since I met him at a house party back in 1998, I've always thought that he and I were meant to be together.

'Do they have guns?' he asks unexpectedly.

'Why do you ask that?'

'Just curious.'

'They're not supposed to and we're all technically searched before we enter the interview room . . .'

'But?'

'But I've seen flashes of firearms before, so clearly some searches are more equal than others. Although, for the people meant to be doing the searches, they're kind of in a tough spot . . . I mean, if the big boss of one of the top departments wants to carry a gun, are you – Mr Security Guard – going to stop him or are you going to decide you didn't see nuffink?'

Jeb is silent, just nods, clearly disturbed by this revelation. 'Why would they take a gun to an interview, though?'

'Who knows? I suspect it's a silent threat. A show of strength? Like, you know, look at me, I can be dangerous, don't mess? Something like that.'

Jeb is silent again, nodding like before. 'You were whimpering in your sleep again last night,' he says gently, his hand squeezing mine as though trying to comfort and reassure me. 'What were you dreaming about?'

The dream unfurls in my mind: *'PICK UP THE GUN, KEZ!' Brian Kershaw's deathly, ghost-white face screams at me. 'Pick up the gun, Kez!' I shake my head, no. I'm not going to do it. I'm not going to pick it up. Brian's near-skeletal hand grabs my hand, forces it towards the gun that is lying on the ground. It's the gun that has just blasted a hole in his chest, and I don't want to touch it. I don't even want to be near it. 'Pick up the gun, Kez!' he screams. 'PICK IT UP!'*

I force the memory of the dream away and say: 'I . . . erm . . . I don't properly remember.' My husband doesn't need to know that my friend who was shot dead twenty-two years ago has begun to invade my dreams; that every night he comes to see me while I'm asleep and tells me in dif-ferent ways to pick up the gun that killed him. Jeb doesn't need to know that I have no escape, no respite from Brian and how and why he died.

'Kez—'

RINGGGGG . . . My mobile, lying face down on the table beside our hands, intones, interrupting the moment. I withdraw my hand from his, and pick up the phone.

Unknown number calling . . .

flashes on the screen. I check the kitchen clock, the watch on my wrist and the oven clock. All of them say that I should have been in my office, at my desk, over an hour ago.

'I have to go,' I tell Jeb.

'Can you just wait a second?'

'I really can't. I have to go.'

'Kez—'

'Mum, how many GCSEs do you have?' Zoey asks, wandering into the kitchen, closely followed by Jonah. Both of them are wearing uniforms that are too small, Jonah especially looks like an international rugby player who has poured himself into a suit for a formal dinner. I make a mental note to scour the parents' forums to find preloved items that will see them through to the end of the year.

'Why do you want to know?' I reply.

'We were just wondering. Jonah thinks it's three but I think it's four. Or even five.'

'You cheeky mares! I've got ten. Or is it eleven? Well, anyway, it's double figures.'

They both look at each other, clearly not an ounce of belief between them. 'Name them,' Jonah says.

'Name them?' I reply.

'Yes,' my daughter says, 'name them.'

'Come on, Kez, name them,' Jeb adds, smirking.

'Don't you start!' I protest.

'Come on, Mum. If it's all like you say, just name them and we can all go about our business nice and easy,' Jonah states reasonably.

'It was a long time ago, but OK, I've got: Biology, Chemistry, three English—'

'How can you have three English GCSEs?' Zoey interjects.

'Yes, Kez, how?' Jeb ribs.

He and I have discussed this before and he never quite believes me when I explain: 'It's English Language, English Lit and Spoken

English. You had to get your English Language to get your Spoken English, which was a separate half-hour exam. But if you didn't get your English Language, then you didn't get your Spoken English, no matter how well you did.'

Jonah and Zoey look at each other, then at me. 'Nah, we're not having that,' they both say at the same time.

'You don't have to "have it". I've got a certificate somewhere. It's a separate exam. Separate mark. So, where are we?'

'Five, if you count "Spoken English",' Jeb says.

'And, as we have established, we *are* counting Spoken English. Then I have History, Maths, French, RS and one more . . .' My memory fails me. 'Eek, I can't remember.'

'It obviously wasn't Geography,' my son says.

'What do you mean?' I ask, offended.

They all fall about laughing. 'You're so bad at Geography, Mum,' Zoey says, recovering first. 'You never know anything!'

I can't really argue with that, but I try anyway: 'That is not true. I know stuff! I know lots of Geography stuff. Like oxbow lakes and . . . long-shore drift! Coastal erosion!' I'm dragging all of that from my memory of their homework past, of course. 'See, I know Geography stuff. I could well have a GCSE in it.'

'What's the capital of Kazakhstan?' Jonah asks.

I want to shake an outraged fist at him as I glance from one expectant face to another, all of them waiting for an answer, none of them willing to give me a break or a hint. 'Oh, would you look at the time. I have to get to work,' I say, getting to my feet and grabbing my phone and car keys. 'It's a shame I haven't got time to answer your question right now. I mean, I'd love to. But, you know, work and everything.'

'Don't worry, Mum,' Zoey says with a smile that comes from

somewhere intrinsically evil, I'm sure, 'we'll just pick up where we left off, tonight.'

'And no searching it up on the internet,' Jeb says as I kiss each of them goodbye.

'Would I?' I ask, aghast that my husband would suggest such a thing.

'Would you indeed,' Jeb says, receiving my kiss, but holding on to my fingers a little longer after my lips brush his cheek. He hasn't forgotten the conversation we started earlier. I haven't, either, but the difference between us is that while I know it's probably necessary we have it, I also know that we should absolutely leave it alone.

'Capital of Kazakhstan, Mum, can't wait to hear your answer tonight,' Jonah calls. 'Can't wait.'

'Yeah, neither can I,' I call back, wondering how I'm going to find out the answer to stop the Geography shaming that's obviously coming my way.

Robyn

1 January, Secret Location

Just so we're clear, this isn't a confession.

What I am writing here is my last will and testament.

By the time all of this is over, I, Robyn 'Avril' Managa, will be dead. Right now, writing this, I am OK with that. I suppose I have to be. You don't start down the path I am currently on and expect to survive. I have to do this, though.

I have to find my father.

I haven't seen him in twelve years. And I have no clue where he is. I don't even know if he's still alive. There is a group of people who do know where he is. They helped him to disappear and now I need them to help me find him.

I am writing this to give my side of the story. To help you understand why I have to do this. And that's why it's not a confession. A confession means I think I'm guilty, that I believe the ends do not justify the

16

means. That's not true. I have tried in every way I know to find him. I have knocked on so many doors, run so many searches, begged the people I know who could help me, but nothing.

Nothing.

I have to find him. I can't put it off any longer.

So I am going to make the people who could help but won't, help me. By any means necessary.

Let me be honest right here and say that I'm not going to tell you everything. I can't. That's the long and the short of it. There are other people involved that I need to protect. So if anyone finds this before I've found my father, I need to do everything I can to keep their identities hidden and their lives safe. I know that sounds overly dramatic, but that's just the way it is. When it comes to other people, I can't afford to be reckless.

What else is there to say at this moment? Nothing, I suppose, except: before things go too far, or get too out of hand, I hope they give him to me.

I really hope they do.

Kez

18 March, Brighton

I pull into my parking spot in the underground car park of the building where Insight is situated, knowing that even though it's early, I'm late. Which means I have to practically run through security on the ground floor, flashing my pass, and then run-walk-wheeze-pause-run-walk-almost-collapse-get-a-second-wind-run-wheeze up to the twelfth floor.

Insight is a government-ish organisation now located on the east side of central Brighton. I call it a government-ish or a government-adjacent entity because Insight isn't actually, officially a government department. We're based in this shiny, newly established government building in the financial district of Brighton, and our wages are paid from government money, but we're technically an independent group of specially recruited psychologists, therapists, behavioural scientists and profilers who are tasked with assisting the government and intelligence services in many different capacities. Various departments come to Insight for assistance with various problems that no one else can or will help with. Sometimes Insight helps with interviewee evaluation, sometimes with criminal pro-filing, sometimes agent mental fitness assessments, sometimes we assist the police on certain types of crimes. Sometimes we provide therapy for those who are traumatised or emotionally unsettled as a result of their work in the intelligence services. Sometimes we just advise on how to frame messaging of a particular government campaign. We are a broad church operation, with a vast remit, even though, *technically*, we don't exist.

I started working here last October, after I made a deal with the devil that is Dennis. I was in a no-win situation, literally with a gun to my head, and Dennis helped me out on the understanding that I would work for him again. I'd met him when I was twenty-two and recruited to the Human Insight Unit, Dennis's original department in London, and he had done everything he could to stop me leaving when I had decided it was time to be on my merry way out. But after the incident where Brian was killed, Dennis had no choice – he had to let me go. So when, years later, I walked back into his life asking for help, it was too good an opportunity to pass up to force me to work with him again.

I dash into the lower level of the open-plan office with space and banks of desks for forty people. They are all empty, the computers and phones waiting patiently for people to arrive and bring them to life. Dennis is in his glass-walled office, next to mine, and he impassively watches me take the steps two at a time to the mezzanine level where our offices are located. He nods a curt 'good morning' to me as I pass his office, and I pretend not to see it so I can ignore him.

Sumaira Wilson, who I was just telling Jeb about, is sitting on the low yellow sofa in my office when I enter. I met her three months ago when Insight was asked to help with recruiting a replacement head for one of the most secret departments in the intelligence services. The man who originally had the job had lost his wife and children in a fire at the family home and had been signed off long-term sick. Because his family's deaths had been deemed potentially suspicious and were still being investigated, the official story about his departure was that he had been given a position overseas. We were finally at the end of a very long and arduous process, with the final three candidates being interviewed today.

'Sorry, sorry,' I say to Sumaira as she uncrosses her legs and stands in her high, high heels. She smooths down her A-line skirt, pulls her black leather jacket into place and slightly adjusts the large bow of her pink silk blouse that sits at her throat. She then bends to retrieve the box file that was sitting next to her on the sofa. It contains everything I need for today's interviews and she smiles as she goes to hand it to me.

Instead of taking it from her, I hesitate, then I take a step back away from her. Once I take possession of this box, I will be putting myself on a particular trajectory that will be virtually impossible to divert myself away from. Once I take this file, I'll be accepting that I am a real part of Insight, not – as I try to convince myself every day – just visiting until I can somehow escape. Once I take this file, I'll be admitting to myself that I will probably be doing this job for ever, because everything will become set in stone.

'Can I ask you something before you give me this?' I say.

'Of course,' Sumaira replies pleasantly.

'Do you know what the capital of Kazakhstan is?'

She knits together her eyebrows, eyeing me suspiciously. 'Yes, of course. Doesn't everyone?'

'You'd think, wouldn't you?' I say. 'I mean, can you believe there are people out there who don't know?'

'I'll see you in the meeting,' she says, and pushes the box file even closer to me.

I have no choice. I have to, reluctantly, relieve her of the burden. I have to effectively seal my fate.

Robyn

Devoted family man kidnapped, wife killed after armed robbers raid Sussex home

By Ted Hartley

16 July 2012

A 12-year-old girl has been left devastated, feared orphaned, after masked robbers raided her home, killing her mother and kidnapping her father. The girl, who cannot be named to protect her identity, is said to have called the police after sitting with her mother's body for several hours.

Police say the brave youngster told them how her mother had tried to protect her from the intruders, after they tied up her father. The girl went on to say that after killing her mother, the four masked men beat her father and then took him with them when they left.

The break-in occurred while the girl's mother was cooking dinner and the devoted father, 40, was helping her with her homework. Although Mr X is understood to have had a high-level job in a large corporation, police are investigating suggestions that Mrs X, also 40, may have known the armed thugs, who are thought to have been from London.

The young girl is understood to be in the care of family and friends, who have all rallied round and are praying for the safe return of Mr X, described by those who know him as devoted to his family, hard-working and selfless. 'He was a pillar of the community,' said one neighbour, who prefers to remain anonymous. 'This has rocked our neighbourhood and it will take a long time to recover.'

Another neighbour, who also prefers to remain anonymous, added that Mrs X hadn't integrated with the community like her husband had. 'She seemed like a very private person who didn't want to spend too much time around us. I think she missed London and the people there.'

Police are appealing for any witnesses who may have seen or heard anything at the family's semi-remote home in Sussex to contact them on the number below.

Picture caption: Mr and Mrs X with their daughter during happier times. (Faces obscured to preserve anonymity)

A lot of people will know my story without realising it, because names, most photos and the exact location were all withheld to protect me. There was a fear the kidnappers might come back, might try to grab me to use as leverage to get my father to do what they wanted. Or that having seen the story about my family in the press, other kidnappers would attempt to cash in by snatching me. I had to move, I had to change my name and I had to cut my hair. That last part was because I got my mother's blood in it and it was too much trouble for them to wash it out, so they just cut my hair instead.

It's all lies, of course. That story that was published in the papers is nonsense from start to finish. My father wasn't kidnapped; he was there when the first police officer arrived on the scene. And he told that officer a similar version of the story to the one published in the papers. Not the kidnapped bit, obviously. My father told the officer that home invaders had killed his wife and tried to take him. Because of my dad's job, he was immediately whisked out of there to a safe location. After the rest of the police arrived to find the crime scene how it was described in the papers, I was taken to be with him.

Forty-eight hours later, I listened to my father confess to having had what he called a 'psychotic break' and killing my mother during said 'psychotic break', and the people who he confessed to decided to keep the kidnapping story to cover for the fact he'd disappeared and I went into care.

And that journalist guy, Ted Hartley, he wrote my father's initial made-up version of what happened to my mother. Ted Hartley knew it was lies. He sat in a room with my father and wrote the story, so it could be instantly approved by the people who were working on getting my dad into witness protection. He knew it was lies but he wrote it anyway. I'm sure they paid him very well for his efforts.

I've read that article so many times over the years. I know it off by heart but I still read it. I still take in via my eyes the full horror of what it says. Not just the lies and omissions, but the very specific way it lies. When I was twelve and I first read it, I knew something wasn't right beyond it being a pack of lies. I knew there was stuff being said but couldn't decipher what or where my feelings of disgust were coming from.

As I got older, as I learnt to read between the lines of all sorts of things and situations, well, there it was to see: the hint that Mum was involved somehow, that she was in with the 'thugs' and they had turned on her. The framing of my father as an angel who took the time to do homework with his daughter even though he had such a high-powered job. The neighbour – who never existed – who told the world my mum was stand-offish, rude and who preferred rough London over genteel Sussex. The reality was: Dad never spoke to the neighbours. Even if they'd been right next door instead of a fair walk away, like they were because our house had quite a bit of land around it, I'm sure he still wouldn't have spoken to them. He was always sneery and condescending about the people in the village, and he very rarely sat down to do homework with me in all the time I lived with him.

That was all Mum. She would go over to the neighbours, despite the distance, to say hello and bring them stuff she'd baked. She was always entering cakes in the village fete competitions and making them slightly below par so she wouldn't win and cause an incident. She took me to church almost every Sunday, even though people would whisper and stare at the only two brown faces in the village.

They decided to add to the article the formal family photo – Dad at the back, Mum next to him and me in front with Mum's hand on my shoulder – with circles over our faces for one reason only: they wanted everyone to see that the decent, hard-working pillar of the community father was a well-dressed white man, and that the possible gang-connected 'mother' was a Black woman. I was in the room when Ted Hartley said: 'Let's put a picture of them in, tug at the heartstrings, make them realise that the woman could have had gang connections, what with that hairstyle and nails.' By which he meant plaits and nicely shaped nails.

I'm telling you all this to explain that I'm starting with him: Ted Hartley.

It's the logical thing to do. They brought him in to manage our public narrative, to tell this ridiculous story about my dad being kidnapped – possibly dead – and me being cossetted and loved by a whole legion of family and friends. Every few years he'll rattle off a 'whatever happened to Mr X who was kidnapped after his dodgy wife was killed' story and I suspect he does that to make sure they keep paying him for his silence. Oh yes, they kept paying him well after the story was published. So, as I said, I suspect he periodically needs to remind them that he could cause a lot of problems if he ever wrote an exposé about what really happened. I also suspect, since he was brought in so quickly, my dad's story wasn't the first time he's done that sort of work for them. I often wonder if he was ex-intelligence services, who was placed in the media so he could do things like that for them. Either way, those periodic stories tell me that he is in touch with the people running the Protected Persons Service (formerly witness protection). That he knows stuff about my dad.

So he is the one I need to speak to first.

He is the one who I'll try out my new interview technique on first.

Kez

18 March, Brighton

'This is not so much a question, more a comment,' says Ben Horson, lead interviewer, from his place sitting beside me.

We have already spoken to two other candidates for an hour each, and the whole process has been as gruelling for the interviewers as it has been for the interviewees. This third aspirant, Russell Trufton, seated at the centre of the room, facing us, the interviewers, on the other side of the long, solid wood table, is the preferred candidate. He has been since day one. He is everything they were looking for when they began the recruitment process.

Trufton has the background, the schooling and the deep vein of confidence not at all backed up by demonstrable ability, which they gravitate towards. They want him because, as many, many psychological theories tell us – like wants like. They want someone who is exactly like them to do this job. This fella is exactly like them. As I told Jeb earlier, even though, as an experienced psychologist and profiler, I wrote then assessed the psychometric tests all the candidates have taken throughout the process, Horson and his gang have pretty much treated me and my work as perfunctory, a box-ticking exercise to ensure everything *looks* fair because they had already made their decision.

In the corner of the room, sitting silent and still in an uncomfortable-looking chair, is Dennis. When I was first interviewed to train and work at the Human Insight Unit, the original version of Insight back in 1998, he did the same – sat in the corner of the interview room and said nothing. He does that because, behavioural psychologist that he is, he is watching the candidates, making mental notes, deciding what needs to happen next. When all is said and done, although Horson is more senior than Dennis, and technically has the final say, if Dennis decides someone isn't suitable, they will not be employed. Simple as that.

I suspect, though, that Dennis likes Trufton, has been taken in by him just like everyone else. Because of that, everything about this has been very carefully crafted and considered, planned and perfected to give the appearance of propriety. The timing of Russell Trufton's interview, for example, is to make it look on paper that, having spoken to the shortlisted candidates earlier, they went on to choose the person who they spoke to last because he demonstrated all the qualities they are looking for, far and above the others.

Ben Horson tries to hide his smile as he proclaims: 'My comment is that at the conclusion of our process, I think I can say with confidence, there is no reason *not* to offer you the position.'

In response, Russell Trufton chuckles modestly, straightens the knot of his literal old-school tie and says humbly, 'I'm so grateful – and dare I say *relieved* – to hear that.'

Horson, usually-silent Langley, slow-talking Neimeyer and even nice-guy Baxter all chuckle as well, the camaraderie of their laughter filling the room like the wisps of expensive cigars and the aroma of well-aged brandy. Sumaira, who is sitting at the very end of the table, doesn't chuckle. Neither do I.

I know she's waiting for me to speak. And I know, when I do, I'll be setting in motion a cascade of events that I will not be able to stop or reverse. I hesitate, scared. I do sometimes wonder why it always seems to be me who has to do these things? Why I can't simply ignore things and let them pass? Why I can't do what everyone else does and keep my head down? *'Leaving it is an option, you know,' my friend Remi often says to me. And I always have to reply: 'Not for me it's not. It's really, really not.'*

'Mr Trufton,' I say, 'I actually do have a question instead of a comment.'

Ben Horson bristles beside me, unhappy that I am stepping out of my bounds. As far as he and the other panellists are concerned, I am here to tick many boxes – diversity (class, gender and race), as well as psychometric (profiling, psychotherapy and behavioural science) – and none of those boxes involves me speaking beyond introducing myself, much less asking independent, unsanctioned questions.

'Miss Lanyon, the question portion of the interview process is over. I thought you understood that.'

All right, enough now, I decide. Crossly, I rotate ninety degrees in my seat so I am facing Ben Horson. He is older than me, his face lined, his body the product of eating well, travelling in luxury and never really knowing a day of hardship in his life. I am so far beneath him he probably needs binoculars to see me. 'Enough with saying "Miss" like it's a slur, OK?' I snap at him. 'It's completely condescending and really jarring. And anyway, I'm *Dr* Lanyon. But it's interesting, considering the contempt you have for anyone who actually does use the "Miss" title that you would call me Miss when I have' – I raise my left hand – 'the biggest engagement and wedding rings known to womankind.' I lower my hand. 'Also, for someone in the intelligence service, and so high up, too, it doesn't say much about your observation skills that you didn't notice my rings, nor register that I've always introduced myself as Dr Lanyon. Well, it does say a lot about your observation skills, but it's nothing good.'

Horson blinks at me, shocked into silence by my mini tirade. The past three months of me taking meeting minutes in the absence of a secretary, me making tea and coffee like a good little dear, me doing everything asked of me and more, without question, has given him the impression that I am subservient, that I believe, like he does, that I am junior and inferior to him. It has never occurred to him that this is not who I am, and I have behaving in that way for a particular reason. As I said to Jeb, needs must.

With a parting sneer, I spin on my seat back to the interviewee, who is showing mild signs of alarm. 'Now, Mr Trufton, as I was saying, this is not so much a comment as a question.'

Open panic flickers across Russell Trufton's face. His alarmed eyes fly to his ally beside me. Trufton even touches the tie – navy blue with a small, discreet purple crest just below the double-Windsor knot – to ground himself. I'm not supposed to speak directly to him, and he is unnerved because I am. He pleads with his eyes for his kindred spirit to do something. But Horson can't of course. He can't show his bias because this interview is being recorded.

'Do you know what the capital of Kazakhstan is?' I ask.

He double-takes, clearly not understanding why I am asking him this question. I can feel almost everyone else in the room emanating the same confusion.

'Never mind,' I say, 'I'm sure everyone knows what the answer to that is. The question I really want to ask is: how much did your shirt cost?'

More confusion in the room. Trufton frowns at me, but doesn't answer.

'I'm serious, Mr Trufton: how much did your shirt cost?'

'I fail to see what relevance that has to anything,' he replies when he realises that his good buddy Horson won't be stepping in to stop me.

'Good, then you won't mind answering the question, will you,' I state. 'How much did your shirt cost?'

'I'm sure I don't have any idea,' he replies. 'What a ludicrous question and waste of my time.'

'I would just like to know how much your shirt cost.'

'My wife bought it.'

'No she didn't,' I immediately reply. 'You bought it in February of this year. How much did it cost?'

He glares defiantly at me, but me knowing the time period in which he bought his shirt has clearly unsettled him.

'I don't remember,' he says, still defiant but now with a tremor of worry vibrating at the edges of his words.

'Thank you for finally being honest. I'll remind you: two hundred and thirty-four pounds and ninety-five pence.'

'If you knew, why did you ask?'

'To check your honesty, of course. Moving on, how much did your suit cost?' I ask this knowing the eye-watering amount he paid for it. Though, to be fair to him, it *is* a nice, well-cut suit, just like it is a nice, handmade shirt. Both items give him an air of sophistication that contradicts the rest of his carefully crafted appearance and demeanour of a slightly bumbling, boyish rogue, endowed by his messily styled blond hair, flabby jowls and up-late-drinking-expensive-liquor eyes.

'For pity's sake, don't start this again,' he grumbles.

'This will be over a lot quicker if you just tell me how much your suit cost, Mr Trufton.'

'I don't remember,' he spits in disgust.

'Thank you: two thousand, one hundred and thirty-seven pounds,' I

31

reply. 'I have to confess, I was a bit taken aback by how much it cost but I told myself, Kez, it *is* bespoke, it *is* handmade and it *does* suit him – no pun intended – maybe you should back off with the judgey-ness. How much did your shoes cost?'

He all but snarls as he tells me, 'I don't know.'

'Six hundred and seventy pounds.'

'If you say so.'

'Mr Trufton, you are currently wearing nearly three thousand pounds' worth of fabric and leather. And that's before we get to the luxury-brand watch and very expensive cufflinks.'

'I fail to see what business any of that is of yours.'

'And that is the point, isn't it? You fail to see what business it is of mine.' I move aside the box file that Sumaira gave me earlier to get to the pile of papers and folders beneath it. I flip open a beige folder.

'I have here some more information that I am sure you will fail to see what business it is of mine. But let's just go through it anyway. You own a car that was bought new for' – I pause to check the figures – 'one hundred and fifty-five thousand pounds, but for every interview since you applied for this job, you have driven the two-year-old family car that cost less than fifty thousand pounds that you got on lease. Now, you see, I think even someone whose business it *wasn't* to interview you might wonder if you were, I don't know, trying to hide something by not using your "real" car.'

I pause to visually challenge Trufton; he stares warily at me, wondering if I am guessing this information or if I know all this for certain. He glances at the file in front of me, trying to calculate if I do have real knowledge or if I am being a profiler, as he knows I am, and bluffing to get him to expose his secrets.

Keeping eye contact, I flip a sheet of paper over to the next page. It's a small action that taunts him, causes red to rise up his jowls, tenses his whole body.

Horson is frozen beside me, staring at his preferred candidate in absolute horror.

I glance down at the page, run my finger along a line. 'I see that in the last twelve months you have divested yourself of pretty much all of your shares in various overseas companies, you have wound up all the businesses you were connected to that were receiving substantial government funding but were still operating at a loss and you have moved almost all of your property into various family members' names – some of it without their knowledge. Again, I think even someone whose business it wasn't to interview you might wonder if you have something to hide.'

I shut the file before Horson can tear his horrified eyes away from the man in the chair and glance at my file, to see if I do or do not know anything.

'The main problem with all of your actions that point to you having something to hide isn't simply the fact that you did these things – who doesn't tart up their CV or work history now and then? No, the main problem is that you started doing all of this BEFORE the job was advertised. Which does very much point to you having inside information about the job becoming available and when it would be vacant. It points to someone telling you that the job was going to open up and warning you to sanitise your history and your financial affairs before you applied. Isn't that right, Mr Horson?' I say.

'Excuse me?' he responds, outraged. He's not used to feeling like this, to being on the back foot, so the rage flushes his face bright red.

'Isn't it correct that someone told Mr Trufton here to sanitise his background as much as possible before he applied for the job and they would ensure that he had the lightest of light-touch background investigations done, while making sure they sit on the interview panel? Isn't it correct that he was told that no one would look beyond three months of background, but to be on the safe side he should start nine to twelve months before the position was advertised?'

'This is outrageous!' Horson thunders.

Over Horson's shoulder, I notice Sumaira silently get to her feet, her eyes trained on Trufton as she kicks off her high heels. I should get to my feet, too, even though I don't have high heels to kick off. But I don't stand, not yet. My hands are clammy, my breath is ramping up in my ears. The droplet of fear that was with me as I sat at my kitchen table this morning, that grew as I drove to work, that swelled when Sumaira gave me the box file, that expanded even more as I walked into this room becomes a flood. If I get up, then I'll have to do the other part and I want to avoid that if I can.

'It *is* outrageous,' I say to Horson, no evidence of my panic, no signs in my voice of my very real terror. 'It's also treason.'

'How dare you accuse me—'

'Oh, I'm sorry, didn't I make it clear? I wasn't talking about you, Mr Horson. I meant you, Mr Baxter,' I say to the man sitting next to him. Ed Baxter has been pleasant, calm and almost charming throughout the whole process. He has made me and Sumaira coffee and tea, he has bothered to ask us about our day. He has been so completely amiable that it pains me that I have to expose him like this.

At the end of Russell Trufton's first interview, Sumaira and I hadn't directly spoken as we made coffee in the small kitchen, but we'd stared long and hard at each other because we'd both heard it. We'd both heard Trufton say 'the tragic circumstances that led to this position becoming available'. The others had been so high on how perfect he

34

seemed that they'd obviously dismissed those important few words in the thousands he had to share, but to Sumaira and me, unimpressed as we were by him, he gave himself away. No one outside of those in the interview process knew that the position had become available because the person's family had all been killed in a house fire. The official story was that he had been recruited to work abroad. For Trufton to know, he had to have had inside knowledge. And for him to have spent so much time sanitising his background *before* the position became available meant the circumstances of that person's family's deaths really were suspicious: he had been neutralised so that Trufton could take over. Why? I didn't know – couldn't know – why. Just that it was what Baxter wanted.

Without directly saying anything to each other, because we knew everything was being monitored, Sumaira and I decided to investigate the other members of the interview board as well as Trufton – beyond the remit we'd been given. And, while I couldn't do too much without triggering all sorts of questions, I had spent the next few interview sessions and assessments building a profile of him. He was vain, so I researched where his clothes came from. He was arrogant, so I looked at the car he drove to interviews and guessed what sort of car he would *actually* have. He was verbose, so I looked at which companies had previously listed him as a director, which agencies online had him as an after-dinner speaking client. It was all there, in the way he held himself, the way he presented to the world. So, no, I didn't have anything written about him on the papers in the beige file. Everything I said to him had been profiled from his own words; from his belief in his superior intellect – which had given him away time and time again. Trufton was easy to profile. Which meant I had more time to work out from the interviews who was helping him.

That turned out to be quite easy, too. Baxter was nice to Sumaira and me, he was hard on Trufton. Baxter presented as a good, down-to-earth guy, but I knew you didn't get to a position like his, to that top level, without being capable of terrible things. And his department – overseas – meant that there was a lot more to this than we could know.

When I'd worked out it was Baxter, I'd felt my stomach fall away with disappointment. I'd liked him. And that was a reminder that he wasn't necessarily a bad guy – he was just doing a bad thing. But whether or not he was a bad guy doing a bad thing or a good guy doing a bad thing, the net result was, I'd have to deal with him.

When Sumaira handed me the box file in my office earlier, I'd known what lay inside. She was telling me that we couldn't know who would be walking into that room armed. She was also telling me that she was going to deal with Trufton, but I had to deal with the person on the interview panel because she hadn't worked out who it was. That was partly why I'd been hesitant in taking the box file from her. The thought of what she was giving me, what it meant I had to do to someone I quite liked, made me sick. And it also meant, if I took the gun concealed in the box file from her, I was committing myself to this place. I was accepting that I was someone who would sometimes pick up a firearm as part of her job. I did not want to be that person. I did not want that job. But taking the box file instead of walking away very fast meant I had become that person.

All through the interviews, I'd found it hard to pay attention, to focus. What was in the box file caused my palms to become clammy and repeating waves of nausea to rise inside me every time I caught even a glimpse of it from the corner of my eye

*

There's a pause. A moment of stillness as everyone digests what I've just said, and then all hell seems to break loose.

Russell Trufton launches himself out of his chair, ready to bolt out the door, I'd imagine, because he has always profiled as a runner when the heat is on, but Sumaira flips open her box file, pulls out a gun, trains it on him while stepping in front of the doorway.

'Don't move,' she orders before he can properly take two steps.

Almost everyone else in the room freezes, scared in case she turns her gun on them, I'd imagine. Everyone except Ed Baxter, who, even though Sumaira has a gun pointed at his accomplice, leaps out of his seat in an attempt to come deal with me. Horson unintentionally gets in Baxter's way. The pair of them struggle for a bit until he has to pause to shove Horson to the ground. Then he throws himself onto the table, knocking papers and files flying, as he comes for me that way. I push my chair backwards to be out of his reach, but with a wall behind me, there is nowhere to go.

'PICK UP THE GUN, KEZ!' Brian roars in my head. My eyes dart to the box file, to the gun Sumaira had given me, which is on the floor at my feet. *'PICK UP THE GUN, KEZ!' Brian screams again.*

Baxter is a big man who can do me real harm, but he hesitates for a moment when he sees the gun. But then he realises he doesn't care – he needs me gone. I can see the murderous rage on his face, but I am frozen. I cannot use a gun. I can't even pick one up. I can't.

He is in clawing distance of me, and in a moment he will be in reaching distance of the black gun at my feet. And he will use it. He will absolutely use it on me. Self-preservation finally kicks in, and I snatch up the gun, hold it in two hands and point it at him, shouting, 'Stay where you are!'

That stops him, causes him to halt in his tracks. He is still murderous. I can see he is still calculating whether he can get the gun off me and finish me off as he is so desperate to do. He's acting as though it is my fault that he is entangled in some stuff that will probably see him sent down for treason. Like it's my fault he didn't pick a better stooge to install.

Suddenly the air is filled with the thunder of several running feet, and the door is opening, and many people – some in uniform, some not – arrive. Everything becomes a blur, a mass of moving images that happen around me.

Two men tackle Baxter, bringing him down, while someone relieves me of my firearm. I automatically raise my hands to show I'm non-threatening. No one takes the gun off Sumaira – I'm not sure they'd be able to if they tried. Trufton, stupid jelly that he is, looks like he is about to start quietly weeping while declaring everything a terrible, terrible mistake. Now there is no longer a gun trained on him, Baxter starts to try to get to me again, fighting the men who have him on the ground, desperate to come and finish me off. I don't blame him, really. He is going to be investigated to within an inch of his life; he is likely to end up in prison for life. In that situation, I can't be certain I wouldn't also be making like the Terminator and going after the source of my unmasking in an unstoppable fashion.

*

It takes a while, but eventually the room is emptied. The other people on the interview panel have all been led away to be questioned separately. They'll probably launch in-depth investigations into them, no matter how innocent they seem after the questioning. I'm expecting to be investigated as well.

Trufton and Baxter were handcuffed and led away. Not to a police station, I don't think. Before she left, Sumaira, completely unruffled by the encounter, had nodded a thank you at me and I had nodded back. She left then stuck her head back in the room. 'By the way,' she said, 'it's Astana.'

'What is?' I replied.

'The capital of Kazakhstan. It's Astana.' And then disappeared before I could properly thank her.

Only Dennis and I are left in this room that has seen so much drama. He didn't move from his chair during any of what happened. Not the unveiling, not the commotion, not when Baxter tried to kill me even when security arrived. He just sat and watched it happen. Now we're alone, he approaches me where I am shuffling together pieces of paper and files that Baxter had knocked flying when he tried to assault me.

I don't look at him – I simply focus on the task in hand.

'Kezuma,' Dennis says as he stands in front of me, wearing his usual uniform of blue chinos, white shirt, red tie.

'Dennis,' I respond.

'Maybe a warning next time? It would have been good to know what you were planning.'

'You hired me for a very specific reason to do a very specific job, Dennis. I can't do that job if I have to report every little thing to you. So, if that's a problem and you'd rather I left, just let me know.'

He grins at me. Amused by me, on the surface at least, but most probably bubbling under with anger as his type usually do. His type being psychopaths. Proper psychopaths. When I first met him, over twenty years ago, I thought the worst thing he was capable of was sexually harassing me to test my mettle – I had no clue what sort of depths he would plumb to get what he wanted. No clue until I had to make a pact with him to keep my children safe.

39

'That won't be necessary. I do understand why you couldn't tell me what you were planning,' he says reasonably. 'I was just saying I wished I had known. I could have made sure you had the appropriate back-up. But you're right – I did hire you to do a specific job and I should allow you to do it.'

'Good, I'm glad you understand.' I place the last of the blank sheets of paper in the beige file.

'Kezuma,' Dennis says gently, and reaches out to touch my arm. In response, I rip my body away, dropping the files as I leap back to take myself right out of reach.

He doesn't get to touch me. *Ever.* Even if I was in danger of falling off a cliff I'd think twice if he was the only one to offer me a hand to save my life.

Dennis looks momentarily shocked, then hurt. The shock is real, the hurt – not so much. People like him don't feel things. 'Are you ever going to stop hating me, Kezuma?' he asks sadly as he lowers his hand, shoves it in the pocket of his chinos.

I gather the files together again, haul them into my arms. I avoid looking at Dennis these days because it's hard to fix my face enough to hide the hatred. But right now, since he's asked directly, since he's brought it up, I look at him, full on.

'Do you care?' I reply.

He smiles then. And it looks for all the world like a genuine smile. A smile tinged with sadness, but understanding too. I asked him if he cared because I know he isn't capable of caring. He can mimic it, he can have his ego bruised, his pride challenged, but he is not capable of caring in the way I mean. He can't *feel* that emotion.

'Thought not,' I say. My work here, for today, is done.

18 March, Brighton

I know he's watching me. I know that the car park, covered by a network of visible and hidden cameras, is not the place to do this. But I can't make myself drive just yet. I can't sit in my office and do this. I can't go home to the others and do this. I have to do this now. I have to sit and stare at my hands. I have to rub the pads of my thumbs over the whorls and ridges that make up my fingertips to rub away the feel of holding a gun again.

And I know he's up there, sitting in front of the monitors to the CCTV cameras covering the underground car park, watching me, probably getting off on the fact that I am so close to falling apart. I am this close to giving in. That I am not as strong as I make out. That my strength can be diminished sometimes.

I know he's watching me. And I don't care.

Robyn

31 January, Hove

Ted Hartley moved to Brighton seven years ago. He wanted to move to a buzzy city that had lots of writers but wasn't too big, and also had the sea. That's what he wrote on his 'about me' section of his website, and on his email newsletter and his social media group. *'I just need a time out from the London rat race; to reset, recharge, revitalise.'* Yeah, right, and I'm sure your years of taking money for articles from whoever would pay you to write puff pieces about them wasn't about to catch you up, at all, I thought when I read everything he'd written about the move.

I sit at the back of a café in George Street in Hove, watching him sip his double latte with a twist, tapping into the shiny silver rectangle of his laptop. He has one of those monetised email newsletter things that he updates every day with really profound missives from his life. He really is prolific. And full of it. *So* full of it.

Ted Hartley takes his glasses off, rubs the bridge of his slightly hooked nose, returns his glasses to his face and then seems to come to a decision. He snaps shut his laptop, returns it to the expensive all-leather monogrammed laptop bag he always carries over one shoulder with such affected casualness. I don't know why he isn't more embarrassed at himself.

'Cheers, Cherry! Cheers, Jenny!' he calls to the baristas on his way out. They offer him wan smiles as they do every day because their names are Cecelia and Josephine. They used to remind him, but now don't bother because he clearly doesn't think it important to get their names right.

I leave it a couple of minutes before I get up and follow him. I've been watching him for a couple of weeks now, and every day he does the same thing: leaves the café, walks down to the seafront, then along the seafront to get further into Hove, crosses the road and then heads away from the sea, back into Hove. There's an expensive independent off-licence down near what they call Poet's Corner. He goes in every weekday. He spends nearly half an hour impressing (not) the owners with his extensive wine and liquor knowledge, then takes his purchase home to enjoy alone.

'I'd never find anyone to put up with me,' he often writes as a punchline to the tales he tells of his dating mishaps. It's a way of being self-effacing to his followers; he doesn't really believe it. However, it's blatantly obvious to anyone who has come into contact with him that finding someone to put up with him would, indeed, be a challenge. More than a challenge – nigh on impossible, I'd say.

By the time Hartley reaches his home area, which is right at the other end of Hove, pushing towards Brighton, it is well past six thirty. The January dark makes it seem later than it is, and I welcome it. I'm waiting for him at the bottom of the winding, narrow street that leads up from the seafront to Western Road, having parked my car down here earlier. He lives on a road over again when you get to Western Road, and I sometimes feel sorry for him because he's obviously lonely. He obviously fills his hours with working three miles away from home so he can assuage this loneliness. Then I remember how he lied and lied about my mum and I feel my heart harden like granite.

Hartley passes without noticing me. I am standing in the shadows of a mews cottage side return. I am dressed in black, have my hair under my hat, my snood over my nose and mouth, my hood up, my black gloves on.

I've done this a million times in my head.

A million fucking times.

So why am I shaking? Why do I feel sick enough to throw up? Why do I feel like I shouldn't do this like this? *I should just email him again, asking him to please tell me what he knows. Yeah, email him again, Robyn. Give him another opportunity to ignore you. Then to threaten to have you done for harassment. Yeah, Robyn, do that. Do that.*

'Mrs X, also 40, may have known the armed thugs, who are thought to have been from London' jumps into my head and before I know it, I am stepping forward, I am raising my weapon and I am swinging down. I almost miss. He is walking faster than normal so I catch only a part of his head. But he feels it, the touch from my club. He turns in curiosity, which becomes alarm when he sees me. He's about to run

when I bring the club up again, this time catching him on the side of his head. And that's all it takes. One blow to the side of the head and he's out. I pick up his laptop bag, and his glasses, but I leave what looks, by bottle shape and the colour of the liquid seeping out, like whiskey on the ground.

Before anyone appears, I have to work quickly. I unlock my car boot, then hook my arms under his arms and start to drag him. He's heavy but I've done this a million times in my head, too. I've trained for this. I can do this, I can do this. I can drag an unconscious man a few metres and then bundle him into the boot of my car.

One thing I mustn't do, I realise as I get nearer to my car, is think about what I'm doing. If I stop to think about that . . . well, nothing would get done.

Kez

18 March, Brighton

'So, Mum, the capital of Kazakhstan is?' are the first words out of my son's mouth when I arrive home.

The house has a party atmosphere: Jeb is cooking dinner, chopping up the veg into giant pieces that drive me round the bend; Zoey is not in her and Jonah's downstairs office, she is at the kitchen table, her books spread around her with some of them on the floor; Jonah is on the sofa in the corner of the kitchen, reading a novel, while twiddling bits of his hair round his finger. There is music even though Zoey usually likes silence when studying.

I'm so lucky, I decide. *I'm so lucky I have this to come back to. I have this to remind me that no matter what I commit to outside of these walls, no matter how many guns I have to hold, I have these three to keep me grounded.*

'Well . . .' I begin.

'You don't know, do you?' Zoey says smugly.

'Give it up, Kez,' Jeb says. 'Just admit you don't know Geography stuff and we can all move on.'

I turn to my son, waiting for his version of 'you don't know shit, Mum'.

46

'The question is there, Mum, for you to answer.'

'Well, you all of little faith, I happen to know that the capital of Kazakhstan is Astana. So neh, neh, neh!' I point at each of them in turn.

'We said no searching it up on the net,' Jeb says.

'And I stuck to that pledge, oh sweet husband of mine. No internet searches for the capital of Kazakhstan for me.'

'I can't believe you knew the answer,' Zoey says, suspiciously. 'And that you didn't search the internet for it?'

'I did not, oh daughter of mine, search the internet for the answer.'

'What's the capital of Uzbekistan?' Jonah fires at me.

'Tashkent.'

They all look at each other in shock.

'Turkmenistan?' Zoey asks.

'Ashgabat.'

'Whoa!' Jeb says, abandoning his chopping. 'Azerbaijan?'

'Baku.'

'Malawi,' Jonah tries.

'Lilongwe.'

'Finland?' from Zoey.

'Helsinki.'

'Brunei?' from Jeb.

'Bandar Seri Begawan.'

'Sri Lanka?' from Jonah.

'Sri Jayewardenepura Kotte. I can keep going if you want. But I think you should all accept I do know Geography stuff and issue me an apology.'

'Sorry, Mum,' Zoey and Jonah intone.

'Apology accepted.' I turn to my husband, who is eyeing me up suspiciously. He can't work out how I did that when usually I am use-less with country and capital names. It's been a running joke in our house for years – Mum doesn't know countries or capitals except Ghana because that's where my and Jeb's parents are from. 'Anything you want to say to me?'

'Yes. I would like to apologise unreservedly for doubting your Geography skills, although I would still like to know how you man-aged to do that.'

I tap the side of my head. 'Not just a pretty face,' I say.

'You've conned me somehow. I just know you have,' Jeb says.

It's not often I profile my family, but in this instance, my reputa-tion was at risk. I was true to my word and I did not look up the capital of Kazakhstan, but I did look up other countries. Knowing them like I do, I knew they would go for three or four neighbouring countries, then they'd try Europe, then Africa and then Asia. The Europe one would be one that sounded like it came from somewhere far removed from that continent. The African one would be a coun-try a good distance from Ghana. And the Asian one would be one that had a long name that I would have no chance of knowing. I didn't con them, I just went into training. I smile at him and mouth, 'You like that?'

Jeb grins back at me as though he likes pretty much everything I do.

*

'Was it awful?' Jeb asks me in bed later. We've had a wonderful even-ing, the type of night where I could almost forget the events of today. I could almost completely shed that skin and ease myself into the skin of being Kez.

48

'Yes,' I reply. There's no point pretending it wasn't. I can't tell him what happened but I can tell him it was terrible.

'Have you crossed that line, now? The one where you know you can't get out of it any longer and you know you're there properly and not just visiting?' Jeb knows me so well – I forget that. He knows so much about me without me even having to say the words.

'Yes.'

'I'm sorry,' he says. 'I'm sorry that I caused this.'

'You didn't. And I can't talk any more. It hurts.' I hate it when he apologises for this. It was a choice that I made, that I was forced to make, but the final choice was still down to me.

'Where does it hurt?' Jeb asks quietly, thankfully changing the subject.

'Everywhere,' I reply.

Gently, he untangles himself from me, then moves to undo the small white buttons of my nightshirt. 'Do you want me to kiss you better?' he says.

I want him to fuck me. To make love to me in that way that takes my mind off everything. To screw me like he used to. But those moments, that type of sex, doesn't exist between us any more. Now, it's things like this. Soft and gentle, which I need, but I also need the other type as well.

'Yes, please,' I reply.

He starts with the right side of my neck, his kisses so tender they feel like the brush of an angel's wing on my bare skin. I take it back. I prefer this right now. I prefer him to kiss the pain away. And when he's finished, I want him to go back to the beginning and do it all over again.

Robyn

31 January, Secret Location

I sit backwards on a chair, patiently waiting for Ted Hartley to wake up. When he does, it's easy to see how much pain he is in. It's easy to not feel sorry for him, as well. Oh, I feel bad for him in an objective sense, like I feel sorry for anyone for whom things have gone horribly wrong, but like before, reminding myself of what he did is enough to act like a flood barrier and hold any guilt at bay.

Clumps of his wavy brown chin-length hair are stuck to the still-bleeding gash on his temple where my weapon connected with his head, splitting and peeling back the skin. It looks excruciating.

'You really are one of the most unpleasant people on earth, aren't you?' I say to him as he continues to come round.

He jumps when he sees me, what with my face being covered and my hood being up. I have been holding some press clippings while I wait for him to awaken, so we can discuss the story he wrote about my family.

'Who are you?' he groans. He hasn't yet discovered he is restrained – wrists secured with zip ties and rope to the arms of the chair, ankles zip-tied twice individually to the legs of the chair. I've gone overboard on keeping him immobilised because I will not be able to fight him for very long if he gets free before I've found out what I want to know.

'I'm the . . . what was it you called me in your last email? Oh yes, I'm the "delusional little runt" who dared to think she could "question one of the country's most eminent and successful journalists".'

Hartley discovers he's tied up at that exact moment, when he tries to move and can't. He tries a couple more times, but realises he is securely bound.

If he remembers saying those words to me via email then he does a very good job of hiding it. He looks confused, properly perplexed. 'I don't know what you're talking about,' he says, his agony making his speech long and drawn out.

'I'm talking about some of your greatest journalistic hits,' I say, ignoring the modicum of doubt creeping in because he genuinely sounds like he doesn't know what I'm talking about. What if it wasn't him emailing me back? What if it was an assistant who took it upon themself to tell me to go do something unpleasant to myself and they replied without any input from him? No, no, it was him. I'm pretty sure it was him . . . Pretty sure . . .

I hold up the collection of papers in my hand so he can see. Some are the original clippings, others are printouts. 'Most journalists say they don't write the headlines for their articles, especially if they get dragged for it, but I know you do. You've said in your newsletter and blog so many times that you don't allow anyone to change your headlines because you will always stand by the integrity of your words. You will always believe what you have written is right.' I pause to look at him and he seems clueless as to what I'm talking about. I plough on: 'And you are master of the passive voice when it comes to men's violence against women, aren't you?

'You always seem to find just the right words to downplay and minimise any situation where a man harms a woman or girl, don't you? You always find a way to cast aspersions on the character and purity of the women involved to make it seem like they somehow deserved it or brought it on themselves. It's quite something. I mean, look at this—' I hold up one of the cuttings. '"Heart-breaking sobs of devoted family man as jury reaches verdict in trial on his family's deaths" . . . I mean, yes, I feel for him – who wouldn't after that headline? Let's ignore the fact he killed his family because his wife took their youngest child to the doctor and forgot her phone so he decided she was having an affair. Let's ignore the fact he killed her and their three children in a particularly brutal way and instead, thanks to you, let's focus instead on how "heart-breaking" his crocodile sobs are when he is found guilty of brutal murder.' I pull out the next headline. '"Off-duty officers convicted of sex with young woman in back of police car". Again, killer headline. But let's break it down by reading the article and, oh, oh, here we go, they were off duty because they left her in the back seat of their car and took it in turns to go in and clock off. Oh, what's this, she was on the at-risk register so already vulnerable and, oh, wait, yes, there we are, she had turned fourteen on the day they picked her up, so underage. So, not only was she not able to consent to sex, especially with two adult men, but they were abusing a child. Who would have guessed it from your headline and the slant of your article?

'And what do we have here? "Olympic marathon hopeful dies after being hit by motorbike". Her abusive ex-husband chased her down and ran her over. "Home Office agent arrested on suspicion of involvement in prostitute deaths". None of those women were in fact prostitutes – you just conjured up this idle speculation because they were vulnerable Black women. But even if they were, how does that detract from the fact he actually killed five women before he was accidentally caught? How does that excuse his crime? And here, this one, "Devoted family man turned to sex with underage girls after marriage broke down". Where to start with this one – this man groomed his daughter's friends for sex and molested the ones he couldn't groom when they came for sleepovers. But sure, let's blame it on his marriage breakdown.'

It's obvious from the nonplussed look on his face that Hartley doesn't have a clue what's wrong with anything I've just read out. He doesn't seem to understand that the way he wrote those articles and headlines were just ways of absolving terrible men of responsibility for their criminal behaviour. Or maybe he does get it, but still doesn't see anything wrong with what he did.

I push back my hood, remove my face covering, take off my hat. He looks at me like he doesn't recognise me. And I'm sure he doesn't. I look like my mum now. She didn't have large corkscrew curls like I do, but my skin is almost as dark a brown as hers, and I have her broad nose, mouth fullness and eye shape. I'm like my mum and that is one of the things I'm most grateful for in how I look. I wasn't allowed to take any photos – or *anything* – after we left the house that night she died, so I don't have any pictures of her. I don't know what happened to those things, what they did with everything when they cleared out our family home. Just that I don't have any of them.

'Who are you?' he asks, clearly confused.

'I'm the brave little girl whose mother was killed and whose father was kidnapped after a home invasion, back in July 2012.'

Horror flashes up in his eyes – he remembers. How could he forget? After all, he does receive £400 a month from an unknown source, these payments beginning back in July 2012. (It was relatively easy to hack his home computer where he stores all his banking information and statements.)

'Look, 2012 was a long time ago. I don't remember writing that story,' he states. Gosh, how smoothly and believably he lies.

'Wow. I've always thought over the years, even knowing how lie-packed that story you wrote about my family was, that you couldn't be that big of a truth-twister in real life. Thank you for proving me wrong. Thank you for showing me you are just a massive, massive liar.'

'No, no. I think I might remember something. Vaguely. What do you want from me?'

'Information,' I say simply. I drop the newspaper clippings and leave the circle of light that surrounds us, so I can wheel my trolley of tools even closer. 'I need you to tell me everything you know about my father and witness protection.' I pick up an old-fashioned steel tooth extractor. It's dramatic-looking, the head twisted at a ninety-degree angle at the top, with big serrated teeth. 'And before you say you don't know anything, I know you do know something. And I will be more than willing to use every single one of these tools to make sure every bit of information that is there in your brain is revealed.'

His eyes are fixed on the tool in my hand. That's the problem when you tell your followers and blog-readers and the world in general intimate, private things about yourself to get and maintain a following – you make yourself vulnerable by sharing far too much about yourself, which is how I know this guy is terrified of dentists. This tool, if I use it on him, will add an extra, petrifying dimension to this. From his face, I can tell just the idea of it is painfully terrifying.

'What's it to be? The easy way, where you tell me everything you know? Or the hard way where I use this?' I move the tool closer to his face. 'As you can imagine, I'm good either way.'

'I'll tell you everything I know,' he says, breaking down into quivery tears. 'Everything. I'll tell you everything.'

Music to my ears. I'm grateful he didn't decide to tough it out, because it would have been difficult to inflict any more pain on him. I would have, obviously, but it would have been challenging.

In a twisted way, I'm grateful to him for not making me do it.

Part 2

Robyn

Beloved veteran journalist murdered in own home

By staff reporter

Top journalist Ted Hartley, who worked on several national newspapers, as well as founding the very successful newsletter, 'The Hartley Of The Matter', was found dead in his home yesterday lunchtime following a police welfare check after no one had heard from him for ten days.

Mr Hartley, who was confirmed dead at Brighton General Hospital, is thought to have been tortured before his death and may have died as a result of his injuries. A source close to the investigation said a note was found pinned to his chest, but police are keeping the exact contents of the note confidential at this time. Mr Hartley's wider family have been informed of his death and funeral details will be shared when more information is available.

Several colleagues openly mourned his passing on social media, with one saying he was 'a top bloke, who was really quite brilliant at what he did'.

Police are treating the death as suspicious and ask that anyone with any information related to the crime call the number below.

*

I can't believe Hartley is dead. I didn't think I'd hurt him enough to kill him. I thought he'd be fine. I gave him his phone and computer back. Why didn't he call for help? And why didn't anyone notice he was missing earlier?

That's the problem with someone like Hartley – sure, *now* they're all saying he was a top bloke, but no one actually liked him enough to keep in touch with him properly. If they had, he might have got help before this happened.

I feel sick. I can't believe I did something that led to someone's death. If it wasn't so important that I find my father, I would try to explain to the police what happened. That I didn't mean for him to die.

I can't do that, though. I just have to be careful from now on. I just have to take them to the brink, but make sure they're found in time so they can get help.

Actually, I *am* going to be sick. I am.

Robyn

16 February, Brighton

My father always said my mother was the most beautiful woman he had ever seen, that she was the love of his life. He also used to say that for as long as he lived he would always love her. I think – actually, I *know* – he meant it . . . right up until the moment he killed her.

I won't ever know when their relationship started to unravel. Mum's not here to tell me, and neither's Dad, in a way. Dad used to talk all the time about how he first saw Mum when they were at Oxford Uni and he turned to his best friend and said he was going to marry her one day. So, on that day, he set out to win her heart, to make her his, but it was years before it worked. He didn't manage to convince her to go out with him until their final year. Mum always used to smile and not say anything when he told that story. Away from him she confessed that she hadn't actually liked him when she first met him. He seemed arrogant and full of himself, wouldn't take no for an answer, didn't ever consider what she wanted in any situation. She didn't say it out loud, but he wore her down. What she did say to me more than once was, 'Never let anyone encroach on your boundaries. Once you shift them to accommodate someone else it's incredibly difficult to push them back out again.' I had no clue what she was talking about at the time. But I remembered what she said because it seemed important to her.

Ted Hartley was actually really helpful. He gave me information that allowed me to connect the dots on other people I need to speak to. He gave me confirmation on a couple of names that I have on my list. He also told me that the £400 he received every month was essentially hush money but also payment to make sure he would tip 'them' off if anyone else came sniffing around the story. 'Them' being an email address.

His face had been a picture when I explained that by my calculations, he had made over £50,000 from my father murdering my mother and how that was a problem for me. His face became an absolute tableau when I told him to transfer all that money to a charity that looks after abused women. After he claimed not to have it, I used his facial recognition and fingerprints to get into his phone to check all his bank accounts and he had £45k across all accounts that we could immediately access. After a bit of *persuasion*, three different charities woke up £15k better off the next morning.

One name he gave me that I hadn't quite remembered was this guy: Gene Talamon. I remembered him, but couldn't recall his name.

I'm sitting at the bus stop at Old Steine, the large patch of green in central Brighton, surrounded by a busy ring road that leads to different parts of the city. They've changed the configuration around here so many times that driving around it has become an extreme sport of throwing yourself into the system and praying that you'll spot your exit and be in the right lane to reach it at the same time. From the bus stop I'm watching Gene Talamon smoke outside the big old pub on the corner of the road opposite the one-way system. He comes here every Friday night. He has a wife and two young children, but he comes out every Friday, whether his friends are here or not.

When he leaves, he'll cross all four roads of Old Steine/Grand Parade and head up to Edward Street, past the new hospital, then on towards the Marina. There's an area between the hospital and the Marina that is quiet and so a perfect place to pick him up, which is why I've parked my car up there. I'm hanging out here a bit longer to double-check nothing has changed with his plans, though.

Gene Talamon is a police officer. I met him when I was nine and my mother walked into a police station to tell them her husband was abusing her. Gene Talamon was the person they assigned to talk to her.

May, 2010

'I would like to speak to a police officer, please,' Mum said to the woman behind the desk at the police station. We'd had to take a taxi from near Pitchingfield to Horsham because there wasn't a police station in the village.

Mum had to bring me with her because it was half-term.

'What is it regarding?' the woman behind the counter asked. She wasn't very friendly-looking or acting or sounding.

Mum looked scared for a moment, then she said in a strong voice: 'I need to talk to someone about my husband and what he's been doing to me.'

The woman kind of nodded her head, told us to 'wait over there' on the plastic seats and then picked up the phone to talk to someone. About twenty minutes later, a tall man with a wide frame, brown hair and brown eyes appeared. His cheeks were quite red, like he'd been running or something.

'This way,' he said in an unfriendly tone.

Mum got up and so did I. 'Sweetheart, could you stay here a moment while I go and talk to this nice man?' Mum said.

I was suddenly really scared. I could tell Mum was also scared by how tightly she was holding my hand, but she was being brave, too. She was brave and determined to do this. There was no way I was letting her do this on her own. I clung to her hand and shook my head at her.

'OK, OK,' she said. 'You can come with me.'

The man led us to a room with a table and four chairs and a tape recorder on the table. 'Take a seat,' he said. Again, not sounding friendly or kind, like I thought police officers were meant to.

I sat in the chair next to Mum. The police officer slapped a notepad down on the table, clicked the button at the end of his pen and held it to the paper in front of him. 'Name?' he demanded.

'Erm . . . Rose. Rose Managa.' I knew without really knowing why Mum had used her maiden name instead of Dad's surname.

He wrote it down, misspelling the surname but Mum didn't correct him.

'What can I do for you, Rose?' he asked. 'They said it was about your husband?'

'Yes. My husband, he . . . he abuses me.'

'What do you mean by abuse?'

'He pushes me, he pinches me sometimes. He shouts at me. Comes right up into my face and screams at me. Threatens to kill me if I do something wrong.'

'Pinches you? Pushes you? So he's never actually hit you?'

Mum took a deep breath, looked at me, then looked back at the man sitting opposite us. 'Yes, yes he has. Several times.'

'With his fist open or closed?'

She stared at the centre of the table as she said, 'Both.'

The police officer wasn't writing anything down. 'When did you come to this country, Rose?' he asked gently.

'What?' Mum said, looking at him through slightly narrowed eyes. 'I was born here. I was born in London. I'm British.'

'What about your husband?'

'He was born here, too.'

He nodded, the red that had been sitting on his cheeks was starting to spread down his neck. 'You see, Rose, isn't it common in your culture for men to not treat women very well? You know, they think it's normal to knock the missus about a bit?' He opened his hands as though that was going to get Mum to agree with him. 'I'm not saying it isn't bad – it's just a cultural thing that I'm not sure we can do anything about.'

'My husband is a white man who was born in the Home Counties,' Mum said, sounding disgusted with him. 'He went to private school and studied at Oxford. He's the head of a big corporation that has government contracts. Is that the culture you mean?'

'Calm down, calm down,' he said, sitting back.

I didn't know why he was saying that – Mum sounded disgusted, not angry. She hadn't even raised her voice. Why was he telling her to calm down?

'I was just asking questions, there's no need to get aggressive,' he added.

66

I was so confused. Being aggressive meant shouting and raging and being threatening. Being aggressive was what Dad was like all the time. Mum was never aggressive. And she wasn't being that way now. But the way he said it, with such conviction, I wondered if I had got the meaning of aggressive wrong.

'I understand you must be very upset to have come here today, Rose. Do you think you might be being a little oversensitive? Maybe misunderstanding some of the things your husband says and does?'

Mum didn't say anything, she just stared at the table.

'Marriage is hard. I mean, me and my missus, we get into some real humdingers. If you talked to her, I'm sure she'd have a thing or two to say about me. Do you think your husband loves you?'

Mum nodded her head.

'Well, then, you owe it to him to give it another try. Maybe try not to wind him up as much. Get yourself something a little silky, keep him occupied. If you keep his mind on the bedroom, it leads to less arguments in the kitchen.'

Mum immediately stood up. 'Come on, Avril, we're leaving,' she said, and shot the policeman a really filthy look.

'Fine, fine. Just trying to help.'

Outside the police station, Mum took several deep breaths in through her nose and out through her mouth.

'We can't tell your father we were here today,' she said to me. I already knew that. I might have been nine years old, but I knew Daddy could never know about this. 'Let's go down to the high street,' she said. 'I think there's a pottery café there. You can make something.'

16 February, Brighton

Gene Talamon could have helped my mum. He could have helped her to escape. But no, instead, he was racist then he was creepy. He went on the list of people I needed to target not because of that meeting with Mum, but because he was there the night she died. I don't remember seeing him, but according to Ted Hartley, he was there. And when he was writing up his piece, he'd talked to Talamon, who told him that Mum had got aggressive when he suggested that she try to be a bit nicer to her husband. It was Talamon who suggested that the police were going to investigate whether Mum had any gang affiliations. This was all *after* they knew that it was Dad who killed my mum. They all knew, but they all tried really hard to find a way to make it Mum's fault. Hartley gave me Talamon's name because he was sure Talamon knew more about my father's journey into witness protection than he should have – Hartley said there was no real reason for Talamon to spend so much time at the safe house, they could have just erased his limited files. I couldn't know for sure if Hartley was just trying to throw other people under the bus, and I might, in the end, have to use the tools on him to make sure he was telling the truth. But there is a whole galaxy of people who let Mum down, and I'm not going to go after them all. I might want to. I might want some kind of restorative justice, but I'm only going to focus on the ones who might know where my father is. No one else.

Talamon stubs out his cigarette, but rather than head back inside, he drains his pint and then slots his phone and keys into his pocket. He's leaving early. That's a pain. That's a huge pain. I wonder if he's meeting someone?

Rather than go to the lights to cross the road, to come closer to where I am, he turns and starts to head towards the other part of Brighton where the Lanes are.

Damn! I get up from my seat, pull my hood up and go to dash across the road. Even at this time of night it's busy and I have to wait for several cars to go past before I can get to the side of the road where Talamon is. He's disappeared into the dark side road near the pub, and I have to move quickly. I can't see him as I turn into the road. He can't have disappeared, he can't have got up the road – I sense the movement before I see it, a blow from the shop doorway. I step backwards, out of reach and Talamon falls forward, unable to stop the momentum of his swing.

'Who are you?' he shouts, righting himself. 'What do you want?'

I have to twist out of the way while stepping back to avoid his second swing. I've only just learnt how to properly fight an opponent and the main lesson I learnt was to avoid getting into a fight with an opponent.

'I've seen you following me. What do you want?' he demands.

69

He throws another punch, but I'm not quick enough to avoid it and it connects with my stomach. I stagger back, winded, hurt. I'm resting against the front of one of the little mews houses that populate this road, unable to move.

Talamon comes for me again, and I just about avoid his punch aimed at my face but not the next one he delivers to my ribs. 'What do you want?' he shouts.

I'm still winded and clutching my stomach; my side is on fire, feeling like it is collapsing in on itself. The road is narrow, the pavements narrow, too. This is one of those roads in Brighton that I've always been awed at them being able to squeeze in so many properties. It means, though, I don't have space to escape from this man's rage.

'Who are you?' he shouts again. I have to get away. He's a big man, but he looks unfit and with the booze and cigarettes, he won't be able to keep up with me if I run.

Summoning up all my rage, all my strength, all my hatred of him, I launch myself at him. My whole body weight comes up against his solid form and I manage to push him back and away, so I can run. Shocked at being shoved with force, Talamon stumbles backwards into the road . . . then has a second to come to a standstill before the car that has just flown round the corner hits him.

I jump. Watch in horror as he is thrown up in the air before landing several metres away from the car. The car screeches to a halt, the young male driver looking horrified by what has just happened. He took that corner too fast; he didn't have time to brake or decelerate – there was nothing he could have done to avoid hitting him. There was nothing Talamon could have done to avoid being hit.

I should try to help him. But I can't, not properly. If I stick around here, I'll be caught and that can't happen. I hate to do this, I hate to leave it like this, but I have to. I reach into my pocket, take out the note I was going to eventually leave and, still clutching my middle, I walk over to where Gene Talamon is lying.

His eyes are wide open, but he is moving so he's not dead. Blood trickles from his mouth and nose. I bend down, reach into the pocket where I saw him stash his phone. I pull my snood up over my mouth and nose before I dial 999. I ask for an ambulance, give them the road name and minor details. 'Please hurry,' I say. 'Please.'

I then unfold the note, place it on his chest, before leaving on top his still-connected phone. The driver has finally got over his shock enough to climb out of his car and is coming towards me.

'What are you doing?' he asks.

'Calling an ambulance,' I say before I get to my feet and then start to run. It's hard going at first. Talamon really hurt me when his punches landed, but the thought of being captured before I find my father spurs me on and soon I find a gait that doesn't cause huge amounts of pain to spike through me. Soon I'm able to run and I dart down different roads until I can get back to where my car is parked.

The note I left is the same as the note I left with Ted Hartley. It's the one I plan to leave with everyone I talk to. It's very simple. And it's for a very specific set of people. They are the ones who can give me what I want. They are the ones who know what I mean when I write:

GIVE
HIM
TO
ME

Part 3

Kez

22 April, Brighton

'Kezuma, come in and shut the door,' Dennis says to me when I put my head round his door. He has just instant-messaged me to come into his office for a moment. I had no idea he had a guest – Ben Horson from the interview disaster a few weeks ago.

Horson, who is installed on the sofa to the right of Dennis's desk, frowns at me and I realise that I was probably meant to knock before I entered my boss's office, but that's not something I do with Dennis. Ever. I probably should, but I don't. I only ever come in here if Dennis asks me to, so he knows I'm coming – why would I knock?

The frown, Horson's presence, makes me hesitate. Do I really want to rehash the disaster that was the Trufton interview? It was a nightmare, it had ended badly and Horson had had to endure a few uncomfortable hours being questioned about what he did and did not know. What else is there to talk about? I honestly don't have the energy for this. I'm formulating a meeting that I can tell them I desperately need to be at when Dennis says, 'Please, Kezuma. It's important.'

It's the please that does it. I could count on one hand the number of times Dennis has said please to me. Well, actually, on three fingers.

Once I am installed in the chair opposite his desk, my profile to

Horson, Dennis says, 'What I am about to tell you cannot leave this office in its entirety.'

I try, and probably fail, not to roll my eyes. *More espionage bull-shit*, I realise. If I don't have energy to rehash old disasters with Horrible Horson, I certainly don't have the energy to be dragged into Dennis's latest spy fantasy.

'We will be telling the team and everyone else a version of what I'm about to tell you,' Dennis says. He stands to hand me an unremarkable beige cardboard folder. 'Do you remember the Managa case from twelve years ago?' he asks.

I search my memory briefly to see if I remember but I don't. Twelve years ago I was dealing with a toddler, a boisterous teen and had just had my second baby. I couldn't remember my own name, let alone worry about what was happening to anyone else.

I shake my head. 'No.'

'They weren't called Managa but I'm using it here instead of X for ease. The Managa family were a mother, father and young daughter who lived over near Horsham. One evening a masked gang carried out a home invasion that left the mother dead, the father kidnapped and the daughter traumatised and barely able to communicate. The father was never heard from again.' I open the file in my hands and on top is a newspaper article from that time. The image has the family's faces obscured. Below the article is a 5x7 version of the original photo. In the photo, the family look happy enough. The father is a respectable-looking white man with dark brown hair, and light-coloured eyes. The mother, who stands beside him, is a beautiful Black woman, with shoulder-length plaits and a radiant smile. Every-thing about her smile is too much, too bright. She has her hand on the shoulder of their daughter who stands in front of them. The daughter

76

is staring at the camera and smiling, but her smile does not match the look in her eyes. If I didn't know better, I'd say this photo had been taken after what had happened to her parents, not before. She looks haunted, despite the sweet-girl smile that creates dimples in her cheeks.

'I still don't remember,' I confess, pulling my eyes away from the traumatised girl with curly pigtails.

'That's actually very helpful,' Dennis says. 'It means you will look at this case with fresh, untainted eyes.'

I glance at Horson, find him watching me intently, his disdain apparent on every part of his lined face.

'Do you want me to go over the case because new evidence on who the father's kidnappers are has come to light?'

'In a way . . . This is the part that cannot leave this room, Kezuma. The repercussions would be untold and catastrophic.'

'OK.'

'The father's kidnappers were in fact, us. Well, the government in a way. Mr Managa is in the Protected Persons programme. Previously known as witness protection.'

'Just him, not his wife or child?'

Dennis looks uncomfortable, which immediately chases wary goosebumps up my spine and along my arms. 'Not his wife or child. The events detailed in the paper are not an accurate reflection of what happened. There was no home invasion.' I look down at the article in front of me. 'Mr Managa was actually the perpetrator of the crime that left his wife dead.'

'You mean, Managa was an abusive man who killed his wife? Probably because she was about to leave him?' I clarify. I feel Horson bristle and I shoot him a look so poisonous, he knows not to contradict me on this. Managa was abusive, that is why his wife looks like she is wearing a mask, and their daughter is traumatised.

'We don't know he was an abusive man, per se,' Dennis responds. 'It's likely there was abuse in the household. But we don't know who from. Mr Managa explained that there was an argument that evening in July 2012 and that he snapped. His explanation and description of what happened that night is a classic case of disassociation. Simply leaving his mind and body and making the horrific discovery of his wife's death when he became "conscious" again.'

The bullshit of every word of that could not be more evident. Dennis knows that. And knows I will not fall for any of the nonsense he has just spewed. 'If that's the case, then everything's cool, yes? Managa is living the sweet life in witness protection. Why do you need to tell me about it?'

'He isn't living the sweet life,' Horson interjects, a snarl so deeply scorched into his voice, and scored into his features, anyone would think I was talking about him. *Have you ever thought of getting help for your chronic case of projection?* I desperately want to say but don't, because I suspect Dennis will pull me up if I do. 'He has not been able to contact anyone from his former life. He had to leave his very successful career, his home, his family, friends, community – his whole life was destroyed because of that one solitary incident.'

'The incident being the one where he murdered his wife?' I reply. 'The one solitary incident being the one that he avoided going to prison for, when most people would be locked up for life? That incident?' I turn back to Dennis. 'What happened to his daughter? There's been no mention of her so far.'

'His daughter is the reason why I need you on this.'

'Go on,' I say cautiously.

'His daughter, Avril, or Robyn as she is now called, has decided she wants to see her father. We believe she has been kidnapping and torturing people to get the attention of those running witness protection.'

'How do you know this?'

'The people she has hurt so far were all connected to her father's original case.'

'That could be a coincidence.'

'It's not. On each of the bodies she leaves a note that says, "Give him to me".'

'Bodies?'

'Yes, she has killed three men. The fourth was found dead this morning. She's escalating. And we need you to get into her head as quickly as possible so we can find her before she kills again.'

Robyn

When the waitress with bright orange hair and shiny red lips put the doughnut down on the table in front of me, I felt my eyes grow large. It was the biggest doughnut I had ever seen. Fluffy and brown and topped with cracked white glaze. Inside was smooth yellow custard.

When she placed the white cup of hot chocolate with squirty cream and marshmallows on top beside the doughnut, I licked my lips. We hadn't done this in ages and ages. I knew Mum had been saving as much money as she could so we could walk down into the village during the summer holidays for a treat near my birthday. The waitress placed a tall glass of tap water in front of Mum and asked, 'Are you sure that's all I can get for you?'

'Yes, thank you,' Mum said with a smile. 'I'm watching my figure.' She patted her slim, actually skinny stomach and made her smile even wider.

'There's not a pick on you,' the waitress replied, waving her hand dismissively. 'Not a spare ounce anywhere.' She smiled at us and then went back to her counter. My eyes couldn't decide which deli-cious thing to try first – the doughnut or the hot chocolate. Hot chocolate or doughnut?

I went for the doughnut first. Used two hands to bring it to my face, bit into it, feeling the thick glazing crack and my teeth sink into the soft pillowiness beneath it. It tasted even better than it looked. A hint of custard oozed into my mouth and I had to lick my lips as I chewed. I closed my eyes, the sweetness and texture making me feel like I was floating. I put it down carefully, then picked up the cup. I brought it to my nose, the smell of chocolate filling my senses. I tipped the cup to my mouth, my top lip gently bumping the swirly cream and marshmal-lows out of the way as the hot liquid poured in.

I settled the cup back onto the table and went to reach for the dough-nut again.

'Hello, you two,' Dad said, pulling out the chair next to me and oppos-ite Mum. Mum froze. I froze. He was meant to be at work. He had said he was going to be working late. How could he be here when he was meant to be at work?

'Are you having a good time?' he asked quietly. Then he smiled. He smiled in a way that told us that he wanted to check if we were having a good time because later we were going to get punished for what we were doing.

I immediately pushed the cup away. Then the plate with the doughnut. I didn't want him to know that I had eaten the doughnut, had drunk the hot chocolate. He hated me having sweet things. 'Indulgences' he called them. 'Indulgences make her weak. And when she's weak, she becomes lazy and rude. Do you want our daughter to be lazy and weak and rude?' he would say to Mum. That was why I wasn't allowed birthday cakes any more. Or to go to other people's birthday parties. And why Mum had brought me here as a birthday treat.

'Are you having a good time?' he asked again, this time without the smile. This time with a frown. His lips were set together over his teeth, which I could tell were clenched in anger. This was how he looked just before he smashed something, punched something. This was how he looked just before he came towards me with his fist raised.

I pushed the doughnut and hot chocolate even further away. Dad's lip curled back, and he was ready to say something else.

'Well, hello there.' The waitress with the bright smile and bright red lips appeared. 'What can I get you?' she asked Dad.

Dad smiled, a proper, happy smile. 'Hello,' he said. 'How are you? Lovely day, isn't it?'

'Yes, I was saying that to your wife. It's such a beautiful day.'

'This day is as beautiful as your smile,' Dad said. 'Don't you agree, Rose?' Dad was still smiling. Looking at Mum and smiling, nodding. He wanted her to agree with him.

'Yes,' Mum said, her voice sounding tight and small.

'Thank you!' the waitress said, tucking her hair behind her ear and looking very pleased with herself. She looked so happy, so flattered, that she stood a little taller. My dad had done that. He'd made this nice lady feel good about herself. 'What can I get you?'

'I think that doughnut looks so delicious – I'll have one of those. And one of those yummy-looking hot chocolates.'

'Sure thing,' the waitress said, and flashed an extra smile at Dad before she went away.

Once she was away from us, his face changed. 'Are you having a good time?' he asked again, and this time his voice and words made me feel sick. Absolutely sick with worry. I pushed the plate and cup even further away from me.

'I would hate to think you weren't having a good time when you're out spending my money on these indulgences.'

'It's her birthday,' Mum said. 'It's just a doughnut and hot chocolate.'

'Just a doughnut and hot chocolate,' Dad said. 'Just a doughnut and hot chocolate.'

'I'm sorry, Daddy,' I said. I put my hand on his to show how sorry I truly was. And to stop him. To stop him shouting. To stop him raising his hand. 'I'm sorry.'

'Sorry?' he snarled at me. 'Sorry?'

83

'Here we go: one doughnut and one hot chocolate,' the waitress said, and put the items in front of Dad.

'Well, don't they look delicious,' Dad said, taking his hand away from mine. He was smiling his happy smile again, and the waitress smiled back at him.

'Oh, don't you want these any more?' she said when she saw how far away from me my plate and cup were.

I shook my head.

'Was there something wrong with them?'

I shook my head again.

'She's . . . she's just not that hungry now,' Mum said. 'We'll take them to go home, if that's all right?'

'Of course. Of course.' She took them with her as she left.

As soon as she walked away, Dad's snarl was back. 'You don't know what sorry is,' he hissed at me. Then he turned his look on Mum. 'Neither of you know what sorry is . . . but you will. You absolutely will.'

We sat and watched Dad eat the doughnut, drink the hot chocolate. And then we watched him flirt with the waitress a little as he gave her a huge tip. And then we followed him out of the café. He drove home

84

and we walked. We walked all the way home, Mum holding my hand but neither of us talking.

And when we got back to the house, he did show us what sorry was. He showed us what sorry really was.

Kez

'I don't understand why you need me? Or Insight? If everything is as you say, just put the people who worked on her father's case originally into witness protection or whatever it's called until you find her.'

'It's not that simple.'

'How can it not be that simple?'

'We didn't keep a comprehensive list of people who worked on the case. All those details were destroyed to make sure no one could trace him.'

Bullshit. 'So how has she got them, then?'

'We don't know. When the police picked up the first case, they weren't sure what to make of it because the note didn't make sense and no one could understand why the first victim was killed. But when the details were entered into the database, it triggered alarms. Which brought them to Horson's departments, which brought him to Insight.'

The maths ain't maths-ing with this, as Zoey says all the time when something doesn't add up. None of what he's telling me is adding up.

Dennis continues: 'You need to create a profile of Robyn Managa that will allow us to predict what her next move might be, how she is finding out information about these people and how we can find her.'

86

'You need to do this as soon as possible,' Horson barks, his tone that of a sergeant major ordering his foot soldiers to complete a task that will most likely end with them dead. 'We are authorising overtime and you can have as many team members as you want within reason, but you will have to keep the government's part in the Protected Persons programme portion of this to yourself.'

I frown at Horson, wondering who exactly he thinks he's talking to, then I return to focusing on Dennis. 'I think I'm going to politely demur on this one,' I say to Dennis, even though I'm mainly talking to Horson.

'Demur?' Horson rages. *'Demur?* What do you mean, *demur*? This is your job and you can't "demur" on something you've been asked to do.'

'You didn't ask me – you ordered me. But I can demur and I am demurring. If you don't like that, then please do sack me.' I am talking to Dennis right now. He knows I'm talking to him because he ghosts up a smile.

'Why are you demurring?' he asks, the smile still haunting his lips as we both gear up, ready to get back to the battle we've been fighting with each other for nearly twenty-five years.

'Partly because I do not want to do anything to help protect an abuser and murderer. He should be in prison for what he did, not protected because of who or what he knew. From what little you've told me, I can see why this young woman would take matters into her own hands. I don't condone her killing people. I don't condone any-thing she's done, but I can understand it if she's spent a lifetime with no one listening to her. And this isn't my fight.' I hold my hand up to Horson to stop him talking, because I know he is about to jump in with some guff about me being part of a team and loyalty to the

87

organisation. 'It is not my fight. I don't care who the people harmed are to you personally, Mr Horson, or this organisation generally, but your fight is not my fight. And it is certainly not my job.' I lower my hand to continue arguing with Dennis. 'And I know for a fact you are hiding something. Actually, I know you are hiding a lot and that means I can't do my job properly even if I was willing to do it. Which I'm not.'

This is why you're my favourite, I hear Dennis silently say. *This is why you've always been my favourite.* He grins at me, his white, straight teeth gleaming. I've never thought of Dennis as vain, but his teeth are telling me a different tale about him. 'Managa was very knowledgeable about many things related to national security. Including defence contracts,' Dennis begins. 'He was CEO of a company that decommissioned and dismantled defence equipment and former military sites.'

'She has no clearance to know this,' Horson splutters. He really is the most ineffectual, ludicrous person. Jonah would call him an NPC – non-player character – if I ever allowed him to be so mean about another human being. Horson's presence in this is so unnecessary. This is for Dennis and me to fight out; we don't need to be constantly interrupted by this fella.

'He couldn't have gone to prison,' Dennis continues, ignoring his technical boss. 'He knew too much about too many things. He always profiled as someone who, if he had gone to prison, would have sold what he knew to anyone in exchange for freedom. When it was determined that he had killed his wife, he made it clear that's exactly what he would do if he was even put on trial.'

'Big shocker – psychopath who was hired solely because he would do things normal people wouldn't turns out to be a complete liability because he promised to act out should anyone dare to try to make him face the consequences of his misdeeds.'

Dennis and I are still engaged in open eye-contact warfare. Neither of us is going to look away first.

'I was involved with tidying up Managa's timeline and life. The information in the file and in the newspaper articles about his wife's death and his kidnapping are not accurate. His name is not Managa – that was his wife's name.'

'What was his original name?'

'I can't tell you that. Virtually no one knows it now, not even Horson.'

'What is his new name?'

'I can't tell you that, either. Again, virtually no one knows, not even Horson. What I can tell you is Managa's position meant a lot of people were involved in building him a new identity and erasing the old one. We made sure to erase his name and all mention of him, Rose Managa and their offspring from everything official and unofficial that we could. It's hard to keep track of all the people involved. And we have never had this situation before: they were all professionals so ordinarily we know they wouldn't talk, but if someone goes after them directly, we don't know how long they'd keep quiet.'

Dennis stops talking and waits for me to say I've changed my mind. He's got a long wait on his hands. Surely he realises the more he says the less I want to get involved. What I want to know, though, is: 'Was he worth it? Really? Was he worth erasing the lives of a woman and her daughter, both of whom I can only imagine endured more than any person should have to? Was all of this really worth it for a man who can kill the person he's supposed to love and then feel entitled to demand being allowed to get away with it? Was he really worth it?'

'To the right people he was,' Dennis replies, still waiting for my acquiescence.

'You said it's hard to keep track of those people, but not impossible. You must have had a list.'

Dennis wants to look at Horson, he's desperate to, but he can't look away because then I'll win the eye-contact battle and he would find that intolerable.

'We did have a list. However, there was a data breach two years ago. No one thought anything of it at the time because even though all sorts of files were accessed via a Trojan horse virus, nothing was ever done with that information. Security was obviously increased, code names changed, sensitive information reclassified and altered. Given what she is now doing, we are beginning to suspect that Robyn Managa was the one who accessed the list at that time and has waited until now to use that information. That data contained – among other things – the names of everyone who was involved and their whereabouts at the time. Unfortunately it does not exist in that way any longer.'

I get to my feet. 'Don't you feel better now that you've told me so much more of the truth?' I say. 'But I'll still demur, thank you very much.' I don't need to keep eye contact with Dennis right now, because, unlike him, I don't find victory or dominance in things like winning staring wars. I fight them, but I also know when to walk away.

I am at the door, my hand on the handle when: 'She's a vulnerable young woman. She watched her mother die, her father abandoned her to start a new life and she grew up in care.' I lower my hand from the door handle. 'Who knows what horrors she experienced there? And because one of the people she hurt was former intelligence services, while two of the others were police and ex-police, when they catch her, they're . . . they will not be bringing her in alive, Kezuma – I can promise you that. If they find her first, she will not survive. If you help to find her first . . . well, she may just have a chance.'

I hate Dennis.

I hate that he knows that my weakness, apart from Jeb, is injustice, especially when it comes to young people. Especially young people who have had to grow up too quickly, or who are in danger because no one is looking out for them. Because he knows my weakness, he is able to bend me to his will. No, I don't know Robyn. But even hearing her story from her killer father's side shows me that she has endured more than any child should endure. She could have easily gone with her father into witness protection, but would she have been safe with a man like him? Doubtful. But they wouldn't have cared about that. All they would have focused on would be how to protect that man because he had so many connections. Which means Dennis is right – they will think nothing of erasing her just like they erased her true past.

And all of that so they can save a terrible human being.

Brian's face comes into my head. '*Pick up the gun, Kez.*' His voice from my dream echoes in my ears. I do not want to do this, I do not want to get involved in any of this, but I do what I do to make up for what happened to Brian.

If I can find her before they do, she may just get a chance of life in prison, or even – ironically – I'm sure I could put together a case for her to go into witness protection. But most importantly, she will not end up like Brian.

'If I do this, I'm going to need complete autonomy. I have to be the one to decide what to tell the Insight team and if that means sometimes giving them classified information, then I can do so.'

His silence tells me that he agrees.

'And I want your word, your solemn word, that if we bring Robyn into custody before the police find her, you will not allow anyone to harm her. No matter what.'

Dennis continues to listen in silence, agreeing to that condition.

'I need you to say it out loud,' I say to him. I am standing here, ready to tear my skin off because I do not want to be involved in this. This is going to go so horribly wrong, and I do not want to be involved in this. But I have no choice. Leaving it is not an option.

'You have my word,' Dennis says. 'You have my solemn word.'

I open the door and leave his office, slamming the door behind me.

Robyn

19 February, Secret Location

My ribs and abdomen still hurt. Gene Talamon did some serious damage to me – even on my brown skin you can see the extent of the bruising. This has delayed moving on to the next target, which I'm not pleased about. But there's nothing I can do. I have to rest now. If I don't allow my body to heal, I'll be at even more of a disadvantage next time.

I lie back on the bed, force myself to relax and close my eyes. No one knows where I am, so I can relax here. I can take it easy. I have to take it easy.

'You have to be more careful,' Holly, who used to run the children's home, would say to me at times like this. 'Think of what your mother would say. Would she want this for you?'

'I'm doing this for you, Mum,' I say out loud because no one can hear me. 'I'm doing this for you, just like you said.'

Kez

23 April, Brighton

'She's clearly a psychopath,' pronounces Bruce Stevens as though that is the last word on the matter. He does that a lot. He half listens to what I say, what I brief him on and then he makes a pronouncement that we're all supposed to agree with.

Or, if we don't agree with his pronouncements, he will sit back with his arms folded and utter the real-life version of 'prove me wrong'. He rubs me up the wrong way. This whole group do, to a certain extent. They could be so brilliant, they could achieve so much beyond what Dennis expects of them if they weren't so determined to be the next Dennis, if running this place wasn't the end goal that they were desperate to reach by any means necessary. If being good – no, *excellent* – at their job was the end goal, they might actually be in with a chance of running this place one day. As it is, their ambition superseding self-development will always scupper their chances.

Dennis hates them. He hates everyone, to be fair, including me, even though he constantly claims I'm his favourite. He hates them but he doesn't treat them how he used to treat Brian, Maisie (now upgraded to MJ) and me. When we were training back in 1998, he put us through every level of hell that he could, but after Brian died, they wouldn't allow him to keep on treating trainees in that way.

While he – quite openly sometimes – shows his contempt for them, they all look up to him, like little birds in a nest, waiting for their mother to feed them pieces of regurgitated worm. They preen before him, trying to show that they're the best and they deserve to be fed the juiciest bit of worm.

I, on the other hand, despite being Dennis's second in command, despite being their boss, am treated like a little old lady from down the way who they need to speak slowly and loudly to, who they also regularly need to condescend to because I might not understand English. *'Don't patronise me; don't talk to me like you think I'm stupid,'* I sometimes want to scream at them. *'I was you when Dennis was allowed – no, encouraged – to sexually harass and assault me, as well as bullying someone else until she almost broke down, and ultimately driving a man to his death. You are all amateurs compared to the baptism by fire I went through.'* I want to scream this at them but never do.

I muster all my patience and say, 'She's not a psychopath, Bruce. How can you listen to everything I've told you and think she's a psychopath?'

'We're behavioural scientists,' Bruce replies, 'and her behaviour says she's a psychopath.'

'What's a psychopath, Bruce?' I ask patiently. I need to get this out of the way so we can move on.

'According to *Diagnostic and Statistical Manual of Mental Disorders* and *Psychopathic Personality Index*, and other academic texts,' he says slowly and deliberately because clearly he's dealing with an idiot, 'a psychopath is someone who exhibits no empathy. Has few sincere complex emotions including remorse and does not take responsibility for their actions. They will lie to get what they want and they are extremely selfish. They very rarely think long-term and they are overconfident.'

'Right. And which of these traits can you apply to the behaviour that I've just told you about? The fact that she called an ambulance in one case, displays clear evidence of empathy and complex emotions. As the notes suggest, she is looking for someone, so clearly she can think long-term. The fact her victims were tortured before death kind of suggests that she told them what she was going to do to get information, and she did it, meaning she probably didn't lie to them. I might be able to concede a little ground on the over-confident part. But . . . Bruce . . . I regret to inform you that *she is not a psychopath*.'

He does not look convinced, sticking his nose in the air, and folding his arms across his body to show his displeasure, but he does shut up. Maybe I was like that at one point. Maybe I was an annoying dickhead who thought they knew it all and wouldn't think to listen to those who had been working in this area for multiple years. Either way, whether I was like them or not, I need them, so I have to restrain myself – no eye rolling, no harsh words.

'Gang, I'm going to be honest with you here – we are up against it,' I say. 'We need to find this woman before she kills again. We are going to be joined by the police, who are also looking for her, and some other members of the intelligence services. This is one of those multi-department task-force things you probably dreamed about being a part of when you applied to work in this field. And when you were told you'd be working on a behavioural insights team, you probably thought you'd be profiling murderers all day long, not working out what type of government messaging can be created to make people recycle their rubbish.' That is mostly what we do here. We profile the behaviours of individuals and groups to help make them easier to understand . . . and persuade. We help to shape policy and government messaging; we help to make life better for people. And, yes, we help to influence people to do what certain bodies want them to do. Helping law enforcement is only a fraction of our work.

I look up at Dennis, sitting at the head of the table but silent as usual, pretending he's not there. He gives me an encouraging scowl because he can't dent his image by smiling. All those years ago when I first ended up here, I'd been naïve enough to believe that I had any choice in being recruited to work on the Human Insight Unit; I also didn't realise I wasn't just training to be a therapist who worked with agents, I was training to work deep within the intelligence services.

'We have little to no time. We also have a lot of people who are relying on us to do this, while at the same time thinking this is a whole load of nonsense, so they don't know why they've been saddled with us. As you know, people can believe two completely contradictory things at the same time. What I need for you to do is to read through these files we have on Robyn Managa. And then draw up a list of people to speak to. Between us we're going to interview as many people in her life as we can. And we need to do that quickly. You'll be in twos, paired with either a member of the intelligence service or a police officer. Your job is to get an idea of who she is. But obviously don't tell those you question that she's killed people and don't let your partner tell them, either.'

'But she has?' Bruce says.

'Yes, I know she has, Bruce. And the second they find out that she has, it will become about that and nothing else. They will start to "remember" instances where she showed her killer side. They'll have stories that may or may not be true about her, which will not be

97

helpful. We need to find out what she's really like. So what we need from them beyond finding out if they've seen her is to work out what sort of life she lives. This will help us work out where she is and where she might go. Even if all you find out is her favourite drink, that will be something.

'Your job is to be proper behavioural scientists, to watch the interviewee's behaviour. Find out from the way they answer the questions who could be helping her. See who has an affection for her, who says via their facial micro-expressions they would help her if she came to them.' I smile at them. 'I don't need to tell you all that. You know what you're doing.' They do not know what they're doing. This is so far beyond their abilities, so not what they're ready to take on, but I have to trust them because I can't do it all. I can't see it all. I can't interview everyone. The urgency of this cannot be understated. I do not want anyone else to die. And I do not want someone to harm Robyn, either. Because I know that is on certain people's agendas. She has been let down by multiple people, and I want to help her. Yes, she'll have to go to prison for her crimes, but I want her to live. I want her to get help, find some sort of peace. To do that, I'll have to look for her father, too. But first I have to get a handle on who she is.

We leave clues about who we are in the communications we have with the external world: the people we like and don't like, the way we move through the immediate environment, the interactions we have, the connections we make and break. We are who we do and don't interact with.

We need to get to know Robyn so we can know how to stop her when we find her.

'I cannot express enough how confidential everything you've been told is,' Dennis says. I hadn't thought he would speak, but now he has, everyone is sitting up to attention, beaks up, eager for their morsel of regurgitated worm. 'No one outside of this room will know as much as you do right now – not the police officers who will be joining us, not the intelligence officers. There is one other person who will be working on the case who will be told everything. Other than that, you are all tasked with finding this woman. Every bit of information you gather will further that goal. I am relying on you. All of you. Don't let me down.'

Kez

24 April, Brighton

'Kez, why is there onion salt on the box in the corridor?' Jeb calls up the stairs.

I've been awake most of the night thinking.

GIVE HIM TO ME

keeps running through my mind. The threat, the promise of what will happen to the 'him' in the note is so present it is visceral. I can't dislodge it from my brain.

I call back to Jeb: 'I, er, bought it a couple of weeks ago. Or maybe more. I emptied part of my bag out yesterday and there it was.'

'So you put it on the box that people go in every day to retrieve and return hats?'

'Well . . . there's a funny story about that.'

'A funny story about onion salt?' Jeb has climbed the stairs and is now standing in the doorway, holding said small glass jar of onion salt.

'Well, more a funny story about . . . no, no, I've told you about my bag and emptying it out already. And let's not kid ourselves that it was in any way amusing.'

'Are you going to work?' he asks.

I am lying fully clothed on the bed. I never usually wear outside clothes in the bedroom and definitely not on the bed. But this navy-grey suit has been in the wash so it, along with my white shirt, is clean. I wore these socks yesterday, though, which is why I am lying at an odd angle to hang my feet off the end of the bed.

'I am,' I reply.

Jeb has been out to drop Jonah and Zoey at school, and had said his goodbyes to me, expecting me to have left for work when he got back. Especially since I've been getting to work for seven o'clock most days these last few months.

'So why are you . . . ?'

'I'm thinking.' I'm thinking about Robyn. And murder. And profiles. And interviews. And men who make their wives drive old bangers while they go top of the range. And how Dennis is manipulating me. And how he won't let me speak to the families of the men who have died because – he says – it won't be helpful, when we both know it would be. And I've been thinking about how my life is ridiculous. Which is great because I am a ridiculous person.

'About what?'

I struggle upright on the bed, swing my legs off and stand up. 'Onion salt, of course.'

I relieve him of the condiment and smile at him. Before I can leave, he grabs my hand, clings on to my fingers with his, trying to keep us together. 'I'm sorry,' he says. 'I'm sorry you have to do this.'

'The only thing you have to be sorry about is taking my onion salt from its place in the corridor where it was meant to stay until I decided I needed to go buy another one and realise I haven't used the one I bought all those weeks ago and left in my bag.'

Jeb isn't playing, won't let himself be distracted. 'I mean it, Kez—'

I push my lips onto his to stop him talking. I can't stand it when he does this. Can't stand it. 'I have to go,' I tell him when I stop kissing him.

'Kez, let's talk a minute.'

'I have to go,' I insist.

'Please don't leave just like that. I—'

'I have to go.'

Jeb and I used to be able to talk about anything, but my job has come between us. Not in the way I thought it would, either. But it has. I hold up the onion salt. 'I think this should come with me, don't you?' I grin at my husband, pleading with him to let me go and not make me talk. I really can't face it.

Jeb gives in. Relaxes into a grin. 'Yeah, yeah. Give it a taste of the good life.'

'Very good, *mon ami*, very good.' I peck another kiss on his lips and run away before he decides he does want to talk after all.

Robyn

Could police officer's death be the work of serial killer?

By staff reporter

Speculation is rising that the death of Gene Talamon, a police officer who it is thought was pushed in front of a car and later died in hospital, may be linked to the murder of veteran journalist Ted Hartley, two weeks ago. Although police refuse to confirm or deny this link, they are treating PC Talamon's death as murder.

The link between to the two men's deaths is thought to be a note left on PC Talamon's body, which sources close to the investigation say was the same as the one left on Ted Hartley's body.

The sources say that when journalist Hartley was found in his home two weeks ago, there was a note proclaiming 'GIVE HIM TO ME' on his body. After PC Talamon was hit by a car on Gloucester Villas in central Brighton, an identical note was left on his chest by the person thought to have pushed him into the road. The shaken driver of the car that hit PC Talamon immediately uploaded the note to social media.

Even though police refuse to formally confirm or deny whether the two notes were identical, their similarity could point to the work of a serial killer whose other victims have not yet been identified.

In the meantime, police are appealing for anyone who knows anything about their colleague's murder or the death of Ted Hartley to call the number below.

Kez

24 April, Brighton

I'm staring at the pot of onion salt, sitting in its new place beside my desktop phone and my notepad, when Dennis knocks, waits for me to say, 'Come in,' and then enters. Behind him is Ben Horson and a proto-soldier-looking guy who is easily six foot two, with crew-cut blond hair and a square jaw. If Action Man were to come to life, this man would be the incarnation of him. He is dressed in blue jeans and a white T-shirt, with a black leather jacket, and his entire being could not scream, 'I AM AN INTELLIGENCE AGENT!' any louder if he tried.

'Dr Kezuma Lanyon, meet Aidan Topher, he is going to be working with you on the Robyn Managa assignment. He knows everything you do and he is very eager to get started.'

Horson has taken a seat on my sofa to the left of my desk, without being invited to. *The nerve. The absolute nerve.* I scowl at him. Dennis sits in the chair opposite me, and Big Bad Aidan, as he has immediately become in my head, stands by the door, legs slightly apart, arms behind his back like a soldier who has been told 'at ease'.

'Yeah, no. Not going to happen,' I reply.

'You need someone with you,' Dennis says. 'Everyone else has a partner – you need one, too.'

'No. Way.'

'Yes, way, actually,' Horson snaps, his face bubbling in desperation to say more things to me.

'No offence to Big Bad Aidan over there,' I say, as though Horson hasn't spoken, 'I'm sure he's a great person and all, but I work better alone.'

'It's not a negotiation, Kezuma. Topher was recruited from the air force to join the intelligence community. He is one of our top candidates and you need someone who has the experience in the field to accompany you. It might become dangerous.'

'Again, no disrespect to Big Bad Aidan but I need to blend in while I talk to people. I do not need the equivalent of the Queen's, I mean, the King's Guard following me around. Look at how he's standing. Who is going to freely talk to us if they think it's some kind of military operation?'

'He will relax,' Dennis assures. 'He knows how to relax and blend in.' As if those are the magic words, Big Bad Aidan unclenches and stands like a normal human being, then moves to the sofa, sits himself down a little way away from Horson. He semi-reclines in the seat, resting his arms along the back of the sofa, and his ankle on his knee. I stare at him, alarmed. There are so many things wrong with what just happened, I can't even. Not least of which is the fact a grown man can just change his whole demeanour on demand. That is not right.

'More than anything it's for your protection, Kezuma,' Dennis says. 'I know how you feel about . . . that side of things. You have made yourself perfectly clear about it. And I've found a way to allow you to keep working here without going through the regular training we all must maintain, but as a result, you have to be accompanied by Topher.'

'And I'm sure Big Bad Aidan won't be snitching to you about what I do at every opportunity,' I say.

'Snitching?' Dennis snaps. 'Are you five years old?'

'I'm pretty sure I was more than five years old when I heard the expression "snitches get stitches".' I turn to Big Bad Aidan. 'Not a threat, by the way. Just an expression.'

'Topher is actually good company,' Dennis says as though he's setting me up on a blind date with a person he's convinced I will be a perfect match with. 'He's got a decent sense of humour and he can be trusted to back you up in any given situation.'

'I'm sure he'll make some other profiler very happy,' I reply.

Dennis narrows his grey eyes at me. They are growing colder and scarier by the second. I have baited the bear. I have done what I try to avoid doing and baited the bear. Dennis turns to the sofa area. 'Can you give us the room?'

The other two get to their feet, Horson almost clapping his hands in glee at the thought of me getting in trouble. Who's five years old now?

Once the door is closed behind them, Dennis focuses his full attention on me. He rises to his feet, looms over the desk, then points in my face as he screams: 'YOU'LL DO AS YOU'RE TOLD!'

I jump. I jump and suddenly I'm back there: *I'm twenty-four, it's 1999, Dennis is standing over me at the firing range. He is trying to teach me how to shoot and I am refusing. I am being cheeky and he finally snaps. 'Pick it up!' he shouts. 'I SAID PICK IT UP!'*

In the present, 'You will do as you're told!' he continues to shout. 'Do you understand me?'

In any other situation, I would be gathering up my things and heading out the door, flipping him the bird as I go. But . . . Dennis knows, as I know, that he holds far too many cards in this situation for me to do that. We both know that I need him to keep my family safe. And I'll do anything to keep them safe.

'DO. YOU. UNDERSTAND. ME?' he roars.

I drop my gaze, tell him without words that I understand. That I will do as I am told.

'You may find that Topher is helpful to you,' he says, sitting down again. After the explosion, he is calm, he is collected. This is what it's truly like to deal with a psychopath. They can go from normal to dangerous to normal again in under ten seconds. 'Topher really is bright. I had input in his training, and he stood out to me. That's why I choose him for you. I wouldn't saddle you with someone who I didn't think could be helpful to you. He's one of the best.'

I nod, but keep my eyes lowered.

'Kezuma,' he says in a conciliatory tone, that sounds almost affectionate towards me, 'there's no need to be like this. I want this to be over as quickly as possible. I want this woman found as quickly as possible. Then we can get back to doing our proper jobs.'

I nod again, still not able to face him.

'Topher will meet you here tomorrow morning.' He stands and pushes his chair in. 'I will see you at the team briefing in an hour.' He doesn't wait for an answer before he departs my office.

I look at my hands once he has gone. They're trembling. I pick up the small rectangular onion salt jar, roll it around in my hands. I need to calm myself before I have to go out there and be the Dr Kez Lanyon those people know me to be. Not the Kez Lanyon who is trembling and shaken because she has just taken a step back in time to who she used to be when she was young, naïve and stupid.

Before she had to kill someone.

Part 4

Kez

25 April, Brighton

Big Bad Aidan drives a big car, a black shiny thing with a double exhaust and full-leather seats. He stops to stroke the sleek lines of the bonnet on the driver's side before he presses the key to open the doors. He didn't profile as someone who would spend money on a luxury car, but when I look at his shoes – almost as good as new even though they are last season's trainer-shoe crossover, and the way all his clothes have been ironed inside out to avoid a build-up of shine on the outside, I should have known. This guy is meticulous, organised and utterly focused on his work – he will have lots of money to buy things like this car because he has nothing else to spend it on and he almost certainly doesn't go out with friends. These things, these possessions, mean the world to him.

The car interior is extremely clean, and I see his gaze flick to my navy-blue denim coat, wondering if the colour will transfer to his tan leather seats. 'We can always take my car,' I say to him.

He shudders, the thought of that making him willing to tolerate a little colour transfer. He hasn't even seen my car, so I don't know what he's shuddering about. And my car is very clean . . . for a woman with two children and a full-time job.

We are on our way to see a Dr Guy Mackenzie, a therapist and lecturer in psychology at the University of East Sussex. From the file that Dennis handed over to me, I discovered that Robyn had lived in his house for nearly six years – all the way through university, through lockdowns and a bit after. She rented a room from him, but what the sparse file didn't tell me was whether they had a relationship or not. An internet search on him told me he has taught at the university for ten years and he lived in London before that, working in private therapeutic practice.

'Tell me about yourself,' I say to Big Bad Aidan as we navigate into traffic out towards Moulsecoomb, which is near the university.

'Why?' he replies.

I'm stumped. No one has ever, in all the time I've worked with other humans, responded to that statement in this way. 'Because we're in the car together and I would like to get to know you since we're going to be working together.'

'Why?'

'Because that's what people do?' *Well, it's what normal people do anyway.* 'Did you grow up in Brighton?'

'No.'

'Whereabouts did you grow up?'

'Not Brighton.'

Good company, decent sense of humour. These are things that I was promised from this proto-soldier and all I'm getting is . . . nothing. What a lucky girl I am.

Robyn

From Robyn's Last Will & Testament

You're probably going to meet Doctor Mackenzie, Dr Mac, at some point.

He's a strange one because he's a nice guy. I've been sceptical about men since before what my dad did. Before he killed my mother, I mean. Sometimes I don't like to say that and I have to. If I'm doing what I'm doing, I need to be able to name those things. To remind myself that I do have a reason for it.

I've been sceptical about men for more than half my life. I just always saw them as wanting something – usually from women – and being violent. Not just physically violent, either. Dad wasn't always physically violent. But he was always emotionally and mentally violent. I understand that now. He was a man who would never let you rest. He wanted to make sure that you were always on edge, always waiting to find out how you'd displeased him, always waiting for the next explosion.

The worst part of that was he would go through long periods of time when he wasn't explosive and angry and aggressive. He would go through months sometimes of being fun, funny, caring and loving. He would be gentle and interested as well as engaged and interesting. He would talk to me about school, he would very occasionally help me with my homework, he would talk to me about my interests, about the books I was reading, he would show me how to fix my bike. He would take Mum out for posh dinners, he'd put on music and dance with her in the kitchen, he'd lie on the sofa with his head in her lap.

But you could never fully enjoy anything because you never knew when the other Dad would appear, when something you said would set him off and he would get that look on his face. That look would descend like a mask and he would be on you. His whole body would transform and he would be shouting or talking at a low hiss, or just swinging. I remember one time, he missed a word in a sentence he was reading to me. I said, 'Oh, you missed out' whatever word it was, 'silly Daddy' and he morphed right in front of my eyes. I didn't even have a chance to think before he'd smacked me so hard across the face I was knocked backwards off the chair. He ripped the book to pieces and made me go to bed with no dinner.

When Mum tried to intervene, he knocked her down and kicked her in the ribs. She didn't back down, though. She put an ice pack on my cheek and brought me dinner even though I could tell she was in real pain.

All that is to say I didn't trust men not to turn on me at some point. Even in the home, I was wary of my two male friends because they were volatile anyway and I had seen them turn on other people. Never really on me, but I always felt it was a matter of time.

Then I met Dr Mac.

November, 2018

'Robyn, could you see me after class, please?' Dr Mac, as everyone called him within minutes of meeting him, asked when I came into the lecture hall where we had our lessons. The space was huge for a relatively small class of forty, but that was the only available place at that time, apparently.

I was immediately on edge. I liked his class, I loved psychology and I was having to work a hundred times as hard, never mind twice as hard, for half the returns because of my skin colour *and* where I came from. Coming from care, even though it's meant to make admissions people more receptive, is something they actually mark against you. When I first applied to different universities, more than one person tried to suggest that I wouldn't be able to handle it, that I wasn't a fit for them, that maybe I'd be happier at another institution. I had to overcome all that, I had to explain to them at length that the actual policy was to give fair consideration to those of us leaving care, I had to show them my grades and references from all my teachers and *still* they made me feel like I should be lucky they even considered me. But I had been accepted onto this course to study psychology with computer science as a professional subject. I did not want anything to mess it up. This was the first step along the road to a new life on my terms.

I knew from bitter experience that teachers only ever asked to see you after class if you'd done something wrong. If I'd done something wrong, I'd rather he tell me now so I could get my explanation ready.

'Have I done something?' I asked him.

Dr Mac looked confused. 'I don't know – have you?'

'You want to see me after class. Have I done something?'

He kept glancing away to nod and acknowledge the students coming into the room. 'I don't know if you've done something, Robyn. But I want to talk to you about something after class. Is that OK? Or do you want to do something before I talk to you?'

'No. No.' I was so confused. 'Why do you want to talk to me after class?' I tried again.

'I can't talk to you about it now. That's why I asked if I could talk to you after class. But we don't have to if there's a problem?'

'There is not a problem. I will speak to you after class.'

He narrowed his eyes suspiciously at me. 'Like I suggested?'

I narrowed my eyes at him. 'Yes, like you suggested but didn't explain.'

'Oh-Kay. I'll talk to you after class.' He pointed to a second-row seat on the left. 'Please take your seat.'

Just to be contrary, I took a seat on the fourth right on the right. Which made him laugh before he began the lecture.

*

'So, Robyn,' Dr Mac said, sitting on the edge of the desk in the lecture hall. When I sat down next to him, he immediately moved to stand in front of the lectern. I wondered if he thought I had a personal hygiene problem or if he didn't want to be accused of inappropriate behaviour. 'I wanted to talk to you about something.'

When he didn't speak for a few seconds, I was forced to say, 'Talk to me about what?'

'Look,' he said in that way someone does when they're about to upset you. So maybe I did have a hygiene problem. Which had a simple explanation, but would mean I'd have to redouble my efforts to hide that. 'Look, Robyn, it's none of my business beyond humans looking out for other humans, but are you currently between long-term housing facilities?'

Oh Jeez, for him to think that, I must have a serious hygiene problem. I resisted the almost overwhelming urge to lift my arms and sniff the area underneath. I could usually smell myself, though, so this was beyond embarrassing. 'Why do you ask that?' I replied, bracing myself to hear that I was a big old stinky mess.

'You hide it well, but I can tell that you're displaced. Things like: you bring everything with you to every lecture. You ration the food that you buy in the canteen. I notice you always keep some, presumably for that evening's meal. I notice you stay in the library until it's chucking-out time and you're always there first thing in the morning.'

117

'Why have you been watching me?' I asked, absolutely horrified. Was it him? Was he the newest person who was going to spy on me for my father? This was why I was homeless – I knew that if I didn't live at the home it would be harder for my father to keep tabs on me. When I'd turned eighteen, I was 'given' a bedsit to live in that I had to pay rent and bills on, but I couldn't enjoy it because I was worried sick all the time that one of the senior social workers from the home would drop by for a check-up visit and with no one around, he would finally finish what he started trying to do to me when I was fourteen. So I left the bedsit and put my name down on the waiting list for on-campus student accommodation. In the meantime, I slept at friends' houses as much as I could without pissing people off, I found all-night cafés to do my homework in, I sometimes found places to sleep outside. But I made sure I showered every day, I bought deodorant, I kept myself clean and I kept up with all my work. I wasn't sure how sustainable it would be, especially with winter coming up, but I would work something out. All that would be for nothing if my father had already found another way to spy on me.

'I haven't been watching you,' he said, raising his hands to calm me down. 'I've just noticed. I notice a lot of things. It's a bit of a curse, actually. Because the things I really should notice, I rarely do, which can cause me problems. But, I digress . . . I have a spare room in my house you can stay in. If you're interested.'

'What?'

'Sorry, did I not say that out loud? Could have sworn I did. But, OK, will repeat: I have a spare room in my house that you can stay in. I live a fifteen-minute walk from campus. You would have your own space. It's not a huge room, but it's big enough for you and your things. There's a desk. TV in the room. Two toilets, kitchen in the house. Parking. Sofa.'

'Why?'

'Why? Because I like to sit and watch TV in my living room and the sofa is always comfiest.'

'No, I mean, why are you offering me somewhere to live?'

'Because . . . I'm going to be honest with you. That story you wrote. It reminded me of how I once let someone down. And I swore back then, if I ever got the chance, I would give back by helping someone who needed it. You need help.'

'No I don't,' I said. Needing help made me weak and made me vulnerable. I didn't ever want to be any of those things again.

'OK. No, you don't. I need to help. So if you won't do it to for you, do it for me.'

The thought of a place to stay, a room of my own, was something I would give almost anything for. But what if he was spying on me for my dad?

'Are you spying on me?' I asked him. I watched his reaction, his instinctive reaction to the question. He was surprised – but at the question, not that I'd worked out he was working for my father.

'No, I am not. And, just to allay any worries, I will not be spying on you in the future, either.'

I scrutinised this man in greater detail. He was older than me, probably old enough – technically – to be my father, but he was buff. He had short, dark hair streaked with grey, glasses, kind face, winning smile. Like I said, he was buff. But probably a creep. I didn't hold out much hope for most people being fundamentally good. I just assumed everyone was out for something, and that way I was never disappointed. Dr Mac was obviously wanting to get me into bed, because, I mean come on, why else would he be offering me this? And if I did need to sleep with him to keep the room, well, it wouldn't be too bad. I mean, I'd been nursing a crush on him anyway, so . . .

'How much rent would you want?'

'Nothing for the first three months. That's how long I reckon you'd need to live there to relax properly. If, after three months you don't want to stay, no harm no foul as they say. But if you do want to stay, then we'll work out a fair rent. How does that sound?'

'Almost like it's too good to be true,' I replied.

Kez

25 April, Brighton

'I think it would be best if I do the majority of the talking,' Big Bad Aidan says as we pull up outside the pale blue house in Moulsecoomb. 'In fact, I think it'd be best if I took the lead on this.'

What Big Bad Aidan means is that he is an agent and I am not. So, in situations such as this, he knows what he's doing, how to get information from people and I, with all my skills as a therapist, as an interviewer, as a person who talks a lot, do not know how to get info from people. I mean, sure, Big Bad Aidan, with his angular features and slicked-back hair that makes him look like a 1980s nightclub bouncer whose only means of sexual fulfilment is frisking women on their way into clubs, is far more likely to get this doctor opening up to him than I am. I'm sure whoever this Dr Mackenzie is will be falling over himself to tell Big Bad Aidan whatever it is he wants to know. Even if he is cooperative, Big Bad Aidan has not considered that what he wants to know and what I want to know are different. However, I will do my best to let him do the majority of the talking.

'Sure thing, Big Bad Aidan,' I reply.

'Why do you keep calling me that?'

'Calling you what?'

'Big Bad Aidan.'

'Is your name not Aidan?'

'It is.'

'So you want me to call you something else? Samuel? David? Matthew? Luke! I can call you Luke if you'd prefer? Luke's a nice name. But then so is Aidan and you seem to have an issue with that, so you may not like Luke as well. Either way, I'll call you whatever you want. Just let me know what you'd prefer.'

'What?' he replies, narrowing his eyes at me.

'What?' I reply, narrowing my eyes suspiciously in return.

'What did—'

'Are you going to ring the doorbell or shall I? I mean, you're taking the lead, so I don't want to ring the doorbell and assert my authority in any way, Luke. Sorry, did we decide on whether it was going to be Luke or Aidan, because you weren't clear just then?'

'What?' he asks again.

'Are you confused? You look confused. To be honest, I'm confused. I'm not sure what's going on. Or why you want me to call you Luke. But, here, I'll ring the doorbell and get this on the way. We are up against the clock after all. I'm really surprised at you, Luke. I thought you knew how serious this all is. Anyway, here I go, ringing . . .'

I push the doorbell before he can say anything else.

The white man who answers the door has short, wavy black hair streaked with grey, and wears black-framed glasses. When he swings open the heavy oak wood door, he is immediately on guard, his body tensing, his eyes scanning behind us to see if there are more of us.

'Dr Guy Mackenzie?' Big Bad Aidan asks. Aidan is standing to his full height, giving strong 'I want to start a fight' vibes.

'Might be,' the man at the door replies. 'Might not be. The answer depends very much on who you are.' *The South London vibe is strong with this one*, I would love to say.

'Can we come in,' Big Bad Aidan states rather than asks, trying a different tactic of intimidation.

'You absolutely cannot. *May* not. You can obviously, in the abstract sense of "coming in", but I am not going to give you permission to come in.'

It takes far too much strength not to laugh out loud.

'Would you rather we talk on the doorstep?' Is the threatening response from Big Bad Aidan. 'Do you want all your neighbours to hear what we have to say?'

'Sure. I have nothing to hide,' he replies. His dark blue eyes drill into Aidan's and he increases his voice volume to add: 'And my neighbours? They'll have a new level of respect for me if we talk on the doorstep. They all think I'm weird because I haven't had a visit from the police in all the time I've lived here. So, yeah, bring it on. The louder the better, please.'

I have to raise my hand and pretend to scratch my lip to stop myself openly creasing up. This guy is a trip.

'We are not the police. My name is Aidan Topher. I am . . .'

'An agent with the intelligence services,' Dr Mackenzie cuts in, unfazed. 'Crime and/or missing persons?'

Aidan, on the other hand, is completely taken aback and shows it. I mentally roll my eyes because if he's one of the best agents available, as was sold to me by Dennis, then we're all in much more trouble than I thought.

Dr Mackenzie turns his attention to me. 'And you're Doctor . . .?'

It's my turn to be a little taken aback. Most people don't assume I'm a doctor. If they notice me at all, they assign Mrs or usually Miss as my title if they think they can't get away with 'Hey you'.

'Why do you assume that I'm a doctor?' I ask, genuinely curious.

'You look like a therapist.'

I double-take. 'I have never been so insulted in my life!' I laugh.

He grins, amused by my laugh. 'Are you a therapist?'

'Amongst other things,' I reply.

'Well there you go then, Dr . . .'

'Lanyon. Dr Kez Lanyon.'

'Kezuma Lanyon?' he replies.

He knows me. I do not know him. This is not good. 'Yes,' I say tightly, a fist of worry forming in my stomach. I do not like being on the back foot at the best of times, but right now it is not good for any of us standing here. I do not want to be cornered. 'How do you know that?'

'When I lived and worked in London, years ago, I used to send patients to you that I didn't think I could help. Usually women, especially Black women, sometimes Black men, or other women of colour.' He points to himself. 'Some things I couldn't understand no matter how hard I wanted to, so you were at the top of our referral list.'

'Really?' I reply, completely thrown.

'Yes. I thought your face was familiar. I obviously checked you out before I referred people. And everyone who I followed up with said they were happy with the referral.'

'Wow, I had no idea. Past me thanks past you.'

'Past you is more than welcome, past me says.'

Annoyed that he is being ignored, Aidan aggressively clears his throat. This is clearly not me allowing him to do the majority of the talking. He's obviously forgotten that him doing the majority of the talking hasn't even got us over the threshold. His skills are such that we're very likely to come away from here knowing less than when we arrived.

Dr Mackenzie glowers at Aidan and then looks me over before stepping aside to let us in.

His house has a short corridor to the living room, which is cosy, neat and tidy. Everything is painted white, with a light brown parquet floor. He has a few ornaments, a few bits of art on the walls, a line of framed photographs on the mantelpiece above the cast-iron fire and marble surround. His furniture is weathered but well maintained. His house tells me that he is an outwardly ordered person. There's probably a room somewhere – in his house and in his mind – where the chaos lives. There is a place where the junk has cluttered and gathered, waiting for that day when he can face looking at it, prodding at it, pretending he can ever get around to tidying it all up.

'What do you want?' he asks Aidan. He is hostile, bordering aggressive.

'Is your wife in?' I ask, to steer the conversation away from his control.

He turns his gaze on me then, the hostility in his eyes giving way to a slightly flirtatious one. 'No, she isn't,' he replies. 'Mainly because I don't have a wife. Or a girlfriend or partner.' He glances briefly at Aidan before returning his attention to me. 'But I'm pretty sure you knew that. I mean, what sort of an agent would you be if you rocked up here without knowing that.'

'I'm not an agent,' I reply.

'Of course you're not,' he responds.

I'm not sure how, but this guy has managed to wrest control of this conversation away from me and back into his hands.

It's taking all my strength not to say, *'I am not an agent. No matter what anyone says or who pays my wages, I am not an agent.'*

'I'll try again, shall I? What do you want?' He's staring at me this time. Challenging me to meet him in this space he's creating.

'Coffee, black, two sugars,' I say.

'I would have thought green tea with matcha was more your thing,' he states. 'No milk, no sugar.'

Charmer. Which is not good for Robyn. I can't imagine a young woman would be able to resist a man who uses his reading of her to flirt with her. With everything I've read about Robyn, she is vulnerable; she has been let down a million times in a million different ways. That is why she is doing this. That is why she is willing to hurt everyone in her path to finding and neutralising the source of her pain. The last thing she would have needed was to have a man as charming as this one seducing her.

When I don't say anything, he returns his attention to the man standing beside me. 'What do you want?' he asks, this time his tone softer, modulated to continue the charm offensive. And it is offensive on so many levels. Partially, I realise, because it almost worked. It almost got me on his side. He knew there was tension between Aidan and me – best way to derail questioning is to work on that. Play to it. Increase the divide by getting one person on side; create an us vs them situation, allow that to help mitigate questioning. It's exactly what I would do if I were in his shoes. *Exactly.*

Aidan glances uncertainly between Dr Mackenzie and me. He's not sure what's happened but he knows something has and he's not sure what to make of it. I should say, *'Aidan, what's happened is that this man got the jump on me. He read me for filth, and I fell for it,'* but I don't.

Giving up on trying to work out what is happening, Aidan asks: 'How well do you know Robyn Managa?'

Dr Mackenzie winces, physically reacts, at Robyn's name. It's momentary, but it tells me so much. It tells me that he knew she was going to do something and that he feels guilty about it. Guilty for what exactly isn't clear, but he knows that he contributed to this situation in some way.

'She lived here for a while. For quite a long while. I'm sure you know that, since you're here.' He is avoiding looking at me, probably because he fears I might see his guilt.

'Do you think it's appropriate for a young woman, who by all accounts is unstable and vulnerable, to be living here with an unmarried man?' Aidan asks, and it's my turn to wince even though I'd been formulating that thought in my head.

'If I was the sort of "man" to seduce a young woman simply because she was under my roof, then I don't think a wife or other female partner would stop me, do you?'

Nice deflection.

He turns to me then. 'You could just ask, if you want to know if I was sleeping with her,' he says.

'And what would your answer be?' I ask.

'None of your business,' he says, looking at Aidan.

'When did you last see her?' I ask.

'Has something happened to her?' he responds. 'Is she all right?'

'We don't know how she is. We only know that she is . . . she is looking for someone,' I say. I am about to take a calculated risk by being upfront with him, because his reaction will tell me if he is helping her or not. 'And she is hurting people to try to make it happen.

That rattles him, causes blood to drain from his face and he has to step back, find the sofa and sit down.

'You would do well to help us find her before the other people after her do. We'll protect her, keep her safe, get her all the help she needs. The other people who have been sent to find her will think nothing of putting her down.' Aidan's tone is nasty.

And when Dr Mackenzie blanches at the idea of Robyn being put down, a look of satisfaction passes fleetingly across Aidan's face. He really enjoyed sticking that particular knife in Dr Mackenzie.

Dr Mackenzie clearly cares about Robyn. I don't think he was sleeping with her, not from this reaction. I think there is something else. Paternalistic, but not quite. I need to speak to him, but not with Aidan around. Dr Mackenzie stops staring into the distance and instead focuses on me. I think he's trying to work out if he can talk to me; wondering if I might give him a proper insight into what is going on or whether I truly want her put down.

'I'll take that coffee now, Aidan,' I say. I turn to face his outrage at the very idea that I would ask him to do something as menial as make me a drink. 'I mean, Dr Mackenzie looks too shaken up to make it, so if you have to search through the cupboards for stuff, that'd be under-standable.' I widen my eyes at him, hoping he gets what I'm saying. 'Didn't you also say you needed the toilet? You'll probably have to *search through the whole house* to find it.' I widen my eyes again and nod to the doorway, trying to communicate with him that this is his chance to search for evidence or anything else that might be helpful in finding Robyn. Finally, eventually, after an age, Aidan catches on and says, 'Oh right, two sugars was it?'

'Yeah, sure, whatever. Do you want anything, Dr Mackenzie?' He stopped staring at me and now doesn't raise his gaze from where he is staring desolately at the ground. 'Nothing for the doctor.' I nod at Aidan again, telling him to get on with it before Dr Mackenzie snaps out of it. Big Bad Aidan, now on the same page, almost bolts out of the room, saying he needs the toilet, and heads upstairs.

Once his footsteps hit the top of the staircase, I move to close the door and turn my attentions to Dr Mackenzie, who is watching me suspiciously.

'We don't have much time. That won't keep him occupied for long. Tell me what I need to know so I can help Robyn.'

'So you and your friends can put her down?' he replies, watching every single reaction, trying to gauge who I really am. 'I don't think so.'

'They're not my friends. I don't want to harm anyone. I am only involved in this so I can stop them harming her. It takes three minutes, if that, to realise that Robyn has been dealt a shitty hand in life and is doing what she thinks will bring her peace. I don't want anything to happen to her. I just want to help her in any way I can. So I need you to tell me what I need to know to help her.'

'I can't, not right now. There's too much. You'll have to meet me somewhere.'

Not at all what I was expecting him to say. 'Where?' I ask. I can hear Aidan coming to the end of his time upstairs. His footsteps have gone to one room and are now circling back. I suspected he would not be good at searching, but not this bad. Though he's probably just realised that doing the search has meant him potentially missing out on vital conversation.

'My university office, tomorrow night. Nine o'clock. I have an online lecture so no one will find it strange if I'm there late.'

'How will I get into the building?'

'I'll meet you in the car park. Wait in your car near the back right corner. I'll come to you.'

'For someone who isn't an agent, you seem very adept at subterfuge.'

'I was thinking the same thing about you,' he replies.

'Yeah, well, it's complicated,' I say.

'You do want to help Robyn, don't you?' he asks so earnestly it throws me off guard.

'Yes,' I reply.

'You aren't just trying to get me to help so you can hand her over to that lot, are you?'

'I want to help her. I want to do everything I can to help her,' I reply.

His body unclenches, his face showing relief. Given the work he does, I'm surprised he doesn't seem to have considered the fact that I might be lying. That I might just be the type of person who would say anything to get someone to give them what they want.

This Dr Mackenzie, who seems to have taken me at my word, isn't the Svengali-like professor I thought he was going to be when I first heard about him. Nor is he the slightly creepy menace that he could so easily have turned out to be. In fact, he is nothing like the negative expectations that had been in my mind when we pulled up outside his house.

He is nothing like I first thought he was going to be. At all.

Robyn

February, 2019

My bare feet made no sound as I entered his bedroom. Light fell on the bed, showing his sleeping form, highlighting the contours of his muscled torso.

I had been living at Dr Mac's place for nearly four months now. Inside the house he was 'Guy', outside he was Dr Mac or Dr Mackenzie. It became easier to call him Dr Mac in and out of the house. Even now, four months in, it still felt odd living here. Mainly because he didn't ask me for anything. I took the piss, to see if he would send me packing. I'd leave the kitchen in a state, I'd come back at all hours and I'd sleep in till midday sometimes. And he just ignored it. Literally ignored it. If I was in and he was in, he'd talk to me but he wouldn't scold me or ask me not to leave the kitchen in a mess. If I left the kitchen with plates, pans and dishes piled up, he'd ignore it and work around it. He'd wash up what he needed, use it, then wash it up again. Which made me feel bad, so of course I would tidy up. If I left my clothes or books or stuff lying around the living room or dining room, he'd leave it where it was until I retrieved it. He didn't complain about the hours I kept, the times I slept. None of my 'bad' behaviour seemed to bother him in the slightest.

But I was here in his bedroom now to get it over with. I'd been waiting for him to make a move, to come to my room in the middle of the night and screw me, but he hadn't. So I decided, before I got too comfortable, before I started to believe I could stay here long-term, I would just get this over with and see how I felt about him and being in close proximity to him afterwards. I was hoping that I could stand it, that I wouldn't hate him too much, so I could stay.

Standing beside the bed, I tugged my T-shirt over my head, pulled down the straps of my one good bra set – white with red roses – then I carefully lifted the duvet and slid in. The bed was cold because he slept on the far side, and my skin tingled for a moment on the cool cotton sheets. This was the best way, I had decided. He hadn't done it yet, so I was initiating it and that meant it might not be too bad. I might even enjoy it. I slid across the bed, and pressed my body against his sleeping form.

Guy's eyes flew open and then, without waiting even a heartbeat, he shot out the other side of the bed. He grabbed a pillow, placed it over his front, covering up his boxer shorts and bare chest. 'What are you doing?' he asked in a slightly manic tone. 'What are you doing?'

I flicked back the sheet, showing off my bra set and naked body underneath. 'What do you think?' I said huskily.

He quickly turned his head away, throwing his free hand up over his eyes. 'Oh my . . . Please can you cover yourself up? And quickly. *Please.*'

'Don't you want me?' I asked coyly.

'I don't, I really, really don't,' he said loudly and quickly. 'But I do want you to get yourself dressed. Please. Please.'

I was wounded. Why didn't he want me? What did I do wrong? Wasn't I pretty? Desirable? Embarrassed, I reached down the side of the bed and picked up my T-shirt. 'I'm dressed now,' I said, feeling foolish as well as embarrassed.

He sighed in relief then cautiously turned his head towards me before peeking between his fingers to check I was indeed dressed. Once he was certain I was covered up, he lowered his hand. But he clung on to the pillow as a barrier between us.

'What are you doing, Robyn?' he asked. He didn't close the gap between us.

'I thought . . . I thought . . . You asked me to live here. You don't charge me rent. And you just let me do what I want. I thought you wanted . . . well, *that* in return.'

'If you can't say sex then you probably shouldn't be having sex. But no, I do not, have never and will never want to have sex with you. . . . And no, before you ask, I'm not gay. I am interested in women. But I don't see you that way. Never have, never will. I respect you. I think you're funny and intelligent and beautiful. But I will never want to have sex with you. And certainly not as a condition of you living here.'

'I don't get it.'

'What don't you get?'

'Why you're letting me live here.'

'I told you. I'm sure I told you? I made myself a promise that if I could ever help someone in need I would. "Need" meet "Help". That is all it is. I want nothing in return. And I'm sorry that you've come across so many shitty people that you think that you may need to provide sex to be treated with a bit of compassion.'

'Do you have a girlfriend?'

He shook his head. 'No. No, I don't.'

I really didn't get it. If he didn't have a girlfriend, then why would he stop himself? 'Do you just not like sex?'

'I like sex very much. One of my favourite things, in fact. I just . . . Robyn, you're a nice girl, but you're young enough to be my daughter and I just don't do that sort of thing.'

I pulled my knees up under the covers. 'What was the thing you did that made you decide to help someone?'

His whole demeanour changed then. He looked utterly bereft and he seemed to have a heavy weight bearing down him. 'I don't want to talk about it.'

'Did you hurt someone?'

'Indirectly, yes. But not in the way you might think.'

'And you really don't want sex from me?'

'I want nothing from you other than for you to be yourself. To think of this place as your home. To sleep in, go out at odd hours, leave the place in a mess once in a while. I want you to be a teenager. I get the impression you've never really had the chance to be a teen, so do that here. But my bed is off limits. And sex between me and you is not on the cards.'

'Does that mean I can bring someone back here for sex if I want?'

'I'm not your parent so I'm not going to tell you what to do, but if you do want to bring someone back, then make sure you practise safe sex – physically and emotionally.'

I nodded. That was fair enough. I had no one I wanted to bring back. Since the home, I'd stopped with the promiscuity. I stopped having sex with anyone who was nice to me. And now it looked like I didn't have to have sex with Dr Mac, either. He was buff and I suspect I wouldn't have minded being under him a few times, but it was actually cool that he didn't want sex or anything from me. It was spectacular, actually. It meant I could be free. I could relax. Like, really relax. I didn't have to calculate what someone wanted all the time; I didn't need to figure out what I had to do to stay safe. If I could stay in my little room, study, go to college, hang out, then I might just be able to do the one thing that I needed to do. I might just be able to get to him.

I might be able to plan how to go after my father once and for all.

'Can I get my bed back?' Guy asked me. 'I assume we're done here, so . . .'

'Oh, sorry, shall I go?'

'I'd love it so much if you did.'

He didn't move until I shut the door behind me, then I heard him cross the room and lock the door so quickly I was sure there would be burn marks in his carpet. He obviously didn't trust me not to come back and try again.

Fair play to him – the thought had occurred to me.

Kez

26 April, Brighton

Dr Mackenzie taps lightly on my car window, even though he knows I have watched him walk across the car park to where I have been waiting. Jeb was not happy about me coming out late at night to go and meet someone. He'd been even less happy about the fact that I couldn't give him any details or tell him where I was going. He'd been almost angry with the fact that once again I wasn't being open with him. When I took this job, I think he thought that I would *say* that I wouldn't share any information with anyone outside of work, but I would secretly let him in on what I was doing. If only it was that simple. He doesn't realise that anything I share with him puts him and our family in danger. This was part of the deal I made with the devil that is Dennis. I have to shut a part of myself off to my family. I have to be removed from them.

I lean over and open the door. He climbs in.

'Do you want to stay here or go elsewhere?' I ask.

'Here is fine,' he replies. 'Here is not covered by cameras.'

'Good point. What can you tell me about Robyn?' I ask.

'Wow. You're just jumping right in, yes? No preamble. Can't even buy a boy a coffee to soften him up before the main show. Just, let's get down to it. Pow!'

I have to choke down a laugh, hide it behind clearing my throat. Wasn't expecting his demeanour from yesterday afternoon to continue. Not when things are so serious. 'Dr Mackenzie—'

'Call me Guy. You can call me Dr Mac, if you really want to, but I'm fine if you want to call me Guy. In fact, I'd prefer it. Guy. Dr Guy Mac doesn't really work. Or Mac, if you so choose. Although I hate that, really hate it. But it's the one that people find the most comfortable – go figure as they say.'

I stare at the manufacturer's badge at the centre of my steering wheel. Dr Mackenzie is an unserious person. He can't seem to stop himself flirting with me. The only time people tend to flirt with me when I encounter them in the course of my work is generally because they're trying to hide something. They think they can throw me off by being charming. They never can, it just makes me more focused on what they're not saying. Maybe Dr Mackenzie isn't the good guy I thought he was. Maybe he has been sleeping with Robyn; maybe he is a master manipulator. Maybe he and Robyn are in it together, because I'm starting to suspect she might not be working alone.

'You do know that every time you flirt with me I assume the worst about you, don't you?' I say, then turn to stare right at him. Watch how he receives this declaration.

He shrinks a little, lowers his gaze and looks abashed. 'I can see why you would think that. It's more nerves than flirting, though. I messed up. I thought I'd got through to her and I hadn't. I'm trying to externalise the part of me that's pretending that I haven't been responsible for this.' He lifts his large hands, stares at them for a moment, then sits on them. 'How many people has she . . . how many people has she killed?'

'I only said she'd hurt people, not killed them.'

'You wouldn't be doing all this if she'd simply hurt people. Please, just tell me how many people has she killed?'

'You don't want to know.'

'I do. I have to know.'

'Four. One may have died as a result of an accident.'

The news hits him like a blow, and he almost whimpers in frustration, despair. Anguish. I don't know if he's helping her – this reaction seems to say he isn't, but I've been wrong before. I've been fooled before.

'It's likely she's going after some others. That's why I need your help. I need to know about her so I can work out where she might be and how I can stop her.'

'She's never going to recover from this,' he says bleakly. 'She'll never get over it. I could see she was clinging on, trying to make sense of everything that's happened to her. And I thought she was doing OK. She graduated with a first-class honours degree. She was getting interviews. When she was in class or studying or building a computer, she was so . . . Happy isn't the word but it's close. She was so outside of herself. She would smile sometimes. She'd sit and twirl her hair. She'd lose herself in a book. She'd sleep through the night sometimes. She was coming out the other side, I thought. I could see the person she could have been if her father hadn't . . . And I thought the longer she lived that life, the more she got to see that the world could be a good place, the more she would give up on the idea of revenge. Some therapist I am.'

'Is that the relationship you had with her? You were her therapist?'

'No.' He shakes his head. Stares into the distance in a way that suggests he barely registers I'm there. 'I was . . . I was trying to help her.

When I first met her she was practically homeless but still managing to come to every class, still completing every assignment. So I told her to come and stay in my spare room for as long as she liked. We would talk. Sometimes late into the night. Over time she opened up. Told me all of her story. About how her father murdered her mother, how she saw it happen. How she went into care because none of her family on either side were around to step up. She talked; I listened. Sometimes I would challenge her, get her to explore her true feelings. And I thought I was getting through to her. That she was starting to see the possibility of a life without the burden of her past. Clearly what I was actually doing was feeding my ego.

'I seriously thought a few words from me and she wouldn't do what she has promised herself she would do since she was a child. My ego is going to be the death of me, I'm sure.'

'You must have got through to her, even a little bit. It's taken her until now to act. She has probably been in two minds about it. She would have acted a lot earlier if you hadn't got through in some way.'

'That's very kind of you to say so. It's probably more likely that she's spent the last few years finding everybody she wants to target. Learning about them. Finding their routines, studying their lives, working out when they were most vulnerable. That's much more likely why she's waited. Even though it fits my internal monologue to believe I'd helped her through her trauma.'

'You did get through to her. I'm sure you did.'

He stops staring into the distance and focuses on me. 'Really invested in getting me to accept what you're saying, aren't you?' he replies.

Of course I am. How many times in the past have I thought I was on the right track, thought I had got through to someone only to find that

I hadn't? That it was my ego getting in the way of understanding what they were trying to tell me without words. 'What can you tell me about Robyn?' I ask him, navigating myself onto surer territory – the last thing I need to do is revisit mistakes of Kezuma past. 'What information do I need to know that will help me find her before she does this again?'

'What information do you have?'

Guy Mackenzie – Dr Mac, Guy, Mac – is frustrating. Dealing with someone who is so much like me is an exercise in frustration. I had no idea I was this irritating. 'I have information given to me by the people who asked me to look for her. I need to find out more from people who actually knew her. Those other people have information – you have knowledge.'

'And you're not going to try to harm her?'

'I wouldn't do that.'

'But the others might?'

'I'd say they definitely will. Which is why I need to get ahead of them. I need to know as much as possible so I can work out her next move.'

'You know her next move – she's organised and she is meticulous; she is going to go after the next person on her list.'

'Do you know why she's going after these people?'

'They were the ones who let her down. Who, instead of prosecuting her father, let him go into witness protection.'

'But why these specific people? There were so many people involved in the process of him going into the Protected Persons programme – why pick on *these* ones?'

'My guess is they weren't just cogs in the machine. She told me how so many people tried to convince her that her father going into witness protection, whatever you called it just now, wasn't a terrible thing. One of the police officers who attended after her mother died had been to the house before. Told her mother she was overreacting and to stop nagging her father, when it was obvious her father had been violent. He could have helped her mother but didn't. It wouldn't surprise me if he was one of them. My guess is, if you know it's her committing these crimes, then she wants to use them as stepping stones to get to her father.'

'She told you that, didn't she?'

'When her blood was up, when everything got too much, when she was about to fall into a depression, she would tell me how she wanted them to feel as scared as she used to all the time.'

This is not good. None of it was good per se, but this is bad. She is a goal-orientated killer. But she also sounds like she has put many years into this. Someone who has spent so much time organising themselves to achieve this is going to be hard to stop even if I do find her.

'What is she like?'

'Funny. Clever. Organised. Focused. Kind. Principled.'

The words he has used, they tell me that he has more than a deep affection for her. But his feelings aren't paternal, nor are they sexual. There is something more to Dr Mac's connection to Robyn, but this isn't the time to explore that. I need to stay focused on finding out what I can about her.

'I'm wondering why now?' I say. 'Did something happen in her life recently that could be a stressor that lit the touch paper?'

'I haven't seen Robyn in a while,' he replies, quietly, shame in his voice. 'In a long while. I've been deep in delivering a research paper and project. Robyn has always been welcome to treat my place like a hotel and she hasn't checked in for a few months. I've left her messages, but she never returns them. I mean *never*. She sometimes does this and I leave her to it. Accept that she needs her space. I'm not her parent or her significant other. I don't need to know where she is every minute of every day . . . And that is how I convinced myself that she was fine and I didn't need to try harder to look for her.'

'We all convince ourselves of things like that,' I say, just above a mumble. Last year, when everything happened with my foster daughter, Brandee, and my oldest son, Moe, I had convinced myself they were fine. That text messages and the occasional returned voicemail message were enough to constitute me parenting adult children. If I'd been more involved, if I'd not deluded myself into believing that they were doing OK, I may not be in this situation. In fact, I *know* I would not be in this situation. 'We all take our eyes off the ball and have to deal with the consequences.'

Dr Mac's dark blue eyes run over me in that way they do when new information forms a new facet of what he thinks of me and he adjusts his profile of me. 'I sense there's a story or two to tell,' he says.

'You sense right.'

He's taken aback by my candour. 'And I sense you're not going to tell me any of those stories.'

'You sense right again.'

A partially hidden smile crosses his lips, and another adjustment is made of the profile of who Dr Kez Lanyon is to him. 'It's good to be right, I suppose.'

'What did she say she'd do after she'd found her father? Did she ever talk about an exit plan?'

He stops staring at me and instead bows his head, his worry billowing out and filling the car. 'No. Never.'

Oh.

Oh.

No exit plan, no talk of a life after her mission is complete means she doesn't plan to survive it. She probably only intends to stay alive long enough to take him with her. No wonder he is concerned.

'When I say I'm not an agent, I mean it. As you've probably guessed, I'm a profiler as well as a therapist and I work at Insight, a behavioural-sciences unit that's been drafted in to create a profile of Robyn to try to stop her before she kills again. There are a couple of other agents working on this, as well as a couple of police officers who are investigating the murders Robyn committed. I need you to come in to speak to the team at Insight,' I say.

'*The* team, not "my" team?' he questions, to avoid answering my request. It really is frustrating dealing with someone so much like me.

'All right. I need you to come in to talk to *my* team at Insight. Better?'

'Much . . . But I'm not going to do that. Why would I do that?'

'Because feelings are high. With every passing day, people are winding themselves up just that little bit more. The sooner we can construct and deliver as full a profile as possible, the sooner we can find Robyn and get her the help she needs. Right now, "my" team and the other people working on this see Robyn as a killer who is coming after people like them. They see an aggressive woman who needs to be stopped at all costs. To find her, they – and I – need to understand her.

'And they need to see her as a hurt person who is hurting other people. You need to humanise her for them. You need to show them who she really is so they stop thinking of her as a monster and instead see she is human and she is hurt and she is acting in this way because of that hurt, not because she is a psychopath or narcissist. She needs to

144

become a real, multi-dimensional human being to them. Only you can do that.'

He still wants to say no, partly because he doesn't want to give away anything that might harm her. He knows that he has to, though. He knows that I'm right. 'Where and when?' he eventually concedes.

I give him the details of how to get to our building and how to get in, and with each word of explanation, the fledging rapport that we had built is dismantled, a wall of frost growing in its place. He doesn't want to do this, but he has no choice if he wants to help Robyn. He resents me for those being his only choices. He resents me so much.

'Tomorrow,' he says. Without looking in my direction again, he pops open the door, shuts it behind him and walks across to his car. He doesn't pull off straight away; he sits staring out of the front windscreen, as though bracing himself for the onslaught he's about to face.

I feel for him, I really do.

And, I realise as a treacherous little thought starts to wiggle in my head, I'm bothered by the fact he's cooled towards me. I'm bothered by that a lot.

The whole drive home, I try to banish that thought. No good can come from thinking like that, no good at all.

Robyn

July, 2012

When I arrived at Maddox Hall, the group home where I was to live, I was not in a good way. Every time I closed my eyes, I saw it happening. I would try to sleep and instead I would be watching it happen all over again. His face, his hands, her struggle, the noise, the way I tried to help in the only way I could. His face afterwards. Like he was shocked, but also that he'd finally got what he wanted all along.

Since the second I knew what he'd done, I was scared all the time. My stomach was in knots that pulled themselves tighter and tighter and tighter. I couldn't breathe properly. The air would not go to the bottom of my lungs. It would only go to the top and then rush out again, as though I was only allowed enough oxygen to keep my life support going but nothing more.

The first night at Maddox Hall, they showed me to the room I was going to be sleeping in. It was small and neat, with three other girls asleep in their bunk beds. I was to be on the bottom of the left-hand-side bunk. When they had all thought my father was a victim, they'd taken him away to a safe house, then took me there later. And when

146

they found out he wasn't the victim of masked intruders and he had in fact killed my mother, everything went into overdrive to help him. So much talking was done until the decision was made to take him to another safe house while they brought me to Maddox Hall.

I moved as though in a dream, wide-eyed and wild-haired, those knots tying themselves tighter and tighter.

'You'll be safe here, Charlotte,' the social worker who brought me here kept saying. She'd said it the whole drive over. As they took me further and further away from him, she kept saying you'll be safe here. I didn't know what they'd told her. Maybe the truth because she seemed to be saying I'd be safe now that I was away from my dad. My father. The murderer. But she was using my new name. They had asked me what I wanted to be called now that I wasn't able to be Avril any more because he wasn't going to be Henry any more. I'd picked Robyn. My father had protested, said I was to be called Charlotte. Charlotte Draheh.

Dad had always planned to do it; he'd planned to wield the ultimate power over my mother all along. It wasn't an accident, it wasn't spur of the moment, he always knew that this was his exit plan if she dared to defy him too much or if she created an exit plan of her own. He would make sure that he got the final say. Like with my name. They told me that I wouldn't see him again, that it was the best thing to keep me safe, but even when I was going to be apart from him, he wanted control over me. He wanted to dictate what I was called.

All I knew was that this thing, this thing that he had done, kept playing and playing behind my eyes. I would never know peace.

The other girls didn't stir when I entered the room, towel, cotton night-dress, toothbrush and small white bar of soap piled one on top of the other in my arms. They slept on as I sat on the lower bunk and the social worker whispered to me to try to get some sleep, said good-night and reassured me that she'd return in the morning. I never saw her again.

I knew the other girls weren't asleep. You can always tell when people are pretending to sleep, their aura and energy move differently in the world. They didn't move once they heard the door close, though. I didn't know why. (I'd find out several years down the track, when it was me who was feigning sleep, that you don't move when a newbie arrives because she's almost always traumatised. She almost always feels like she's been brought into prison and is being punished for the simple crime of being a child who can't make her own decisions – and the last thing she needs is someone staring at her and asking what happened. There was always plenty of time for that. Plenty, plenty.)

I sat on the bottom bunk, these new possessions in my arms, and stared into the dark, my eyes wide open, because closing them was horror. Closing them was being back there. Watching him do it all over again. Watching him do it all over again and knowing nothing I did could stop him.

I think, being away from him, not having to pretend any more, was why I started having these flashbacks. Because it was that night that I started having sleep problems. It was from that night I couldn't close my eyes without seeing my father murder my mother.

Kez

26 April, Brighton

When I enter the kitchen after washing my hands, Jeb is sitting at the table with a full whiskey glass. He also has his mobile phone, the house phone and his tablet – all the ways he would get a notification that I am dead – lined up in front of him like soldiers on parade: present and correct, ready and waiting.

He has been sitting in semi-darkness, with only one under-cupboard light on, going through several circles of hell. He thought I wasn't coming home, he thought he'd lost me. And that is Jeb's nightmare. His terror – that I will be harmed and he can't stop it – is especially heightened right now because he feels responsible for putting me back in harm's way on a daily basis. And because he feels responsible, he can't really tell me off. When it was my choice to march into situations that could end my life or seriously injure me, he could gently pull me back from the edge by reminding me how much he loves me, how much they all need me. Now I am back in this world that he's not allowed to know anything about, he's feeling powerless.

'See, I told you I'd be fine,' I say, pushing sunshine into my voice. I twirl with my arms up, show him my body is intact, unharmed. 'No injuries, no pain, I am completely whole. No need for you to worry.'

He refuses to look at me for a long time and I know it's not because he's angry – it's because he's worried. And not just about my physical safety. We have no way of navigating this part of our lives where I have to keep secrets. Jeb has always known everything about me. After the house party where we had a one-night stand, we didn't see each other for eight years. Then he walked into my therapy room, back into my life, and a year after that we got together properly. At that point, I told him everything. I told him where I had worked, what I'd been forced to do, what I went through as a result of what I was forced to do. One of the basic, unspoken rules of our relationship is that we share. Even when I know he won't like something, I share it with him. The same with him. But last year, I discovered that he had been hiding something huge from me. Something huge about his son with his ex-wife – my stepson – and if I'm honest, I don't think we've fully recovered. Last year's damage led to many fractures and fissures in our relationship, it led to me having to take this job, it led to us having moments where I can't talk to him. And it's led to here, me needing to keep stuff from him to keep him and our family safe.

Jeb finally forces himself to look up at me. There's no fury on his face, only anguish. Only fear. And hurt. I rush to him, take his hands in mine. 'I'm fine. I'm really fine. I'm going to stay fine. I promise you.'

He gets to his feet, takes me in his arms. 'I'm sorry you have to do this,' he says quietly. 'I'm sorry you have to do this because of me. I'm sor—'

I stop him talking with a kiss. I can't hear another sorry from him. He already says it too much. Even when he doesn't verbally say it, his demeanour around me is contrite, cautious. I want him to go back to normal. But our normal doesn't work right now. I can't be as open as I usually am and that reminds him of how guilty he feels. And because of that, we are spending our time together in suspended animation. Some of the time, we can forget and be who we were, but at times like this, we are stretched, febrile. He tries to speak again and I kiss him a little harder to stop him.

He hesitates for a moment, then he kisses me back. And the feel of his lips pressing firmly against mine pours sweet molasses through me. This is one of those moments where we are back to normal. He picks me up off my feet and kisses me more firmly. I feel the blood gushing through my veins. It hasn't felt like this in months. Months and months.

He moves me back to the kitchen counter, and I wrap my legs around him as his hands go to my face and his kisses become even more passionate. And then I'm clinging to him, accepting his kisses as passionately as he receives mine. He reaches down and unbuttons my jeans, I do the same to him.

We have children upstairs, but neither of us seems to remember or care. We're moving on each other like we've been deprived of something we need to survive and now it's been given back to us we're going to devour it whole. He almost rips my jeans and knickers over my hips and then steps back to fully open his flies and take his jeans off while I kick off my jeans and knickers. And then we're back together again. He's lifting me to rest on the side and he's wasting no time pushing into me. I tip my head slightly so I can see him staring into my eyes as he moves inside me. My body starts to almost melt as he ignites pleasure all over me. He groans, pushing and thrusting into me. I tip my head right back, close my eyes, enjoy the pure, pure ecstasy of being with this man. I moan softly.

'You like that?' he murmurs.

'Yes,' I whisper back, moving my hips to match his. My body starts to unclench. Relax. 'Yes.'

'Oh, I think you like that,' he says.

'Yes,' I say.

'I think you like that.'

'Yes.'

I feel him speeding up, hurtling towards the end and I bite down to stop myself crying out. The rush rises through me, the bliss stretching out through every nerve. All I can feel and be is pleasure. Pure pleasure. 'Yes,' I whisper again. 'Ye—' Guy Mackenzie's face flashes up behind my eyes. The 'yes' dies on my lips, my body stops mid-stroke. Jeb pauses, wonders what's happened, why I've stopped. My eyes fly open and Jeb frowns slightly. 'Are you OK?'

I grab his face, kiss him, encourage him to keep going so we can finish. When he starts to move again and I pull away from the kiss, I keep my hand on his face and I stare directly into my husband's eyes. I stare into his eyes and don't look away, don't allow anyone else to enter my thoughts as my husband moves quicker and quicker until we're both groaning and moaning, faster and faster until we're both clinging to each other, on and on until the pleasure ripples and pulses outwards through every nerve in my body.

*

'Can you imagine what would have happened if one of the children had come down?' I say to Jeb as we gather up our discarded clothes.

'A lot of very awkward conversations,' Jeb replies.

'"Awkward conversations"?' I scoff. 'I think it'd be a lot worse than that.'

Jeb lets out a laugh. 'Yeah, just trying to downplay it cos I didn't think of them at all in the heat of that moment and the thought of them walking in . . . wow.'

'Neither of us thought of them in that moment,' I say. 'Not like us at all.'

Jeb stops before pouring his whiskey down the plughole, comes back to me and kisses me again. He was about to say something, probably sorry again, and he knew I couldn't stand to hear it, so decided to do the next best thing. He hands me the glass and I take a sip, the fire burning almost straight away as it enters my mouth. Jeb kisses me, takes the heat away. He hands me the glass again and we repeat me drinking, him kissing away the fire. A few more goes and the glass is empty, a warm fuzz throbs through my veins.

'Go,' he whispers, lightly tapping my bottom.

I creep upstairs while Jeb stays behind to finish tidying things away and wiping down the surfaces. I go straight to the shower, shut and lock the bathroom door. It's only when I'm alone, when I can collapse against the door, that I think about what happened. Who I saw right in the middle of what I was doing with my husband. The way that other man's navy blue eyes danced with the intensity of him adjusting his profile of me, the flirtatious smile that always seemed to sit on his lips when he was talking to me.

It doesn't mean anything, I say in my head, pushing away that image of a man I've met twice for a few minutes in my life. I march to the shower cubicle, reach in through the glass door and switch it on, watch water spurt out of the dinner-plate-sized showerhead. I strip off the rest of my clothes, step into the water stream. *It doesn't mean anything. Seeing him when I was with Jeb doesn't mean anything. Of course it doesn't. It doesn't mean a single thing.*

Robyn

July, 2012

Tommy was slightly younger than me and smaller than me. His brown hair had been butchered by someone and stood out at odd angles all over his head. He was quiet but vicious. He would look at you and you would know he wanted you dead. He got slapped around for it. A lot.

The first morning, I woke up alone in my room and the woman who ran the place, Holly Banks, told me where I could wash and gave me some clothes. She also told me to come down for breakfast when I was ready and she would make introductions later.

After a quick shower, I walked into the breakfast room, which was pretty much the kitchen, dining room and hang-out room, that took up most of the ground floor, and a big guy with a cigarette behind his ear and a black leather jacket was smacking Tommy round the back of the head.

The sound of that guy's hand hitting the back of the poor mousey-looking boy's head made me feel sick. The sound of hand on flesh was so common to me. The feel of hand on flesh, the smack delivered

154

to the back of the head for saying something stupid, for looking upset, for breathing too much was something usual to me. It lurched my stomach.

I knew where this was going to end. I knew what I was going to have to play witness to again. I marched right up to the leather-jacket guy who was walking away from the mousey-haired boy and shoved him. Hard. So hard. He went flying forward, bashed into one of his friends and ended up sprawled face down, spread-eagled on the floor. His friend wobbled on his feet but didn't fall. The other six people in the room were shocked silent and then they all burst out laughing.

'What the fuck?' leather-jacket guy exclaimed, and jumped to his feet. He whipped round to find out who had pushed him, glaring at everyone who was laughing.

When he saw it was me, he turned to his mate. 'Who the fuck is this?'

His mate, still laughing and holding on to the other person beside him as he did so, shook his head, shrugged.

He came up to me, lowered his head and peered at me as though I was under a microscope. He wasn't angry so much as confused. 'Did you just push me?' he asked.

'Just leave him alone,' I declared. My hands were in fists down by my sides. My feet were planted into the ground, ready in case I needed to fight.

'You did push me?' he asked, incredulous.

'Just leave him alone,' I repeated.

Leather-jacket guy rubbed at his eyes, clearly not believing what was happening. Everyone around us had stopped laughing, now they could feel the rising tension, the coming danger. I could feel it. I was attuned to it but I didn't care. I just didn't care.

'It's like a munchkin decided to take on Mike Tyson,' he said, still confused.

His friend stepped forward and whispered in his ear. When their chat had finished, he returned to glaring at me.

'You're the kid whose dad was kidnapped, ain't ya?' he said, now fascinated as well as confused. 'Offed your ma, took your pa. What's that like?'

I didn't know what 'offed' meant but I could guess. And I wanted to howl. I wanted to curl up on the floor and scream my head off. It still didn't seem real and I couldn't believe this person was saying things like that.

I wanted to hurt him. To do something to him and then go: 'See, that's what it feels like. That's what it feels like to hurt in every way possible.' But I couldn't do that.

'Just leave him alone,' I said again. 'Stop bullying him.'

Leather-jacket guy was confused again, didn't understand what I was doing. 'You're weird,' he eventually said. 'You're really weird.' He then came right up to me, got right in my face. 'But don't do that again, yeah? I'll let it slide this time cos of your ma and pa and all, but don't do it again. It won't go well for you if you do.'

He brushed past me to leave the room and everyone stared at me for ages. Then they all went back to eating their food.

The boy who'd had his head slapped was staring at me, wide-eyed, obviously not expecting anyone to stand up for him. I didn't know what to do with myself. I hadn't intended to come down to breakfast. I was and wasn't hungry at the same time. But then I could hear noises outside the room and downstairs, and started to fear I was imagining them because I was alone in this strange place. And that I might never see another human being as long as I lived. And what if they couldn't see me? What if I became invisible and no one ever saw me? Because the last few days before I ended up here, everyone had ignored me – they'd had conversations about me but acted as though I wasn't in the room. I thought, sitting upstairs, that I could waste away and no one would notice. So I had come downstairs.

The boy with the badly cut spiky hair continued to stare at me then pulled out the chair next to him. Patted it for me to sit. With nothing else to do, I slid my bottom on the hard wooden seat. He turned a small glass with bobbly sides in front of me the right way up, then got a jug of juice and poured some into the glass. He poured it right to the top and I stared at it, agog. Its orange colour looked so vibrant, inviting. It looked like it was for me, this glass of bright liquidy goodness. That couldn't be right. I wasn't allowed juice. We were never allowed juice. Only Dad could drink it. We didn't do anything to earn the money that bought it and we didn't do anything to earn the right to drink it, either.

If I could be a little less clumsy, if I could get just that next grade up – from A to A* – if I could get the one above A* that we weren't sure existed, if I could remember to brush my teeth for two minutes exactly (not one minute thirty, not two minutes ten, not three minutes), if I could remember to dust the living-room table without being reminded, if I could polish my school shoes without a prompt, if I could hang my satchel the right way on the hook behind the front door, if this, if that, if this, if that, then he might possibly consider letting me share some of his juice. And it was his juice. He had bought it; he had earned it. What had I done exactly?

The boy with the badly cut hair pushed the glass of juice towards me, nodding at me to take it.

I looked around me, checking Dad wasn't going to appear from nowhere, slap the glass out of my hand, tell me that I was awful and that I was not going to get dinner for the next two nights, that he would deal with me later – that 'dealing' involving the broadside of his brown leather belt. I never even drank juice at school on the special occasions they had it because I knew I would go home and Dad would know I'd had something special and he would take it out on Mum before he took it out on me.

Go on, the boy seemed to say with his nod. I picked up the glass. It felt alien and cold in my hand. I slowly raised it, trying to stop my hand from shaking. I brought it to my lips and tipped, just a little, enough to allow a small drizzle of juice to dribble into my mouth. I took the glass away, allowed the liquid to seep into my mouth, then the tip of my tongue came out to dab up the rest of the juice that sat on my lips. It tasted like happiness. Like how I always imagined happiness to taste. Sweet and tangy and something else I could not name. I did it again. I put the glass to my lips, took a bigger swallow this time. And again. And again. And again. Again and again and again and again until the glass was empty. I put it down, wiped my mouth with the back of my hand, then immediately looked around again. Checking my father wasn't about to appear.

He had before, not just like that time after my ninth birthday when he'd showed up in the café. It didn't matter where we went, how far we tried to get away, he always seemed to find us. He always seemed to know where we were.

I looked around again, just to be doubly sure he wasn't coming. I pushed the glass towards the boy, wanting him to give me some more. Some more of that sweet orange nectar.

He filled the glass again. And while I gulped down the juice, he watched me intently. Then when I had finished it, put the glass down and wiped my mouth on the back of my wrist again, he opened his mouth and said: 'I'm Tommy. What's your name?'

I was meant to say Charlotte. I was meant to say Charlotte Draheh. I was meant to be a good girl and use the name my dad had picked.

'Robyn,' I said to the boy. That was the name my mum had picked for me when I was born. It was going to be my name right up until they got to the register office and my father had started to sulk, said he hated Robyn, wanted Avril instead. Mum, not wanting to cause a scene, and wanting to please him, put Avril. I wasn't allowed to be Avril any more, but I didn't have to be Charlotte, either. He wasn't here. He wasn't here, so I could drink juice and I could call myself whatever I liked. 'My name is Robyn Managa.'

Part 5

Part 3

Kez

27 April, Brighton

'This is Dr Guy Mackenzie,' I say to the assembled people in the Insight main room. They consist of two police officers who are working the murder case but have no clue what we know at Insight, the four psychologists who work at Insight, and Dennis, Ben Horson and Big Bad Aidan. Big Bad Aidan looks pissed.

Properly pissed. Probably because it's now obvious that Mackenzie and I formed an alliance when his back was turned. He was meant to be supervising me – even though I have more experience than him in pretty much every area of life – and I've gone off plan. I'm not sure how he thought our dynamic was truly structured, because spend three minutes with me and you know I don't listen to a word anyone says, much less defer to them on anything. It was obvious that I was going to go off and do something on my own.

'Dr Mackenzie is a clinical psychologist and therapist, as well as a lecturer in psychology. He knows Robyn Managa very well. She lived in his house for a few years while at university. If there is anyone who will be able to give you an insight into who she is, it's him. You can ask him anything you want, the wilder the better, as far as I'm concerned.' I feel Dr Mac's head creak round to look at me as he realises that I've stitched him up. I haven't though, not really. Not in the way he thinks. 'We need to know everything possible to find her. Do bear that in mind when you ask him questions. He isn't a suspect though, he hasn't done anything wrong. And he doesn't have to answer any of your wilder questions, so if you want to go off-piste and be rude, expect to get it back or to be banished from the room by my good self.'

Horson, who is wearing what looks like his best suit, and is sitting beside Dennis, bristles at this. He doesn't like me, not that that makes him unique. But he *hates* the way I do things. He thinks I'm undisciplined and uncouth; he believes I have no respect for tradition or hierarchy. He's right about my lack of respect for tradition and hierarchy, certainly. The first two, well, I think *he's* undisciplined, rude and uncouth, so one or none or both of us could be right on that score. I know Horson will have told Dennis what he thinks, and I know Dennis will have told him that he finds me invaluable. That the way I do things is the reason I am here. That my position here is non-negotiable. That's why Horson hates me. Usually, when Horson takes against someone they are gone in short order. Dennis has let him know that isn't going to happen with me.

By the end of this session with Guy Mackenzie, Horson will be spitting feathers. I saw his face when he was explaining about Robyn in that first meeting. I know he identifies with Robyn's father and wants Robyn 'put down', as Big Bad Aidan so delicately put it. If this works, people will be less keen on that happening by the time they walk out of here, and Horson will have *another* reason to want me gone.

'I'll start.' I move to stand in front of the people opposite Dr Mackenzie. I am stitching him up here, but it is for a good cause. I hope he realises that. And if he doesn't, I'll apologise to him afterwards. What's that saying about it? Oh yes: better to beg forgiveness rather than ask permission? Never realised I would one day need to apply that to myself.

'Were you sleeping with Robyn, Dr Mac?' I have to get that one out of the way. Take away anyone else's chance to ask it, so it'll be removed from people's minds and they can focus on other parts of the profile. I have to call him Dr Mac to remind them of his professional standing but also to soften him, make him seem approachable and likeable.

When Guy Mackenzie stares at me, anger ripples like snakes in a sack across his jaw. 'No, Dr Lanyon, I was not sleeping with her. She was a vulnerable young woman who walked into my lecture hall and tutor groups and excelled at every module she studied. I worked out that she was pretty much homeless and I offered her a place to stay. She misunderstood my intentions one time but when I explained that all I was offering was a place for her to stay and space for her to study, things settled down. She had a key and would come and go as she pleased.'

Mackenzie glares at me for a moment before looking away. His disgust and fury are hidden but there. I guess he won't be flirting with me again.

'Dr Mackenzie, as a psychologist, in the time you knew her, did Robyn exhibit any psychopathic, narcissistic or sociopathic traits?' Bruce asks. Even though I explained to him why she wasn't any of those things. Even though he seemed to accept what I said, he clearly had not let his theory – his pronouncement of who she is – go. He knows better. Always. Although, I did say to ask anything and he wouldn't be Bruce if he didn't seize on the chance to prove himself right and me wrong.

Dr Mackenzie – Mac – glances at me before he says, 'No. Never. Not in the way you think, anyway. She was more vulnerable than angry. She didn't believe she was right and everyone else wrong. Most of her anger and rage was at herself. She spent a lot of time depressed – and as I'm sure you know, many believe that depression is rage turned inwards.'

Bruce remains unconvinced. 'So if she didn't exhibit any of those traits, how do you explain her current crimes?'

'She . . . she disassociated a lot. She has been through a lot and leaving her mind and body for stretches of time was how she coped. A lot of people do that, especially when they have been through even a fraction of what she has been through.'

'You believe that a bad childhood made her a serial killer?' This is Cherelle. She has all the traits of caring about people, she is sharp and astute; however, she has a deep disdain for any type of reasoning behind the things people do. Which is not great in a behavioural scientist or psychologist.

'Robyn didn't just have a bad childhood,' Mac says, calmly. 'She watched her father murder her mother. As in, she was in the room and saw him do it. That's way beyond a "bad childhood". She also watched as her father wasn't given a prison sentence, but instead was given the keys to a new life while she was sent to live with strangers. I think "bad childhood" might just be underplaying it.'

'Did she tell you any part of her plan?' Big Bad Aidan. I'm impressed – I thought he might just stay strong and silent and pissed off, but he's got over himself enough to contribute.

'Over the years, we talked a lot about what might bring her closure. She often said confronting her father, looking him in the eye and telling him what she thought of him would maybe make her worries go away.'

'What did you think about that? Did you agree?' Iris asks. She's more open-minded than some of the others, which will make her a good profiler and therapist if she continues on her current path.

'I thought her father was an abusive bastard who spent all his life terrorising his wife and daughter. I thought Robyn went through hell from a very young age so it was a miracle she turned out so normal. I thought I wouldn't blame her for doing terrible things. But she didn't. Not in the time she lived in my spare room.'

'Psychopaths are really good at hiding their true nature,' Bruce asserts.

Mac turns to him, his jaw rippling with the snakes of anger again. I know how he feels when it comes to Bruce. 'Psychopaths are also very good at not listening to someone who knows what they're talking about when they say someone isn't a psychopath, or a sociopath or narcissist. They're very good at trying to assert that they are right despite all other evidence.' *Ouch.*

'Do you know where she is?' I ask because I sense the people around me are flagging. Also, I'm not sure why, but none of the non-Insight people – except Big Bad Aidan – are asking questions. Are they all too scared that their question might reveal that they want to have sex with their mothers or something?

'No,' he replies curtly to me. He really is never going to flirt with me again. Which is probably a good thing, given . . . *Nope, not going to think about that.*

'Does she have any family that she mentioned that she might be staying with?' Dennis asks.

'No. She has no one.'

'Apart from you,' Cherelle says.

'She doesn't have me. At one point, maybe, but not now. Not any more. Especially not after this.'

'Which drugs does she take?' one of the police officers asks.

'None. That I know of. She smoked occasionally when she could afford it, but I never saw her take any drugs or seem intoxicated.'

'So she didn't even drink?' I ask.

'Not really, no. She was very keen on not losing control.'

This is at odds with what she's done, what it looks like she is promising to do. I hope people can see that.

'What makes her tick?' Iris asks.

Mac stops for a moment to consider this. I sense he wants to reply *What makes anyone tick?* but instead eventually says: 'Finding a way to be at peace with what happened to her, what her father did to her and their family. Robyn is always seeking peace. Which is why it was unusual that she had very few crutches – she wouldn't drink, drug, sleep around, over- or under-eat. She didn't seek solace in anything other than the search for peace. Which is why—' He stops himself talking, clearly he was about to reveal too much.

'Which is why?' Iris pushes.

'Which is why all of this is alien. She said more than once she just wanted to talk to her father. But even if she wouldn't be able to control herself in front of him, I can't see her hurting other people.'

'And yet she did,' Dennis says. 'Do you think you are allowing your very clear and obvious affection for the girl influence your judgement?'

Mac is silent for a while then says, 'She's not a girl, she's a woman.'

'Where do you think she would go, especially if she doesn't feel she can come back to your home?' Big Bad Aidan.

'I have no idea. She would sometimes disappear for days at a time. But I just assumed she was with friends or had a boyfriend. It was none of my business. So I have no idea where she might go.'

'If she is not a psychopath, then what do you think she is?' Bruce *again*. Collectively, the people in the room sigh in frustration.

'I think she is a hurt young woman who grew up from being a hurt girl. I think she is very goal-orientated, and she will do everything she can to confront her father. I don't know why she harmed those people' – I hear Horson whisper, '*Killed. She killed those people*' – 'but I don't think it's because she got any enjoyment from it. She is not grandiose, she does not take pleasure in the misery of others, she doesn't blame everyone else for her failings. She was always keen to look after others, protect others. She is not a psychopath. Nor is she a sociopath. Nor is she a narcissist. And if you bring that up one more time, I am walking out of here because you're clearly not listening to what I'm telling you. Just accept she is a little more complicated than the theories you've read about and she is more than the few actions you know she's taken.'

'They're more than a few actions,' I say. 'Please don't downplay what she's done.'

He glares at me again – oh, he *hates* me now. 'I didn't mean to do that. I was trying to say that she isn't what you'd expect. And what she's done is beyond anything I thought her capable of. But I seriously doubt she is gaining any enjoyment from it – she simply wants information that will bring her closer to her father.'

'Is there anything else you think we need to know?' Dennis asks.

Mac glances at me, wondering if I'm going to tell them that she has no exit strategy, that she has hit the destruct button with no real thought of how she will get out or what she will do afterwards. Of course I'm not going to tell them that. It would undo everything that has been gained here today.

'Robyn is organised, methodical and intelligent as well as resourceful. There will be a logic, a reason for the order in which she is doing this. It may not seem obvious, and I doubt you'll have a clue about everyone on the list. But . . . I'm going to say this as someone who knows her, the best thing you can do is find a way to get to her father and then hand him over. She's going to keep going until you give him to her. That's all there is to it.'

Robyn

August, 2014

Cindra and Brad came to one of the open afternoons the home sometimes had and they looked like my mum and dad – Black mum and
white dad.

The 'Meet the Children' type thing they held at Maddox Hall was
like an open house. We made cakes and added fizzy water to the
squash. We – most of us – dressed up in nice clothes and made
sure we smelt nice. I was sitting in the corner of the living room on
a beanbag, reading. I'd been to three of these things now and no
one was ever interested in me. They smiled at me because they
smiled at all the children, aware that they were potentially being
watched and people wouldn't want them to adopt a child if they
were mean to children.

I had found a copy of *War of the Worlds* that one of the older children
had got from school, and was sitting on the red-and-blue beanbag,
transported to a world where aliens were trying to take over.

'Hello there,' Cindra said to me, crouching down to get my attention. I looked up briefly because I couldn't believe anyone would be foolish enough to interrupt my reading, then went back to my book. Then my brain kind of caught up with my eyes and I realised it was a Black lady with a soft voice and kind eyes talking to me. I looked up again and she grinned even wider. Behind her stood a white man who wore glasses and smiled too. 'I'm Cindra,' she said, pressing her hand to her chest, 'and this is Brad, my husband.' She indicated the man. 'What's your name?'

'Robyn,' I said. I was suddenly shy, nervous, a little scared, even. I'd been jealous of the other children who people wanted to talk to on other family days. I'd wanted someone to do more than smile at me. I wanted someone to want me and now here they were and I was scared. What of, I didn't know. I just knew that I was.

I put down the book and started to pick at my nails. I'd stopped biting them the year before and now just picked at them and tore at my cuticles instead. 'Do you like reading?' Cindra asked. 'Because I do. I used to drive my mum round the bend because I always had my head in a book. Not always school books, either.' She laughed. 'Cindra!' she continued in a light Jamaican accent. 'Let me catch you reading a book instead of doing your chores. Just let me catch you!'

'That's quite spooky,' Brad said, looking unsettled, 'because that does actually sound like her. I mean, *exactly* like her.'

'What sort of books do you like to read?' Cindra asked while her husband continued to look a little freaked out.

I shrugged. I liked to read whatever I could get my hands on. Before I came to this place, I would sneak home more books than I was allowed from the school library. We would never buy books. Even though we had at least two bookcases or shelves in almost every room in the house – even the bathroom had one and it was usually Mum who had to make sure they were all perfectly clean and dust-free – none of the books were mine. None of them were Mum's, either. Even though she used to tell me how she loved to read, even though she said they'd each moved into the house with enough books to stock a small village library, only Dad's books made it to being displayed. She said she didn't mind. Not really. It'd started with getting rid of her versions of any duplicates, she'd explained. 'We didn't need both copies. And mine were usually a little tatty because they'd been read so much, which made sense for them to be the ones that went to charity.' After that, Dad, she said, would regularly question her about the books she might never read again. It had been just casual conversation, chat among all the other things they talked about. But a few days after the chat, the books that related to that chat would mysteriously disappear. When Mum asked about them, she would get the reply: 'You said you wouldn't want to read another book about that subject. I was just saving you the trouble of having to dispose of them.'

Mum would never have 'disposed' of her books. She brought them everywhere, she'd told me. They were like her friends, her little doorways to escape when times got tough.

This kept happening, though, until the conversations stopped happening and Dad was deciding which of her books should go because they were too predictable, written with unstable science, too far-fetched, too depressing, too this, too that. I could tell as Mum mentioned it, almost in passing, that she was upset at the loss of her books. But if she ever said anything to Dad, he would be hurt, he would be angry, he would ask her where she was getting all this time to read when she had a house to look after, he would say that she would soon have a child to take care of, if only she could get the getting-pregnant part finally right. Eventually, our house was a house full of books – Dad's books – and Mum could only remember the books she had. They'd become like the friends you grew up with – you loved and remembered them, but had to accept them as pieces of your past you could never revisit, friendships you could never revive.

Mum could never restore the extensive personal library that she'd had before she met Dad because she couldn't remember half of them, and she would have had nowhere to put them. And where would she get the money to buy them, anyway? They had to be careful with every penny; they couldn't just waste it on books when they had to budget carefully for food and bills. Yes, Dad had expensive clothes, a sleek car and drank top-quality whiskey, but that was only because he knew how to budget. He earned the money and so he deserved it.

'Well, do you like this book you're reading?' Cindra persisted.

I nodded. It was interesting, not like anything I'd ever read before.

'I used to love that book when I was little, about your age. I loved H. G. Wells. My favourite was *The Time Machine*. Have you read that?'

I shook my head.

'Well, OK, maybe I can lend it to you?'

That would mean she was intending to come back. I checked her out again. She had long thin plaits, an indentation on her nose like she normally wore glasses but wasn't now. She had straight white teeth and soft-looking full lips. Her nose was like Mum's. Broad and cute. She had big silver hoop earrings. I'd seen similar in Mum's jewellery box, but she'd never worn them, not even when Dad got us to pose for formal pictures. I was sure one time I heard him say they made her look cheap and she should never wear them.

I checked out Brad. He didn't seem to mind his wife wearing those earrings. And I noticed she had her nails painted. Those were cheap, too. Something only harlots had done. Brad didn't seem to mind that, either. And it sounded like Cindra had her own books if she could lend them to me.

'I'll just go and talk to someone about maybe coming back to visit you,' Brad said, and wandered off.

'You want to see me again?' I asked cautiously.

'Yes. I know we've only talked for a little bit, but how can we not come visit when you're a book girl like me?'

I glanced over at Brad, who was talking to Holly, the main care worker at the home. I checked he was out of the way before I whispered to Cindra, 'Do you have your own books?'

She frowned at me, confused. A lot of people got confused by the things I asked. 'Yes, of course.'

'And they're yours, not Brad's?'

She frowned even deeper. 'We've both got books. Our house is full of them.'

'And Brad doesn't mind?'

'Why would he mind? It's our house.'

It was my turn to frown. My turn to be confused. The way my dad would make it seem like a big deal if we encroached on his space. Everything we owned – toys, clothes, books, shoes, food – had to be always tidied out of sight or there would be trouble. We never displayed any of the pictures I drew. It was our house, but we couldn't have our things out in the open, ever.

Brad returned to us. 'All set. Holly said, if you're interested, we can come back for a visit, take you out for ice cream. That's if you like ice cream.'

Ice cream was another thing that I'd eaten, waiting for Dad to appear and scream at me. 'I like ice cream,' I said.

Kez

27 April, Brighton

Outside the building, with the occasional car going past and our images reflected in the mirrored walls, Mac stands with his hands in his blue trouser pockets, his head lowered to avoid my eye. He seems wounded, which I regret, deeply. I'm about to explain myself when he says, 'I'm assuming you must love sewing.'

'Sorry, I don't get you?' I reply.

'I've never seen anyone stitch someone up as expertly as you did to me back there. I'm assuming you must have a side-hustle as a professional sewist, or at least it's one of your hobbies.'

I say nothing to that because I do actually like sewing. And he's back flirting with me.

'What, did you think I'd stop flirting with you just because you threw me to the wolves?' he teases. 'It'll take more than that to stop me, sorry.'

'I'm not sure what to say to you,' I admit. 'I was about to apologise for sort of throwing you to said wolves but you're acting as though you half expected what happened so you don't mind but also like I've mortally wounded you. I don't know what I'm supposed to be doing or saying.'

'You could make it up to me,' he says, his tone dipping his words in lasciviousness. He folds one arm across his body, rests the other elbow on top and then partially covers his mouth with his hand – a classic case of hiding from what you're saying.

'And how would I do that, then?'

'You can tell me what you're going to do next.'

'Oh, well, that's easy. I'm going to go back and talk over everything you've just told us and then I'll put together the proper profile.'

'No, I mean, tell me what *you're* going to do next. I saw something ping on your face earlier when I was talking. Almost missed it because you're so beautiful as well as beautifully distracting to look at, but I did see it. You realised something about where to find Robyn, but you're not going to add it to the profile. You are going to pursue that lead yourself. Tell me what it is or, better yet, take me with you. I can help.' I now realise what he's doing – the way he's standing, the reason he's covering his mouth is so that no one can use the footage from the video cameras trained on this area to lipread what he's saying. Again with the spy-like behaviour. He must have done a job like mine in the past. Surely. 'Let me help you. If you do find Robyn, I can help talk her down. You need help, especially if you're going to go it alone.'

'I'm sure you're keen to help,' I say for the cameras, because I'm pretty certain Dennis is watching me right now. 'And thank you for your time, Dr Guy.'

'You do realise that is my first name, don't you?'

'If you say so.'

That makes him laugh and it feels good to have done that. I stick out my hand for him to shake. 'Thank you for your time, Dr Guy. I will let you know if there is anything else I need from you. And call me if you think of anything that you think I might find helpful.'

He removes his hand from his mouth area and then shakes my hand. 'Thank you for your time, Dr Kez. Please, let me know if I can be of any more assistance.'

'With my sewing skills? Are you sure?'

He laughs and while he laughs, I nod slightly at him. Hopefully he'll understand what I mean with that nod. Hopefully he knows I will be in touch. If he doesn't, then fine. I can follow up this lead on my own.

*

'What did Mackenzie want with you after the debrief?' Dennis asks after knocking and entering my office. He's been strangely respectful of my space since I started working for him again. I didn't expect him to start sexually harassing me like he used to, but I thought he would just walk into my office any time he wanted, like I do to him. I expected him to treat me with contempt and disdain, that he would put on a united front for the other team members to keep them off kilter and always wondering just how much they can trust me, but that he would let how he really feels about me show when we were alone. But none of that. If I didn't know better, I'd almost think he liked and respected me beyond his declarations that I was his favourite recruit in all the years he's recruited people.

'Oh, he was trying to flirt with me.'

'Was he now? Interesting.' Dennis is amused by that idea.

'He's been doing that since I met him. He thinks it will help him insert himself into the investigation.'

'You think so?'

'I know so.'

'Do you think he's helping her?'

'I don't know. I didn't originally profile him as someone who would help a killer. But you said it yourself: his deep affection for her could be swaying his judgement. I absolutely think he will help her if he gets the chance. If he manages to insert himself into the investigation, then he may feed her information if she gets in touch with him. I don't think he's in touch with her right now – he seems too anxious about her to have had recent contact. But if I let him think I'm flattered, he may tell me if she gets in touch with him.'

'Not a very Kez thing to do,' Dennis says.

'Since when do you call me Kez?' I reply.

He smiles like a man who has been caught with his hand in the till. 'Not a very Kezuma thing to do,' he corrects.

Dennis doesn't make mistakes like that, so I wonder what is going on in his head that would cause that? All the same, I sit back and fold my arms across my chest. 'How would you know what is and isn't a Kez thing to do, exactly?'

He shakes his head, shrugs a little. 'I think I've got more than a little insight – excuse the pun – into who you are and how you do things. And this doesn't seem to be very you.'

'It doesn't seem very me to want to do anything to stop people being killed? Or to use anyone I can to try to save a young woman from herself? I thought I profiled a lot clearer than that, to be honest.' Before he can say anything else, I push out my chair and stand up. 'Speaking of which, I think we should go hear what the team have come up with in terms of the profile before I put it all together.'

Robyn

September, 2014

Cindra and Brad's home smelt of vanilla and cinnamon. I was nervous when they opened the door after Holly dropped me off. We'd had two visits – one where they took me out and we went to the high street for ice cream and the other where we had ice cream in the park. And now a home visit.

We made popcorn and watched *The Princess Bride*, sitting on the sofa in the living room with the bowls of popcorn on our laps. I'd never done that before and I kept looking at Brad, waiting for him to shout at me, to ask me what the hell I thought I was doing sitting on his sofa and eating.

When the film ended, Brad and Cindra asked if they could talk to me.

'We've really enjoyed spending time with you,' Cindra said as we sat at their kitchen table. They had a warm kitchen, clean and tidy but homely too. I hadn't realised how cold my parents' kitchen had been until I came here. This was lived-in, with stuff on the sides, papers sticking out of a letter holder, books piled up, a first-aid kit in a small black zip-up case sitting on the area beside the sink, a couple of dishes wait-ing to be washed up, an errant can of spray deodorant waiting to be returned to its rightful place. It was weird since I'd only been there a couple of hours, but I felt like I'd come home. I hated myself for thinking that, because nowhere could be home without Mum.

'And we were wondering if you would be interested in possibly coming to stay with us on a long-term basis?' Brad said.

'We're really sorry to be springing this on you, but I just love being around you. And I – we – get really sad when we're not with you,' Cindra said.

'So we wondered if you might like to make this placement a bit more long-term?' Brad finished.

Did I? Did I want to make it long-term? I knew so many kids at the home who would jump at the chance. They would love to have two wonderful people who were kind and patient and generous to ask them to live with them. They'd shown me around the house and there were four bedrooms. One of the bedrooms had a single bed and a desk and a wardrobe and pretty cream curtains. I'd lingered in the doorway of that room, imagining it was mine. That I could live there. But, Mum. How could I live with anyone else when my mum was still a big part of my life? I didn't see what happened to her every time I closed my eyes any more, because I had forced myself to remember her as she had been. To remember the times when Dad was out and we had the run of the house and we could have fun. I loved my mum, still. Totally. What would she say about me going to live with two new people?

'We realise this is a big thing, so don't feel you have to say anything right away,' Cindra reassured. 'We will completely understand if you think it's too fast.'

'We'll take everything at your pace. You get to decide what happens when,' Brad added.

'We're really aware that you don't have much say over what happens to you right now, so we want to make sure that you know this is a hundred per cent your choice.'

I started nodding, because I didn't know what to say. Whilst nodding, I reached for the glass of juice that sat just out of reach. My nervous, trembling fingers brushed it, and I moved forward to grab it but misjudged and the whole glass fell over, loudly clinking onto the wooden table and spilling its juice all over the smooth surface.

'I'm sorry!' I cried, jumping to my feet and slamming my hands on my face. 'I'm sorry, I'm sorry, I'm sorry!' My eyes flew around the kitchen, searching for where the tea towel was so I could clean it up. 'I'm sorry! I'm so sorry!' I continued to cry and dashed over to the double oven and snatched up the tea towel hanging on the handle, ran back to the table and started to mop it up, all the while telling them how sorry I was.

Their confusion filled the room and Cindra got to her feet, came to me and steadied me by placing her hand on my arm to stop me cleaning. Brad carefully took the tea towel out of my hand.

'It's OK,' Cindra said. 'It's only a bit of juice.'

'There's no harm done here,' Brad said, mopping up the juice in no time because he wasn't frantic. 'It's just an accident.'

'I'm so, so sorry,' I began to sob. Why were they saying these things? I knew they didn't mean it. I knew they thought I was a bad girl. Stupid. Clumsy. An embarrassment. I knew they were going to take me back and demand I was punished for wasting their money by spilling the juice and messing up their tea towel. They were going to tell Holly that I was not worth the time and effort they'd spent on me, but they were being nice right now and I didn't understand why.

'It's OK. It's really OK,' Cindra kept saying. She sounded so confused. She took me in her arms, hugged me close to her. 'It's OK. It's OK,' she hushed. 'It's all OK.'

*

Later, back at Maddox Hall, I pretended to go upstairs to get ready for bed. In reality, I crept downstairs to hide by Holly's office so I could hear what they said. So I could confirm that they were going to demand money from Holly and explain why they were not going to see me again.

'What happened to her?' Cindra asked Holly. 'Who did that to her?'

'I don't have details,' Holly replied. 'She was a very traumatised little girl when she arrived. As I told you before, her mother was murdered, and her father was kidnapped. No one knows what happened to him.'

This was the story that kept being told. People would repeat it and I would look at them without saying anything because they believed it. And I wasn't allowed to explain that it was my father. That he was the one who murdered my mother. That instead of going to prison, they took him away. That the story they were telling was the one I heard him tell the first police officer who came to the house. I didn't correct the people who repeated this story because I knew no one would believe me. It was easier, I knew even then, for people to believe that a group of masked strangers had devastated my family than to believe that my father had done it. My father was respectable-looking. He was well spoken and well dressed. He came from a 'good family'. And everyone seemed to love him.

That was proven when they still spoke softly and kindly to him, even after he'd told them what he'd done. They didn't put on handcuffs. They just took me away and made sure he was OK.

'I know you told us that, but her reaction today, that wasn't the result of one night. She was so scared over a little spillage. I mean, I knock things over all the time. It was like she was expecting to be beaten over a normal accident,' Brad said.

'I hate the thought of that,' Cindra said. 'She's so fragile. We asked her if she wanted to live with us, but after the spillage, we weren't sure she would. She was so distraught. We don't want to upset her. She might not want to come back to ours.'

'Do you want her to?' Holly asked. 'Because you don't have to do anything to progress this. We can tell her that it isn't the right time.'

I held my breath. Closed my eyes. It had been nice, dreaming that I could have people who wanted to spend time with me. That it could work out. That I would be away from the home. My heart was beating so hard in my chest it felt like it was throwing itself against my ribcage.

'Of course we do!' Cindra and Brad said at the same time. 'We want her so much. But I don't want to do anything she's not ready for. I don't want to be upsetting her. She might not want us.'

I do! I was screaming inside. *I do, I do, I do!*

'Well, if you're sure you want to go ahead, I'll start on the paperwork that will allow her to come and stay with you temporarily at first and then we can look into long-term.'

'Really?' Cindra said excitedly. 'Really?'

'I didn't dare hope,' Brad said. 'Didn't dare hope.'

I snuck away upstairs again, climbed into bed in the empty bedroom. I was like Brad: I didn't dare hope. Some of the other children here, that's all they did. They spent every waking second hoping for a foster family to walk in and find them. They did everything they could to make themselves perfect so when the foster parents of their dreams walked in, they would be ready. I didn't dare hope I would get a home again. Because unlike most of the other children here, I knew my mother wasn't coming back and that was because of my father. I didn't dare hope I would get another family because the first one I had was taken away.

I had to be careful, though. It might have been a trick. They might have been saying it was fine and they were worried about me to get me into their home. Once there, they could do whatever they wanted to me to teach me a lesson for spilling the juice. Dad did that all the time. He made you feel that something was OK. He made you believe that spilling something, dropping something, forgetting to shut the door was no big deal. He would comfort you, say nice words, sometimes even clean up.

And then . . . hours later, sometimes, you would be sitting at the table, doing homework and he would slap you round the back of your head. You would be walking past to go to the toilet and he would kick one of your legs out from under you. You would be thinking about bed and he would grab a handful of hair and drag you to the ground.

I didn't think Cindra and Brad were like that. But they could be. That was the thing I had learnt – even the person that everyone likes, that no one suspects, could be like that. Anyone could be like that. I was going to live with Cindra and Brad, but I had to keep my wits about me, just in case.

Robyn

October, 2014

I'd accumulated a little bit of stuff since I had arrived at Maddox Hall. Some more clothes, a few books, shoes, a couple of friendship bracelets the other girls made for me. I packed them up in a bag that Andrich, leather-jacket guy, got for me. We'd become quite good friends because he, Tommy and I had been at Maddox Hall the longest and so were constantly around each other while others came and went.

I packed all my stuff into the holdall and sat on my neatly made bed, waiting for Cindra and Brad to pick me up. I was trying to keep a lid on my excitement because I was the only one who had found a family after the open morning. I wasn't one to shout about things like that anyway, but I didn't want to rub anyone's nose in it.

Outside, I heard a car pull up, its tyres crunching on the gravel driveway into the small parking lot where the carers parked overnight. I grabbed my bag, my cuddly toy that I'd managed to keep from my house and ran downstairs. It was Saturday, which meant almost everyone was home unless they had a weekend job or a class. Most of them didn't have those things and just hung out at the weekend. I spent most Saturdays doing homework.

I could hear people in the garden and knew immediately that they were keeping out of my way. Most people here don't like goodbyes – it just adds another one in a life when they've already had to leave people and loved ones behind. Another goodbye to someone who is going off to a life that you want must be especially painful.

Holly had one of those faces that couldn't hide anything. And when I saw her standing at the bottom of the winding staircase, I knew I wasn't going with Cindra and Brad that day. Or any day. Holly nearly jumped out of her skin when they rang the doorbell. She let them in and they too could tell something was wrong, because their grins fell off their faces when they saw her.

'Has something happened?' Cindra asked, looking from Holly to me. She saw I had a holdall; she knew I hadn't changed my mind.

'No, no, not exactly,' Holly said.

What does that mean? I wanted to ask. But I knew to keep my mouth shut. If I didn't, I would start screaming. If I started screaming, I would not be able to stop.

'What's going on?' Brad asked.

'Well,' Holly began, and stopped. It was obviously terrible news because she didn't even think of ushering us into her office. She was just doing it standing here. 'The thing is, when I filed the paperwork to allow Robyn to come and live with you, even just temporarily, something was flagged on the system.'

'What was flagged?' Cindra asked, obviously as keen to get to the point as I was.

'It seems . . . it seems Robyn isn't allowed to be fostered.'

'What? Why?' Cindra almost screeched.

'I'm not sure exactly. It's come back because of her status as a ward of the court, because her mother died in suspicious circumstances and her father is still missing, presumed dead, that she can't be fostered until the status of her father is established.'

'But that doesn't even make sense,' Cindra said disparagingly. 'If both her parents have sadly passed, then surely there can be no objections? It should be smoother not more difficult.'

'But we're not sure of her father's status, so that is why there is a problem, I think.'

'What does this all mean?' Brad asked. His gaze kept swinging between me and Holly. Cindra suddenly dashed across the small hallway and up the stairs until she reached me. She snatched me into her arms as though she was going to be dragged away at any moment.

'It means . . .' Holly didn't want to say anything else. You could tell she just wanted the ground to open up and swallow her whole. 'It means I can't allow you to take Robyn with you today.'

That made Cindra cling even tighter to me.

'We're only taking her for a few days and extending after that if it all works out. Why do you need to stop her coming today? Everything's ready – we've got her room ready. We know what we're having for dinner. We've picked out tonight's movie. Why can't she come, even for a few days?'

'I'm sorry. I'm so sorry. But the rules mean I can't allow that to happen. Not now, not ever.'

My face was wet, and it took a moment to realise that was because Cindra was crying. She was clinging to me and crying big, quiet tears. I was crying too and my tears were mingling with Cindra's, causing a tsunami of emotion on the right side of my face.

'This can't be happening,' Cindra sobbed. 'This can't be happening to us. We've got everything ready,' she added, echoing Brad. 'Her home is waiting for her.'

'I'm sorry,' Holly repeated.

'There must be something you can do. Something.'

'There isn't – I'm sorry. I've never been in this situation before. I've never seen a message like that before. I've talked to my supervisor and his supervisor and every senior person I can think of. I've called everyone I can and they've all said the same – that I have to comply and I can't allow you to take Robyn with you today.'

Those words seemed to break Cindra. She engulfed me with her arms and started sobbing proper. Brad came striding over. He climbed the stairs to where we were and grabbed us both into a hug. He wasn't crying but he might as well have been. We stood there, the three of us, holding each other, two of us openly crying, the other silently sobbing. Eventually we had to break apart; we had to let each other go.

'We're going to fight this,' Brad said, helping Cindra down the stairs and towards the front door. 'We're going to fight it and you're going to come home to us.'

I nodded and said, 'Thank you.'

I was saying thank you because they wanted me. They truly wanted me. It would do no good for them to fight it. There was nothing to fight. I knew this was all down to my father. He used to say, 'If I can't have you, no one else will,' all the time to my mum. Usually when he was threatening her. Mainly after he'd hit her, so she'd know that he would never let her go. He never said it to me, but it was true all the same.

I didn't know where he was – I hadn't heard from him at all since I had been moved here – but the message was clear: I don't want you, but no one else is allowed to have you either. With Mum, he meant he'd take her life; with me, he'd taken my home. And this was a reminder that he would keep taking my home until I knew my place. If I wasn't with him, then I wouldn't be anywhere that made me completely happy, made me feel whole again, made me forget for minutes at a time that I was away from my family.

'He can't be that powerful,' Tommy would say all the time if I talked about my dad. But here he was proving Tommy wrong – my father was that powerful. He was the most powerful man in the world.

I didn't see Cindra and Brad again. Occasionally, Holly would give me a book and say it was from them, sent without a note. I suspected that Holly kept the notes because she knew they would upset me, but I didn't physically see either of them ever again. I hoped that they found a child to complete their life. That a child out there got to experience being loved by those two like I had.

Part 6

Robyn

January, 2015

The Henwrights were brought to Maddox Hall by a stern-faced senior social worker called Mr Fikowsky who smelt of damp wool and year-old Polo mints.

Mr Henwright was a big tall man with brown hair and reflective sunglasses. Mrs Henwright wore white high heels, a leopard-skin skirt, a black leather jacket and a white button-up blouse under the jacket. She was so beautiful with her platinum-blonde hair and ready smile. She loved kids, she gushed when we sat in the small room set aside for things like this. But they couldn't have them, so they'd decided to adopt.

Tommy, who no one had ever had any interest in, didn't want to go in alone so had made me come in with him. 'Is she up for adoption, too?' Mrs Henwright asked when we sat down on the sofa. The social worker looked at Holly and Holly glanced away, looking pained. She hated this part. It truly agonised her to have to explain: Robyn is unfosterable.

'No, Robyn isn't up for fostering,' Mr Fikowsky said.

'Oh, I love the name Robyn,' Mrs Henwright said. 'Are you sure you don't want to be adopted, too? You and Tommy seem very close.'

'Leave the girl alone, babe,' Mr Henwright said. 'Tommy, do you like rugby?'

Tommy nodded. He was so nervous. He told me last night that he wanted to be fostered so bad, but he was scared that what had happened to me would happen to him. That he'd do something to make them change their minds. I told him that Cindra and Brad didn't change their minds and I didn't do anything wrong, but a bit like the thing with people preferring to believe that masked men killed my mother and kidnapped my father over my father being the killer but him not going to prison for it, the kids in the home would prefer to believe that I did something to put them off rather than think my dad was far, far away but somehow still ruining my life.

'Tommy's nervous,' I said to the Henwrights. 'He likes to watch rugby but doesn't like to play it. He prefers football and cricket. And he's really good at it. And he's really good at climbing.' I turned to Mrs Henwright. 'And he's really polite. He looks after people. And he's a really good singer even though he hardly sings because he thinks people will make fun of him.'

The social worker was glaring at me. He thought I was making this all about me when I wasn't doing that. I was trying to make them see that Tommy would fit in with their family.

'Football and cricket?' Mr Henwright said, seemingly impressed.

'I played football back in the day,' Mrs Henwright said. 'What position were you? I was a striker. Top scorer in my team. I always joke that Mr Henwright had to chase me extra hard because I was so quick.'

Tommy couldn't help but grin.

'I'm the singer in the family,' Mr Henwright said. 'Opera for a few years.'

'He's being modest. He's sung all over the world, starred in a few shows. That's how he wooed me – he used to sing to me. Serenade me. I felt so special.'

Tommy's eyes grew wide with surprise and happiness. These two were perfect for him.

'Would you be interested in going out for ice cream?' Mrs Henwright asked. I could hear her nervousness, despite the huge pang that had echoed through me as I remembered Cindra and Brad asking if I liked ice cream. Sometimes it felt like a fever dream, like I had been deathly sick and hallucinating when all of that happened. It was like that but worse with what happened to my mum.

Tommy nodded, too shy, too excited to speak.

'You need to speak to them, you know?' I said. 'I've just told them you can sing but how are they going to believe me if they think you can't talk?'

'Sorry,' Tommy said to me, even though I knew I'd catch hell later. 'Yes, please, I would like to go for ice cream. When?'

'Any time you like, lad,' Mr Henwright said. Both of them were grinning; they must have been so nervous. I didn't really think about what it's like for foster adults, coming to meet someone who may or may not live up to their expectations, who might put an end to their childlessness and complete their family. What it must be like to lay yourself bare and to find that the person you are meeting doesn't feel the same way. That instead of coming home with you, they'd rather stay where they are.

'Erm, well, we will have to arrange things a bit more formally,' Mr Fikowsky said, jumping in. He was glaring at me again. What did I do? If anything, I got these people together because I didn't see him doing anything of use.

I swear I saw Holly roll her eyes at Mr Fikowsky before she said, 'It's OK. I'll arrange everything. I know Tommy's timetable.'

'That's that, then,' Mr Henwright said. He clapped his hands together and stood up like he had come to a decision. He held out his hand for Mrs Henwright to take so she could stand up, too. That moment of affection, like so many I saw between Cindra and Brad, reminded me that my parents weren't like that. Dad would mostly treat Mum with care, affection or respect when other people were around.

Tommy stood up and stuck his hand out to Mr Henwright, who happily shook it after shooting a look of admiration to his wife. Tommy did the same with Mrs Henwright. She was equally impressed.

'Are you sure you're not interested in being adopted?' Mrs Henwright asked me.

'I'm sure,' I said. 'I get much more satisfaction from watching my friends finding new parents.' The social worker looked like he was going to spontaneously combust.

'You're a sweetie,' Mrs Henwright said. 'If it all works out with Tommy, you can come visit us. Stay over. That'd be nice, wouldn't it?'

We all nodded and agreed it would be nice.

While Holly started searching for a date for when Tommy could go out with the Henwrights, Mr Fikowsky showed them out. I went to the kitchen since they didn't need me any more. I stood at the sink, sipping a glass of water. Through the window, I watched the others playing with water guns and the small paddling pool we'd all put our money together to buy. I turned to go join them and found Mr Fikowsky was standing right there, glaring at me.

'*What?*' I wanted to snap at him but didn't dare. I was aware that if he wanted, he could get me moved. I could end up anywhere.

'Next time, keep your nose out of adult business,' he snarled, his voice low and threatening. I backed up to the sink, scared. I had seen that look in a person's eyes before and I knew what came with it.

His look mutated into one of triumph because he'd got what he wanted – a fear reaction. With a sick, sickening grin smeared across his lips, he advanced on me.

I tried not to be scared, tried to push down my fear, but I couldn't help it. I was right back there. Dad pulling the book out of my hands, his hand across my face, my split bleeding lip that I had to say I got from running indoors and tripping on the hallway rug. The fear of it all came flooding back. I hadn't had this properly in so long, so long, that I'd forgotten how fear can freeze you, how it can shock you still.

And fear can also make you clench your teeth, it can tense every muscle in your body when a man standing in front of you sticks his hand up your skirt. Terror can stop your heart when that same man, with his hand up your skirt, clamps his hand around your leg, then uses his thumb to roughly stroke your inner thigh.

'I know who you are,' he said quietly, menacingly, his hand moving higher. 'I know you're not Robyn Managa or Charlotte Draheh. I know who you really are, *Avril*. And I know I can do whatever I want to you.' His hand moved even higher. 'Because no one would believe a word you say. Not the daughter of a murderer. Not the word of a girl even her murderer father didn't want when he started his new life in witness protection.' His fingers brushed against my knickers. 'Are you that much of a bad girl?' he sneered. 'Are you that naughty?'

I wanted to push him off but I was as scared by his words as what he was doing. He knew my father. And if he knew him, then he probably knew that nobody would care if something happened to me.

'Robyn—' Tommy called as he came running into the kitchen. He stopped at the kitchen door when he saw how close the social worker was to me, that he had his hand up my skirt. Tommy instantly knew something wasn't right. When you grow up in care, you get an instinct for when things aren't right, when you could be in danger. Tommy's instinct was much better honed than mine – he'd been there so much longer than me. The social worker removed his hand from where it shouldn't have been and stepped away.

'What's going on?' Tommy asked loudly to make sure Holly heard.

'Our little secret, *Avril*,' the social worker hissed before he tugged a smile into place to face Tommy. Just like Dad used to do. Smile at a stranger, hiss threats at me. 'I was just telling Robyn here how helpful she was with the Henwrights,' he said. 'It's a shame she can't be fostered, too. They seemed very keen on the pair of you.'

Tommy's hands balled into fists, ready for fight or flight. I shook my head at him. This man could ruin both our lives.

Tommy was still poised to fight, his stance rigid, his face screwed up and focused on the social worker. The older man, in his tweed jacket with leather patches at the elbows and neatly ironed white shirt and black trousers, tried to smile at Tommy, tried to convince him that all was well. When Tommy didn't smile back nor unclench his hands, the older man decided to show us who was boss, who was really in charge here.

'Tommy,' he said calmly, 'if you don't want to be fostered by the Henwrights, I can always call them. Say you don't want them. I'm sure they'll understand. I had another boy and girl lined up for them, actually. I think they'll be a much better fit. I just thought, well, you've been here for so long and you're approaching that age where no one will want you.' He sneered in satisfaction when naked panic streaked across my friend's features. He knew how to get to Tommy. To most of us.

'Just say the word, Tommy, and I can make sure you are here for ever.'

Tommy's fists unclenched, his whole body unclenched, his fight stance fell away. I was grateful. I didn't want Tommy to fight him. I didn't want a fuss of any kind. I knew how dangerous this man was, on so many levels.

He knew my dad was alive. He knew what Dad had done. He knew the name I was meant to use. He knew the name I had before. Before they dragged me, literally kicking and screaming, away from the so-called safe house, they told me over and over that no one could know that Dad was still alive. They told me over and over that no one could ever know my 'real' name so not to tell anyone. They told me that no one would ever know what had happened that night.

And I believed them because Holly certainly didn't know. I told her when I arrived that I didn't like the name 'Charlotte Draheh' that had been chosen for me and that my mum had wanted me to be called Robyn and Managa was her maiden name, so could she put that down as my name? She had been fine with that and had gone through and changed all the documentation without question. She didn't know I had been called Avril before. How did this man know? How did he know so much?

Logically, there could only be one reason: my father had told him to watch me. My father was proving once again that he was more power-ful than I could imagine. And I was never going to get away from him. Even here, I was never going to be free.

Three months later, Tommy left Maddox Hall to live with the Hen-wrights. They asked a couple of times, apparently, if I wanted to be fostered, too. Mrs Henwright really liked me and was really keen on having both of us. But, no deal. Obviously, no deal.

We were all of us happy for Tommy because he'd been there the long-est out of everyone – he'd arrived when he was two years old, having been abandoned as a baby. So when it came to his time to leave, we all congregated in the living room and hall, hugged him, told him we were pleased for him and told him not to come back. Even Andrich punched him lightly on the shoulder and said good luck. Holly was inconsolable, her tears coming in floods – he was almost like her child, I heard her saying on the phone; letting him go was fantastic for him, but awful for her.

He and I were the last to hug, by the car. 'I'll see you,' I said to him.

'I'll see you,' he said to me, both of us knowing that we wouldn't. We absolutely wouldn't. And that was OK. That was simply the way things were.

Kez

29 April, Brighton

Profile of Robyn Managa

Name: Robyn Managa

Address: Whereabouts unknown. Thought to be in Brighton area

Place of birth: London

Grew up: Brighton, East Sussex, West Sussex

Eye colour: Dark brown

Glasses: Unknown

Hair colour: Black (assumed) according to eye-witness testimony

Body type: Athletic

Occupation: Unknown. Graduated from University of East Sussex, January 2020

Relationship status: Unknown

Age: 25

Significant others: Mother (deceased), father (whereabouts unknown)

Significant information: Robyn has killed four people – three directly, another died as a result of falling in front of a car during the assault.

Background

Robyn Managa is the child of Rose Managa and her husband, whose name we're not allowed to know. For the purposes of this profile, I am calling him John Doe. Robyn grew up in West Sussex, where her parents moved when she was two years old.

Information from the sparse files we have on Robyn's early life show that her parents were unhappily married. In the year that Robyn was to turn twelve, her parents' relationship broke down completely. From what was reported in the press, on the night in question, a group of masked men broke into the family home in Horsham, killed Mrs Managa and kidnapped Robyn's father, John Doe. At the time, John Doe was high up in a large corporation. It was believed the kidnap was to coerce him into stealing funds from the corporation.

The kidnappers left eleven-year-old Robyn behind. John Doe was never seen again.

This is the official story. The one that was released to the press.

The real story is that on the night in question John Doe claims to have 'snapped' and had a psychotic break. When he recovered from this break, he discovered that he had killed his wife, and called the police.

He claims to have no memory of the crime. However, the assessment we made of the crime-scene photos and his subsequent actions suggest otherwise. It is my belief that John Doe was abusive throughout their relationship and did in fact plan to kill his wife – if not on the night in question but at some other point.

He committed the crime in full view of Robyn and I suspect he did not offer her any comfort or explanation. He also originally lied to the police and told them that several intruders had committed the crime. It is not clear how, but in the early days of the investigation, John Doe managed to strike some kind of deal with the government, for whom he was an important contractor, that meant he was not charged with the crime. Indeed, a story was fabricated to ensure unknown assailants were blamed for the crime and the world was made to believe that John Doe had been kidnapped and was feared dead. This allowed John Doe to be placed in the witness protection programme.

John Doe began his new life in witness protection not long after that. He was furnished with a new name and identity. From the scant documents we can get hold of from that time, it seems he decided he did not want to bring Robyn with him. However, there might have been a decision made that Robyn would not be safe with John Doe now that he had already escaped prosecution for murder once.

Robyn, by now twelve – her mother died on the eve of her birthday – was put into care because no family was available to take her on. I suspect the truth of that is that John Doe, being an abuser, would have already damaged and destroyed all his wife's close relationships. And, if some family or friends had been found, I am sure they would not have been allowed to take her on because they may have speculated about the truth of the multiple-intruder story.

Little is known about Robyn's time in care. Her records have yet to be located and anyone who might have known anything is consistently unavailable for interview. I suspect there is some deliberate obstruction going on to prevent us knowing how badly she was treated. And whether her father was in any way influencing how her life went at the home. One of the people Robyn killed was a former social worker who had been investigated multiple times for sexually abusing some of the children in his care. He was also found, after his death, to have had many different types of payments going into his bank account, and it seems likely that he may have been charging people for access to the children. It stands to reason that how he treated Robyn may have contributed to his death. It's unknown, however, if one of the payments he received was from Robyn's father or someone else to keep an eye on Robyn.

Robyn resurfaced again in 2017 when she enrolled at the University of East Sussex on a psychology course. One of her first-year tutors,

Dr Guy Mackenzie, deduced that she was vulnerable and possibly homeless, so, against university protocol, he offered her a place to stay in his home.

From different rounds of questioning, Dr Mackenzie has explained that despite Robyn getting the wrong end of the stick when she first moved in, nothing sexual happened between them. Several background checks have been run on Dr Mackenzie and have come back clean.

Robyn graduated, passing with first-class honours. All university records state that she was a diligent, hard worker. That she focused determinedly on whatever task she set her mind to. She was very hard on herself when she got things wrong. Her time at university was unremarkable. The only incident of note involved a friend of hers who accused a fellow student of sexual harassment and a minor sexual assault. Having originally denied the allegations, the student then returned to university authorities and confessed to the crime. The university authorities suspected that the accused, sporting a broken hand, had been coerced into the confession by Robyn Managa. Nothing was ever proved either way and the matter was dropped.

Robyn's final-year thesis was on the psychological effects of trauma on perceptions of justice.

Present situation
After university, Robyn worked in temporary jobs, and nothing was heard of her until earlier this year when it appears she kidnapped,

tortured and killed a journalist who wrote the original fabricated news story about her mother's murder.

At an as yet unknown location, it seems she continually tortured and beat the journalist – who was originally an intelligence agent – presumably asking for information on the whereabouts of her father. When she dumped the body of the journalist back in his flat, she left a note saying 'GIVE HIM TO ME'. All capitals.

She has repeated this pattern of violence and demands for information with three other people. The crime-scene photos seem to indicate that she is escalating the violence.

She is demanding in her notes that 'they' give her father to her. It is almost certain that she will kill her father if she meets with him again. Her finding him through her current means is not an option for that reason.

This profile is to assist in finding Robyn. We are using the information we have on her to find her before she kills again.

Information gleaned so far from:
*victimology – those she targets are people who she believes wronged her thirteen years ago and, crucially, may know where her father is

*the nature of her crimes

*the note left as her calling card

*the length of time she has waited to begin this campaign

*the possibility of her learning to fight and strengthen her body in order to carry out the attacks

*the fact she has avoided the police so far

*the certainty that she will not stop until she has what she wants

leads to the following conclusions about Robyn Managa

*She is highly organised

*She is determined

*She is intelligent

*She is meticulous

*She is methodical

*She has forensic and criminology knowledge

*She is disciplined

*She is patient

*She has significant IT skills that allowed her to hack at least one government database in her search for information

Other observations

Psychopathy, sociopathy and narcissism have been ruled out. Her actions do not point to and have not historically exhibited signs of any of these conditions, although other mental health concerns are very likely. Dr Mackenzie spoke of depression and sometimes raging at the world.

Witnessing her mother's murder will very likely have traumatised her and left her with lasting emotional and mental scars, if not physical ones. It is likely that untreated Post Traumatic Stress Disorder will, for the most part, be driving this behaviour.

Her levels of organisation, patience and planning all suggest that she has a complete list of people she intends to attack. Her determination suggests that she has studied the victims over a long period of time to work out their weaknesses, routines and pressure points.

She will have a base of operations where she has been planning and preparing for this. The place will be remote, but not completely isolated. This base will be clean and tidy. She will have work-out equipment, space to spread out her information, access to the internet, easy access to the motorway – M23 or M25.

It's my belief that we need to concentrate on finding this base of operations first. It will be easier than trying to find her. Finding and neutralising her base of operations will allow us to identify her future victims and take them into protective custody.

Neutralising her base of operations will also slow her down. Her personality needs certainty, to work through things at a logical pace – everything needs to be done in a particular order. Removing or at the very least destabilising that order will be our best chance to make her slip up and allow us to capture her alive.

If we do not find the base of operations in the next few days, I would suggest that we seriously reconsider finding her father and facilitating a conversation between them.

I am not saying we should do it – I am merely saying we should consider the possibility. Because Robyn is so good at what she does, I think there may be a real possibility that we may not be able to stop her before she finds him, which would be catastrophic.

Offering the possibility of a conversation with her father may be enough to allow us to control what happens and spare other people's lives.

Also, you people who decide these things should consider making her a part of one of your teams. I know she has killed people, but we all know that doesn't disqualify people from working in your teams. I say that because what she has achieved on her own so far puts a lot of your 'brightest and best' to shame.

Kez

29 April, Brighton

I deliver the profile to everyone who was there when we questioned Guy Mackenzie.

No one speaks for a few seconds. This is the first time anyone other than me has heard the whole thing together. Each person in the room knew a bit; no one knew it all. Until now. And they are all shocked. These less experienced psychologists/behavioural scientists have to confront the reality that humans might be one thing – serial killers – but might not exhibit the expected traits of psychopathy or sociopathy, which means they cannot be as easily profiled, categorised or 'cured'. They are also probably shocked that Robyn's father, who does sound like a psychopath, had help getting away with his crime.

The police officers are shocked that they can't neatly classify Robyn's behaviour as the work of a sicko or psycho, and that everyone now knows that the police can and will cover up crimes if it benefits them.

Big Bad Aidan is shocked because I've just said without saying the actual words that he's doing a terrible job and should be replaced. He is also coming to realise I'm not as 'woo-woo' and 'out there' as he thought I was when he first met me. I suspect his dislike of me is grow-ing at an exponential rate.

Horson is shocked because I can actually do my job and, of course, he is PISSED OFF because I've just leaked confidential information to a room of people he doesn't trust.

And Dennis is shocked because everyone now knows how Insight really rolls – that we are potential supporters of a murderer. That's just the way the cookie crumbles sometimes. Nothing I can do about it.

'So,' I say to the room of shocked, silent faces, 'does anyone have any suggestions on how we go about finding her base of operations?'

Part 7

Robyn

28 February, Crawley

Boris Fikowsky was the first person who told me that my father was keeping an eye on me from wherever he was. He was the man who glared at me when I tried to help my friend get himself parents. Who shoved his hand up my skirt and would have done worse if my friend hadn't walked in. Who threatened my friend when he wanted to help me. Boris Fikowsky was always very clear about knowing who I was and how he could do whatever he wanted to me and that I had no way of fighting back. I lived with the constant fear of the day that he would finally force himself on me. Whenever he was in Maddox Hall my heart would beat in triple time, my stomach would be in knots, I'd jump at every shadow.

It's taken me a while to recover from Talamon's punches, and in that time I've been watching Fikowsky.

He has thinned hair on top that is lightly grey all over. He has a paunch and bad posture. He wears blue-and-white checked shirts and belted light-beige chinos that sit below his paunch. His arms and top half are slim so he convinces himself that he still has the physique of the man he used to be when he wielded so much power over young lives. I have often wondered how many young girls didn't have a Tommy to walk in and stop his hand going further. How many times did he do more than just touch? How many times did he threaten to snatch away someone's future if they didn't let him do what he wanted with their body?

He still wears that tweed jacket, its leather-patch elbows badly worn. His face now has glasses and he still sports a gold wedding band. He is high, high up in the social-services ranks now, which means he doesn't deal with the children any longer. Probably because they knew what he was doing, but didn't have the guts or the leverage to get rid of him completely. Creeps – like flotsam, like liquid sewage – almost always rise to the top.

He leaves his house every weekday morning at 7.30 a.m. He goes to his vintage red mini with the Union Jack flag roof and shiny alloy wheels. He tosses his leather briefcase onto the passenger seat, then takes a deep breath to allow himself to concertina himself into his car. The car is too low for someone as creaky as he walks. He drives forty-five minutes to work, probably listening to audiobooks or podcasts or the radio, feeling smugly superior to everyone else. On Mondays, he makes a detour. He stops off at a house just out-side Crawley. The house's owner welcomes him in a red silky dressing gown that she wears over a black lacy teddy. She acts like she's delighted to see him, but get close enough and you can see the disdain in her eyes, the forcedness in her smile; get close enough and you'll see she's only acknowledging him at all because she's getting paid.

He leaves twenty minutes later, arrives in time for work at 8.45 a.m. His job title tells me that he spends all day supervising others, checking the quality of their reports, allocating funds, overseeing the way national policy is applied on this local level. At 5.45 p.m. on Monday, Tuesday, Thursday and Friday he leaves work, drives home. His wife often has dinner waiting. Sometimes she goes out to supper with friends and leaves the house looking cold and unloved. She is pretty, his wife. She takes care of her appearance. I suspect she wanted children, he didn't and now she has accepted her fate. I could be wrong, but him firmly clinging on to his mini and her having a bigger, almost family-sized car tells me I'm more likely to be right. He hates children. He would never willingly share his home and life with one.

Wednesday evenings, like today, he leaves work at 5 p.m. He goes back to the house near Crawley. He spends more time (and therefore money) there. He comes out looking especially smug, his step is noticeably lighter, his posture far more upright.

I almost feel bad as I tug up my mask to cover my mouth and nose, pull up my hood over my hair under its hat, tug gloves onto each hand. I almost feel guilty as I pick up my weapon and, holding it down by the side of my leg, I advance on his position. He looks back at the house every time leaves, trying to catch a glimpse of his 'friend' waiting in the doorway to blow him a kiss goodbye, I suspect. He does it every visit, and every time I think he truly believes she'll be there, so awed by his prowess she'll show him some off-the-clock affection.

The dark surrounds us like an invisibility cloak and I almost can't see him until he opens his car door and light shines out onto him.

I hesitate.

I wasn't expecting that. I wasn't expecting to have second, third and fourth thoughts while approaching him. Maybe I'm a little bit scared? After what happened with Talamon, I'm a bit nervous he may get the upper hand.

Feel the doubt and do it anyway, I decide. *Feel the fear and hit him across the back of the head anyway.*

When I do, he unceremoniously falls to the ground.

Kez

29 April, Brighton

'Tell me the truth about why you helped Robyn and I will tell you what I worked out.'

I am sitting on the steps outside Guy Mackenzie's house, where I've been waiting a while. It doesn't matter now if I'm seen with him – Dennis knows what I said about trying to exploit his attempts at flirting with me to find out if he's in touch with Robyn, so Dennis will think nothing of it.

'You're a professional. We both know that there would have to be a very good reason for you to risk everything by having a vulnerable young woman living with you. I believe you when you say nothing happened with her, but I need to know why you took her in instead of directing her to services that could help her. I need you to tell me the truth.'

'Hello to you, too,' Mac says.

I meet his eye as I say, 'And don't start flirting with me. Or pseudo-flirting with me or whatever it is you're doing. It's not going to do anything other than make me think I can't trust you and that you're hiding something.'

'You're no fun,' he says to me.

'Fair enough,' I say, and stand up, dust imaginary dirt from my hands and descend the steps.

Before I can walk away, Mac steps beside me, far too close for someone I don't know, and puts an arm out to stop me in my tracks. 'I'm sorry,' he murmurs. 'I'm sorry. It's deflection. I think you know that. It's not easy. Robyn reminds me . . . she reminds me of how wrong I got it. How I thought I knew it all, how I was this big-time therapist who could fix anyone and everything . . . and someone died as a result of it.' He looks at me then, and even in the dark I can see the torture. I know that torture, the pain of getting something so cata-strophically wrong because you thought you were almost superhuman. I've been there. And Jeb has said more than once that it is the reason why I am the way I am, why I take the risks that make him so worried. 'Will you give me another chance? Please?'

*

'One of the first tasks that I ask my first-year students to do for the Principles in the Therapeutic Process module is to write me a story.'

Mac and I are walking towards the university buildings along a main road. It's occasionally busy and as the night progresses into blackness, I'm comforted by the steady flow of cars. He had gone into his house to leave his bag and computer while I waited outside.

'Any particular reason why?'

'Well, you know how pivotal storytelling is in our lives and in help-ing to make sense of our reality. I want to get an idea of the type of people who are taking my class. It's a thinly veiled chance for them to talk about themselves without actually talking about themselves. I get to see what sort of people they are and see how I need to approach teaching them.

'I don't actually ask them to write a story about their lives. I ask them to write a short passage from the perspective of someone who is at a crossroads in their life. Robyn's story was from the perspective of a police officer who has been assigned to work on a case where a father has killed his wife. And the police officer is at a crossroads – does she take the father into custody and get justice for the wife or does she decide to let him off so their son, who was witness to the act, doesn't have to take the stand in court.'

'Pretty on the nose,' I say. 'How did you know it wasn't just a made-up story?'

Mac stops walking and stands in front of the house on the corner of the street. He folds his arms across his chest and tries – and fails – to stop a look of pure contempt taking over his face. 'How do you think I knew?' he asks, hostility coating every word.

He knew because you can just tell. You can tell when someone's story is personal to them, if they are writing something that comes from a deep place inside them. No matter how much they try to dress it up, you can tell. You can always tell. 'Fair point. But I'm pretty sure there will have been other stories that were just as harrowing and revealing. You didn't ask them to come and stay with you.'

He starts to walk again, uncrossing his arms and dropping them to his sides before he sticks his hands in his pockets. It's such a desolate action that my heart skips a little for him. 'Do you remember when you were newly qualified how you felt when you realised you'd helped someone? How incredible it felt to know that you'd given someone their life back?'

I remember. It felt like I could fly, that I could do anything and everything. It was the strongest drug I'd ever experienced.

'I felt like I was superhuman. That the world should bow down at my feet. Not really, but you know what I mean. I thought I knew best. There was this couple . . . Really nice couple, two kids. Came for therapy. I remember, in the first session, he said something. Huge red flag. I realised it was an abusive situation. And what are you told about abusive relationships and therapy?'

'Couples, family and group therapy is not suitable where abuse is present,' I reply, feeling the dread of what is coming.

'I thought I knew better. I thought I could work with them. I thought that recommendation couldn't possibly apply to me. Not to me. Again, that wasn't what I was consciously thinking, but it was how I acted. I thought I could sort them out and fix their relationship. Find a way for them to stay together, keep their family intact.'

'What happened?'

'I fixed them. Every week things got better and better. They both worked really hard; they both accepted their part in making the relationship as difficult as it was. They both committed to working harder.' His voice quietens a fraction, almost as though he is slowly withdrawing, hiding from what he is about to say. 'They finished their sessions and they walked out of my office hand in hand. I mean, I did that, right? I saved their relationship; I kept that family together.'

I feel sick for him, properly nauseous for what he's about to reveal. I'm tempted to help him, to not make him say it. But I get the impression that he hasn't talked about this in years and just like me and the Brian situation, sometimes you need to say it out loud. You need to hear it so you can own it. 'It was six months before I heard about them again. I got a call in the middle of the night. The husband wanted to speak to me. I got to the police station and there he was.' He runs his hands over his head. 'He gave his solicitor my name and number because he wanted me to tell them. He wanted me to explain to his solicitor and to the police how it was all her fault. I had told him that, week after week. I got her to admit that she was the one who wound him up. She made him do it. She made him control her. She made him hit her. She made him kill her in front of her children.'

I feel his pain – sharp, acute – as he reaches this apex of his story. I have to put a hand on his arm to offer some comfort, as small and inconsequential as it is.

'She'd tried to leave. She'd tried to remove herself from that situation. She'd packed a bag and was going to stay with her sister.'

'The most dangerous time for a woman is when she tries to leave an abusive relationship,' I say. He doesn't need me to say that, but I say it anyway, to let him know I understand. I really do.

'I did that. I got her killed because I didn't want to listen to what people wiser than me had said. Reading Robyn's piece just brought it all back. I haven't forgotten – I could never forget – but I have been determined to help people ever since. Trying to make up for it. And Robyn needed help. She needed someone to give her a break. And I could do that. I could do that. I can never make up for what I did. How I took those children's mother from them, but I could do my best to help Robyn.'

It's like listening to myself. Listening to myself talk about why I do the things I do.

'And now I'm faced with the things that Robyn is doing and how I'm partially responsible for that.'

'You're not responsible for those things. She is. Just like the man who killed your patient is responsible.'

'If we were talking about you, would you believe that?' he replies.

My turn to stick my hands in my pockets. 'But we're not talking about me, are we? We're talking about you. And the fact that you couldn't have stopped Robyn. Especially not when you see the lengths they went to, to cover up what her father did. Like I said, you probably stopped her from doing all this earlier.'

'Yeah, maybe. Maybe.'

We walk in silence a little longer.

'So, are you going to tell me what it is that you worked out?'

'Looking at the minimal information that I had for John Doe as I'm calling him, I realised that he was a narcissist and psychopath. That he would have enjoyed what he did to Rose Managa and he would have revelled in getting away with it. The last thing he would do is get rid of the place where he did all that stuff. He controlled every moment of Rose Managa's life there and he controlled her end there. I checked after I realised that and it seems he does still own the house. It's owned by a consortium, officially, but I'm sure it's still his. I mainly think that because it's been empty all this time. It's protected by a private security firm, but I think it's where Robyn has set up her basecamp. I doubt the police would think to look there, especially since it's now officially not owned by him. It's the perfect place, too, because she can retraumatise herself by being where all of this began. Whenever she starts to have doubts – which she will because she's not a psychopath – she will have a sensory reminder of what happened and why she's doing it. I also think that's where she takes people. That does suggest, though, that she's got help. But I can't see who would help her with this.' Apart from the man next to me. 'Apart from you, of course.'

'I wouldn't help her to do that. I might help her in other ways, but not to do that. I hope you believe that. I think you may be right, though. I think that's where she is. Let's go there.'

'What, now?'

'Yes, now. It's not that late. I can drive us up there. We'll be there in under an hour at this time of night.'

'I can't go now. I've got a husband and children to get back to.'

'I thought you wanted to stop her.'

'I do, but I'm not going in there unprepared. Especially not when I told my husband I wouldn't be out too late.'

'I'll go on my own, then.'

'No, don't.'

'She could be up there right now, torturing someone. I don't want to live with that on my conscience, do you?'

'No, of course not.'

'Then let's go.'

'No. She has been leaving at least two weeks between incidents. It's been seven days since the last incident. We have seven more days. And this would be the worst time to go. If she is there with someone, how are we going to stop her? We'll be forced to call the police and you know what they want to do to her. If we go, we're going to have to pick a time when she's most likely to be asleep. I think she's probably been sleeping during the day so she can grab people at night. We need to catch her when she's not in full-on fight mode.'

Mac is still wanting to go, but he knows I'm right. 'OK,' he eventually concedes. 'But tomorrow. First thing in the morning.'

'Yes. Fine.'

'I'll pick you up.'

'You most certainly won't. I keep all of this shizzle away from my family. If my husband knew even half the stuff I do he'd never let me work there. He would make me leave straight away. There's no way in hell that you're coming to my house.'

'Well, come here, then.'

'Can you cool your jets? I have to work out a way to get out of work. Do you think my boss will just be like, "fine, Kez, go off and do what you like"? I'll answer that for you. No, no he won't. I will ring you when I have found a way out of work tomorrow and we'll head up there.'

'Fine.' He shakes his head. 'I just want to see her. Talk to her. Get her to stop.'

'I know, I know. I do, too. We've just got to do it carefully. If we mess this up, Robyn is dead. And neither of us wants that.'

'No, no we don't. OK, I'll try to hold back.'

'Thank you. Let's walk back so I can get my car. I need to try to be home for bedtime today.'

*

'I'll see you tomorrow,' Mac says when I am back in my car.

'Yes, I'll see you tomorrow.'

'And thank you for listening,' he says before I pull off.

I'm startled. Not many people thank me for listening. 'No worries.'

'And thank you for understanding.' Mac gives me that look, the one where he tells me without words that he knows I've been where he is. That I carry the huge guilt of someone's death with me wherever I go and whatever I do.

I nod, push the button to close the window and leave before I start blurting out exactly how I understand what he is going through.

Robyn

28 February, Secret Location

'Hello, Mr Fikowsky,' I say when my former social worker finally prises his eyelids apart.

'Whaaaa—?' he mumbles, trying to remember how to speak.

'You scared me there. I thought I'd hit you too hard or in the wrong spot or something. You've been out for quite a few hours.'

He blinks his bleary eyes and then moans loudly because the pain in his skull has obviously just made contact with every single nerve in his pain centres and they are not playing nicely together. He moves his right hand to his head, trying to check the areas of particular tenderness even though all of it hurts. He realises quickly that he can't touch his head. He can't in fact move either of his hands because he is tied to a chair in the middle of the darkened space we are in.

I watch terror bolt across his face, pooling in his eyes – he's just discovered his feet are bound to the chair, too.

'Who are you?' he demands. 'What do you want from me? I don't have any money.'

'I don't want your money, Mr Fikowsky,' I reassure. 'I want something far more valuable.'

'What are you talking about? What do you want? I demand you let me go. Right now!'

I step into the light then. Allow him to see me, dressed all in black from my skin-tight jeggings to my black T-shirt to my black utility jacket, my hood up and my neck scarf in place over my nose and mouth.

He quivers, properly scared now. Now he feels what I felt every time I knew he was in the children's home. Now he knows what it feels like when someone cruelly exercises the power they have over you

'Please, please don't hurt me,' he begs. 'Please.'

'That all rather depends on whether you answer my questions in the way I need you to or not.'

'Please, I haven't done anything.'

'We both know that's not true,' I say. 'But we're not here about that. I have some very specific questions. If you answer them, I'll let you go.'

'Please, I don't know anything about anything,' he begs.

'But that's just it – you do. You told me years and years ago that you do.'

I pull down my hood, take my hat off and shove it into my coat pocket, then I lower the black snood from round my face. 'Hello, Mr Fikowsky,' I say with a wide smile.

'You!' he says. 'I know you!'

'You sure do.'

'Untie me this instant! How dare you! Untie me!'

'Weren't you listening to me? I told you very clearly that I would let you go when you give me the answers I need.'

'Untie me, you silly little bitch!'

My shoulders sag. He used to call me that and other stuff when we were alone. He obviously hasn't changed his attitude towards me, so that means we're doing this the hard way. I move out of the circle of light and grab the silver trolley, wheel it into view. I stop it right in front of Mr Fikowsky. It has an array of dental tools as well as a hammer and a screwdriver, a wrench and pliers, and a few other D.I.Y. tools, including a blowtorch.

'I hoped it wouldn't come to this. But you tossing around the B word like that means this is clearly needed.'

233

I pick up the pliers, hold them right up as I examine them, moving them this way and that, making sure Mr Fikowsky sees them, *properly* sees them. I know the exact moment when he understands what he is seeing, the precise second when all the scenarios about what I might do with them click into place in his brain. I know because that's when he sits completely still, when he stops being angry and indignant, when he stops thinking he can bully me into being fourteen again so I'll comply with his every demand. It's when he becomes very, *very* afraid.

I finally have his full, focused attention.

'Now, Mr Fikowsky,' I say, approaching him with the pliers, 'where the fuck is my father?'

Part 8

Kez

30 April, Brighton

'So your husband doesn't know you're an agent?' Mac says two minutes into our journey. I arrived at his house at ten o'clock to find him standing by the front window, looking out, and as I pulled up at the kerb, he came skipping down the steps.

'I'm not an agent,' I reply simply. 'And, anyway, you're one to talk. You seem to have all the experience and tricks of being an agent. Covering your lips so the cameras can't pick up what you're saying. Knowing where the CCTV blindspots are in the uni car park. You're either a master criminal or an agent. I'm not sure which I have you down as yet. Nor which I'd prefer you to be.'

I feel him smile a little, and something lights up inside me that I've managed to make him do that when he looks so serious and seems so burdened most of the time. 'I can neither confirm nor deny if I may or may not have had the tap on the shoulder at some point.'

'Right. So you were recruited. What happened?'

'I can neither confirm nor deny that I saw what they wanted from me and I wasn't willing to give it. Much like you, I'd imagine, I mean, since you're not an agent and all.'

I think about my career, and how I ended up here. How I was

recruited while doing my master's degree in psychotherapy because my tutor passed my name on to the Human Insight Unit as it was back then. I consider how my naïveté of the world led me to meeting Dennis. And meeting Brian, and Maisie as she was at the time before she became MJ. I never really got the chance to walk away, to decide what I was and wasn't willing to give. Every time I tried to walk away, Dennis sabotaged me. Did everything in his power to make those other jobs go away, even the ones I'd been practically offered. Dennis was determined to never let me go, never let me escape. And then, when Brian died, I – and Dennis – had no choice in my leaving because they needed me gone to cover up what had happened. None of that was a conscious choice to walk away or stick around. Much like this situation I'm in with Insight – not much choice in walking away. 'I'm not an agent,' I reiterate.

'Of course you're not,' he teases. 'You said your husband wouldn't let you carry on working where you did if he knew what you did. Does he often tell you what to do?' His change of tack is jarring, like brakes suddenly applied when you're cruising at 70mph on a motorway so you can take a sharp turn-off. I did wonder if he would ask me about that, given the history he told me about. Given how things like that must sound to anyone who isn't in my relationship. If Mac knew what our sex life used to be like, how raw and close to the bone it used to get sometimes, I'm sure he'd have quite a few more reservations about the safety of my marriage.

'No, he never tells me what to do. He just gets me to agree not to do certain things. And, yes, I'm aware how red flaggy that sounds. But he's not controlling. He . . . he only ever gets me to agree not to put myself in danger. And even then he only tells me what he thinks, like he shines a light on what I'm doing. He doesn't try to stop me in any serious way.'

'Still not hearing how he's not controlling.'

'I apparently have an unhealthy disregard for my own safety sometimes,' I confess. 'I can't really see it – things happen to me and I just accept them as part of my life. Jeb, that's my husband, he's like the self-preservation widget that regularly doesn't go off in my head. He kind of pulls me back when I go too far.'

'All right, that is sounding a bit less controlling but go on . . .'

'That's it, really. He isn't controlling. At all. I can do whatever I want. It's just sometimes he has to say "stop" before I fall off the edge. Like when an inmate punched me in the face during a prison group-therapy session. I was like, "Well, that's not ideal, but I can understand why he did it," but Jeb was like, "No more prison visits, Kez." And I didn't see the big deal, but he explained how once I'd been assaulted in that environment, it could trigger other people to do the same. If I had decided that I still wanted to do them, he would have accepted it eventually, but he would have made me have several conversations beforehand. He struggles with what I do and how I do it. He's told me that more than once. But it's never a problem if I want to do something. I don't sit there and think, "How am I going to spin this with Jeb?", which is how I see the difference between being in a controlling relationship and not, I suppose. I can do whatever I want. And I have him there to pull me back sometimes.'

'How did you meet?' he asks.

'Why do you want to know?'

'Because you're beautiful as well as endlessly fascinating to me and I want to know everything I can about you.'

'I thought we agreed you weren't going to flirt with me any more?'

'No, you said me flirting with you stopped you trusting me.'

'The implication from you then telling me your story being that you'd agreed to stop it.'

'All right, sorry. I wanted to know how long you've been together.'

'I met him at a party, when I was in my early twenties.' By *'met at a party'* I, of course, mean *'fucked him in a bedroom upstairs without even knowing his name'*. 'We didn't see each other for many years, then we met again in London and got together after that.' By which I mean *'he walked back into my life with his wife who he'd married a week after we did said fucking'*. I've erased for the most part that I could be considered my husband's stag weekend indiscretion, that he used me to try to get out of getting married. At the same time, he kept my number and when his marriage broke down I was the person he came to. Our relationship origin story is wildly unromantic and romantic at the same time. Or just wild. I've never really worked out which.

'Why aren't you married or partnered?'

'Because no one will put up with me, is the short answer.'

'Why, what's wrong with you?'

'An unhealthy disregard for my own safety,' he replies. Our eyes meet when we both give each other side-eyes. I look away back to the road first and he continues: 'For a long time I tried very hard to destroy myself because I was so eaten up with guilt. I did the drinking and drugs thing. But I became obsessed with helping people. With seeing things that weren't necessarily there in patients' lives. I signed up for every volunteer programme available, I worked for half the price I should have, I was always on call. After that woman died and her husband was sentenced, I tried to burn myself out to make up for my role in it. I didn't see it at the time, of course. I thought I was doing good, that I was helping, but really I was just trying to end myself the long way round. And for anyone who is close to you, that way of living is . . .'

'Terrifying,' I say at the same time as him.

Terrifying is the word Jeb uses to describe how I am. Terrified is how he looks sometimes when I walk through the door later than I said I would be. '*I never want to have that type of conversation with our children*,' he's said more than once. '*I never want to tell them you're not coming home.*'

'Yeah. "I got someone killed and I'm so consumed with guilt you'll never come before my need to right that wrong" is not exactly something to put on a dating profile— Hang on, this isn't the way to Horsham. Where are we going?'

'Worthing.'

'Why are we going to Worthing?'

'I told you we need to see Robyn in her down time and she doesn't stay in one place for too long. She has evaded detection because she has multiple places.'

'How did you work that out?'

'I put myself in her shoes. I worked out what I would do to avoid being caught, while being allowed to do what I need to. Having several boltholes and identities would be essential.'

'Identities?'

'Yes, she's got lots of different identities and formal ID to match. Mainly credit cards. And she could do that because she had a permanent address that was linked to her but not, as well.'

'You mean she used my address to set up multiple credit-card accounts?'

'Yes. And your name. One of her identities – I double-checked on people linked to your address – is Avril Mackenzie. Avril was her original name.'

'I don't know whether to be furious or impressed.'

'You can be both, I think. She's been very good at erasing as much as possible of her digital and real-life footprint, though.'

'What was your stressor?' he asks, again forcing our metaphorical conversation car to take a sharp turn.

'I don't get you.'

'What was the stressor that triggered your unhealthy disregard for your own safety?' Brian's ghost-white face flashes up in front of my eyes. Brian's ghost-loud voice screams, *'PICK UP THE GUN, KEZ!'* in my ears. He is my stressor. He is the reason why I am doing all of this. Brian, the one I couldn't save. Brian . . .

'I don't want to talk about it,' I reply. 'I never want to talk about it.'

'Does your husband know?'

'Yes. He knows pretty much everything about me.'

'But not your job.'

'But not my job.' Nor this thing that's going on right here with this man in my car. I haven't told Jeb that someone is charming me when I thought – always assumed – I was immune to that kind of approach. Over the years, in every single iteration of my working life, no one I've met during the course of my job has flirted with me unless they wanted something – be that to distract me, to get me onside to use against someone else, to get me to overlook what they've been doing. Sometimes the person doesn't even realise they're doing it. Sometimes they just want me to like them so they can carry on doing whatever it is that they're doing with impunity. But with this man, with Mac, it's different. He is obviously trying to distract me, he is clearly trying to get me onside so I will let him accompany me wherever I go, he is possibly trying to keep me off the scent of him helping Robyn, but I get the impression that he likes me, too. I could be completely wrong, but I sense I'm not. I sense a part – a large part – of him seems to be genuinely interested in and attracted to me.

His face popping up in my mind during sex aside, I've been avoiding thinking about whether I'm attracted to him or not. Which is not ideal. The more I avoid thinking about it, the bigger an issue it's likely to become. And if I think about it, it won't likely become a big issue, it will *be* a big issue. I know it's all tied up in what happened last year. In the damage it's done to my relationship with the world as well as to my marriage to Jeb.

We're approaching Worthing, Brighton's older cousin from down the way. When one of our parents or siblings would come to look after the kids for us, Jeb and I would opt to come here overnight instead of going into Brighton or going further afield. We loved the anonymity of it, because Brighton felt like home – Worthing felt like a place we could disappear and just be us. We'd play slot machines on the pier, sit on the seafront eating ice cream and snog each other's faces off in the cinema. We'd sometimes spend all night drinking fizz and fucking in a tiny hotel room. We haven't done that in years. Not just because of the pandemic – we seem to have just let life get in the way.

'What's the plan?' Mac asks as we come closer to the seafront.

'I've found an alias of hers registered at three hotels. I can't find out if she's actually there. And they wouldn't tell me how long she'd been staying. I just had to keep ringing back and asking to be put through to the alias's room.'

'Tell me again how you're not an agent.'

'The plan is to go to the different hotels and see if she's there.'

'And if she is?'

'We talk to her, I suppose. You talk to her; I talk to her. Get her to turn herself in.'

'I don't think that will work.'

'I don't, either, but we at least need to try. Maybe I can convince Dennis and Horson to let her see her dad. Get a sit-down with him so she can at least talk to him. Communicating to the person who is the source of her pain is what I think she ultimately wants.'

'What if she's just building up to killing him?'

I take my eyes off the road to look at him for a moment.

'I know that's crossed your mind,' he says. 'She's working her way up to it. That's why she's going through those people first. She's getting herself comfortable with killing. That's what's keeping me awake at night. That's what I'm really scared of.'

Me, too. She wants to kill her father so she has to get used to doing it first. I hope we're both wrong about this. 'We'll talk to her. Between the two of us, we must be able to talk her down. We must be able to.'

'I hope you're right, I really do.'

Robyn

1 March, Secret Location

Fikowsky didn't know where my father is. I didn't actually think he would. My father is very good at charming people, at getting them to do what he wants by making them feel important. By making them feel like, without them, nothing would work. Nothing would happen.

So, although he kept an eye on me via this hideous man, he didn't tell said hideous man anything. I suspected that would be the case. But I also knew that he would know something. He would, for example, know who else had been involved in my case. I knew some of them, but not all. Not all. And once he told me who they were, I could add them to the board. The board of research that had begun as one sheet of A3 art paper and which is now creeping right across the wall.

From Fikowsky I managed to get five names, two of which I already had. The other three, I wrote on the board. I knew I had to start the process of finding them, working out when I would approach them, how I would approach them.

I have two weeks until the next approach. That gives me enough time to recover, and find these new people.

I really wish, though, that they would just give him to me. They have no idea how determined I am to get him. If I fail, it'll only be because I'm dead.

Because I want him. And I will do anything to make sure I get him. That's a promise I made to myself and to my mum. I will get him. And I will not rest until I do.

The next name on the list is Julian McDermott, someone I hate even more than these other guys I've spoken to. Someone I hate almost as much as I hate my dad.

Robyn

17 March, Brighton

Julian McDermott has become a keen gardener since he retired from the police force with full honours, full pension, full log book of stories of his heroism.

He is beloved by everyone.

Except me, obviously.

Before I started watching him as the next person I speak to, I had met him properly four times in my life.

The first time was when, at ten years old, I called the police because Mum left a water ring on the dining table. She'd been in a rush. As a result, my parents got into an argument. Fine. Normal. What most couples did. But my parents were not most couples.

November 2010

Mum came running to the table. Mistake number one.

She hadn't wiped off the glass in her hand. Mistake number two.

She put the glass, dribbling with a few rivulets of water and con-densation, on the table without a coaster. Mistakes number three and four.

Mum thought it was safe to tuck in her chair, pick up her knife and fork, to start eating. We hadn't started eating – if there is one person who isn't at the table when the meal starts, the meal doesn't start. Dad was always very clear: we all eat at the same time. If Mum was running around trying to finish washing up – Dad hated a sink full of dishes – we had to wait until she was finished.

'What on earth do you think you're doing?' my father asked Mum. His voice, low and controlled, brought goosebumps out all up my arms. I knew that tone. I knew that look.

Mum would usually jump in terror, her eyes flying around, trying to work out what was wrong, figuring out how to fix it before things escalated. This time, she sighed, hung her head, just looked thor-oughly worn out. Terror tumbled through me, the goosebumps becoming painful pinpricks of panic on my skin. That note in his voice always meant someone was going to get hurt.

'Please,' Mum said quietly. She wasn't pleading; she wasn't begging. She just sounded tired, exhausted. She looked it, too. Mum's beauti-ful brown skin that used to glow was dulled, her sad eyes had bags underneath them.

'Please?' Dad hissed. 'Please? You sit there and say please? While that water is damaging the table that I paid good money for, you are saying please?'

'I bought the table,' Mum said quietly, defiantly.

'What did you say to me?' Dad said.

Mum looked up then. She faced him and she was not scared. Usually when Mum looked at Dad, she was scared, fearful of upsetting him. I had worked out a lifetime ago that Dad liked that. He liked her to never question, never speak up. She only ever did when he came at me. Then she became a physical barrier. But I didn't remember her ever doing this – just looking him in the eye and saying something.

'I bought the table. My money that you took. My money that you made me sign over to you. This is my table. And if I decide to let a couple of dribbles fall on it because I have been on my feet all day and I have been cooking and cleaning all evening, I don't think it's a big prob-lem.' She took her time, picked up the glass and plonked it on the place mat. Then she used her fingertips to wipe away the moisture. 'There. See? It's like it was never there.'

I held my breath, hoping it would make me smaller, less noticeable. And praying it would hold back what was about to happen. If I held my breath, the look that was coming over Dad's face wouldn't take root, he wouldn't rise from his seat, he wouldn't clench his fists on the edge of the table and he wouldn't flip the table. If I held my breath, the moment where everyone seems frozen would linger – nothing would happen; nothing would go wrong. If I held my breath, we would all be OK.

My chest was burning, but if I let go, if I exhaled, I knew everything would detonate. They sat staring at each other and even though I was holding my breath, even though I was trying really hard, I could see the lines setting on Dad's face, I could see his muscles tensing, I could see him lifting himself from his seat. I kept on holding my breath, even though it was agony. I had to stop him. But, no, I couldn't. I didn't breathe out, but he was still on his feet, he was still grabbing the table, his face was still contorting as the scream of rage erupted from deep inside. Mum just managed to dart out and away from the table before it went over on its side.

She stood staring at him, again not cringing like he expected. I knew, despite being a child, that he would stop if she was scared, if she shrank and pleaded and begged like she often did. But she wasn't doing that. She stared at him, and he saw it as a challenge, her goading him.

He went for her, running round the table to try to grab her. She darted the other way, running out of the room into the corridor and then into the downstairs bathroom, the only place with a lock on the door.

I stood and watched him scream even louder with rage and then run out of the room after her. He got to the bathroom door, and started kicking at it. Standing back, raising a leg and kicking at it. Kicking, kicking, kicking.

250

With those kicks, he was threatening her, promising that he was coming. He wanted her to have time to think, time to be properly scared before he delivered the final, decisive kick. The one that smashed the door open and allowed him to march in.

I didn't see what he was doing. I heard it. And I knew I would never forget it. I knew those noises would haunt my dreams, my quiet moments, the times when I was having fun – that noise would storm in.

Moving slowly and calmly, I went to the navy-blue phone that sat on a little glass table in the corridor, I picked up the receiver and I dialled 999. When the lady asked what service I wanted, I told her police. Then I added ambulance.

'I hope this isn't a prank call,' she said to me.

I thought it was odd to say that. I thought it was odd that someone who was terrible enough to make a prank call would admit to it.

'My dad is hitting my mum,' I said. 'My dad is hitting my mum and he won't stop. He's hurting her.' I spoke calmly. I remember at school they told us that if you ever call the emergency services, stay as calm as possible so they can understand you. They can't help you if they can't understand you. I needed them to help my mum so I needed to be as calm as possible.

The sound didn't stop. Each moment of it made me feel sick. My empty stomach lurched, I wanted to vomit so much. It seemed to take for ever for the sound of a siren to arrive. For the car to screech to a halt outside our house, and for a car door to open, car door to shut. Feet on the drive, a banging at the door.

The noise from the downstairs bathroom had stopped by then. It was quiet and Dad walked calmly to the door, barely glancing at me on the way to answer it. His shirt was slightly torn, his hair was slightly ruffled and he absent-mindedly wiped his bloodied knuckles on the bottom of his shirt. Just before he opened the door, he deliberately swiped the back of his hand against his cheek.

The man on the other side of the door was tall, white; he had pushed-back brown hair and quick, inquisitive eyes. 'We've had a call about a disturbance,' he said to my dad. He reared back a little, seeing the blood on my father's face.

'Officer, it's my wife,' Dad said, opening the door to let him in. 'She's gone crazy. She attacked me. I locked myself in the bathroom to get away from her and she kicked the door in. I had to defend myself.'

'Where is she?' the policeman asked. He looked a bit unsure, especially since Dad didn't look like he'd been viciously attacked. But he did sound sincere, and I think the policeman latched on to that.

'In the bathroom, down there.'

The policeman moved quickly in the direction Dad pointed. Dad followed him. When I tried to follow too, he scowled at me. But for the policeman he said in his nicest voice, 'No, darling, stay here. I don't want you to upset your mother any more. I don't want her to get angry all over again if she sees you.'

*

Mum sat leaning heavily on me on the sofa in the living room. Dad stood near the door, too scared of Mum to sit down, or so he said.

'What's this all about, eh?' the policeman asked, looking from Mum to Dad, but clearly expecting Dad to answer. Despite being 'scared', Dad had done most of the talking since the policeman had arrived. Despite Mum being unable to hold herself upright properly. Despite her face being a bloodied mess, her clothes being ripped, scratches on her arms and legs. Despite all of that, Dad kept insisting that he was the one who was scared and needed protection.

'Don't blame my wife, officer,' Dad said. 'She's been so stressed recently about . . . She wants a second child. And it's just not been working. And she gets so upset, so frustrated. She takes it out on us. My daughter and me.' Dad looked at me. 'Doesn't she, Avril?' The policeman looked at me. I shook my head. That was not true. None of it was true. Dad would give me hell later; he would slap my legs, grab my arm, shake me and scream in my face. But I didn't care. It was not the truth and I was not going to say it was. Mum didn't want another baby. I heard her telling my auntie Meryl that she would never bring another child into this mess. She felt guilty enough with bringing one child into this – she wasn't going to make that mistake again.

I shook my head again, just so the police officer would know that this wasn't the truth.

'She's nervous,' Dad said. 'As you can imagine, she's seen things a child should never see.'

The police officer looked at Mum. Hurt, damaged, injured, but not broken. Dad had tried, but she wasn't broken. She was still defiant under all of the pain; she was still strong.

'What have you got to say for yourself?' he demanded, obviously believing Dad because Mum wasn't broken. Despite her injuries, she still had defiance in her and the policeman probably didn't expect that.

Mum struggled to speak, what with blood beading on both her split top and bottom lips and the bruising around her jaw. 'I didn't hit him. I didn't do anything to him,' she managed to get out.

'Well, he says you attacked him,' the officer said. 'He says you broke down the door to get at him.'

'I didn't,' she said.

'God, Rose, I've covered up for you enough. I'm really frightened of what you'll do next.' He moved his head, showed a scratch I hadn't seen before. 'Look what you did to me. Look what you started so I had to defend myself.'

The officer looked at the scratch on Dad's neck and that seemed to upset him. 'He has a right to defend himself,' the officer said coldly to my mother.

'I didn't do anything to him,' she said. 'I didn't hurt him.'

'Rose, it's clear to see what you did,' Dad said.

'I didn't do anything to him.'

'Stop it, the pair of you. What sort of example are you two setting for your child there?' the officer snapped at both of them. 'Squabbling like naughty school kids. I should bash your heads together. Grow up.'

Dad didn't like that. I could see his fearful expression dropping for a moment and he looked absolutely furious. I wondered if he would give himself away then. Would show the policeman it was him, not Mum that was the danger here.

But Dad hid his anger and instead, in a meek voice, said: 'You're right, officer. You're right – we need to grow up. Rose needs to feel the consequences of her actions. I think, I think I need to charge her with assault.' He showed his neck again. 'And actual bodily harm. I don't want to, but' – he lowered his head, looked sad and scared – 'it's the only way to stop her.' Dad looked like he was going to cry. 'I can't do it any more. I can't cover for her any more.'

'I didn't do anything,' Mum whispered. The police officer stared at her with suspicious eyes. I wondered if he was seeing what I was seeing. How could he look at her and think that this was just Dad defending himself.

The officer stared at Dad, who was trying to look brave, trying not to cry, showing that he was the victim even though she was the one who was hurt. Dad had inflicted that much damage on her while he literally only had a scratch on his neck. And, of course, his bruised and bloodied fists.

I realised what was happening, then. The policeman expected Mum to be crying and broken, he expected her to be begging him to help her, but because she wasn't, because she kept herself together despite how beaten she was, he could believe that my dad was the victim. Even though everything was showing that Dad was the violent one, he could convince himself that Mum was the one causing the problem.

Which made the idea that he might arrest my mother all the more terrifying. I didn't know what I would do if this policeman did arrest her. How would I cope without her? She was everything to me. I couldn't spend a night without her, with just him. I couldn't.

'You need to keep your temper under control,' the police officer told Mum. 'Stop nagging him. Stop provoking him. Come on, what sort of example are you setting for your daughter? Do you want her to grow up thinking this is normal?'

I would never think this is normal. Never. But I would think it was normal to not trust men like him. How could anyone, especially a policeman, sit and look at someone who had been beaten, who had been hurt and then tell them it was *their* fault for provoking the person who looked barely hurt? Why couldn't he see what had actually happened? It was so clear. So obvious. Even I, ten years old, could see. And he couldn't.

Was it also because he looked like Dad? Was it because he thought this was normal? Is this what this policeman did to his wife when she put a glass of water on a table that she'd paid for without a coaster? Is that why he couldn't see who was the real danger and who was really *in* danger?

'If I have to come back here again, I will arrest you,' he told my mum, pointing his finger in her face.

Mum glared at him from her closing eye and, with her split lips said, 'I didn't do anything.' She wasn't going to let him make her believe that she was the bad person here. And I loved her, fiercely, for that. I knew it made the police officer believe my dad that bit more, but I loved her for not being cowed by these two horrible men.

'If you ever need anything, anything at all, here is my number. Call me any time.' The police officer gave my father a business card. Then, 'Stay safe,' he said to my father and shook his hand. I watched him do that, I watched him shake Dad's hand with its full set of split knuckles, and realised that life really wasn't fair. That if you were my dad, you could do anything, create the type of noises that would haunt your daughter's every moment, and people like that police officer would tell you to call them if you needed anything and then shake your hand. They wouldn't arrest him, they wouldn't bring him to justice like they did on the television, they would just threaten my mother and tell *him* to stay safe.

After Dad shut the door behind him and returned to the living room, a satisfied grin took over his face. I never knew what the police officer said about the 999 call I made, how he squared it so they likely registered it as nothing, but I knew now I couldn't call the police again. I knew now that they wouldn't help. I knew that. Mum knew it now. And, most importantly, Dad knew it as well.

I saw that police officer again twenty-two months later. Twenty-two months later he walked through my front door into the living room and I was sitting on the floor, holding Mum's hand.

July, 2012

That police officer walked into the living room, and made eye contact with me. He stared at me, stared at my mother, then looked at my father, who had called him. The 'any time' of 'call me any time' turned out to be right then. Dad needed help and he called this man. I could tell by the look on his face that the police officer knew what my father had done. He knew what had happened.

I wanted to run at him. To punch and scratch and hurt him in any way I could because this was partly his fault. If he had stopped my father last time instead of shaking his hand, this wouldn't have happened. My father was sitting on the sofa, the place where he'd dropped after he called this policeman. He'd called him almost straight away while I sat and held Mum's hand.

And then I'd watched him get himself ready for this visitor. I'd watched him trying out facial expressions – moving his eyebrows down, turning his mouth down, but not too down. I'd watched him test out wringing his hands and his eyes filling with tears. I'd watched him nod and sigh as though in pain. Then he'd sat back and examined his nails until the urgent knock on the door. I watched my father go running outside, dragging the police officer in, pointing at Mum and screaming, 'Help her, help her, PLEASE!'

Mum's hand didn't move, it wasn't as warm as it had been earlier, but it wasn't cold. She often had cold hands when she was moisturising my body, putting cream on my eczema, when we walked into town because Dad had the car and we had no money for a taxi or a bus. She would laugh about always being cold. She was getting colder, but she wasn't cold cold yet.

That policeman walked slowly and carefully across the carpet. People weren't allowed in here with their shoes on and now look at him just wandering in. Dad would have screamed at Mum for that. He would have called her names and made her clean every part of it with a toothbrush. He'd ordered her do that before – then went to bed saying he expected it done by the morning. I'd crept out of bed to try to help her but she'd said no. She'd said I had to sleep so I would be able to go to school in the morning.

I watched that policeman watch my father. My father looked up at him, his eyes filled with tears, his hands wringing themselves together, his mouth slightly downturned – just like I'd seen him practise.

'Look what they did to her,' he whispered. 'There were five of them. They had ski masks and guns. They tried to hurt my daughter and she got between them. Look what they did.'

That policeman's whole body seemed to relax. He seemed relieved that it wasn't Dad. That it was five men, five strangers, who had done this thing. He was an adult and he couldn't see that my father was lying? Or was it like last time? Did he just want to believe that some-one like him was a good person so he ignored all the evidence right in front of his eyes?

'They tried to kidnap me. Take me with them. I think they might come back.' As Dad spoke, he raised his voice, started to act like he was panicking. I clung tighter to Mum's hand, even though she didn't do her thing – the quick squeeze, squeeze before she tightened her grip – to show me that she was there, that she'd always be there.

'They got scared when Rose wouldn't wake up. They got scared and they left.' Dad was wild-eyed now. 'What if they come back? Try to take Avril? What will I do then?'

'I have to call this in,' the policeman said.

Suddenly there was another man in the living room. The man wasn't very tall; he had light brown hair and he wore glasses. He was the type of man you were instantly wary of but you didn't know why. I hadn't seen him before and I stared at him, wondering how he'd got in and what he was doing there. Our house was far away from every-thing else. You only came here if you meant to come here.

Dad gave the man his sad look again and the police officer asked, 'Who are you?' He looked scared, like this man could be one of the gang that Dad had made up, come back.

'I-I called him,' Dad said, his voice weak and shaky. 'Because of my job. I've been told that if anything happens, I have to call him.'

The policeman looked suspicious and slightly scared, but the man who had walked in didn't care. 'What's happened?' he asked Dad.

'Masked men. They tried to take me. They hurt my wife.'

The man looked around, then stared right at me, holding my mum's hand. He knew. I could tell he knew the truth. But instead of saying that, he returned to looking at Dad and said, 'We need to get out of here. Now.'

'You can't leave,' the police officer said. 'I have to call this in. They have to investigate. They may be able to catch the men if we hurry.'

'No, I have to get him out of here,' the man said. 'Masked men tried to take him. No doubt because of his job. They may come back. We need to get him to safety. If there's even the slightest chance that they'll return, I have to make sure he is safe.' He looked at me again, then at the police officer. 'You need to stay here, call it in. But say he was gone when you arrived.'

'I can't do that.'

'You have to,' he said, his voice suddenly all nice instead of stern and slightly rude. 'Listen, I know you must mean a lot to him if he called you at the same time he called me. You have to help him. You're the only one who can save him right now.'

The man went on to explain that he was going to take Dad to somewhere safe. That the police officer had to stay, call the rest of his police friends in and say he'd received a panicked call from Dad but by the time he got to our house, Dad was gone. 'I'm only taking him with me, to make it look like they kidnapped him after they killed her,' he said. He nodded in my direction. 'We'll arrange reuniting them in a few hours. If she tries to say anything, just tell them she's been saying all sorts of things that don't make sense, including that aliens did it.

'Right now, I just have to get him to safety. We're relying on you to help us out. Can you do that?'

The police officer could. Of course he could. The man told Dad to leave everything and come with him. Dad barely looked in my direction before he followed the man out of the house. I hadn't stopped holding Mum's hand, hadn't left my place by her side. I sat and watched all of this happen – watched my dad leave, the policeman stay, him using his radio as soon as we couldn't hear the sound of the man's car any more. I listened to him speak about a murder. And then I watched him look around, watched him realise the place didn't look like five masked men had broken in and killed my mother, saw him start to push things over, tear things apart, make it look like a proper crime scene, I guessed, instead of the scene of a man killing his wife.

I didn't let Mum's hand go while he did all this. I just sat and watched.

I hated my dad. He was my dad, that should count for something, but I realised then that I hated him. He had taken my mother away. And he had taken my life away with his lies and violence. I hated him.

And I hated that policeman who could have stopped all this. I didn't know his name, but I *hated* him. Almost as much as I hated my father.

17 March, Brighton

I've watched former uniform sergeant Julian McDermott for a few days. It's harder with him than Fikowsky because he doesn't have a set routine. He doesn't have a wife – he got divorced a lifetime ago – and he spends a lot of time pleasing himself. I suspect that might have preceded the divorce, though, and indeed had something to do with the marriage's demise.

He goes to his allotment sometimes; he works in his extensive back garden at other times. He rattles around in the home he shared with his wife – four bedrooms, two bathrooms – and rarely has visitors. All his three children live abroad and none of them have visited England in years. I found out that his wife has three foreign holidays a year – probably to visit the children – but McDermott doesn't.

I found out by obsessively combing through their social media accounts that McDermott kept the house in the divorce and his wife was all but destitute. That's what Dad used to say to Mum – you'll be nothing without me. If you want to go, you go ahead and go, but my daughter stays here.

Mum never had any money. Even though my auntie Meryl – a woman who was married to one of Dad's oldest friends but never seemed to like Dad very much – tried to help her, it was never enough. She always feared that my dad would find the money Auntie Meryl gave her, which would cause even more problems. But it's clear that the policeman wasn't very nice to Mum because he recognised himself in my father. He could justify what my father did because he had been in my father's place.

I'm not sure where to pick him up. The allotment is private enough, especially because he goes there late at night sometimes, but it's too far for me to drag him to the car from inside the allotment.

Outside his house is too risky. People look out for other people in their own neighbourhood, even if they dislike them. I need to be careful, too. He is a lot bigger than me. He was a police officer so might be prepared for a surprise attack, like Talamon. He doesn't go to the gym, and the only other time he is out is when he does his weekly shop, but there are far too many people around then.

I sit in my car, watching him get ready to move from his car across the road to the allotment and I see an opportunity. I pull silently out of my space, creep forward and as he gets near the centre of the road, I put my foot down. The car jerks forward and he doesn't have time to move. The last thing I see are the widened whites of his eyes as he throws his hands up to protect himself.

I grab my weapon and come to check he is still alive. He is. But he is hurt. His left leg is busted, it lies at an odd angle to his body. He is out cold so will only feel the real pain of it when he regains consciousness. Which reminds me that I need to get a move on. I should turn the car around so it'll be easier to get him into the boot, but I don't. Because I'm an idiot sometimes. No, instead I drag his body to the boot of my car. I'm proper tired by the time I've hoisted him up, the bruising from Talamon's punches starting to nag a little, and bundle him into the boot.

I don't think I've ever been more satisfied to close my car boot in all my life.

Kez

30 April, Worthing

After driving around for a bit, trying to remember the best place to leave the car, I park and we walk over to the first hotel. She's registered in three hotels that are close together near the seafront. Good plan because she can move easily between them and no one will think anything of her coming and going at odd times. I'm not sure where her money is coming from, though. Possibly the credit cards but there must also be another source of income because none of this is cheap.

I know I profiled her as smart, but she is super smart. Scary smart. We are playing a type of catch-up with her that I'm not used to. I'm sure the police are used to this, and I'm sure they'd probably be able to do this a lot quicker than I can, but I can't let them get to her first. They won't take the time to talk her down; they won't be able to promise her that they'll try to get her some time with her father. They'll just stop her by any means.

The first hotel is set back from the seafront, on the other side of the main carriageway. Only some of the rooms have a sea view. I'm guessing Robyn would have a sea view. It gives you a better view of the surrounding area, which helps to avoid being ambushed. A room high up would give her an additional vantage point, but would make it hard

266

for her to get out of the hotel quickly. Ground floor would be easy to escape, but you lose the vantage of height. I'm guessing she has a room on the second floor.

The person behind the desk is dressed in a black suit with a white shirt, no tie. He looks up and gives us a barely controlled eye roll before he plasters on a polite smile.

'Good morning,' I say, pushing sunshine into my voice. 'I'm wondering if you can help me? I'm looking for a Cindi Reid? She's a guest here at the hotel. I think she's been here for a while?'

'She might be. But I'm not authorised to give out any information about guests.'

I sigh internally. I really would rather not do this. I reach into my jacket pocket and take out the slim black wallet that I hate to carry. 'I'm from a special task force that has been set up to investigate Miss Reid.' I flash him my badge, my ridiculous badge, and I can feel Mac silently saying, *'Not an agent, huh?'*

'How do I know that badge is real and not something you've just printed off the web?' he says.

I look him over and notice, peeking out from under the lapel of his jacket, the slightly discoloured area of his white shirt where he'd spilt coffee and hadn't been able to get it out. His fingernails are uneven, but clean. His eyes are bloodshot, probably from spending lots of time on his phone, watching videos. This is a man who has spent a lot of time recently hearing that nothing is as it seems, that there are conspiracies working against average men like him, that guys like him just cannot get a break.

'To be honest, you don't know. And I respect that you're wise to that. But what I will tell you is that the investigation into Miss Reid is to do with her using hotels as a way of running drugs. Now, I'm the advance guard, as it were. I'm here to try to scope out what she is up to before everyone else turns up mob-handed. I mean, if I say, have a look in her room or speak to her first, you may be able to avoid all the fixtures and fittings being torn apart while they look for her stash. And, of course, the hotel being cordoned off and not being able to open for weeks. The last place this happened to, they were out for months and the employees didn't get paid.

'It's really unfortunate since they didn't actually find anything. But the hotel kind of got a reputation as a place where drugs were bought, sold and trafficked and nothing they could do, not even changing the hotel's name, could stop it.' I pause to check what effect this is having on him. If I told him the truth, he's much more likely to be fascinated than horrified and keen to help. Suggesting his job is on the line was always far more likely to work. This is what we mainly do at Insight – find ways to present information that will nudge and encourage people to behave in certain ways. We study human behaviour and try to influence it sometimes. Usually for the greater good. Usually. It's become so clear in recent times, to get most people to get on board with doing something, you have to make sure they understand what's in it for them, first. The greater good is very rarely enough of an incentive for people to do things nowadays. It has to personally impact them, they have to know what's in it for them, before they care. What's in it for him is to not have his work – and pay – disrupted if it doesn't need to be.

'So what's it going to be? I am more than happy to go call in the others, or to just have a quick look in her room to see if I can spot anything that might lead me to find her – away from here. What works best for you, bud?'

He's unsure. I thought he might be a little hesitant, but he seems a bit more unsure than I expected. Maybe he knows the owner, possibly he knows he'll be taken care of if the hotel is out of action for a bit.

'All right, I can see you're conflicted,' I say. 'Let me take the matter out of your hands.' I pull my mobile from my pocket, bring up the keypad in clear view of him and start to dial. The first ring, sounding out from my handset, brings him to life, pushes him to make a decision.

'I guess it'll be OK for you to have a look. But a quick one. And you can't touch anything. She hasn't been here in a while. Maybe two weeks? But you can't touch anything.'

'We can't touch anything,' I echo.

*

The small room is pretty much dominated by a double bed and the glass coffee table that sits at the foot of it. The whole space is immaculate – probably more sparkling than the cleaners left it. You couldn't tell someone had ever stayed in here.

Ray, the guy from reception, stands outside the door, probably so he doesn't have to see if I violate our agreement and touch anything. I stand at the foot of the bed, scanning the room, trying to see if she has made any attempt to personalise the place. Not really. I open the wardrobe door and at the bottom is a selection of cleaning items – bleach, glass cleaner, cleaning cloth, magic eraser, furniture polish wipes, Dettol wipes, black bin bags, yellow rubber gloves. This is why the room is so pristine. She makes sure to clean up before she leaves, in case she can't come back. She wants to make sure all traces of blood – hers or other people's – is gone.

'I have to use the loo,' Mac says, 'I'm busting.'

He goes to the bathroom, shuts and locks the door. I try not to listen, but it's so hard with the bathroom being so close. I stand awkwardly, looking around to see if anything else will give me a clue as to her state of mind. She's sticking to the 'organised' and 'meticulous' parts of her profile. She certainly seems to know what she is doing.

Mac seems to be taking a long time in the bathroom, and it's getting more and more awkward trying not to hear what he's doing. The toilet flushes, the taps run and he softly hums 'Happy Birthday' as he washes his hands. I jump, embarrassed that I've been listening, when he unlocks and opens the door.

'Sorry about that,' he says, as embarrassed as I am.

'It's Ray you'll have to say sorry to – he told you not to touch anything,' I reply.

'No, he told *you* not to touch anything. He didn't give me any instructions at all.'

'This is true. Let me go look at the bathroom in case there's anything—' As I move, my shin catches on the lower ledge of the bed that is covered up by the bedcovers, tipping me off my feet. I go flying forward, heading for the clear glass table that sits at the foot of the bed. My arms come up to break my fall but I'm going to be— Suddenly, I'm not falling but being held up and pulled back. Suddenly, one of Mac's arms is circling my body and pulling me backwards to counterbalance the fall.

'I've got you,' he murmurs. 'I've got you.' And time stops for a moment, freezing us with it. He is holding me against his body, so close his breath is moving the small hairs at the back of my neck. I'm not breathing. If I breathe, I'll put myself closer to him. 'Are you OK?' he murmurs, the vibrations moving through my body in a terribly pleasurable way.

I swallow and then nod my head, not trusting myself to speak and sound normal.

'If I let you go, will you be OK?' he murmurs again, the vibrations having the same effect.

I nod. 'Yes. Thank you. Yes,' I manage.

He lowers his arm and I immediately step away, start to push my hair behind my ears, straighten my clothing.

'Sorry,' I say, avoiding his eye while trying to calm my breathing. I don't want to see what look he has on his face. 'Clumsy.'

'As long as you're OK?' he says, his voice tight, as though stretched to its limits, as though he's trying to speak without breathing.

'Yes. Fine. Fine. My shin may not be. Who puts a frame around the base of a bed then covers it up with a bedspread?' I babble. Babbling is good – it's calming, it's me and it's normal. I have to act normal.

'Are you finished here?' he asks.

'Yes, I'm finished here.'

'Let's go, then.' The same tight voice.

I take the chance to look at him and he is staring at me. Glaring at me, actually. He's clearly angry with someone – possibly me, but also possibly himself. I look away again. This is not good at all.

*

After I have thanked Ray and reassured him several times that his hotel will not be raided looking for drugs, we step outside. Mac's anger seems to have dissipated and we stand on the pavement. The sea air seems different over here. In Brighton there is a slightly frenetic edge, something that says nothing sits still for long. Here, the seagulls seem to fly slower, the water takes its time and meanders up the beach before strolling out again, the clouds move like overweight tumbleweeds across the sky.

The other two hotels are a couple of streets away. I take out my phone to call up a map so I don't get lost on our way to our next destination. As I do so, I spot him from the corner of my eye. Well, the shape of him. I pretend to focus on my phone but tip my head slightly so I can properly check. It *is* him.

Across the road, sitting at the bus stop, trying to blend in with the surroundings by pretending to read a newspaper is Big Bad Aidan.

Robyn

17 March, Secret Location

Julian McDermott wakes up in pain.

I had to tie his broken leg to the chair and that was enough to wake him up. He groans loudly and obviously thinks he's at home because he lets out a howl of pain. Real pain. That's what I wanted to do when Dad killed her. When I was sitting holding her hand. When they all believed Dad's lies. I wanted to scream out loud all the agony that was submerged inside.

Once McDermott has screamed a couple more times, his vision clears and he finds me sitting on the floor in front of him. I'm not wearing my face disguises with him. There's no need. For him, knowing it's me straight away will be far more scary.

He was there when they were taking me to the children's home. 'I hate you,' I spat at him just before I got in the car. 'I hate you!' He had been surprised, hurt even. He didn't think I knew what he'd done. How he'd let my mother down.

He didn't think that I would hold any animosity towards him when he had sat there and listened to Dad's confession. No one told me to leave the room, so I heard him finally tell a version of what happened that they would find palatable. That all those men around the table could nod their heads at in understanding: *Nagging wife, brat of a daughter, just snapped. Didn't really know what he'd done. Made up the story about the masked intruders because he panicked, couldn't believe he'd done such a thing. Couldn't believe she was gone.*

On the television, they were supposed to arrest people who confessed to murder. But not those police officers with my dad. The story about the kidnapping was out there now. Everyone thought he'd been kidnapped, probably killed, anyway, so they decided to use that as cover for being put into the protective person's programme/witness protection, so, even though he confessed, they were going to keep to that story. They were going to let him get away with it.

The only thorny issue, the only fly in the ointment? Me. I was an inconvenience to my father. He didn't want me staring at him with my mother's eyes, reminding him what he had done. He wanted to be free. He did not want a living, breathing conscience to hold him back. I often wonder as an adult: if he had known how I would react to what he did, would he have killed me, too?

And then it was decided. I would go into care. He would start a new life and would never be heard from again – kidnapped, presumed dead. They made sure everything was good for him, good for how he wanted his life to go. Not for me.

Is it any wonder I spat, 'I hate you!' at that police officer? Is it any wonder I want him to remember that it was me who said those words? They weren't simply a statement of fact – they were a promise. A down payment on a return showdown where I would have as much, if not more, power than him.

'Hello, former uniform sergeant Julian McDermott,' I say to him. I even smile because I have all the time in the world to be pleasant. I have all the time in the world with him.

'Who are you? What are you doing to me? How did I get here?'

'So many questions!' I say. 'Old habits die hard, yes?'

'Who are you?' he demands. I can see he is in pain and, weirdly, I take no pleasure in it. Maybe it's because I inflicted it indirectly with the car? Maybe.

'Oh, come on now – that's really hurtful. You ruined my life and you can't even remember me? How is that fair?'

He blinks a few times, obviously trying to clear his blurry vision. I wonder for a moment if he has concussion and if I should take him to get help. But how would I explain it? I hit him with my car, I tied him to a chair and it was then that I noticed he might be concussed? Yeah, no, not going to happen.

'I know you,' he says. 'You . . . you were that—'

'Yes, I'm that girl whose mother you allowed to be murdered by her father. And when you found out what he'd done, you were all so understanding and put him into witness protection. Or Protected Persons as they call it now.'

'What are you doing?'

'Isn't it obvious?'

'No, no, it's not.'

'OK, all right. I've had this plan for so long I just kind of assume that everyone will understand what I'm doing. But if you want me to, I will spell it out, so it's simple: I am looking for my father, who is in the Protected Persons programme, because I think it's time for a family reunion. And I'm torturing everyone who I think might have the slightest inkling of where he might be until they tell me what they know. I mean, I don't *want* to torture them, but I think most people will definitely be backwards about coming forwards with the necessary information unless I do, so needs must.'

He doesn't say anything, which I'm surprised about because I thought explaining what I was doing would at least get him to declare he doesn't know anything and so necessitate me bringing out the equipment. 'Don't you have anything to say about that?'

He shakes his head, mumbles, 'No.'

'I am surprised. I thought you'd at least ask why I chose you?'

'I know why.'

'You do?'

'You blame me for what happened to your mum. You think it's my fault.'

'But it is your fault.'

'It wasn't. There was so much doubt. There was bad behaviour on both sides. You could tell. I'm sure your mum was a nice lady, but women . . . You don't know when to leave well enough alone. You just don't. I don't mean to speak ill of the dead, and she was your mum after all, but she didn't do herself any favours.'

'That's what I love about "normal" misogynists like you – you're literally at my mercy but you still can't stop yourself being awful about women in general and my mum in particular.'

He glowers at me, resolute in what he's said.

I get to my feet, move to the trolley, wheel it into view. I see his eyes widen in utter horror but he quickly hides his fear. He thinks I'm a psychopath, that his fear will give me enjoyment and will spur me on, so he needs to control his facial expressions, hide his emotions from me. I sit in front of him again, but this time with the hammer in my hands. I weigh it in my palm, smoothing my fingers over its rubberised handle and cold, solid top.

'That night, the first night you came to our house, I called the police because he had upturned the dining table and chased my mum because she had put a glass on the table without a coaster. And instead of rushing to make it right and crying until he forgave her like she normally had to do to keep me safe, she decided to tell him it was no big deal.

'I was sure when the police arrived they would see from the state of her what he had been doing to her. But no, not you. You took the time to believe him, to understand him, to tell my mother to behave. I called the police because I could hear him raping her in the bathroom.' I tap the side of my head with my forefinger. 'I can never get that sound out of my head. No matter how hard I try, I can still hear it. And afterwards. After you left, telling him to stay safe, he did it again. After that night, he knew he could do whatever he wanted because no one would stop him.

'Before you came into our lives, we could always believe that he would stop if the police came. You, the police, were the one thing that was meant to keep us safe. And you didn't. In fact . . .' I stop to strike the hammer against the stone floor, the sound loud and echoing around the room, and he jumps, immediately regrets it because he has so much pain in his body. 'In fact, you made it worse. You gave him everything he needed to eventually kill her.'

McDermott's demeanour has changed. He was indignant before, despite his pain. He was very keen to 'both sides' this and pretend it was too complex for a person like me who hasn't lived to understand. Now he seems shaken. Probably because the excuses he has used

278

for over a decade to square in his mind getting my mother killed aren't valid now. Now I've told him what really happened, he is unsettled.

'Believe it or not, I'm not here to get revenge on you or to hurt you. Even though you are hurt. No, I just want you to tell me where my father is.'

'I don't know.'

'Yes, you do.'

'It's called Protected Persons for a reason – and that reason is no one can know where the person is being protected.'

'Yes, I know. But I also know you were completely fooled by my father. You would have done anything for him. I find it hard to believe he didn't keep in touch afterwards.'

'He wasn't allowed to—'

'Forgive me, are you trying to tell me that a man who broke one of the most fundamental rules of life when he murdered someone is not going to break the "not speaking to someone from your old life" rule? You expect me to believe that?'

'It's the truth, so, yes, I expect you to believe it.'

'Well, OK. As I said, I don't want to torture you. I thought you being in pain would act as a truth serum and you would just tell me. But that doesn't look to be the case, so, with regret, I am going to have to harm you to get what I need.'

For the first time, he looks scared. He's obviously realised that I mean business.

I stand up, move towards him, take his hand and hold it flat against the chair's armrest. Raise the hammer. 'I just want you to know, it really isn't completely personal. It's only a little bit personal. Most of it is purely business.' I raise the hammer even higher. 'It's only to get you to give him to me.'

Kez

30 April, Brighton

'What happened to your shin?' Jeb asks. My poor shin is swollen, the skin slightly broken where I hit it against the bed base. It's not the only thing feeling bruised and damaged, swollen and a little broken by today's events. My mind is still reeling from the effect Mac is having on me. And I can't help but suspect that is by design. That he might possibly be helping Robyn and doing a number on me to keep me distracted enough to allow her to finish her mission.

'Work injury,' I reply. We are in bed. A rare moment has occurred this evening where we've been able to get everyone – including ourselves – upstairs into bed at a decent time, so we've got a chance to cuddle up. I decided not to work on the Robyn Managa case tonight. I needed a break. I needed to step away so those little things that are niggling at the back of my mind can show themselves. Once in bed, and with Jeb not working either, we'd just snuggled up together, our limbs draped over each other until he'd accidently touched my shin and I'd quietly yelped while snatching it away.

'What work causes such an injury?'

'What work doesn't cause such an injury?' I reply.

*

Earlier...

When I thought about it, it made perfect sense for Big Bad Aidan to be in Worthing. He'd been pissed that I'd had contact with Mac between that first meeting and Mac showing up at Insight. He probably decided, since he had been assigned to 'supervise' me, that he needed to properly keep tabs on me and had put a tracker in my car or on my phone. Most likely my car since he's never been alone with my phone. Or maybe he did it before my secret conversation with Mac. I remembered how he had shuddered at the thought of going to see Mac that first time in my car. He couldn't have known what sort of state my car was in unless he'd known which one it was – which suggested he'd put a tracker on there already.

The next two hotel visits went much the same way as the first, with slight adjustments to the story – credit card fraud and possible money laundering – depending on who I was speaking to. In each hotel room the cleaning material cluster at the bottom of the wardrobe was repeated, as was the extreme level of cleanliness. Neither of them had seen her for a while, either. As we walked to the second hotel, I'd told Mac about seeing Big Bad Aidan and he'd said he wasn't that surprised, given how badly Big Bad Aidan had reacted to Mac turning up at Insight.

We'd both been impressively stoic about ignoring what hadn't happened in the hotel room, since nothing had happened but very obviously did happen.

As we buckled ourselves into my car, Mac asked me: 'What are you going to do next?'

'Well, I'm going to take my car in to the people in the know at work and ask them to check for trackers,' I replied.

'No, I mean—' he began.

'You know, one time, one of my clients put a tracker on my car. One of those airtag things,' I cut in.

'What?' he replied, thrown by me doing his type of sharp turn in the conversation. 'Why?'

'This is well before I went to work at Insight. I'd been asked to come in to assess a business that had a high turnover of staff. Everyone — I mean everyone — who left went on to slag off the company to anyone who would listen. He was quite high up in the company, and he thought I'd humiliated him in one of the sessions when trying to find out his role in creating the frankly terrible atmosphere of the place. He decided he wanted to know where I lived to have a "private" word with me.'

'How did you find out?'

'It started to randomly beep when I was at a petrol station. The police told me they'd had a real problem with them because a lot of abusive exes and partners used them to stalk their partners or ex-partners. A lot of the time, women — and it is usually women — have no idea how their exes find them all the time or how they track their movements.'

'So you did go to the police?'

'Jeb made me. I was just going to brush it off, but it was apparently one of those "unhealthy disregard for my own safety" moments, so he said I should.'

'What happened to the guy?'

'What always happens to men like him — he got a slap on the wrist and a promotion.'

'*Are you serious?*'

'Deadly. They said there was no way for me to prove that it was him. Even though my oldest son, who's a whizz with computers, had traced it back to him, right down to where and when he purchased it and the credit card he used. But, according to them, there was no way of *actually* knowing it was him. I mean, *really* knowing.'

'And he just got away with it, just like that?'

'I believe I mentioned the wrist slap? That involved him apologising to me by saying if he'd ever acted in a manner that would make me mistakenly think he was hostile towards me, then he was sad and distressed that I would assume that. And he was not that kind of person and he felt sad that I would ever think that of him.'

'That was his apology?'

'That was his apology and so-called "slap on the wrist". The pain of me thinking that him stalking me meant anything bad about him was unbearable, apparently.'

'I'm rarely shocked, but wow.'

'For a long time I couldn't go anywhere in the car without obsessively checking for trackers and I wouldn't let anyone speak in the car in case there was a listening device.' I hope he gets what I'm trying to tell him. 'I had to sell the car in the end. Well, Jeb suggested I sell the car. He couldn't stand to watch what it was doing to me and our family.'

'Right,' Mac said. And I knew he understood what I'd been trying to tell him because he didn't say a word until we got to his road.

As soon as I pulled up on his road, Mac shot out of my car as though it'd bitten him. I took my time getting out and walked a bit of a way towards his door, leaving my phone and bag in the car.

'I'll meet you at Pyecombe services tomorrow,' I said to him quietly. 'Take a taxi. I'll do the same. We can get a taxi from there. If he is still tracking me, it'll be harder for him to keep up.'

Mac looked as though he was going to say something, not related to what I'd just told him about arrangements for tomorrow. Something else. Then changed his mind and mumbled a goodbye before walking up the road to his house.

*

And it's been bugging me ever since. What happened in that hotel room. Everything, every little thing, makes me trust him less and less, but also makes me trust myself less. I'm being led down a path – several paths – here. Obviously by Dennis – it's what he does. But what is Mac doing? Is he meant to distract me but it's backfired because he genuinely likes me? The similarities between us, the way we could very easily bond over our shared experiences, how we could seamlessly slip into finishing each other sentences, seems to have thrown him. It's thrown me. And it's distracting me. I'm not as focused on Robyn. I'm not putting together what I saw in her rooms at the hotels because I'm too aware of not getting sucked into something – even a close friendship – with Mac.

And I can't help thinking that might have been the plan all along. Even if he isn't working with her, maybe he's trying to delay me finding her so she can have more time to find her father. Because someone is going to talk. It's only a matter of time. They are going to decide that his life is not worth their life, and they will illuminate the path to whoever it is that can find Robyn's father.

'Seriously, though, how did you hurt yourself?' Jeb presses.

'All said and done, it was a collision with a stupid piece of furniture.'

'Clearly the furniture won.'

'It may well have, but it wasn't a fair fight because it was hiding a

285

big part of itself away and it was that bit that took out my shin. And, anyway, I didn't go down without a fight.'

'I knew you wouldn't have.' He pushes his lips against mine in a soft kiss.

I shift my whole body so I can properly take in my husband. I drink in his smooth brown skin, his warm, sparkly eyes, his broad nose, his sensuous mouth. I drink him in and I can't help myself – I grin at him. He's so beautiful, so handsome and so perfect. I'm so lucky. Jeb's face creases in surprise at the way I'm smiling at him. He cups my face in his hand and grins back at me.

I'm so lucky, so why is this other man constantly in my head?

Part 9

Robyn

October, 2015

'I still think you're weird,' Andrich said to me.

We were the only two left in Maddox Hall that day because the others had gone to the circus in Brighton. I wasn't up for the circus so said I had a headache, and Andrich was in trouble again for God knows what so he was grounded. Andrich was always in trouble. I think he didn't know how not to be in trouble, sometimes.

Since that first day, when he warned me not to shove him again, I hadn't shoved him. And he, miraculously, hadn't bothered Tommy again. It was as though all someone had to do was stand up to him and he would back off. He had piercings on his nose, through the middle of his lower lip and above his left eyebrow. He now wore black leather and decorated blue denim. He had bright hazel eyes and skin a shade or two lighter than mine. He was mixed race like me and spent a lot of time twiddling his hair to get it to dread.

I often found myself thinking about him. He made my stomach flip, and I always had to stop myself staring at him. We sat at the table. He was eating a bowl of Shreddies instead of the pasta we'd been told to cook. I was eating the pasta.

'I still think you're weird,' he declared again, even though we'd had tons of conversations since he'd told me that on the first day. He gave me stuff all the time. We'd started to hang out even more since Tommy left because we were the only ones left from the old days. We were the only two who hadn't been fostered or adopted.

'I know. I don't care, though.' I shrugged. I cared very much. I was crushing hard on this boy and he had gone out of his way to tell me – twice – he thought I was weird.

'What happened to your pa?' he asked. He had a slight Scouse accent. He'd been at the home almost as long as Tommy but he was still in touch with his mother. She would come by sometimes to take him out and promise him they'd live together again one day. No matter how many times Holly gently told him not to get his hopes up, that his mother was unwell and they would have to go through a lot of processes for him to be able to live with her again, he always had a meltdown when the request for a home visit was turned down. Always.

'What do you mean?' I asked. The only person I had told that my dad hadn't really been kidnapped was Tommy. Everyone else still believed that old lie.

'I mean, were you there when the men took him? The papers said you were found all alone with the body of your ma. No sign of your pa. Is that true?'

'Do you want it to be true?' I asked because I hated lying. I hated it so much. I knew I had to. I knew it was the only way to make sure no one looked too deeply into what happened and found out it was my dad. But I still resented having to lie for him.

'Well, I don't care either way, do I?'

'So why are you asking if you don't care either way?'

'Something to say.'

'What happened to your pa?' I asked.

A look of pure revulsion came across his face. 'He bounced when I was a toddler. Went back to his rich family. Pretended me and me ma didn't exist. Saw him once at a train station in London. Called him a bastard and gave him the finger.'

'When was the last time you'd seen him before that?'

'When I was about two.'

'And you remember him?'

'Yeah. Me ma's got pictures of him as well. She used to go to bed hugging one and crying and that. I'd never forget that bastard's face.'

I got scared sometimes that I'd forget my mum's face. I wasn't allowed any pictures of her, any reminders of her. When the other police officers arrived, they took me kicking and screaming from the house into what they probably all thought was care. It was actually to the safe house where my dad was. And because of that I had to leave almost everything behind. Except for the bunny someone had shoved in my hands on the way out, everything was lost to me. So I didn't have pictures of my mum to obsess over. And sometimes I'd close my eyes and try to recall her and the image would be blurry, time having faded the edges and definition.

I pushed the still half-full bowl of pasta away. I didn't have an appetite any more. I was wishing I'd gone to the circus now, even though clowns and ringmasters freak me out, wishing I was there and not here thinking about my mum. It was half-term so I didn't even have any homework I could be getting on with.

'Do you have a boyfriend?' Andrich asked. He watched me carefully as he waited for my answer.

'No,' I replied with a shake of my head.

'Have you ever had a boyfriend?'

I should probably have lied, should probably have pretended to be more experienced than I was, but what was the point? I already had enough lies going on in my life. 'No.' Another shake of my head.

'Do you want to listen to music in my room?' Andrich asked.

He was staring at me. He was staring at me in a way that told me he wasn't just asking me to listen to music, he was asking me if I wanted to do other stuff while listening to music.

'Yeah, all right,' I said with a shrug.

Andrich had a room that had its own bathroom – toilet, sink and shower. He was the oldest person and had been there the longest, and he was also really antisocial most of the time. He left the shared bathrooms in a state, and he would spend hours in there if he could. No matter how many times Holly told him, he still behaved in a selfish manner. Odd, then, that when he was given a room with a bathroom, it was pristine and he spent the normal amount of time in there. He was a master at psychological warfare I realised – he had worked out what to do to get the room he wanted.

Once he'd put Biggie on the CD player and his music filled the room, Andrich came and sat next to me on the bed. 'I still think you're weird,' he said. 'But pretty, too.'

He moved his face closer to mine, and I closed my eyes, waited for him to kiss me. I was tense, ready, almost excited, but mostly scared that I was going to be kissed for the first time. I waited and waited. But nothing happened. Eventually, I opened one eye, opened the other. When I did, he smiled at me. That surprised me. He mostly looked the pissed-off side of normal, but here he was, his features all relaxed into a dazzling smile. 'You're really pretty,' he said, and kissed me before I could say anything.

I resisted for a moment, not sure if I liked what was happening or not, but then he was putting his arms around me and I liked it fine. I liked it a lot. We kept kissing until he was pulling us both down onto the bed. Then he was pushing me gently onto my back and climbing on top of me. Then his hand was moving up inside my T-shirt and stroking my breast. I tensed for a moment, not sure if I wanted him to do that. He immediately took his hand away, then pulled away from the kiss to look at me. It was like he was silently asking if he could touch me there. I didn't hate it – I was just unsure. I grabbed his hand and placed it back on my breast and he grinned at me before he started kissing me again.

As he kissed me, he moved aside my bra strap and pushed his fingers into my bra, teasing my nipple. I gasped and he pulled away again, stared into my eyes as he played with my nipple, smiling in satisfaction at the noises of pleasure I was making.

I'm going to have sex, I realised. *If we carry on like this, we're going to have sex.* Did I want to have sex with Andrich? I hadn't thought about it. I thought about him. I had been crushing on him, but did I want to do it with him? He moved his hand away from my nipple and traced it down my chest, over my stomach, down to my jeans waistband. Carefully, he pushed his hand into my knickers, his eyes on mine the whole time. Then he pushed lower, between my legs, then inside me.

I gasped again, unable to look away from his eyes. He was grinning at me as he did this. *Yes*, I decided, *I do want to have sex with Andrich.*

I wanted to keep on feeling this good. This free. This blissed out. It must have shown on my face that I'd decided to do it with him because Andrich's smile widened and he pushed a bit deeper, the intensity in his eyes growing. Oh yes, I wanted to have sex with Andrich. I really, really did.

*

'Was that OK for you?' he asked me afterwards. 'I didn't hurt you, did I?'

I shook my head. He hadn't hurt me. The opposite, in fact. It'd opened a whole new world to me. I didn't know that sex was like that. That it was all about pleasure and enjoying being with someone. I don't know what I thought it was, but not that. 'It was OK for me,' I said. We were cuddled up together, like they did on the television. 'It was good for me.'

'Me, too,' Andrich replied.

'How many times have you done that?' I asked him.

'Dunno. Loads of times.'

'With the same girl?'

'No. Not really. I had a girlfriend a while back, but it was hard to be alone together because she lived with her folks and they weren't up for having me over at all, let alone to sleep in her room. And Holly wasn't letting her stay over here. So we kind of broke up.'

'What do you think Holly will do if she ever finds out about this?' I wondered out loud.

Andrich sat up suddenly. 'You can't tell her,' he said seriously. 'You can't tell anyone.'

'OK,' I said.

'I'm serious here – you can't tell anyone. If they find out they'll separate us. They'll send us to different homes. I've seen it happen. Two people started having sex here and they were sent away. And I can't be sent away from here. It's the home closest to me ma. If they send me somewhere else I'll never see her. I'll never be allowed to live with her.'

'I'm not going to tell anyone,' I reassured him. The last thing I wanted was to be sent away. I'd had enough upheaval in my life. I liked it here. I liked almost everyone who lived here and I liked Holly. I loved Holly. The thought of living somewhere else with other people made me feel physically sick. I couldn't. I just couldn't.

'You'd better not,' Andrich said, an edge to his voice.

'I said I wasn't going to, didn't I?' I pulled away from him. I didn't like how he was being.

296

'All right, sorry,' he said. 'I was just panicking, you know? I can't be sent away from me ma. I'm just waiting until I hit eighteen then I can be out of here and I can go home and take care of her. I can get a job and look after her properly.'

'What about school?'

'What about it?'

'Everyone says you—' I stopped talking because I could hear a car pulling up outside. It sounded like the minivan the others had gone to the circus in. Both Andrich and my eyes widened in horror. They were back early or we'd lost track of time, or both. We leapt out of bed, and I grabbed my clothes. I decided to run back to my room that I shared with another girl before getting dressed. It'd be disastrous to be caught naked in here. I was just about to run for it when Andrich grabbed me, stared into my eyes for a second and then kissed me. Softly, tenderly. Then he let me go and I ran for it.

I dumped my clothes in a pile on the floor by my bed, grabbed my nightshirt from under my pillow and pulled it on before I leapt into bed. I had just shut my eyes and pressed my head deep into the pillow when the door opened.

'Robyn,' Holly called from the doorway. 'Robyn?'

I pretended to be asleep. I didn't really want to speak to anyone right now. I hadn't had time to think about what I'd done with Andrich.

I didn't want to speak to Holly, who might be able to tell something had changed. Holly was nice and interested – if she saw me now, she'd definitely know. And if she got closer to me, she'd probably smell Andrich's Lynx Africa on me. I could smell it and I liked it, mingled with my scent.

'Robyn?' she called a little louder. She hung on for a few more seconds before giving up.

'Did you see Robyn earlier?' Holly asked Andrich outside my room.

'She's weird,' he replied.

'I didn't ask you what you thought of her. I asked if you'd seen her?'

I could almost hear his shrug. 'She's weird.'

And I could almost hear Holly's eye roll of exasperation. 'Thank you, Andrich, Mr Not Weird,' she said, then stomped away.

I told myself that I heard him pause outside my door and press his fingers against it, in a moment of tenderness and affection, just like he'd done when he kissed me earlier. I told myself that it happened, so I was smiling when I finally drifted off to sleep.

Kez

1 May, Pitchingfield

The old Managa house hasn't been lived in for years, not since what happened the night Mrs Managa was killed. However, it does not look like a derelict place. It looks like someone has overseen the care of the grounds around the home. The windows are boarded up, but that looks like a recent thing.

The house sits in a plot of land out between Horsham and Crawley, in a village called Pitchingfield.

The road it is on is long and winding and leads down to the village, which has a couple of cafés, a post office, library, shops and a supermarket. But it is isolated. I'm sure that is how Robyn's dad liked it. Out there, no one could hear you scream. Out there, you couldn't have friends and family just drop by to visit or check on you, you couldn't make friends or form alliances with neighbours. If you didn't have a car, you would have to make a trek into the village every time you wanted something.

Rose Managa must have been so lonely. So scared, too. There was nowhere to run, no one to easily call on for help. Her whole life must have been centred on that one place. I wonder, as we approach the house, like I have been thinking more and more about her life, if she knew she would die here? I wonder often what she felt in those last few moments, whether she tried to be quiet because she knew her daughter was in the room and she didn't want her to be scared? When I have those thoughts, I always feel pain, physical pain, that marrying a bad man brought her to this. Marrying a man who she wouldn't have known was evil, who she would have loved with all her heart at one point, ended her life. And then I think of all the people currently going through what she went through and I hurt all over again.

I met Mac at Pyecombe services like I'd suggested, but we didn't take a taxi. We walked along the dual carriageway to where I'd parked a hire car a little way away. We'd been silent for the walk to the car, then when we were safely shut in the car, we made the most excruciating small talk while I drove. We lapsed into silence again when we got nearer the village.

There are vistas over the surrounding area that are breathtaking, and if I didn't know how Rose Managa's story ended, I might have felt envious of her, being surrounded by all of this beauty.

The house is at the end of a long, gravelly track, and it's not easy to approach without being seen. I park the car quite a distance away, on the other side of the road to the village, and we walk up to the house. If the person who has been maintaining the gardens is around, the last thing we need to do is tip them off that we're approaching. And if Robyn is there, we definitely don't want to alert her to our presence before we have to.

'What are we going to do when we get to the house?' Mac asks as the building becomes more solid and present in front of us. Before, it was almost an apparition on the horizon; now it is very real.

'Always with the hard questions, eh, Dr Guy?' I say. I actually don't know. I don't know how far gone Robyn is, if it's still possible to reason with her. She's not like other people who do this. She's not doing it for ego; she's not doing it for financial gain – well, not that I can see. It's revenge. Pure revenge. She only really wants to hurt one person and that is her father. The people she is hurting aren't even substitutes for her object of pursuit, they are necessary steps to get to the person she really wants.

'I've been thinking and thinking. I don't know if talking to her will be enough,' he explains. 'She's focused. She has one thing on her mind. I'm not sure there is anything we can say at this point to stop her.'

'We're here to see if this is where she has her list,' I admit. 'I don't think it'll be possible to stop her. Just delay her, delay her enough to get her to turn herself in. And we'll only get her to do that if we can convince her that it's the quickest way to get to her father. We were never going to stop her.'

The closer we get to the house, the more we can see that I was right: the boards are new – they haven't been up long enough to be weathered, swollen from rain, their nails rusted up. The roof looks recently repaired, too. The gutters are clear of leaves. The windowsills that are visible around the boards have been painted white. I have a feeling that I am right about this – this is where Robyn has based herself.

We walk around the house, looking for points of entry. Nothing. It looks hermetically sealed. But it mustn't be because I am sure this is Robyn's base. The lack of car in the drive suggests she is out, too. I look over at the double garage. I don't know if she has a car in there. There are no fresh tracks to the garage, but there are some leading to the back of the house. On the wall is the dark green box of a security firm alarm.

We do another circuit of the house and just as I'm about to say that we should think about ripping the board at the back off, Mac says, 'All right, was hoping it wouldn't come to this.' From his pocket he produces a small, blue velvet roll and steps up to the front door.

'Oh please tell me that's not what I think it is.'

'You didn't see nuffink,' he says, and begins to work on the bottom lock.

'But you're not an agent, right,' I scoff.

'You didn't see nuffink,' he repeats. I listen to him working, the light scraping, the constant pausing to listen, his sigh as he finally gets what he wants. He then works on the top lock, the same routine, the same sigh at the end when he gets in.

We gently push open the front door. And I pause, wait to see if an alarm goes off. If it does, I don't hear it. We move quickly inside and shut the door behind us. Still no alarm sounds. But I notice at the back of the front door there is a white alarm contact sensor, one that is set off when the door is opened. I can't see the keypad to cancel the alarm, but that doesn't mean there isn't one. And, besides, we'd have no clue what the code would be. 'There was an alarm box outside and there's a sensor on the back of the door. I don't think there are motion detectors, but there is definitely that sensor. We have to be aware that an alarm might have gone off somewhere so we need to move quickly.'

'Agreed,' Mac replies.

The lack of post behind the door, the lack of dust all over the floor and stairs suggest someone comes in here regularly to tidy up. It doesn't look expert or anything, so I suspect someone local has been coming in to maintain the place. And if they are simply cleaning and dusting, then they won't have gone to the attic. They would clean the rooms that are visible and probably not even all of those are done every time they visit. 'Attic is the most likely place for her to put her stuff up,' I say.

We move up the stairs, the thought of being raided any second making us move quietly but quickly. We go up the second staircase to the second-floor landing with three bedrooms. In the ceiling of the hallway is a wooden slatted hinged door. I'm guessing there is a pull-down ladder up there. Neither of us is tall enough to reach the door. I push open the bathroom door, which is on the right at this part of the landing. Bingo! Sitting by the door is a long wooden pole with a metal hook on the end. I grab it and then open the door. As I suspected, a wooden staircase is lowered as the door flips open. We open the con-certinaed ladder and push it into place. I pause, I'm sure I can hear a car coming towards the house. There must have been a silent alarm.

'We need to move,' I say, and go up the staircase into the loft.

Mac looks down at the pole I handed him, moves quickly to return it to the bathroom before climbing the stairs after me and pulling the door shut behind him. I haven't put on the light, but from what I saw before Mac closed the hatch, the loft is partially boarded and some beams are still exposed.

We stand in the dark, close together, scared to move for long sec-onds. I'm being paranoid, I decide. I didn't really hear a car. It was just my imagination. I'm about to say as much when Mac presses his fin-gers on my lips to stop me talking, because . . . 'Hello?' a voice calls through the house. 'Hello? Is there anyone there?'

We both stand rigid in the dark, too scared to even breathe.

'Hellooooooo,' the male voice calls again. 'Is there anyone there?'

They call out a few more times, wander from room to room, look-ing and checking. After a while, they seem to give up. We still don't move. We stand still in the attic, barely breathing, Mac's fingers on my mouth, our bodies too close, far too close. I can feel the heat radiating from him and he can probably hear my racing heart. After more of a while, we hear the car outside starting up, and eventually it pulls away. Still we don't move. Still we wait. Until the car is a distant sound and we feel rather than know that we are alone.

Once we realise we are alone, Mac takes his hand away, but can't step away because we can't really see in here. I reach into my pocket and take out my phone, flick on the light. The loft has been cleared, everything piled up in the corner, to make space for its new purpose: being Robyn's base of operations.

Along the longest wall, she has created something similar to a police crime board. There are pictures, printed-out text, addresses, lists, green string linking it all together like a web.

'Can you put on your light so I can take pictures of this?' I ask Mac. He moves away from me to flick on his mobile's light. I need to take pictures because once I call it in, I'm doubtful they will share all of it with me.

It takes an age to get as much of the information down as possible. She has been scarily accurate, terrifyingly detailed. She has people's schedules, routines and whereabouts. She has names, aliases, employment histories, known associates. This must have taken years to amass. Years and years.

The more I learn about Robyn, the more scared of her I am. Her not being a sociopath, a psychopath, nor a narcissist makes her unpredictable. Her being this single-minded makes her dangerous. Seriously dangerous.

Although Mac doesn't say it, I can tell he is taken aback. I can tell he's becoming as scared as I am.

There is no blood in the room, which suggests that she doesn't work on them here. I suspect she uses the garage or one of the outbuildings that are set further away from the house for that.

But with all the security, how does she get in and out without being discovered? I can only imagine she's paid someone for the security code, slipped them something to look the other way.

'I'm going to have to call this in,' I whisper to Mac as we stand in the dark, staring at Robyn's work.

'This is beyond me,' he says. 'I honestly thought I could possibly talk her down. But this just tells me that I have no chance. I never had a chance. She's been doing this for years. That's obsessive – at this stage, it's also compulsive. All of this is so wrapped up in her identity, in who she is now, I don't think anyone will be able to get through to her.

'I had no idea. I had no idea at all. This is where she disappears to. This is what she's been doing. Some therapist I am.'

'But she wasn't your patient, not your client. You were talking to her as a trusted friend. Someone who was trying to help her. You weren't giving her therapy. Things would have been different if you had.'

'Some friend. How could I have not known?'

'Robyn is a traumatised little girl. She grew up in a violent, abusive household that ended with her mother being killed by her father. I hate to think what she went through. Not only that, he didn't get put away. She grew up in care knowing he was out there living his life. There was no way that she was not going to have issues. You helped her. I know you did. But we can't focus on that right now. I have to call this in. And cross my fingers that my delay hasn't meant someone else is killed.'

'Yes, of course, of course.'

We lower the ladder and climb down, Mac first. At the bottom, he reaches out his hand for me to take. I pretend I don't see it and continue to climb down unassisted.

At the bottom, we move away from the hatch and head for the stairs, descend to the level below. As we go down to the first floor, I realise with an unpleasant start that I'm not thinking about Robyn, nor what happened in this house. I'm thinking about the touch of Mac's fingers on my lips, how natural they felt there, how I wanted them to stay there that bit longer. We move towards the staircase to the ground floor but before we descend, we both simultaneously pause. Mac turns to me and my breathing becomes shallow. He seems to be desperate to map out my face, his gaze lingering on my mouth, then rushing up to look into my eyes. I know I'm doing the same. I know I'm staring at him and feeling . . . something I shouldn't be feeling for someone who isn't—

He cuts off all thoughts by moving closer still, lowering his head to look deeper into my eyes. My lips part and he brushes his nose over my nose, pausing to savour the moment before his lips find mine. I hesitate for a moment, too, trying to think twice, trying to think three times before I give in to the inevitable and kiss him back. His arms wrap around me, and my hands go up to his face. Our kissing is deep, involved, it sends sparkles all over my body, it causes my heartbeat to quicken, my mind to cloud over. He pulls me into the bedroom we're standing beside, his arms tightening around me as he starts to kiss me a little harder, almost like now he's allowed to, he wants to do this as much as he can. I match his intensity, the heady vibration of sex pulsing through every second of our kiss.

We stand beside the stripped bed, enjoying the sensation of our lips moving together, our bodies being desperate to be together. Eventually Mac sits on the bed, pulling me down on top of him. We break apart, and he lies back, staring up at me as I sit astride him. His hands move over my breasts, skim down my waist and then he links his fingers with mine. We keep eye contact, both of us softly moaning, our hands gripped tight together as I grind on top of him. He places his hands under my jacket, pushes it off my shoulders. I tug my top off over my head, and his hands are immediately on my breasts again, this time teasing my nipples through my bra, making me writhe harder.

I tug his T-shirt out of his jeans, unbutton them and reach inside his boxers, take him in my hand. I love the feel of him, how thick and long he is, and I start to stroke the full length of his erection. He convulses in pleasure, moaning, 'Don't stop, don't stop.' I want to feel him inside me, I *need* to feel him inside me.

I stumble off the bed, and he sits up to rest on his elbows as he watches me. 'Slowly,' he whispers when I begin to fumble with my clothes. 'Slowly.'

Carefully, tantalisingly, I pull my jeans and knickers over my hips.

'Yes, like that,' he says huskily. 'Just like that.'

I keep my eyes on him as I slowly take off my jeans, my knickers, my bra, enjoying how much he loves the tease of what I'm doing.

He pulls his boxers and jeans over his hips, and then holds out his hand for me to come back to him. I return, take his erection in my hand and then slowly, carefully, guide him in—

'I'd better get on with calling this in,' I say, loudly, shoving away the vivid fantasy playing in my mind, while trying to break eye contact with Mac. Trying and failing. I'm hypnotised by him, completely in his thrall. *What nonsense is this? What am I doing?*

'Yes, you'd better,' he replies, still staring deep into my eyes. *I wonder if he can tell? I wonder if he can tell that a whole fantasy about him and me unravelled itself inside my head. Fully formed. I* hadn't thought of it at all, but the way it just unfolded in my mind, you would have thought I'd spent weeks and months perfecting it.

I reach into my pocket to retrieve and then hand him the car keys. 'Take the car. I'll have it picked up tomorrow. I have a feeling I'm going to be here a while.'

He holds out his hand and I drop the grey metal bundle into his palm. 'Thanks,' he says, and pockets them.

A rush of embarrassment overtakes me and I'm finally able to tear away my eyes from his. I want nothing more than for him to disappear. And to never see him again. Being around him is dangerous for my work and my marriage. This man is a distraction I didn't expect and certainly don't want. 'I'll contact you when I've got a proper lead on where Robyn is,' I say to him.

'No, don't. I don't think it's a good idea for me to be around this.' By which he means me. It's not a good idea for him to be around me. 'I'm not helping. And it's not good for you to be distracted. If you're going to help Robyn, you need to be focused.'

'I think you're right,' I say, staring at the honey-coloured varnished floorboards and grey painted skirting to avoid his gaze.

'Kez,' he says quietly.

'Yes?' I reply, my eyes still averted.

He steps forward, hand out to touch my face, I think, and I dart backwards out of reach. 'No, don't,' I plead. 'Just don't.'

'It wasn't meant to go like this,' he says. 'I genuinely only wanted to help you find Robyn so we could bring her in safely. I didn't expect this to develop between us. For us to—'

'Take care of yourself, Dr Mackenzie,' I cut in. I can't have this conversation. Not when I'm married and I love my husband. I can't betray Jeb by doing this externally, even in abstract. A fantasy is one thing, talking to the object of the fantasy about the fantasy, even tangentially, is dangerous. Too dangerous. 'And thanks for all your help. It's been invaluable.'

He inhales deeply, holds the breath while he nods and tucks his disappointment behind a neutral expression. Eventually he exhales as a sigh. 'Take care of yourself, Dr Lanyon. I hope I get to see you again.'

Robyn

February, 2016

Andrich and I did it whenever we got the chance. We didn't get that many chances because Holly lived as well as worked at Maddox Hall with her husband, Clyde. There were three other care workers who came and went, but she was there all the time and she was always on high alert for shenanigans.

Sometimes I'd sneak out of bed and down to his room, which thankfully was on the opposite side of the large building to Holly and Clyde's room. I also had to be careful because Marnie, who I shared with, and who had been here for three months, was a bit of a bitch and had told me she had a crush on Andrich so I wasn't allowed to go near him. She even made snide comments if I spoke to him, so if she found out, or suspected that's where I went when I crept out, she would have snitched on me for sure. Sometimes, to throw her off the scent, I'd go sit in the bathroom and read for a couple of hours, so if she did suspect and go looking, she would see where I was.

I loved doing it with Andrich. And he said he loved doing it with me. It was kind of exciting, too, having to be quiet, having this thing between us that no one knew about. We'd been doing it for about four months when he got news that he'd be allowed a long-term home visit if he wanted to still do that. Just like that. None of us were expecting it and he'd thought Holly was winding him up when she told him. But no, it was true, he was allowed to go and be with his mum, and so another person I cared about started packing to leave me.

Holly slung her slender arm around my shoulder and rested her head on mine as he said goodbye to the others. 'I'm sorry he's leaving you, but I'm happy that he's getting what he's wanted all this time,' she said.

'He's leaving everyone,' I replied, a lump in my throat. He'd stopped himself from crying as he hugged everyone, but had almost broken down when we briefly hugged goodbye.

'You lot think I'm thick, don't you?' Holly replied. She lowered her voice: 'I know you've been sleeping together for months.'

'Pardon me?'

'It's against the rules and I would have stepped in if I'd actually caught you in the act or had overwhelming evidence you were. But I'm like your parent, and I have to do what's best for you. And you two were good for each other. If I didn't suspect it was something going on with you, I would have thought Andrich had been body snatched because he became such a sweetheart.' She squeezed me tight, her floral perfume comforting and reminding me of my mother. I wondered if I would have told Mum about Andrich. About my first kiss with him that led to my first time with him on the same day. I wondered if she would have approved after everything she went through with Dad. Holly gave me another close squeeze. 'Don't do it again, though, there's a good girl. I can't look the other way again, OK?'

'OK,' I replied.

Of course I did it again. Why wouldn't I? Sex made me feel good. I thought it was because of how much I liked Andrich that I enjoyed it so much, but it turned out I could enjoy it without the emotional connection. I mostly did it with older boys from my school. We'd go back to their houses to study and we would study – after they'd screwed me in their narrow beds with football-themed duvet covers and posters of busty women on the wall.

I liked how sex took me out of things, got me out of my head. I liked having another person's skin so close to mine. I liked orgasming. I always made sure I enjoyed myself and that the guy wore a condom.

The boys all swore me to secrecy then told anyone who would listen what we'd done, so obviously I got a reputation. I honestly didn't care. I had watched my father murder my mother, did anyone really think 'Robyn Managa is a dirty slut' scrawled on a blackboard or on the back of a toilet door was going to touch me? Did they think whispering as I walked past or blanking me in the dinner hall was going to wound me? Did they really think that tripping me up or pulling my hair was going to harm me? I liked sex because I could feel something. I could get out of my usual mode of numbness, shock and terror and feel something.

Sex released me from the cage of horror I'd been locked in ever since that July night in 2012. I didn't care what anyone said about me.

Holly did care, though, and when she heard about my reputation, when the school told her that lots of the girls refused to work with me because I'd slept with their boyfriends, she pulled me out of school and sent me to an all girls' school that I had to get a bus to from the edge of the village down from Maddox Hall. I didn't think it wise to mention to Holly that a couple of the girls who refused to work with me were actually girls I'd slept with, too, so an all girls' school per se wouldn't stop me.

But I did stop. Holly sat me down when all the other children were in bed one night and said to me she understood. 'I grew up in care, you know, Robyn? I get where you're coming from. I was just like you. I was promiscuous, and I got a reputation. A lot of the other girls I was in the home with got pregnant really young. Others got hooked on drugs or booze or both. You, like me, are getting hooked on sex. And it's not even sex, is it? It's feeling wanted. Feeling loved. Getting out of your body and head while you're with that other person. But you know what I eventually realised far too late?'

In the darkened dining room, I shook my head.

'I realised it wasn't going to bring my mother back. It wasn't going to stop her being gone. And avoiding that fact was just going to lead me on a journey of self-destruction. And, if there was one thing I knew about my mum, it's that she wouldn't want that for me.' She smiled sadly in the dark at me. 'Would your mum want that for you?'

No. No she would not. She wouldn't want any of this for me. And I had made her a promise. I had told her what I would do if she was gone. It wasn't sleeping around, getting hits of pleasure from anyone I could. It wasn't letting my grades slide at school. It wasn't not living up to my potential and pretending I was OK with that.

Mum had made me promise what I would do if she was gone. And I had to keep that promise. I had to find him, no matter how long it took.

Part 10

Kez

14 May, Brighton

It's been two weeks since we found Robyn's base of operations and thankfully there haven't been any more bodies or deaths or victims. As I suspected, finding the base of operations slowed her down, since everyone on her list has been placed under police protection.

I don't think for one moment that she has given up, but it has bought us time. The task force such as it was has been moved to the back burner, most of Insight are back working on other projects and I am waiting. Waiting for something to happen.

I think she's going to strike again soon. Who, I don't know. Where, I don't know. I just know it's going to happen.

I'm also waiting to hear back from the application I've put in *again* to have them tell me something about her father. Just his name. If he's alive or dead, whereabouts in the country he is. Anything that will give me something to bargain with. Dennis keeps patiently explaining it doesn't work like that. I keep, just as patiently, explaining that he needs to find a way to make it work like that because the only way she'll stop is if she talks to him.

I'm also waiting for the nonsense that is going on in my brain to go away. Because I miss Mac.

Urgh, just thinking like that makes me cringe and want to throw up. I was getting a steady dose of ego boost by simply being around him. I was spending time with someone who did and didn't need me at the same time. My need to be needed, my need to atone for Brian, has clearly made me susceptible to the particular blend of charm that he was dispensing. It was good, satisfying, to be around someone who spoke my work language, who challenged me in one of the ways I challenged other people, who I would catch staring at me with such intensity it made my temperature rise just thinking about it. He wanted me on so many levels and that was intoxicating.

I hate myself for thinking like that. About any of that. But I can't stop myself. I constantly check my phone to see if he's messaged, and I always . . . *always* feel a heady combination of terror and euphoria when I sometimes see the three dots appear because he's typing something to me. He never finishes the message, never presses send, but it's sometimes enough to know he's thinking of me. And I hope when I type the messages that I never send – that I would *never* send – that he realises I'm thinking of him, too.

Part of me wants to go over to his house and fuck him. Just get it over with and live with the guilt and the destruction of my family, afterwards. The other part of me, the sensible part that would never allow me to do what the stupid part of me wants to do, knows what she has to do.

I have to stop this in its tracks. I haven't done anything, but before it becomes an issue, I need to face it full on. And the only way to do that is to confess.

I have to tell Jeb.

Robyn

From Robyn's Last Will & Testament

I should be in bits right now, horrified and scared that they've found where I've mostly been hiding out and where I've been taking the people I question, but I'm not.

Not really.

I'm more relieved than anything. It'll be harder, yes, not having a proper list to work from, and not having the element of surprise because they'll either be expecting me or they'll be guarded, but maybe that's for the best? I mean, if I don't have the chance to torture them in the way I have been, maybe no one else will have to die?

I hate that people have died because of this, because of my mission. Don't misunderstand – they were terrible people – but I still don't think it's right how they met their end. Yes, it was because of me, but I still feel turned inside out about it.

And while I don't want anyone else to die, I do need to do this to find him.

Those two things are wreaking havoc with my mind, causing constant conflict in my head and chest.

That's why I'm not as upset as I should be about them discovering my board and where I was getting those men to talk. It means doing things that way has been taken out of my hands and I need to do things differently going forward.

I wish there was someone I could talk to and tell everything to. There is so much I can't write here because, as I said, there are other people involved and things would be catastrophic for them and me if this was found before I've done what I need to.

What I can say, though, is the policeman, McDermott, told me about someone who might know Dad's new name. It's a very real lead, so I hope when I find this new person that I won't be forced to hurt them. That they'll just tell me what I need to know so I can walk away cleanly.

What am I even trying to say? I can't walk away cleanly. I'll always have the literal blood of those men on my hands and their deaths on my conscience.

That's why it's annoying and inconvenient that they've found the board, but it's also for the best.

It really is for the best.

Kez

20 May, Brighton

'Something's happened and . . . and you're not going to like it. But I have to tell you about it,' I say this to Jeb from the doorway of his office, six days after I made the decision to tell him.

My husband's handsome face draws in; he is concerned and scared all at once. He's sitting on the sofa in his office, reading some work papers, so pushes his glasses to the top of his head and studies me, searching for a clue as to what I'm about to say. He won't be expecting it – he'll have no clue. I've decided to do this because it's the only way to stop it. If I don't . . . If I don't . . . I don't trust myself is the bottom line. Since our split last year, Jeb has been on tenterhooks around me. He has spent hour after hour trying to make it up to me. Which is probably part of the reason why we are where we are. Why I've had my head turned in such a decisive fashion.

'What is it?' he asks. I can tell he is trying to modulate his tone, to sound calm.

I step fully into his office, shut the door with a big split in the wood of the left-hand panel behind me. Then I walk like a woman approaching the gallows to the centre of the room. 'There's no easy way to say this,' I begin. Then I stop talking because my brain is racing, panicking, screaming at me not to do this. Once I do this, I am probably going to upend my whole marriage.

'Kez, you're really scaring me here. What's going on?'

'This thing I've been working on, another one of those things I can't tell you about, I've had to work with another psychologist . . . therapist. And . . . I . . . I felt . . . I've been attracted to him.'

He frowns at me, his mouth tense, his eyes wary. 'What do you mean?'

'I mean . . . I mean I've been attracted to him. I've found myself kind of liking him. Kind of.'

'Did something happen with him?'

'No, no way.'

'But you wanted it to?'

'In a way—'

'It's a yes or no answer, Kez. Did you want something to happen with him?'

'It's not th—'

'Yes or no, Kez.'

'Yes, but only vaguely. It wasn't—'

Jeb is on his feet, then. He snatches his glasses from the top of his head, throws them onto his desk. Then he comes towards me until he is right in front of me. He looks so betrayed. Because he *has* been betrayed – by me. I've hurt him and I hate myself for that. 'Why are you telling me? If nothing happened, why are you even telling me?'

'Because I want to be honest with you. I always want to be honest with you.'

'Oh, that's it, is it? Because I wasn't honest with you over that stuff last year, you're showing me how I'm supposed to behave?'

'No, I didn't mean it like that.'

'Then how did you mean it?'

'I meant I just want to be honest with you.'

He shakes his head in disgust. 'Why did you really tell me?'

I flap my arms up and down in frustration. 'I just want to be honest, like I always am. If I can tell you something, I do. I just want to be honest.'

'No, Kez,' he says sternly, leaning right down to face me, 'no. You told me because you want to stop yourself. You told me because it's the only way to stop yourself doing something with him.'

I stare furiously at the floor, at the carpet neither of us has had the time to organise being changed. I can't say anything to that.

'Tell me I'm wrong,' he says.

I can't meet his gaze. I have to continue staring at the ground in shame. Why do I forget how well my husband knows me? How obvious this would have been to him.

'Thought so. Tell me the truth – have you fucked him?'

'No! I wouldn't. I wouldn't do that. I wouldn't do that to us. To our family.'

'Have you kissed him?'

'No! I told you I wouldn't do that.'

'But you've come close to it, haven't you? That's why you're telling me. You came close, you're still thinking about it and now you're expecting me to be the reason you don't go through with it when the opportunity arises again, aren't you?'

'It wasn't like that.'

'Then what was it like? Come on, tell me, how was it?'

I still can't look at him and I can't explain that moment at the Managa house, the other moment in the hotel room. I can't explain it without it becoming a bigger deal that it is. Rather than say anything about what has almost happened, I hang my head, mumble, 'It's not like that.'

Throwing an 'urgh' of disgust in my direction, Jeb strides out of the room and down the stairs. Seconds later, I hear him pick up his car keys and then the front door opens and shuts.

I put my head in my hands, rub my fingers over my eyes. *What have I done? What have I done?*

Robyn

From Robyn's Last Will & Testament

'Tell me what you would say to me if I was your father?' Dr Mac said. 'Imagine right now that I'm him. What do you want to say to me?'

I shook my head.

'Come on, tell me. You can say whatever you want to me. I will not say a word. Just tell me whatever it is you want to say. Come on, you can do it. Come on.'

'You didn't have to do that to her,' I whispered. 'You didn't have to hurt her like that. I . . . I'm sorry, all right? I didn't mean to talk back to you. I didn't know that when I said I wasn't going to do my homework right then it would upset you so much.

'That's not true. I knew it would upset you, but I didn't care. You were always upset. Everything made you unhappy and angry. Everything made you mad. I was just doing what I had to do. I know you were paying money for me to go to school. But you didn't have to get so mad. You knew why I was doing what I was doing. You didn't have to knock me off my chair and put your hands around my throat and try to choke me.'

'Keep going – tell me. I'm listening to you. Tell me.'

'You didn't have to choke me. And when Mum came and grabbed you, tried to stop what you were doing, you didn't have to . . . you didn't have to turn on her. Knock her down, start hitting her. You didn't have to put your hands around her neck. You di—'

I couldn't keep talking. I couldn't. I'd never said that much out loud before. I'd never admitted before that it was all my fault. That if I hadn't cheeked my dad, I'd still have a mum. I'd still have my family.

'It's not your fault,' Dr Mac says. 'It's not your fault and it's not your mother's fault. It was his fault. It was all his fault.'

I knew that. On so many levels I knew that. But on the level where I operated, on the level of my everyday life, it was my fault. It was all my fault.

Kez

20 May, Brighton

About an hour later, the front door opens and then Jeb's footsteps are on the stairs.

I stand when he enters the bedroom. 'I'm sorry,' I say quickly. 'I'm so sorry. It came out all wrong. I was trying to explain that we're not—'

Jeb watches me speak for a moment or two, then pulls me to his body and pushes his mouth onto mine in an all-consuming kiss, the first time he has kissed me with this desperate *need* in months.

Still kissing me, he pushes me back onto the bed, pulls away and starts to almost rip at my shirt, trying to get it open. And this, he hasn't been this rough with me in an age. Since I started working at Insight, after our break-up last year, he's been overly cautious with me – gentle and loving like always, but always too careful. That passionate way he used to be with me, the desperate-to-devour-me way we sometimes used to have sex, just didn't happen any more. Whenever I tried, Jeb would half-heartedly join in, but he would mostly look worried and would hold back, so I stopped.

Jeb tears at my shirt until it is open – I think it lost a couple of buttons on the way. Immediately he takes my nipple in his mouth through my bra and I moan far too loudly at the shot of pleasure that fires through me. He moves to the other breast, does the same and makes me moan just as loudly. He goes for my jeans next. In response, I reach for his fly, but he pushes my hands away. He doesn't want me to do that. Once he knows I understand and lie back, he goes for my jeans again, tearing at them, until he strips them from me. I lie still, watching as he stands back to undress himself. Then he is back, a storm of emotion swirling in his eyes as he thrusts as hard as he can into me. When I moan too loudly again, he captures the tail end of the moan with a kiss, whilst threading his fingers into my hair, pulling slightly on it. I moan again against his lips as he drives himself into me, as he continues to bring us back to where we used to be, how we used to relate to each other. Jeb used to fuck me like this because he saw me as so much more than one thing. Jeb has always seen me as fragile, as strong, as beautiful, as complex, as this whole flawed human person who needs to be brought back from the brink sometimes for her own safety. When he wasn't treating me like that, when he was always concerned and cautious, we started to fracture.

RINGGGGG ... My phone starts, from its place on the bedside table. *RINGGGGG* ... I look in its direction, wondering if it's important since it is quite late on a Monday night, and in response Jeb covers my nipple with his mouth and bites enough to cause the perfect mix of pleasure and pain to flood my senses, convulsing my body and banishing all thoughts of the phone from my mind.

I give in to it then, I lie back and let him do what he wants to me. I let him move and thrust and fuck because he needs this, I need this. *We* need this.

Eventually the ringing stops. And Jeb carries on. Carries on and on and on ...

*

'You haven't done that to me like that in an age,' I say as we lie breathless side by side afterwards. 'I've missed it. I've really missed it.'

'Are you going to leave me, Kez? Like last time?' he replies. 'Are you going to leave me and then go be with him?'

RINGGGGG . . . My phone starts to ring again. I glance in its direction but decide to ignore it. *RINGGGGG* . . . I turn my head, instead, to look at my husband and he is staring back at me, worry and fear daubed all over his face. The phone's ring is loud and insistent and I wait for it to stop before I say, 'It was never about . . . I would never leave you for him. Or anyone else.'

'But you might still leave me,' he replies.

'No. Jeb, it was—'

RINGGGGG . . . My mobile starts to ring again and Jeb uses its intrusion to say: 'Since you started that job, you've changed. And I feel guilty about that. About why you had to take the job.'

'I haven't changed. It's just the way I work has changed. I can't tell you everything any more and I hate that, but it's necessary. And then I met this person and I kind of connected with him.' The phone stops and I rush to add: 'And it scared me. I haven't had that kind of connection with anyone since I met you, and I told you because I wanted to bring it out into the open. If it was a silly crush, I wouldn't have said anything. But this wasn't just a crush.'

RING-RING-RING! The house phone starts. No one but our immediate families have that number, so my hackles rise, scared that something has happened to someone important. But the only charged receiver is downstairs, which means by the time I get down there, it will have stopped ringing. *I'll pick up when my mobile starts again*, I decide.

329

'This wasn't a crush,' I say to Jeb. 'And when I told you, I realised it wasn't the big deal I thought it was, either. It's just I don't want to be connecting with anyone but you. When I thought I was, it scared the life out of me.

'But as soon as I told you, I realised what I actually have is a damaged connection with you and this person came into the picture when I was feeling particularly vulnerable.'

'What are you saying? You don't have a thing with this guy?'

'I have a desperate need to get you and me back to where we were. For us to be together again properly. You treat me like I'm made of glass, like I'm fragile, and you don't let me be who I am with you any more. Like just now, that's the first time in months and months that you've just let go and fucked me as though I won't break. I need that sometimes. I need you to be like that with me as well as being gentle.'

'Kez, you're around people who carry guns all day.'

'Not all day.'

'How am I supposed to treat you when I don't know what you're up against? I'm worried for you all the time. I want to stop you going there but I can't. I feel powerless to protect you or even support you.'

'It's not just that, though, is it? You think I hate you for what happened last year and you're waiting for the day that I tell you it's over.'

Jeb exhales, finally breathes out. He's been holding his breath, metaphorically and probably physically at some points for more than ten months. He's been waiting for me to say I'm going to leave him again. And now I've voiced his fear, he can let go. He can face that terror.

'Do you hate me?' he asks quietly.

RINGGGGG . . . Into the silence where my reply should be, comes my mobile phone again. *RINGGGGG* . . . I stretch out to pick it up.

'Don't, Kez,' he says, desperate to know the answer to his question.

I look at the screen and '***Unknown caller* . . .**' greets me.

'Don't answer it,' Jeb says.

'I have to,' I reply.

'Right now? Right at this second?'

'I have to.'

'Jeez!' Jeb spits as I press the green answer button and put the phone to my ear.

'Kez Lanyon.' Without a hello or even a proper greeting, the person on the other end starts to speak and I listen with an increasing dread that twists my stomach, then I hang up without saying goodbye.

'I have to go,' I tell Jeb, sliding off the bed and reaching for my dressing gown behind the door.

'Go? Go where?'

'I can't tell you.'

'Right this second, in the middle of *this* conversation, you have to go.'

'Yes.'

'And you can't tell me where?'

'No.'

'Or why?'

'No.'

'Kez—'

'I have to go,' I state firmly. I know this isn't the best time, but there will never be a right time to exit this conversation, and the longer I stay, the worse it will be when I do leave. 'I . . . I have to go. We can finish this conversation when I get back. But right now, I have to go.'

331

Jeb flops back on the bed in frustration and I leave the room shrouded in guilt. But I have to go.

Without her base of operations, without her board of information and without her list, Robyn has struck again.

Kez

20 May, Brighton

The crime scene hasn't quite been processed, so I have to put on gloves, blue plastic overshoes, a face mask and push my hair under a hat before I'm allowed to enter the house in Stamner Park. I am here – along with Dennis and Big Bad Aidan – as members of the task force hunting the perpetrator of this crime.

Robyn was waiting for them when they came home, apparently. She'd disabled the alarm without tripping it, and she had waited in the study for the person to return. I understand why she would wait in the study – it's one of the last places you visit when you get in. If the alarm is off, you think you've forgotten to put it on. If the living room and kitchen look untouched, if the bathroom, where you're very likely to head to is fine, then you're unlikely to head to the study.

Once the person was settled, had been to the toilet, had washed their hands, had gone into the bedroom to get changed, Robyn snuck out and waited outside the bedroom door. When the person had come out, she'd hit them over the head with a baseball bat. Not too hard, just enough to incapacitate them while she dragged them into the bedroom. I walk the scene, starting in the study, standing in the doorway, examining the angles and places she would have hidden. How she

333

must have had so much patience not to move, to wait in the dark until they came home.

Then I move to the bedroom, to the space outside the door, where I can almost see her form, dressed all in black, her hair tucked away, waiting for the person to finish changing. Then I move into the bedroom, look it over. She dragged a chair in from the study. She closed the blinds, drew the curtains. She had the big overhead light. No, no . . . she turned the side light on. It is sitting on the floor on the other side of the bed to where the chair is. She put it down there to make the room scarier, more threatening. The person, already disorientated, would hate the shadows cast, the not knowing where the next attack is coming from, if there is more than one person outside the small pool of light.

Once I have seen the set-up, I go back to the front door to walk the route again as the victim.

Opening the front door, frowning because the alarm doesn't sound. Pressing buttons to check it's working, getting the usual beep. Thinking back, kind of remembering not pushing the button to set it. Mentally kicking yourself to make sure you do it next time.

I look at the off-white keypad, its bottom hinge down from where the person checked it was still working. Beside the door is an umbrella stand with two big umbrellas in the four slots, the third umbrella is propped up next to the door.

You flip down the bottom hinge of the off-white keypad, check it's still working. From the umbrella stand by the door, you slowly, quietly pick up one of your large golf umbrellas, leave the other two in place, because despite sort of remembering not setting the alarm, you're still cautious. You move slowly to the living room, stand in the corridor, trying to see in via the crack in the door, then ever so carefully push

334

the door open with the tip of the umbrella. When nothing happens, no one rushes you, you push the door open wider. You stand and look in, trying to see around the corner into the library area, to see if there is someone there, or if anything has been disturbed. It's clear. So you move on to the kitchen, keeping an ear out in case you hear anything that shouldn't be there. The kitchen door is shut, so you have to turn the handle and then push it open with the umbrella in case someone is waiting for you. But no, it's all undisturbed. You go to the back door, check there's no one there. All clear. Relief.

I look around the kitchen, trying to work out how much time they spent in here. Did they put the kettle on? The water level indicator reads full – suggesting it was filled up recently – if you make yourself a drink before you leave for work, you don't go to the sink and fully fill the kettle. No, must have been filled after work. An empty pan sits on the stove.

My eyes sweep over the surfaces. Kitchen drawer partially open, bottle opener on the worktop above it. No bottle cap, must have tossed that in the recycling bin by the back door. A ring of moisture sits on the countertop beside the beer bottle opener.

You decide that everything is fine. It doesn't look like anyone was here. You decide to have pasta for dinner. You get the pan out of the cupboard, you fill and put on the kettle. Instead of getting the pasta out, you go to the fridge and get a beer. You remember when you start to drink that you were busting to go to the toilet when you came in. You take the bottle and head upstairs. Leave the umbrella by the front door. You put the bottle on the bedside table, then leg it to the loo. You wash your hands, dry them on the towel, go into the bedroom.

I stand at the bedroom door, looking at it how the victim saw it. On the floor by the bed is an umbrella.

You're still a bit nervous when you come up the stairs so you grab an umbrella again from by the front door (that turns out not to be the original one) and bring it up with you. You drop the umbrella to strip off your clothes, pull on a light grey tracksuit.

The house is quiet. Too quiet sometimes, but not at times like this when you can hear the kettle boil, you can hear the beep of the fridge saying you've left the door open. No, scratch that. *The kettle boiled while you were on the toilet. If you heard it, you heard it then.*

You finish getting changed. And you hear it. Something. A little noise. You stop, you listen, you wait for it to come again. But nothing. Nothing comes. You must have imagined it, it must be the age of this house, it must be next door. I look at the TV at the foot of the bed. It is on, switched to an action-movie channel, but it is muted. Probably because it was too loud for anyone on forensics to bear. *You don't flick on the TV. That comes later.*

You leave the room, forgetting your beer bottle because if you hadn't, it'd be lying on the carpet outside the bedroom.

But it's not. And it's not in the bedroom either. I make a mental note to look up the list of items taken from the bedroom.

You go to leave the room. And suddenly there's someone there. Dressed in black, face partially covered. You draw back, just as the person swings and hits you over the head. You only saw it coming at the very last minute.

I turn back to the bedroom. I look at the umbrella, the chair lying on its side on the blood-dappled carpet. Not too much blood. Not hours and hours and hours of torture took place. Hours, yes, not hours and hours and hours. One of the handcuffs is still on the chair.

You wake up, disorientated. Not sure what's happened. Your head is splitting in two. You can't get your bearings. You don't know

336

what's going on. You try to touch your head. That's when you realise you're handcuffed to the chair, and your middle is tied with a dressing-gown tie.

No, not that. She will have brought rope or tape with her.

As things become clearer, as the fug is absorbed by the pain in your head, you realise that even though you're in your own bedroom, the lights are just that bit too low. Your mouth is dry. And there is someone here. Just before, there was someone there. Before you can speak, the figure in black steps out of the shadows. You can only partially see them. But that is enough. Because at that very moment, you realise that this is the day you're going to die.

Except it's not.

This person survived.

Even though she's escalating, even though she is determined and has more reason to go overboard with anger at having her list taken away, she didn't. She showed restraint. She even waited until she was far away and called an ambulance.

That can only mean one thing.

Once I am on the threshold of 73 Harrick Terrace, I take off my cap, my overshoes, mask and gloves. I dump them in the industrial bin and march down to the end of the path where Dennis and Big Bad Aidan are waiting for me. They were here when I arrived but hadn't even attempted to come inside.

'Who is this person?' I ask them.

'Aren't you the one supposed to be telling me that?' Dennis replies.

'I'm serious, Dennis. Who is this person?'

'No one, as far as we can ascertain. Pretty low-level admin. Has been all their life. They've had one job – two if you count the post room from years ago – and have stuck to that ever since. I questioned them – they had no idea why she targeted them. They simply aren't as important as the other people on the list.'

'The other people weren't any more important than this person, thank you, Dennis,' I say with a glare in his general direction. I then glare at Big Bad Aidan, too, because he probably agrees with him. 'I need to speak to them.'

'No can do.'

'Dennis, I need to speak to them.'

'No can do, Kezuma. They are under police protection in hospital. Only a select group of people can speak with them. I'll do the best I can to allow you access to his statements.'

I sigh in frustration. Dennis doesn't want me speaking to this person, probably because they know whatever it is Dennis is hiding. But I can't get into that right now. 'All right then, he knows something. This person knows something. They came across the information by accident because he had such a low-level job and no one thought there was anything at all important about his position. She let him live because he gave her what she wanted. He gave her information that is going to lead her directly to her father.'

Both of them are openly alarmed.

'How do you know this?' Big Bad Aidan asks.

'That crime scene was nothing like the others. After the initial knockout, she used minimal "persuasion" techniques. This person rightly valued their life over Robyn's father's. Robyn made it look good, but it was all light-touch stuff. Enough that they would need to be hospitalised but not kill them. Enough to not make anyone think he had passed on information.

'This person knew something, possibly from their time in the post room, or maybe from pushing paper. I wonder if they worked some kind of admin for when the Protected Persons programme was being digitised? Or maybe when stuff was outsourced, they saw something that stuck in their mind and hung on to it? I don't know how she found them, but they knew something significant about Robyn's father and they told her. They might even have known his new name? That's why I need to speak to them. I need to find out what he told her.

'Because if she doesn't already have her father's new name, she will do very, very soon.'

Kez

21 May, Brighton

'I don't hate you,' I whisper to Jeb in the dark of our bedroom at 3 a.m. He is flat out asleep, naked in bed with the duvet pulled up to his chest, even though it's warm. He can't sleep without covers so we spend a lot of time with him pushing the covers off in his sleep because he's too hot, then pulling them back on when he realises his body isn't covered.

I kneel down on his side of the bed and link my hands together in front of me to talk to him. 'I don't hate you. I could never hate you. I can't even stay pissed off with you for long and sometimes I need to. But I . . . I need you to give him back to me. I need you to give me the Jeb you were before. I know we all change, and what happened last year nearly broke all of us. But I want my husband back. I want the man who tells me off, who tells me without words but in a thousand different ways that I'm beautiful. I want the man who makes me laugh and who doesn't think twice before he tells me I'm out of order. I know he's in there somewhere. That's who I want back. That's who I want to be married to.

'Because you know what? That's who you are, Jeb. Not this version of yourself. This version of yourself is going to break down if you carry on like this. I need you. I love you. The children need you. Your whole family need you. I know the Jeb you were before is in there somewhere – please can you try? Please can you try to give him back to me? Please?'

Robyn

21 May, Brighton

I have his name. I have my father's new name. Julian McDermott told me about a data entry clerk who had stumbled across some anomalies while entering data for the Protected Persons programme. Someone had attempted to erase all the available background and internet files of one particular person, but whoever was erasing the files didn't really know what they were doing so left behind a mess of partially deleted files and incomplete wipes.

The data entry clerk had decided to double-check before they went ahead and finished deleting the files properly and permanently. The question had sparked a flurry of activity and McDermott had offered to talk to them, seeing as he was working on the murder anyway.

Under McDermott's supervision, the clerk had deleted the files properly, made sure as much as possible was removed about that particular person. But McDermott was convinced that the clerk had kept a copy.

McDermott was right. They *had* kept a copy.

And when I confronted them in their house, they had given me the new name straight away. Straight away. They weren't going to protect my dad, no way! But we agreed I'd have to hurt them a little bit to throw off suspicion, so no one would know that they had told me anything. They were actually a good sport about it.

But I have my father's new name. It's not that unique, but it's unique enough to narrow my search. I could have him in no time. No time.

My father's new name is Brandon Miller.

Part 11

Kez

23 May, Brighton

I hear the footsteps, quiet in the lowest level of the underground car park in our work building, but it's the cadence of them, the way they are moving in time with my footsteps that makes me pause on the way to my car.

I stop, I listen, try to work out if they are just going to their car, or if— The footsteps stop and I have my answer: the footsteps are here for me.

A cascade of fear flows through me, coursing through every vein and artery, setting alight each nerve. This is not simply the fear that every woman walks with, the fear of attack that we're always meant to pretend is irrational. This is not the reality of knowing that round the next corner could be a physically violent racist that Black people and people of colour move with. Working on this case, looking for a young woman who is killing to get what she wants, has added to the usual fears I have. It's a reminder that bad things can happen to you at home, just as easily as in the street. I knew that, but hearing a fraction of Robyn's story, knowing what her father got away with doing behind closed doors, has turned me all the way inside out. Just like hearing

Brandee's story all those years ago made me decide I had to get her away from her mother.

I want to help Robyn. I *need* to help her – but will she believe that? Will she pause long enough to listen? I have a feeling, I realise as the quiet, creeping terror pools in my stomach that I'm about to find out. I am about to be in one of those situations that Jeb is always worried about. He keeps making me promise to do whatever it takes to come home. He makes me promise, and I do – with my fingers crossed in my head because I can't always be sure that 'coming home' will actually be an option available to me.

It's the middle of the day – this is a secure building with over a thousand people in it – but Robyn has still managed not only to gain entry, but also to pick a time when there is no one around. I wouldn't normally be down here at this time, but I have to pick up a prescription for Jonah and the chemist's will be closed by the time I leave work.

I slip my hand into my pocket. My fingers close around the miniature canister of deodorant I carry for protection. It won't deter even the most lightly interested attacker, but it can provide a few seconds' distraction, which can be all you need sometimes to get away. I flip the lid off the can with my thumb. My legs feel like Slinky springs – wobbly and unstable – as I resume my journey to the car.

The footsteps start up again. Light. Careful. Deliberate.

I take a few more steps, stop to make a big show of looking in my bag, just to confirm.

The footsteps stop.

OK, yes, this person is definitely following me. And I'm one hundred per cent certain that it's Robyn. Her modus operandi is surprise attack, overkill violence to make sure she gets and maintains the upper hand. She can't risk allowing the person even one moment to recover, otherwise they might fight back and she may not be able to keep them subdued.

I really don't want to fight anyone right now. Actually, I don't want to fight anyone, ever. I've seen what she can do, how vicious she can be. If she strikes, I am screwed. My fighting days are well and truly over. To be fair, they never really began. Even when I was training all that time ago and they taught us fighting techniques, I didn't really get into it. I was very much all about doing the bare minimum to make sure I passed that segment of the training course. And now look: I'm going to have to drag up what little bits I remember to fight someone twenty years younger than me.

'I don't want to fight you, Robyn,' I say loudly, far away from my car. I suspect that's where she'll attack and I need to avoid going there. 'I DON'T HAVE ANY ISSUE WITH YOU SO I DON'T WANT TO FIGHT YOU!' I say even louder this time. 'I KNOW IT'S YOU. AND I DON'T WANT TO FIGHT YOU. I DON'T THINK I COULD FIGHT YOU. SO, PLEASE, LET'S JUST TALK.'

I turn in the direction of the footsteps, still with my hand in my pocket on the deodorant. She may be too far gone to stop herself, but I haven't hurt her, I wasn't involved with her father's case, so I'm hoping she won't be absolutely set on harming me.

Her footsteps have stopped, so maybe she's thinking about it.

'I want to help you, Robyn,' I say. 'Dr Mackenzie – Mac – believed that I want to help you. He came with me to try to talk to you. He believed I wanted to help you. Please. Let's just talk. Please.'

Robyn doesn't move or say anything for a few more seconds, then she slowly comes into the light. She's not as tall as I expected, her body is slight but solid and her face is hidden by a neck scarf she has pulled up to cover her mouth and nose. She has on a beanie that covers her hair. She's dressed all in black, even down to black gloves.

As she stands in front of me, she pulls down her face covering. 'I hear you're looking for me,' she states. Her voice is not what I was expecting. She sounds a lot older than her looks, mature and certain.

'How did you hear that, then?' I ask. 'I'm pretty sure you haven't spoken to Dr Mac, and I'm not exactly "out there" so how did you know about me?'

Maybe Mac did sell me out to her? Maybe I shouldn't have trusted him. But I didn't get the impression that he would do that. Especially not after he stepped away because he couldn't trust himself around me. Why would he then sell me out to her and put me in harm's way?

'That's for me to know,' she says, and that makes her sound so much like Zoey I have to wonder what she would have been like if she'd had a normal life.

'No, honestly, how did you find out? Because I'm nobody in all of this. I'm not out there in any way. So, how did you know?'

'You have to teach yourself all sorts of things when you're like me,' she says. 'Finding out who's coming after you is always the best way to keep yourself safe.'

Maybe she has somehow got into Mac's phone or computer? Maybe she's been tracking him and through that found out about me.

'Why have you come after me?' I ask her. 'I'm nothing to do with what happened to your father.'

'Then why are you looking for me?' she replies. She comes closer, not too close; now that she has lost the element of surprise, she doesn't want to risk a confrontation starting. Her quick brown eyes also dart to my hand, still in my pocket.

'I want to help you.'

'Then tell me where he is. Give him to me. That's all the help I need.'

'Even if I knew where he was, I wouldn't tell you. That wouldn't be helping you.'

She laughs, mirthlessly. 'Another person who thinks they know what's best for me. I'm an adult, Dr Lanyon. I know my own mind. And I know that I want him. Nothing more, nothing less.'

'You're hurting people to get to him. That isn't . . .' I'm about to say 'that isn't knowing your own mind', when it's actually the very definition of knowing your own mind, especially when your mind is in pain and is desperately seeking resolution. 'OK, you know your own mind, but this isn't the way to get your mind to rest. To stop it screaming in pain.'

'What do you know about it?'

What *do* I know about it? Probably nothing on the surface of it. I didn't grow up in a violent home. I didn't watch my father subjugate and abuse and diminish my mother before he delivered that killing blow. I didn't watch my father get away with his crimes, see him be given a new life with a new name, possibly new face, definite fresh start. I didn't get to grow up alone and in care with varying levels of neglect and abuse, only to find myself on the streets at eighteen. I didn't get to meet the only person who has cared for me in recent times and to even then, *even then* not be sure if I can trust him. I have none of her experiences. And I have none of those specific stressors. But I do understand pain. I do understand constant, unrelenting pain. I do know how it feels to sometimes be terrified that the pain will consume you. I do understand that sometimes you'll do anything to make it stop. That sometimes you will make every deal going with the devil to make it stop, even for a little while.

351

'Nothing,' I say to her. Because she does not need me to pretend that my pain is her pain. That we are in any way equal. I do understand unremitting, unrelenting pain, but I do not understand *her* pain. 'I know nothing about it. But I want to. I want to help you deal with your pain. That's what I do. I help people deal with their pain. I want to help you before it's too late.'

'Oh, really? And there was I thinking you were a profiler who had been brought in to profile me, to help to find me so you can neutralise me.' How *does* she know so much about me?

'I was brought in to profile you, to work out where you would go and what you would do next, but not to neutralise you. I would never take on such a job. As I told Dr Mac, I only took on this job to make sure no one harmed you.'

She glances away to the side for a moment, uncertainty dancing across her face. I'm getting through to her. She's starting to believe me. But my moment of hope is dashed away when a sardonic smile swells on her lips. 'You're good, you know? I almost believed you there for a moment. I mean, you must have been good to have Dr Mac fooled, but I didn't realise how good. I'm actually impressed by how much sincerity you managed to put into that micro-monologue. You're a good actress. You put on a good performance.'

'I wasn't acting. Performing. Everything I just said is true. It's one hundred per cent true.'

'Of course it is. I'm really impressed. I can understand why my uncle Dennis likes you so much, why you're so special to him. He's really done a good job with you.'

What?

WHAT?!

'I'm sorry, *what*?' I say, staring at her as the alarm that is rising in my body is realised on my face, while I suddenly feel like I am burning up.

Robyn double-takes, realises that I do not know what she is talking about. 'Are you telling me you didn't know?' she says with a laugh. 'Oh, that is priceless. Priceless.'

'What are you talking about?' I say. My heart is fluttering, shaky in my chest; my breathing is shallow and painful.

She laughs again, this time the derisory sound is nasty, vicious. 'My father is called, *was* called, Henry Chambers. Dennis Chambers is his cousin and best friend.'

Kez

23 May, Brighton

'My father is called, *was* called, Henry Chambers. Dennis Chambers is his cousin,' Robyn says, watching the revelation filter through my mind. 'That's how I know about you looking for me – I knew he would make sure he was put to work sorting this out. It was him who arranged for my dad to go into witness protection. It was all him. He persuaded people and that's why I've been very careful about who I targeted. They all had to be known to him. It was him I was writing the notes to. I had to get his attention so he would lead me to my father. I knew, too, that Uncle Dennis would put his best people on it to protect his cousin.'

The questions I have are whizzing too fast around my head to actually leave my mouth. *What the actual hell?* I keep saying to myself. *What the actual hell?*

'They were cousins, but they were like brothers, really. They grew up together, did everything together. Even went to the same university, where my father met my mum and Uncle Dennis met his first wife, Meryl.

'Auntie Meryl was actually a really decent person. Not as lovely as my mother, but no one was. They were good friends, Meryl and Mum. They looked really similar and were often mistaken for sisters. When

354

I was really young, she was over all the time. We'd all have so much fun. I remember she used to smell of strawberries and Astral skin cream. She would buy us all sorts of things. She'd come over loads without Uncle Dennis. And when Dad wasn't there.' Robyn looks down at her glove-covered hands. Suddenly she is tugging the gloves off so she can examine her nails. 'She gave Mum money because Dad liked to control her by keeping her short of money. He liked to make sure she couldn't do anything because she never had enough cash. He controlled her bank account and if she earned any money doing ironing for people in the village or anything, he would take it from her. He never let her have more than a few pounds at a time.

'Uncle Dennis was actually all right. He'd play sometimes. Sometimes. But when Auntie Meryl came over on her own, that was when things were really fun. At some point, though, she and Mum would go off and talk alone.

'I overheard them, of course. I was always there with my head pushed up against the door. Lurking. Wanting to know what was going on. And what was going on was Auntie Meryl wanted us to leave. She wanted us safe. Away from him. She was trying to help Mum get out. To protect us. She helped Mum save money; she found us somewhere to live. And then she disappeared.'

'What do you mean, "disappeared"?'

'She just stopped showing up at our house. Stopped coming over with Uncle Dennis. I never saw her again. About two years later, Mum . . . Mum was—'

'Did she show up then?'

'I told you, I never saw her again. I haven't been able to find her. Maybe you should ask Uncle Dennis what happened to her. Because he loved her. You could tell. He couldn't keep his eyes off her. And then she was gone. His current wife, she looks a bit like her. I thought it was her at first, then realised it was someone else. So, yeah, go ask what happened to his wife. Where she is.' Robyn pushes her fingers back into her gloves. Pulls the scarf back into place around her mouth and nose, pulls up the hood over her beanie. 'Can't stand around here all day yapping. Consider this chat, the note I would have left with you.' Her face moves in a way that suggests she has smiled. 'Tell Uncle Dennis, "Give him to me." That's all I want: "Give him to me."'

She disappears into the dark shadows of the car park.

I cannot move.

For long minutes I stand shaking, the information she has just given me spinning my brain. I have lost all sense of balance.

Dennis.

The utter, utter bastard.

Robyn

From Robyn's Last Will & Testament

She is not what I was expecting, at all.

I thought she would be dynamic, cold, single-minded. But instead she's quite homely. I mean, beautiful, but kind of mum-like. I didn't think my uncle Dennis would put someone so *human* on this.

I didn't tell you about my uncle Dennis before because as I said at the beginning, if someone finds this before I'm done, I don't want them tipping off anyone else. I need to keep some stuff back so I'm more likely to succeed.

My uncle Dennis is an odd person. If odd isn't too vague a word. As I told Dr Lanyon, he was nice to me, nice to Mum. He would play with me sometimes, he would make up elaborate games and read me stories and look like he was listening when I talked. When I was young – five or six – I had theories about everything. Everything. I was once convinced we could pay off the mortgage on our house by persuading all our family and friends and neighbours to give us money. Just like that. Uncle Dennis would always sit and listen to

357

me. He would consider what I said, and contribute his thoughts on the matter.

But . . . he changed when Auntie Meryl stopped coming over. He would still play, would still listen, but it was like he wasn't there half the time. His body was, but his mind was elsewhere. By that point, things were awful with Dad. He was angry all the time, he would blow up all the time. The good times when he wasn't awful were so few and far between that it became easier to just accept this hellscape was where we would always stay.

One time, about six months after Auntie Meryl stopped coming to visit, Uncle Dennis waited until Dad was out of the room and Mum was in the kitchen to say to me: 'It won't always be like this, you know, Avril? You won't always have to live like this.'

I wasn't sure what he meant. How could any of this be any different? What was going to change it?

He wasn't wrong, as it turned out. I don't think he meant it would turn out the way it did, but it wasn't always like it was. It was so much worse.

Uncle Dennis turned up at the safe house we were put in after they thought Dad was in danger of being kidnapped. I remember he walked in, his face like thunder. He asked for the room and no one argued, everyone just left. Except me. I sat in the corner with my rabbit on my lap, watching. 'What did you do?' Uncle Dennis said, grabbing Dad's shirt front. 'What did you do?'

358

'It wasn't . . . masked men—'

'Shut up!' Uncle Dennis snapped and pushed Dad back onto the sofa. 'Just shut up! You got that fuckwit Ridge to sort it out and he's cocked it up even more! I'm going to have to clear this up now. We can't have you going to prison. You know too much. If word got out that you were in there, everyone would be trying to get to you. And you know that. You've always known that.'

'It wasn't meant to turn out like this. Things just got out of hand.'

'Just shut up! If you were anyone else, I would have you taken out within the hour. The amount of favours I'm going to have to pull to get you into witness protection. The work we're going to have to do to erase you and Rose and anyone connected to you from existence. I always said Rose was too good for you.'

'Oh, I know how you felt about Rose. Had to settle for Meryl but always carried a torch for Rose. She didn't even know you were alive.'

'Shows what you know, doesn't it?' Uncle Dennis said.

'What are you saying?' Dad snarled. He was suddenly nasty again. He was the nasty that he'd been two days before, the nasty that resulted in what he'd done to my mum. I was scared suddenly for Uncle Dennis, even though he had said the thing that had wound up my dad.

'I'm saying I'm going to call the others back into the room and you are going to confess. To all of it. You're going to tell them about every hospital visit, every excuse you told the neighbours in your old place and this, and you're going to sound upset while you do it. Then we're going to work out how to cover up what you did and create a new life for you, you miserable little bastard.'

Dad was still stinging from my uncle Dennis's remark about my mother. I wondered why he'd said it. Mum never mentioned him unless it was to talk about Aunt Meryl. They had all been best friends in college. Obviously Dad and Uncle Dennis had known each other all their lives since they were cousins as well as best friends. But they'd met, and then years later married, my mum and Aunt Meryl at the same time. Mum used to say how much fun they used to have. Her time at Oxford was so happy because of her large group of friends, the subjects she was studying, the world that was opened up to her. She always glowed when she talked about those days, and I knew Uncle Dennis was a part of that life, but I didn't think it was more than that.

They still hadn't noticed me, and Uncle Dennis went on to explain to Dad that he needed to confess so they could work out how to neutralise any possible leaks that might appear after his disappearance became official. Everyone had bought the police officer's story about turning up and finding Dad gone, and me with Mum. I couldn't believe that they couldn't see he was lying. Just like my father. So, I knew, there was no point talking to them. No point trying to tell them what had really happened. So I sat and listened.

After that, I was taken to 'care', which actually meant being brought to be with him at the safe house. After Dad's confession, Uncle Dennis explained that if Mum had been to the police or hospital, there would be a record. Which would mean, if they heard the story, they might remember her name or the village where she lived. They might type the name into the computer and discover a history of violence at the house and/or with that name. They might realise that Dad killed my mum, not masked men.

Uncle Dennis said everything had to be laid bare so it could be rooted out and erased. They were talking about sanitising my dad's history, his life story, so he could get away with killing my mother.

I started to hate my uncle Dennis right then. I started to really, *really* hate him.

I wonder why, then, he put someone on the case who seemed determined not to harm me? There must be something in it for him. There must be.

I'm going to let Dr Lanyon live for now. But if she gets in my way again, I will have to neutralise her. I will.

Kez

23 May, Brighton

Ben Horson is lounging back on Dennis's sofa when I march into the glass-walled office without knocking. I have run all the way up here to the twelfth floor, such is my anger, such is the power of the adrenalin that fuels me. Even when my heart and lungs complained, I pushed on, desperate to speak to this man.

'Leave,' I say to Horson. I have no time for niceties. I need him to get out. Now.

'I beg your pardon?' he replies, outraged.

'LEAVE!' I roar at him. He needs to leave. He needs to get out. *Now.*

He looks to Dennis, expecting him to do something. Dennis, in return, nods towards the door. Telling him to go because I am not to be messed with.

His outrage rolling off him in large juicy waves, Horson leaves the room, shutting the door behind him.

'WHY ARE YOU ALWAYS TRYING TO GET ME KILLED?' I scream at the man sitting behind the desk. I throw my bag on the floor in frustration. I don't care if the people sitting in the open plan workspace at the bottom of the short flight of stairs up to these offices can see or hear, if they wonder what is going on.

362

'I sense you're upset,' Dennis replies, not at all rattled by my anger. 'WHAT HAVE I DONE TO YOU THAT IS SO AWFUL THAT YOU KEEP TRYING TO END MY LIFE?'

'Take a seat,' he says, calmly, reasonably.

I go to his desk, slam my hands down and lean on it so I can look him full in the face. 'What happened to your first wife, Dennis?' I say, matching his calm tone. 'Why has no one seen her since she floated the idea of leaving you?' He momentarily registers shock that I know this. 'I mean, we all know how much you hate people leaving you. What happened to her? Or should I ask what did you do to her?'

'Sit down, Kezuma,' he instructs.

'Doctor Lanyon to you,' I snarl.

'Please,' Dennis says, dragging that word from the depths of wherever it is that he has to access real-ish emotions when he needs to get people like me – who don't fall for his normal human act – to do what he wants. 'Kezuma. Sit down. *Please.*'

I pull out the chair, sit down in it and glare at him. He isn't going to get out of this. Not this time. It's almost impossible to profile a person like Dennis. He has so many ways of behaving normally that I am still, even after all this time, thrown by him. But he isn't going to get out of this.

When he doesn't speak, I sit back, fold my arms across my body, cross my legs. I will wait him out.

'I couldn't tell you who Robyn is. If anyone knew how deeply connected I am to this and her, they would take me off the case.'

'Bullshit,' I say. 'You can do whatever you want, Dennis. We all know that. Even the people who are supposedly your bosses know that. Look at Horson – one nod from you and he's leaving your office, not demanding that I be fired. So, bullshit.'

'It's not.'

'Look, let's just skip this back-and-forth where you claim you couldn't say anything because you feared being sidelined and I tell you that's crap. Did you kill your first wife?'

Dennis glares at me. And that glare is of someone who is wondering whether the truth or a lie will get them what they want. He doesn't care if I know he's a killer or not – he just wants to make sure that what he says keeps me hooked into his sphere of control.

'I know you think I have no feelings, that I don't care about anyone or anything, but that's not true. My cousin is not a perfect man but he is reformed now, one hundred per cent. He is slightly older than me and was always someone I looked up to. And I . . . I could see what he was doing. I simply didn't know what to do about it.'

'You, who has revelled in breaking the spirits of hundreds of young recruits over the years, who sexually assaulted me, who caused Brian's death, all in the name of work, didn't know what to do about your killer cousin? Is that what you're trying to convince me of, Dennis? Me? After everything you've done to me, you're trying to convince me of that? Really?' I shake my head. 'I know you want me dead, but I didn't think you thought I was stupid.'

'I don't want you dead, Kezuma.' He seems genuinely shocked I think this. 'Far from it.'

'Did you kill your first wife, Dennis?' Was this a family endeavour? Something the Cousins Grim both did?

'I wanted you to work on this because I knew, I *know*, that you would do everything you could to help Robyn. I don't want her dead, either. And I knew, out of everyone who could work on the case, you would do all you can to keep her safe and bring her in.'

'Bring her in to what? You've just said it yourself: everyone wants to harm her – "put her down" as Big Bad Aidan said. Why would I believe you don't want the same thing? How can I trust you or anyone not to just execute her on sight?'

'It's that level-headed reasoning that makes it essential that you keep working on this case. She needs someone like you to look out for her and bring her in.'

'Again, Dennis, why do you think I'm stupid enough to fall for the same trick twice? Or is it five times now? You can try to flatter me all you want, but I'm going to keep asking – did you kill your first wife when she decided she was going to leave you?'

He looks down at his neat desk. Everything lined up and at right angles to each other. If there are no angles on the item – say a cup – he has made sure it is equidistant to each item around it.

'I wouldn't do that,' he says quietly. 'I didn't do that.'

'Where is she, then?' If he thinks quiet words are going to stop me asking, then he's got another several other deep thinks coming.

He can face me again suddenly. 'I would have thought you had other questions to ask me before I clam up,' and, just like that, he's back to taunting me. I thought for a moment that he might be normal, but no, not this man. I remember I once called him 'a disingenuous slime' – and that was before I found out what he was truly capable of. People will think he is a narcissist. They may think – briefly – that he's a psychopath. But I know, if I tried to explain that he is a real psychopath, they would dismiss me. They would say he was more narcissist than psychopath. They would not understand that he is both and dangerous with it. A narcissist needs adulation, they are manipulative, they are attention greedy, they are controlling. But a pure narcissist wouldn't do what Dennis does, they wouldn't go to those extremes. That's what psychopaths do. They go to extremes. And if they are hardwired narcissists, then the psychopath in them will drive them to do anything – *anything* – they can to get what they want. They do not care who gets hurt and who is collateral. All they want, need, care about is what they want.

'What happened to your wife?' I reply.

He stares at me, his grey eyes becoming colder and more deadly by the second.

'You do realise that once I decide to stop talking, I will stop talking, don't you? And you will get no other information from me.'

'What happened to your wife, Dennis?'

'Isn't there anything else you want to know?'

'What happened to your wife, Dennis?'

He glowers at me again, unhappy that I am refusing to play the game his way. We are deep in that dance we do with each other, the dance where neither of us will allow the other to get the upper hand. It hasn't been like this for a while, but now we're back here. Right back here.

'You know I'm going to keep asking so you might as well tell me. What happened to your wife, Dennis?'

'Nothing. Nothing happened to her.'

'What happened to your wife, Dennis?' I ask again.

He frowns, looks down at his desk again, something approximating shame taking over his face.

'What happened to your wife, Dennis?'

'She left. She left me.'

Bingo! 'Just that? She left you? She left you when she was worried about her friend and her friend's child? So worried she was visiting several times a week without you, and encouraging her to leave and she gives up on all of that to leave you? And when her friend dies, she doesn't swoop in and adopt her child? Really, Dennis? Am I supposed to believe that?'

'I'm not sure what you are supposed to believe, Kezuma.'

'Did you kill your wife, Dennis?'

'She left me, Kezuma.'

'She left you and that was it, cool-cool? You? Really?'

'She left.'

Every time I have asked Dennis a question I have been watching. Reading his body language, registering his micro-expressions, noting his voice intonation. He knows this, but hasn't been able to fully hide everything from me. My anger was real, but it was expressed specifically to put him on the back foot a little. It was a way to question him without directly asking him the questions I need to – because that would allow him to think and obscure the answers. He is hiding something else. Something big. There is more to this. Still. It may well be what happened to his wife, or it might be something else, but there is something.

'And you destroyed her, didn't you? You destroyed her and that's why Robyn can't find her, isn't it?'

The twitch above his eyebrows tells me that his first wife is still alive. That he worries about her being found. Possibly that Robyn might harm his current wife.

'If you want me to find Robyn, to bring her in without her being harmed, you're going to have to tell me more. You know that, don't you?'

'I don't know what more you want me to tell you,' he says.

'Tell me what you're hiding, Dennis. Tell me what else I need to know about Robyn so I can find her. Tell me what you did to your first wife. Tell me something. Anything.'

367

He thinks about it. He stares at his desk in silence. I'm not used to this type of silence from Dennis. It is a type of contemplation that I've never been sure he is capable of. I have to hold my nerve, though. I have to not let his demeanour derail me, I have to not speak while he decides what he's going to do. What he answers with will tell me a lot of what I need to know. And what I need to do next.

He eventually lifts his head. 'My wife wanted me to help Avril and her mother leave. I refused.'

Bastard. He knew what was going on, but didn't want to help. Bastard.

'I know what you're thinking, Kezuma. Yes, I was a bastard. Yes, I should have helped her. But I refused because I looked up so much to my cousin. And my wife . . . couldn't stand to look at me, let alone be around me after I said no. She hated me for it. She decided to help them on her own. So . . .' Dennis can't look at me all of a sudden. He can't face me while he explains what he did. 'So I told her to choose. If she wanted to help them, she had to leave our home, our marriage and I would help. If she was willing to stop helping them, she could stay.'

'What sort of a person gives another human that kind of choice?' I ask. 'What am I even saying? You, you're that sort of person. Carry on.'

'She left.'

'And you didn't help? Not even to have a word with your beloved cousin to get him to back off?'

'She left, we got divorced straight away without speaking and she made sure that I couldn't find her so I would keep to our agreement. And after what happened—'

'You mean after your cousin killed his wife, not something that

368

simply happened.' When Brian punched Dennis back in 2001, Dennis made sure Brian took responsibility for his actions. He made sure Brian accepted it was an action not a passive occurrence – and then he had Brian fired. And not only that, he made sure Brian couldn't find another job. So now, today, Dennis doesn't get to try to frame what his cousin did in passive terms – if Brian had to take active responsibility, so does Dennis's cousin.

'After that . . . I didn't want her to get in touch. I couldn't face telling her that I had reneged on our deal, what the result of me reneging was.'

'You were never going to hold up your end of the deal, though? Surely she knew that? Surely? You just thought you could keep her in line by saying she should leave if she wanted to help them. You thought she would choose you over her friend.'

'Do you want to hear or do you want to keep interrupting?'

'Carry on.'

'As I said, she made it so I could never find her and I was grateful for that, because I could not face her, knowing I didn't help her best friend. We didn't communicate again.'

What Dennis has just told me, by choosing to answer that question, which is the type of humiliation that he hates anyone to witness, is that there is a lot more to the Robyn story than he will ever let on to me. Even if it puts my life at risk, he is holding back everything else he knows about his cousin and his cousin's daughter.

It must be bad. I wonder if he helped his cousin beyond helping him into witness protection, beyond making sure Robyn was sent into the care system? I wonder if he helped to cover up something else that he did? It's the sort of thing Dennis would do. It's the sort of thing he did do with me.

'How much contact have you had with your cousin?' I ask him.

'Now why on earth would I tell you that?' Dennis asks, wresting back control of this situation.

'Because I need to know how far you'll go to protect him. I mean, will you sacrifice Robyn to save him? Or will you decide that a killer doesn't get to be protected over the actions of a young woman who has been let down all her life?'

'Robyn is a killer, too, Kezuma. Don't forget that.'

He has just told me that he's using me to get Robyn. He knows young people are my trigger point, that I have an innate need to help vulnerable people, especially ones who have been let down by the adults in their life. He knows I will go all out to find her, which by default means his cousin will remain safe. I wonder if he will try to neutralise her, or just have her locked up? No cushy witness protection for her.

'If you want me to find her, you're going to have to give me some-thing. She's smart, really smart. But you know that. She's going to find him.'

'You're going to have to make sure that she doesn't. You're going to have to convince her to come in. Because the longer this goes on for, the more likely she is to . . . not survive.'

I can't let that happen. I hate that Dennis knows that. I hate that I am going to do what he wants because I can't allow her to be harmed. Or to harm. Because she has to stop this. I know first-hand how killing someone will change you in fundamental ways. This will stay with her for ever. If she doesn't stop, then she will be completely lost. Once her mission is complete, she will have to sit back and think about what she has done and that may well destroy her.

I stand up.

'Stop trying to get me killed, Dennis,' I say to him. It sounds more like a plea than the threat it is. I'm not sure which way he takes it, but I hope he realises that I am serious. He needs to stop trying to get me killed. Or I may just forget why I am here and start to fight back.

Kez

28 May, Brighton

The answer to finding Robyn lies in the files we took from her childhood home. I'm sure it does. I've been over the files – the ones I've been allowed to have – several times. I'm sitting in my office now, going over them again as well as poring over the images I took on my phone.

The special task force has been unofficially disbanded since my encounter with Robyn. It's been decided that it'd be too expensive to take everyone on the task force into police protection and that if we just back off instead, we're unlikely to be targeted. No one, but no one – not even Bruce – argued with that. They'd seen the crime scene pictures, read the autopsy reports. They didn't want to end up like that, especially since she showed that security in our building is a joke by coming in, threatening me and then leaving without being properly detained or detected.

I, of course, can't stop working on it. And neither can Big Bad Aidan, although he just sits in the corner at 'his' desk, glowering at people and working on other stuff for Dennis and Horson.

What is it that I'm missing? I ask myself as I again look over the pictures on my phone.

My eye keeps being drawn to the images that Robyn stuck up of her time in the children's home, Maddox Hall. I searched it up and it was run until a couple of years ago by a woman called Holly Banks. She had been there for nearly twenty years and for the last ten years of her life lived there with her husband, Clyde Olufawu. There was no scandal attached to the home, and she apparently died of complications from Covid. Her tribute page is post after post of shock, upset and genuine grief. Everyone loved her, everyone said what an amazing person she was. Robyn must have known her and I wonder if this was the stressor, if this was what made her decide to go from thinking about finding her father to actually doing it.

Robyn losing two mother figures would have cleaved her heart in two. It wouldn't surprise me if this was what had broken her. On the board, near the picture and profile of the social worker Boris Fikowsky, Robyn had pinned a photo of five people. Centre back stood Holly, a beautiful Black woman with straightened, shoulder-length hair, hoop earrings and a beam of a smile. Next to her, I have guessed, is her husband, Clyde. He is a Black man with close-shaved hair and a close-mouthed, amused smile. Beside him is a biracial boy of about sixteen. He has a pierced eyebrow and pierced lower lip. He's not looking at the camera – he's looking at Robyn. Robyn has her hair in a high ponytail and small hoop earrings. She's wearing a white summer dress covered in a flower pattern. She's beaming at the camera and every time I look at the picture, I get the sense that she isn't putting it on. She is actually happy. And that makes me happy that she did know some good times in the home. Next to her is a boy with long brown hair and haunted eyes. He is the same height as Robyn, but the look in his eyes makes him seem older than her. He isn't smiling at the camera and it's clear he hasn't had a good life in the home. They're standing outside Maddox Hall, a large, redbrick, black-roofed building.

I can't work out why Robyn put that picture next to the image of a man who was awful. So awful she went on to kill him. Maybe it was a reminder of what he'd done? Maybe he abused her and abused her two friends? Maybe she's set it up so if her board was ever discovered, people would know that these are the lives that that man destroyed? I've searched and searched online but I can't find out who those two other boys are. Holly is dead and there is nothing on the whereabouts of her husband. Robyn is so intentional about everything else, why put a happy image amongst all of this planning for death and destruction? Why?

I'm zooming in on the picture again, when someone knocks on my door and enters. Sumaira Wilson walks into my office with a smile on her face. This is not good. She is not someone who just drops by for a chat.

'Am I in trouble?' I ask her, forgetting to say hello.

'No, no,' she reassures. 'Of course not. I'm just here because I've been told that you haven't had time to come for a debrief about the Russell Trufton interview.' So I am basically in trouble.

'The thing is, Sumaira, I've been really caught up in this new case. It's been all-consuming. And . . . I also have a pathological aversion to being questioned by people who could make me disappear if I give them the wrong answer.'

'There's no right or wrong answer.'

'You say this, but how do I know that until I've given the wrong answer and then I get got?'

'The thing is, Dr Lanyon—'

'Call me Kez.'

'The thing is, Kez, I'm not saying that armed people in balaclavas will be dispatched to your house in the middle of the night if you don't come for the debriefing soon but . . .'

'But . . .'

'But let's just make sure you find the time. I like you. I like you a lot. I would hate for stuff to go wrong.'

'OK. I will find time.'

'Fantastic. Shall we?' She holds her hand out to usher me out of the door.

'What, now?'

'Yes.'

'But—'

'But grab your stuff and let's go.'

This woman is not someone to argue with. And I get the impression that she doesn't like many people, so I am honoured on that score. Plus, she's obviously gone out of her way to stop me getting into serious trouble, so I sigh, put down the phone and stand up to grab my suit jacket from the back of my chair.

'Are you going to save me if I give the wrong answer and they want to make me disappear?'

'Well, seeing as I'm kind of in charge of doing the disappearing, I'm confident that if you are disappeared, it'll be to somewhere nice.'

I whip my head round to look at her, alarmed. She grins then laughs at me. 'Your face! You're going to be fine. Promise. We just have to make sure we've checked out all the accounts of people who were there. I will be with you and everything will be fine. We're all just one big family and this is just a tick-box exercise, nothing complicated.'

'Yeah, that's what they all say.'

We're about to walk past Dennis's office when something twangs in

375

my mind. 'Give me a moment,' I say to Sumaira and dash back to my office. I open my mobile and look at the pictures again. The tick-box comment has dislodged something in my head. Not the whole thing, but a part of it. There *is* a reason why Robyn put the picture up there. She was saying something. I'm not sure what, yet, but there is something loose in my brain now, a thought, a connection that I need to hook up to something else before I can get the full picture.

'I'm all yours,' I say when I return to Sumaira. Dennis looks up at us, then looks down again, uninterested. I'm fairly sure he hasn't had a debrief and won't be forced into one. He's kept his distance from me since our encounter last week, but I know he's watching me. I know he's got Big Bad Aidan watching me, too. But he has, at least, avoided speaking to me as much as possible, which is just the way I like it.

Kez

31 May, Brighton

I'm leaning against the sea wall on Undercliff Walk when MJ Hudson comes running round the corner. This is the point of her run where she turns to head back the way she's come. I have been waiting for her for a while.

Even though she – with her very high-level government position – isn't meant to do anything regularly, she can't help herself when it comes to running this particular path on this particular route. I bet it shows up as a nice little pattern on her running tracker app. I bet she gets an immense sense of satisfaction from watching the blue line showing her where she runs; she probably even allows herself a smile of satisfaction because she's run it a little faster every time. Despite the wind, the weather, the way she might be feeling at the start, when MJ does this run she is rejuvenated. No one is going to take that feeling away from her, no matter how against protocol it is.

Of course, that means when someone wants to find her, to speak to her away from prying eyes, they just have to work out her run route. I'd asked Jeb a couple of days ago what route he would run along if he lived where MJ lives, and once he had explained the route to me, I had checked on the map and had seen that this was the best place to meet her. No cameras, very few people milling about. I've even pulled on my running gear – pretty much brand new from how unused it is – to make my presence seem less out of place. I have used Jeb's car and have made sure that Big Bad Aidan wasn't following me.

MJ falters when she sees me. The horror of clocking me standing, very obviously waiting for her arrival, causes her to momentarily lose her footing. She stops then marches past me, assuming I'll join her.

MJ was called Maisie when I met her back in 1998 and we were both signed up to train under Dennis for the Human Insight Unit along with Brian. While Dennis sexually harassed – and eventually sexually assaulted – me, he made Brian feel like he was less than a man, and he made MJ feel like she was stupid and all she had going for her were her looks and posh accent. Even before Brian died she was clear that once she left T.H.I.U. she was going to pretend she'd never met any of us. I could respect that level of scorched-earthing of your past, to be honest.

'I really thought I'd never see you again,' she says quietly, not bothering to hide her naked fury.

'Why's that, then?' I reply, facetiously.

'What do you want, Kez?'

'I need you to get me some information.'

'You say that like it's easy. I'm guessing that if it's information you need from me, then it's not easily available. And if it's not easily available, especially where you now work, then I doubt very much I'll be able to get it for you. Or tell you if I do get it.'

When MJ and I were training, she didn't really seem to have any qualms about her abilities, despite what Dennis tried to do to her. She was very confident in herself; she had the innate self-assurance of someone who had been brought up to run the world. Her current circumstances – a huge house with a pool in a very expensive part of Brighton, a job where she has a driver, a family that has branches spread out across the whole of government *and* the business world – suggest that she could pretty much get whatever she wants. If she wants to.

I have come to her because the thing that was dislodged in my brain has found its footing, has made the connections, and I now need to get this information to make sure I am right.

'I think you're going to want to help me out here, Maisie. Sorry, I mean MJ.'

'Really, Kez.' Even though it was nearly a year ago, MJ is still *really* pissed off with me for not allowing her to cover up what we did the last time we saw each other. 'Am I really going to want to help you out?'

'Yes.'

'And why, pray tell, would that be?'

'Because I need you to find someone in the Protected Persons programme.'

She stops walking and squeezes her incredulous face at me, absolutely disgusted that I would try to get her to do this. 'Have you lost your mind? How am I going to find someone in the Protected Persons programme? How do I even begin to do that?'

'I think, once you find out who it is, you'll be really motivated to get me the information I need.'

'Who is it?' she asks, begrudgingly.

'I don't have his new name. Only the old one.'

'Well, spit it out, then.'

'Henry Chambers.'

Her eyes widen. 'As in—'

'Yes, as in Dennis's cousin and best friend.'

She is both fascinated and shocked at the same time.

'He's in the Protected Persons programme because he killed his wife and Dennis helped him escape justice. Now Henry's daughter is killing people to get to him. I just need you to find out where he is so I can use it as leverage to stop her.'

'Does Dennis know?'

'Of course. He says he doesn't but I know he does.'

'And he won't tell you?'

'Of course not.'

'He'd be so pissed if I told you, wouldn't he?'

'*So* pissed.'

MJ's face lights up at the idea of having the chance to get back at Dennis. All these years later she can finally hurt him. 'Leave it with me. I'll have his new name and location in no time.'

'Thank you, MJ.'

'But this is it, Kez. This is absolutely the last time I am helping you out.'

'I know.'

'I mean it, Kez.'

'I know you do.'

'I really, seriously mean it.'

'I know you do, MJ. I know you do.'

After telling me not to contact her, she'll contact me, she jogs off without saying goodbye. Dennis might predict that I'd go to MJ for information, he might not. But once I have the info that I need, I am absolutely going to pass it on to Robyn – on condition she takes me with her when she goes to confront her father. I'm hoping that if I'm there, I'll be able to convince her not to kill him. I can convince her to just say what she wants to him and then walk away.

I know I'm living in cloud cuckoo land, but I have to try. I have to. It's the only way I can think of that will spare her life and save her soul.

Part 12

Kez

4 June, Hove

Big Bad Aidan jumps when he sees me.

I guess he wasn't expecting to find me sitting at the iron table on his small patio garden at this time of night. He's dressed like he's just been to the gym – tight black T-shirt, tight black shorts that leave nothing to the imagination, socks that stop mid-calf. His blond hair is darkened with sweat and flops on his forehead, and he has a small blue towel draped round his neck and over his shoulders.

Confused, and openly incensed, he unlocks his back door and steps out. He stands by the door, shooting daggers at me. It's a warm evening, darkness is just about to descend, but right now the sky is luscious, a navy-blue velvet, scattered with bright white stars. I always wonder if what they say is true, that those stars are so far away that by the time we see them, they've already burnt themselves out. I feel very much like those stars – now when people see me, they only see the burnt-out shell of who I was before I began work on the Robyn Managa case. This whole case is breaking me down. Making me weary.

'Hello, Big Bad Aidan,' I say pleasantly.

'Stop calling me that,' he snarls.

'Oh, don't start that again. I'm not going to call you Luke or whatever it is you want to be called, so just live with it.'

'What are you doing here?' he demands, a clear and present menace in his voice.

'I need to speak to you. Away from Insight.'

'How did you get in here?'

'You left the side gate open.'

'No, I didn't.'

'Oh, Big Bad Aidan, please let's not do this. You may not have technically left the side gate open, but it was open when I entered it. Go figure.'

'What do you want?'

He is much more 'real' here in his own habitat. I'm not sure why. Out there in the field, in the Insight offices, in his car, he seems unreal, like the idea I used to have in my head of what an agent is. Calling him Big Bad Aidan doesn't seem as appropriate here. Here, he seems like a normal guy. Here, he is less proto-soldier and more little boy who was once seven years old and afraid of the dark.

'When did you stop being afraid of the dark, Aidan?' I ask.

'What?' he asks. A micro-expression crosses his forehead as he wonders how I knew about that. 'What are you asking me that for?'

'Because I want to know if it was Robyn who helped you get over it? And if so, if that is why you're helping her? Or if you're helping her because when she arrived at your group home she protected you from the bullies.'

There it is, the micro-expression that tells me I'm right. Before it settles, Aidan replaces it with anger, disgust, contempt. Or approximations of them. 'If you think for one second I'm helping our target, then you call Chambers right now and tell him.' He pulls his mobile out

386

of his shorts pocket and throws it on the table for me to use. 'Go on, call him.'

I fold my arms across my chest, sit back and study Aidan. 'You're meant to be one of the best, Aidan. Haven't you worked out yet that I'm not someone whose bluff you can call? You've seen me and Dennis go at it more than once. Do you think the "throw my phone down to get her to back off" tactic is going to work on me?'

'It's not a tactic,' he growls.

'Look, I worked out you were helping her a while back,' I reply. 'It didn't register at first, though. When you were in Dr Mackenzie's house? You went to search upstairs but only went to one room. There are three bedrooms, one bathroom and a study up there, but you only went into one room, her room. Because you'd been there before when the good Dr Mackenzie had been out.

'And that's how she knew how to get in and out of the Insight building without being detected. Only someone with your clearance knows about those secret little exits not covered by cameras, where they bring in people who don't technically exist. And obviously that's also how she knew about me. There's virtually nothing online about me, even less about what I do at Insight, but she still found out who I was and thought that I was favoured by Dennis because you told her that he gives me preferential treatment. Protects me from all sorts of shit. You didn't know that Dennis actually hates me, too, so you told her that he had put his protégé on the case.'

Aidan is silent, which is as close to a confession as I'm likely to get.

'When we found the board at her old house, I kept looking at the picture she had pinned up next to the hideous social worker. Kept wondering why she would do that, considering she killed him. And then someone said to me, "I will be with you and everything will be fine," and I got it. She pinned it up there because the person who is helping her will always be with her. And she will be fine because he can get her what she needs to complete her mission. You look nothing like your photo, by the way. What was it? Car crash? Reconstructive surgery?' *Micro-expression says yes.* 'Right, that's why you had to leave the military. You weren't able to continue. They gave you a leg up into the intelligence services, probably to cover up something.' *Micro-expression says yes again.*

'You were adopted when you were around thirteen, fourteen? So I guess you met her when you were around eleven, twelve? If there's one thing I've deduced about her, it's that she can't stand bullying. She saved you, didn't she? Stood up for you. Made them leave you alone. You were both probably inseparable after that, weren't you?' I am reading his facial expressions while I feel my way through his story. He is good, he is able to control some of his micro-expressions, but not all. 'And I bet that the people who adopted you wanted to adopt her, too.

'But because of who she is, that was blocked. That must have broken your heart. It breaks mine to think of it. What that must have done to the pair of you. None of this needed to happen. If they had just let her go to people who wanted to love her, none of this would have happened.' Something flies across his face, so quick I can't decipher it, but it settles into sorrow in his eyes. 'I can't imagine what it must have been like for the two of you, being separated after you had found each other.'

Aidan isn't playing. He is controlling his facial expressions and his body as much as possible, and he is not going to confirm or deny what I say.

I've pretty much accepted Robyn's trigger was the death of Holly Banks. Was that when Aidan agreed to help her? Did they keep in touch over the years or just see each other at the funeral? 'I should have seen it when you were so hostile towards Dr Mackenzie on sight. There was absolutely no need for it. Do you hate him because he gave her a home when you couldn't? Or did you worry that he was taking advantage of her?' His eyebrows tell me I'm right on both scores.

'So what was it? What kick-started all of this?' I have my suspicions, but he will only partially confirm them with his micro-expressions. 'I'm guessing you met Dennis when you were recruited to come to the intelligence service? We all did. You probably told Robyn about it at some point. And she would have realised who he was. I suspect you meeting Dennis seemed like fate to her. The sign she needed that she had to find her father and make him pay for what he did to her mother and the life he left her to.' Again, the micro-expression that says I am right, but also that I'm missing something. 'Did you help her with setting up all the stuff at her house or was that all her?' *All her.* 'Did you help her transport the people back and forth?' *Yes.* 'Did you help her question them or was it all her?' *All her.* That makes sense. He couldn't risk being seen. 'Did she mean to kill those people?' *Not sure, but mainly no.* 'Did you ask to be put on this case?' *No.* 'Of course you didn't. You would never have been allowed to if you did ask.' *Nothing.* 'But you have spent the last couple of years making sure that you're the best at everything so that when the time came, Dennis would think of you.' *Yes.* 'If only you knew how much satisfaction it gives me to think that you and Robyn played Dennis.'

I sit back and sigh. Me being right about Aidan helping Robyn does actually complicate things. A lot. It means what happens next can play out in multiple ways because she has good, solid back-up. Which suggests an escape plan that she didn't share with Mac. Which suggests it'll be harder to convince her to turn herself in.

'I'll be honest with you, Aidan, I was hoping I was wrong about you. Because now when I tell you what I'm about to tell you, I think you and Robyn could very well plan to kidnap and torture me. Which I would not like to happen for obvious reasons.'

'What are you talking about?' he asks.

I get up from the chair. My knees creak, my hips creak. Good luck to me if I think I'm going to outrun him if he goes for me. 'I know where Robyn's father is.'

'What? Chambers told you?'

'No, he would never. I found out another way.'

'Where is he?'

'Do you really think I'm going to just tell you?'

'I could make you,' he says.

'Didn't I *just say* that I don't want you to torture me? But, anyway, I would like to arrange a meeting with Robyn. That's the other reason I came here, as well as letting you know that I know. I want to meet with Robyn and take her to her father. But only if she agrees to turn herself in afterwards.'

Aidan's face tells me that is not going to happen – he and Robyn are much more likely to do me over to get the information than negotiate.

'Like I say, I know you could harm me, but I don't think you will. Especially since I have done everything I can to investigate without putting her in danger. And I'm not going to tell Dennis about you. Well, not right away. I just need you to convince her to talk to me. To think about the deal I'm offering.'

Again, his face says that's not going to happen.

'Just think about it. And let me know what she says.' I start to move towards the exit at the side of the house. 'And before you consider jumping me, let me tell you two things: firstly, I didn't get an address – I got coordinates, for a very specific reason, which is, basically, I can't learn coordinates so even if you do torture me, I won't be able to tell you anything. And, secondly, my husband is sitting outside in his car waiting for me, so he will know if something is up if I don't call him or appear in the next thirty seconds. And obviously he's got the police on speed dial should I not appear.'

With that revelation, Aidan's body physically relaxes. *That guy! He was going to actually jump me! Wow. Did I read him wrong! Or actually, did I read the situation wrong? I'm underestimating how badly he and Robyn want to get at her father. Grossly underestimating.*

My legs are a bit shaky when I get to my car. Jeb isn't in his car, of course he isn't. I would never put him in that kind of danger. I would never bring him, knowing that the kids would be left orphaned if we were both hurt.

Aidan is looking out at me through the slatted blinds of his front window, and with my driving glasses on, I can tell he is pissed that I bluffed him. I can feel his anger and rage the whole drive home.

Robyn

From Robyn's Last Will & Testament

'Well, if it isn't my first true love and my best friend,' Andrich said. 'Fancy seeing you here.'

I'd been shattered when I got the call from Clyde, Holly's husband, that she had passed. I had lived at the home until I had to move out at eighteen and she had loved me right up until the last minute. And beyond. She kept in touch as much as she could. She would send me texts, she would send me emails, she would demand my address so she could send me cards. She always signed off with 'lots of love'. She probably wasn't meant to keep in such close contact, but she did.

I always thought I'd see Holly again, beyond the odd FaceTime call. I always thought I'd get to hug her again, to have her floral scent fill my senses, to be around someone who genuinely cared for me.

The church where they held her funeral was packed, absolutely standing room only. And those who couldn't fit in stood outside instead. So many people came, so many faces I kind of recognised who had passed through Maddox Hall, who had got their dose of Holly magic and had moved on. She was truly loved.

Andrich had come over to Tommy and me after the service. He looked so different, so grown up, a proper adult in a serious black suit with a black shirt and tie. And the leather jacket. He only had the one eyebrow piercing left, and his hair was cut low instead of the dreads he spent years trying to cultivate. Beside him stood a beautiful woman who had waist-length sisterlocks and wore a stylish black dress with a black leather jacket over the top. I noticed their matching wedding rings and felt a pang of nostalgia? Jealousy? I couldn't place it.

'Andrich!' I said, with a huge grin.

'Is that the way to greet the guy whose heart you stole?' he said, and opened his arms. I looked quickly to his wife, wondering how she would receive him saying that twice now.

'Oh, don't worry, Margarita knows all about you. And us. Come here.' I walked into his arms and got flashes of how much I'd loved hugging him, almost as much as I'd loved having sex with him.

Once he let me go, he went to Tommy and grabbed him into a hug, too. 'Good to see you, buddy,' he said. Tommy was frozen for a second or two, not sure what to do, then he hugged Andrich back.

'Why did you say I was your best friend?' Tommy said after they stepped apart.

'Because you were. Why, wasn't I your best mate?' Andrich looked a bit confused.

'You used to bully me.'

'Not after this one shoved me over. After that, I didn't. Mate, you were too cool. I was well jealous of how much you didn't give a shit about anything.' He grimaced. 'Shouldn't be using that language in a church. Let's go outside.'

The church courtyard was full of people. So many people, all dressed in black, all looking distraught, milling around, not sure what to do with themselves. 'So, what you two up to?' Andrich asked.

'I just left the military,' Tommy said. 'Doing something else now. Intelligence services.'

Andrich was impressed. 'That's so cool, man. What happened with the folks that fostered you?'

'Nothing happened with them. They were – are – good people. Took care of me. They didn't like me joining the military, but they still showed up for everything.'

'Did they adopt you?'

'Yes. And they let me keep my surname as Topher. That was the name of the person who found me and I didn't want to give up that connection. They were cool with it, though. I changed my first name officially to Aidan to make them happy.'

'What you up to, Robyn?'

'This and that. I think I'm going to train to be a therapist at some point.'

'Good woman. I can see you helping a lot of people. Margarita and I are full-time foster parents. We provide a home for children who need somewhere to stay in an emergency or long-term.'

'Wow,' I replied. 'That's so impressive.'

'I thought so, but Margarita says we need to be humble, so I'm not allowed to say that out loud.' His wife side-eyed him and then grinned and I felt it again, that pang of something I couldn't quite decipher or name.

'Why don't you three go off and raise a glass to Holly?' Margarita said. 'I have to head back for the kids, but you stay out.'

*

In the pub round the corner, I finally told them the truth about my father, about how my mother died. All of it. Tommy knew some of it, but even he was shocked by it all. Especially about how Fikowsky had used his knowledge to keep me scared and cowed. Andrich was floored.

'I'm going to find him, guys,' I told them. 'I've been toying with it all my life, but Holly passing has just made me think I need to get on with it. I need to do it now or I'll never do it.'

'I'll help you,' Tommy said immediately. 'I'm sure I can get some information once I'm properly inside the intelligence services.'

'I'd love to help you, Robyn, but I can't do anything that will jeopardise our fostering eligibility,' Andrich said.

'I wouldn't want you to.' I took both their hands in mine. 'I love you both. I'm so grateful that I got to meet you two. My mum would have loved you both, too.'

She would have as well. They were, in their own way, strange boys but they were my kind of strange. Mum would have loved them. She was so accepting of people for who they were, and these two helped define who I became.

Hours later, when Andrich had gone home and Tommy and I had started to formulate a plan, I finally understood what that pang was for. It was for the other girl I could have been. The Robyn who could have got married, had kids, lived a 'normal' life. Out of all of us, Andrich had done it. And that showed it was possible and there was hope for all of us. That was what my heart was pining for. The Robyn I could have been if my father hadn't done what he did.

Part 13

Kez

7 June, Brighton

I have told Jeb. Everything.

I am meeting Robyn today to go to her father's house, so I decided I needed to tell Jeb. I told him all of it because if there is a chance I won't be coming back, or that I might be arrested for helping a known criminal or that something might happen to me while I am being arrested for helping a known criminal, I do not want the narrative around what happens to me to be defined by anyone else. I do not want Jeb to have any doubts about how and why I died. Or was arrested. Or died after being arrested.

He took it as well as he could. By which I mean he took it really very badly. He asked me not to do it. Then he put aside his pride and begged me not to do it. He did so knowing that I was going to do it anyway.

I made the children breakfast – wholemeal bagel with scrambled tofu for Jonah, scrambled egg with coriander on toast for Zoey. They'd both looked down at their plates, the good ones I usually get out at Christmas, Easter or when the grandparents come to visit, at the nice stainless-steel tumblers I'd poured their water into and then looked at each other.

'Are you two getting divorced?' Zoey asked.

'Cos something's hinky here,' Jonah added. 'We're thinking divorce.'

'Well, you would think wrong,' I replied.

'Absolutely wrong,' Jeb added. Usually he leaves that to me. Usually he gets up and does stuff to avoid difficult conversations. The entire kitchen was cleaned from top to bottom when I was accidentally forced to give them the sex and reproduction talk at five and eight. And when Jonah had asked what 'wet dreams' were, I've never seen my husband move so fast to get out into the garden to mow the lawn, tidy the shed and dig a whole load of new flower beds. But with this, he sat at the table.

'Is Moe going to come live here again and I have to give up my room?' Jonah asked.

'Well, it'd be my room since mine is slightly bigger than yours,' Zoey reasoned.

'Yeah, but mine's already set up to be for the mandem.'

'What mandem do you even know about?' she replied.

'I know stuff.'

'Yeah, sure you do.' She turned her laser sight on me. 'Don't think we've forgotten you two. What's going on, Mama? Why are you giving us the good plates and the favourite breakfast treatment?'

'Because I love you,' I replied, and jumped a little when Jeb curled his hand round mine. 'Nothing more, nothing less.'

Zoey, who is more like me than I'd like to admit, stared at our linked hands and then looked back at me. She knew something was going on, but had no proof. And she knew that if she persisted, it would upset Jonah. 'We'll be here, Mummio, when you get back from work,' she said. 'We'll be right here.'

'I know you will,' I replied. 'I know you both will.'

'And when you come back, I'd really like you to tell me what the capital of Colombia is.'

'Oh, what?' I said. 'I thought you lot had accepted that I knew stuff about Geography. What is this now?'

'Mum, Mum, Mum . . . you need to stay sharp,' Jonah said. 'Capital of Colombia if you don't mind.'

'I do mind, actually, but I'll get it for you. I'll trawl through my brain and find it.'

'Good woman,' Zoey and Jonah said together. 'Good, good woman.'

After we'd both taken them to school, Jeb and I had ended up in bed. It wasn't intentional – I'd planned on heading out – but he'd been so sad, so broken, so devastated that I'd started to comfort him and one thing led to another. He'd wanted to drive me to work, but I said no. I needed the drive to the office to shed the skin of Kez Lanyon Quarshie. I needed to stop being his wife, their mother. I needed to slip into the skin of Dr Kezuma Lanyon, so I could focus on making sure we had the best outcome for everyone today.

'I'm going to say what I said to you last time: do whatever you need to do to come home. I don't ever want to have *that* kind of conversation with our children,' Jeb had said.

'OK,' I replied. 'Yes.' We both knew that doing whatever it took to come home last time was the reason why I was in this situation now.

'And I'm going to remind you that I love you. I have loved you since the moment I met you. And I'm going to keep loving you for ever.'

I took his face in my hands, looked over every millimetre of it as divine as it was to me, even after all these years. 'Me, too,' I said to him. 'Me, too.'

We were both being overdramatic. It was ridiculous, really, since I fully planned to survive. Just like I'd survived the last two times I was in this type of situation. I'd only warned him so he could brace himself for the very small chance that I didn't survive. And that chance was so small it was miniscule.

Robyn

From Robyn's Last Will & Testament

Twenty-five.

Twenty-six.

Twenty-seven.

Twenty-eight.

Twenty-nine.

Thirty.

Thirty-one.

Thirt—

No, no, I can't do it. I can't do another one. I can't.

I collapsed on the ground, breathing hard, my arms and shoulders and core on fire, burning up with the effort of doing a devil-made combo of planking and push-ups.

'I can't do it,' I panted. 'I can't do it.'

'You can,' Tommy said, a hard edge to his voice. It was the sort of voice he had in the home, when someone did something to him and he would promise them he would hurt them. He very rarely did it straight away. He would promise and then fulfil it later. Much later. Usually when the person had forgotten all about it. At Maddox Hall, he never used that voice with me. But in the past few weeks, I heard it all the time. All the time. 'You. Can.' He got down on his knees so he could get right in my face. 'Get up. Start again. Start. Again.'

When he said he would help me with finding my dad, he said I needed to do two things: get fit and learn to fight.

He told me that I had to get fit, to improve my strength, because I needed upper body strength to incapacitate the people I was going to talk to and to lift them into the boot of my car, then to drag them into the outbuilding where I was going to question them.

And he said I had to learn how to fight, so I could take care of myself, because I needed the confidence that came from combat training that would allow me to attack them in the first place. And then go to extremes when it came to questioning them. 'As you are now, you won't be able to do that. As you are now, you'll change your mind,

404

probably mid-mission and then you'll be done for. You'll get properly hurt. Or you'll stop before you have the information you need.'

I knew he was right, of course. But this training was hard. *Punishing*. I hurt all the time – either from the exercises or the blows he landed on my body. And Tommy wouldn't let up. Not for one minute. Not for one second.

'I can't,' I wailed.

'Get up.'

'I can't.'

'Get up.'

'No, Tommy. No.'

'Robyn. You have to. You have to.'

'I can't,' I begged.

'Robyn, you remember how it was for me at the home? Remember how I couldn't look after myself and then when you came you used to stop people having a go at me? Remember how I got myself fit? How I got myself strong? The military sorted me out. It got me strong. And I did it. I made sure no one picked on me again. I made sure that I put down everyone who even looked at me strange. If you want to find your father, then you need to get strong enough to question those men. If you don't want to find him, then I'll leave you alone. We can leave it at thirty press-ups and you can sit and pretend you want to find him.

'If you don't want to find him, you can stop and we'll never talk about it again. But if you do want to find him, if you *do* want to confront him, then get up. Get up. Get up and do it again. And again and again and again until you get to a hundred. Until you get fit enough to find him.'

He was right. If I wasn't willing to do whatever it took to find him, then I didn't really want to find him.

'Do you want to find him?'

'Yes.'

'DO YOU WANT TO FIND HIM?'

'YES! YES! YES!'

'Then get up. Get up and give me another seventy push-ups.'

I forced my hands flat on the ground, tucked in my elbows, and forced my weight downwards until my body was lifting off the ground. I'm going to do this. I'm going to do this. I'm going to do this.

'And it's sixty-nine!' I shouted at Tommy.

'What?'

'I've done thirty-one push-ups – I only need to do another sixty-nine!'

'Keep talking back and you'll have to do a hundred and one,' Tommy replied as I fixed in my mind the reason I was doing this. I had to find him. I had to. And to find him I had to do this. I had to do push-up after push-up after push-up.

Kez

7 June, Brighton

Aidan and I have agreed we're going to leave at ten o'clock to go and meet Robyn and from there we'll go to her father's house. I'm aware that I'm putting myself in danger. That they could absolutely kill me once they have the information they need. So I have to keep my wits about me and do my best to strike up a rapport with Robyn as soon as possible. I stopped her from killing me last time, hopefully I can do the same this time. There is no chance in heaven, hell or on earth that I can strike up a rapport with Aidan. I remember at the start of this when I asked him to tell me about himself and he replied, 'Why?' No rapport is possible with this fella. And I haven't forgotten how he was contemplating jumping me last night.

At 10:01, as we're getting into the lift to the car park on the lower ground floor, Dennis appears. 'Kezuma,' he says. 'Topher. Just one thing.'

He knows, I realise. *He knows and he's coming to scope me out. He'll then tip off his cousin and all of this will be for nothing.*

'Yes, Dennis,' I say quietly, letting my natural irritation and dislike of him mask the fear of discovery.

'Where are you going?'

I look him straight in the eye. 'I can't tell you.'

'What do you mean you can't tell me?'

'I think I know where she is, and if I'm right, I want the chance to talk to her. I can't do that if I know you're going to come busting in at any time or that you'll be sending police officers after me. You will also have plausible deniability when I'm charged assisting a known criminal.'

'You care what happens to me? Interesting.'

'Of course I don't. I've never cared what happens to you. But you gave me your solemn word that you'd let me try to bring her in without any harm coming to her,' I remind him.

Dennis shakes his head. Hung by his own words and the only bit of integrity I know he has.

'Don't worry, Dennis,' I add, 'if I'm not successful, you'll have all the time in the world to get her because I'm pretty sure – no, no, I'm a hundred per cent sure – you're the next person on her list.'

He ghosts up that partially amused smile. 'And you're taking Topher with you. I suppose that's an upgrade from the therapist.'

The partially amused smile becomes a twitch around his mouth – he guessed about my crush on Mac and that amuses him, greatly. Which is good because he'll think that's what has made me so jumpy.

'We all know that if she attacks me, I have no chance. Toph—Big Bad Aidan has assured me he'll protect me.' I almost gave it all away there. Almost told him that how I relate to Aidan has changed, formalised, because I know something about him and he isn't someone I'm trying to ditch any more.

'Make sure you check in as soon as you can,' he says to me.

'Sure, Dad, I'll make sure he walks me right up to the front door before my curfew,' I say in a teen accent that would have Jonah and Zoey cringing.

Dennis walks away without saying anything else. I don't look at Aidan as I get back into the lift and I'm pretty sure he doesn't look at me. We both of us want to get this over with.

*

'I thought you were going to make me wear a blindfold or some such nonsense,' I say as we head onto the A23 out of Brighton

Aidan says nothing.

'Which would have been pretty crap since I'm driving.' I picked the meeting place, it was nearish to where her father is but not so close they could find him without me.

Still he says nothing.

I never did profile Aidan, did I? Even when I worked out that he was helping Robyn, I kind of let it go. I didn't look at his role in this. I thought he was a cipher for her, someone who did the heavy lifting – literally. But . . . What if it's not like that? What if his role in this is much more involved, central? What if Aidan Topher is not who I thought he was?

What if he is the serial killer in this scenario?

With that thought, it's like the final puzzle piece being slotted into place, like the final bolt being thrown. Everything makes a whole lot more sense when I think of the killer as Aidan. He can easily slip between roles – like when I first met him, he was uber-soldier one minute and then relaxed guy who could be sitting in a café the next. His open contempt and hatred for Mac – probably because he had a significant place in Robyn's affections and people like him do not like to share. And another big one: I have never warmed to him.

410

And the other night, when I asked him if Robyn had meant to kill those people, he had all but said no. What if he came in for the kill shot? What if he returned the people back to their homes or where they were snatched, and instead of just leaving the note, he killed them first? That's why the last guy didn't die, he was in his own home and Aidan didn't get to take him home.

I was wrong. My profile was wrong. Robyn didn't kill people. She might have tortured them to get them to talk, but Aidan delivered the killing blow when he left them in their homes.

'*To do what she's done, she must be a psychopath,*' Bruce had kept saying. He was right, but it was a different person who killed them, a different person who was the psychopath. (That would make Bruce very happy.)

And look at me just driving off to some remote location with the newly unveiled psychopathic serial killer.

I am a ridiculous person. I think that all the time, but I am. Why wouldn't I think that my immediate and innate dislike for him as well as Dennis's affection for him could only really be for one reason?

I have to act normal. I have to not let on that I know it was him doing the killing. People like him are very attuned to shifts in reactions to them. They know when people find out the true them. I'm pretty sure that's why Dennis likes me – I worked out who he was an age before Brian and Maisie/MJ did, probably sooner than his other trainees, and it didn't faze me. I didn't change towards him – I wasn't scared and I wasn't conciliatory. And because of that, he probably thought I was like him – a bit of a psychopath. I am not, and yes I would know if I was, but Dennis thinks I am.

I am in more danger than I anticipated. Aidan will absolutely finish me off the first chance he gets.

'If you don't mind me asking, how did you end up in a children's home?' I ask.

He doesn't say anything for a time and I wait. I need to draw him into conversation so everything seems normal.

'I was abandoned as a baby. Found on the steps of a hospital. No one ever came forward to claim me.'

'And how do you feel about that?'

'What is there to feel about it? She didn't want me. She left me.'

'Do you want to talk about it?'

'With you? What do you think?'

'Fair enough,' I say. 'How is Robyn?' I have to keep talking to him. Annoying him like I normally do.

'She's . . . She's ready. She's ready to see her father. Speak to him. She's ready.'

'Neither of us believe that she is going to talk to him. She hasn't done all of this simply to speak to him. But before she goes there, I want to talk to her, get her to agree to come into custody after she's done whatever she's going to do. As long as she's not going to kill him – I don't want that for her.'

'You really think you're her mother, don't you? You and that "therapist". You really think you can make her do whatever it is you want her to do. That you can control her like her father did.'

'I just want to help her. Just like Dr Mackenzie only wanted to help her.'

'If you wanted to help her, you would give her the address without any conditions.'

'Do you have a girlfriend, Aidan?'

'No.'

'So you and Robyn never . . . ?'

'She's practically my sister. I'm practically her brother.'

'Right, right. Fair enough. Well, you know, I'm married.'

'Good for you.'

'Yes, yes, it is good for me, actually. It's good for me because when I want to do crazy things, he pulls me back. He doesn't let me do what I want without conditions. That's because he cares about me. Sometimes, you need someone to pull you back from the brink. I've been trying to pull Robyn back from the brink. Just like Dr Mackenzie tried. Just like you, I'd imagine, because anyone who cares about someone, wants them to be happy and they want them to be safe. I know that's what you want more than anything – for Robyn to be safe.'

Now that I am profiling him, I know the need for him to appear like the good guy in front of Robyn, in front of the world, actually, but especially in front of Robyn, is what I have to keep pushing on. It's what may be the one thing that stops him killing me once we get to Robyn's father's house. Maybe.

He lapses into silence and I know that I've got him there. He can't very well say that he doesn't give two figs about Robyn because it's not true and he knows I will make sure she finds out about it if he does confess he doesn't care. He does care about Robyn, in the only way that a person like him can. Just like Dennis cares about me and cares about Aidan, this guy next to me is capable of caring about people, in a very particular way. In the way that feeds their ego, bolsters the narrative they have about themselves.

As well as trying to stop him from bumping me off the second he gets the chance, I'm also telling him that I'm not going to just sit back and let him do whatever he wants.

That I will put up a fight. Probably not a long fight, but a fight nonetheless.

Tommy

7 June, Near London

Before he met the Henwrights, Tommy had only loved two people in his life – Holly and Robyn. He had hated so many more. So many.

For as long as he could remember, everyone had thought he was weak and small. They thought he was easy to push around. They made fun of his night terrors and they bullied him even though Holly punished them severely for it.

When Robyn had arrived, she had changed everything. She stood up for him every chance she got. Not just with Andrich, but with the others, too. When he would have bad dreams and night terrors, when he was afraid to go to sleep because of the horrors of the dark, when he would wet the bed and they would laugh, she would push people over, she would shout at them, she would tell them she'd fight them if they didn't leave him alone – and she would always follow through with a punch, kick or shove. She never backed down when it came to protecting him. When Robyn arrived, his life got a million times better. And he loved her for that.

But that didn't take away his hatred for others. That didn't stop him wanting the people who had hurt him to pay. And, more than that, he wanted the people who had hurt Robyn to pay. He knew he could never do that, though. She kept saying that her father was untouchable. That they could never find him even though he was controlling her life and watching her.

The Henwrights were good people. They cared for him; they loved him. Nothing was too much if he wanted it. They gave him the world and more. They hadn't minded when he wanted to keep his surname when they adopted him, and had been satisfied with him changing his first name to Aidan. They hadn't been happy that he signed up for the military, but they loved him enough to support him no matter what. His new mother had asked him why he wanted to go into the military and he had just said because it seemed like something he would enjoy. He couldn't tell her that it was because he might see actual combat. That if there was another conflict overseas, he might get the chance to fight. To kill. More than anything, he wanted to find out what that was like. How it felt to do that.

There were so many people who he wanted to kill, but he would never get the chance to do that without losing his freedom in the process. In the military, in the air force, he would be able to do that and no one would stop him. In fact, they'd encourage him to do it.

He worked hard – he worked so hard. And he got strong, he got taller, he changed his hair, he learnt to fight, he learnt to defend himself, he learnt to focus his rage and anger and hatred into being the best soldier he could ever be. Everything was on track, ordered, precise. Perfect. He was rising through the ranks, on course to be an officer . . . And then one of the generals on his base got drunk, smashed into Tommy's car. He nearly killed both of them and put Tommy in the hospital for weeks. His mother came every day, cried for the first couple of weeks. Holly visited. She told Robyn, so she visited, too. They both cried when they saw that his face had been smashed up, that he'd need extensive surgery, and it would take months and months for him to get back to normal.

It was a terrible time, but it all worked out in the end – to make it all go away quietly, they offered him a job in the intelligence services, said he would make a brilliant agent. Fast-tracked him through. He loved it. Thrived. Excelled at everything and learnt so much. It was like he was born to do it.

Tommy had never felt so fulfilled. His life was back on track, things were looking up. The future was clear. Sorted. Perfect.

And then Holly died. Holly was taken from him.

Everything imploded. His mind collapsed in on itself because he couldn't comprehend how she was gone. She had been his mother for so long. She had been a constant from since he was a tiny baby and now she was gone. Now she had been taken from him.

He didn't show it, but he raged at the world. He raged at everything. He wanted to burn down everything and everyone. He wanted the world to stop spinning so they could acknowledge his loss. He wanted to hurt everyone like he was hurting.

Holly was gone. And the people who had hurt him, had hurt Robyn, were still here. They were still walking, talking, living, when Holly wasn't. How was that fair? How?

Tommy had had enough. He couldn't take any more of this. He had to do something. He had to redress the balance. He had to make someone pay for the pain he was in. He had to make someone pay for those bastards still being alive when Holly wasn't.

When Robyn said she was going to find her father by going after all the people who had helped him get away with murder, he immediately offered to help. Because this was a sign. A way to finally repay the girl who had saved him. This was his sign to stop the indescribable pain he was in by balancing the scales, by delivering *real* justice.

This was his sign that his time to kill had finally arrived.

Kez

7 June, Near London

'Where is he?' Robyn asks the second I get out of my car.

'Nearish by,' I reply.

We are standing a little way away from the bright lights of the Cobham services. That's where I met Jeb to hand over the children when we split up. It's busy, but where I have parked, they could both jump me and drag me off without anyone noticing, so I am being careful to keep both of them in front of me and in sight at all times.

'Don't play with me,' Robyn says.

'I am not playing with you, Robyn. The fact you're meeting me here says that Aidan told you that I said I would give you the coordinates if you agreed to hand yourself in after you've seen him.'

'I'm not going to do that,' she replies.

'Did you even think about it?'

'I'm not going to do that,' she repeats. 'I *can't* do that.'

'I will speak up for you. You may get out of prison early.'

A smile as spiky as barbed wire twists itself on her lips. 'You're not listening to me: *I can't do that.*'

'If you've got claustrophobia or anything like that—'

'STOP!' she shouts. 'Just stop. You may be this big-time profiler

418

who knows everything about everything and everyone, but you don't know me. You don't know what I've had to do. So stop. I just want you to tell me where he is and I'll do the rest.'

'I'll take you there,' I eventually say.

'No. No. Just tell me and you can go.'

'Whether you realise it or not, you've spent a lot of time studying human behaviour. With that in mind, how likely do you think it is that I'll just hand over the address and walk away?'

In unison, she and Aidan sigh in frustration.

'I will take you there,' I repeat.

'We could make you tell us,' Robyn says.

'You could try,' I reply. 'But, honestly, haven't you got bigger things to worry about? You really want to expend your energy fighting me when the cause of all of this is not far away?'

'Just tell me.'

'I will take you there.'

Her soft brown eyes have hardened like tourmaline, her lips have set like resin. She has one purpose and she has accepted internally that she has to let me come with her, but is still fighting it. I'm running out of chances to stop her from killing her father. Now that I know she didn't actually kill those other people, this is going to be even harder on her. I know that I can't actually stop her if she has a mind to do it, but I don't think she has a mind to do it. I think she wants to hurt her father, but not kill him. But if it is just her and Aidan, he will find a way to force her to do it. And once he has got her to do that, he will find ways to get her to keep doing it. I am fighting against a lifetime of shared experiences here, but I am going to fight. I'm going to keep fighting until the last.

She's not my child, but as I'm often saying to Zoey and Jonah, we don't live in a world where we just look after ourselves and screw everyone else (I don't say the screw part to them, obviously). Or, rather, we live in a world where too many people just want us to look after ourselves and that is not what humanity is about. Humanity is about looking out for each other, even if we don't benefit directly from it. When we support each other, when we try to save each other from the worst of our excesses, we create a better world for everyone.

I am not going to let Robyn do this without fighting for her to find a better path first. It's as simple as that.

'I'm sure Aidan here has told you I'm all kinds of irritating. That I don't let things go and I annoy the hell out of pretty much everyone I meet. Which is strange because I'm convinced that I'm a really nice person. But we can get moving a lot quicker if you just accept that my default setting of being annoying means I am coming with you no matter. Well, it means that I'm going to take you to him.'

She and Aidan look at each other, and decide that I'm right – I am annoying enough to keep arguing until they concede to take me with them.

Kez

7 June, Near London

Aidan drives us to the location, a smallish housing development just outside London. Robyn has hired a car but is too nervous to drive. And they were never going to let me drive in case I took them to a police station. Which I wouldn't do, but they weren't to know that.

Since I walked into the Insight offices this morning and saw Aidan sitting at his temp desk, laughing and joking with Bruce, I've had my heart lodged beside my vocal cords while my mind has been fighting the overwhelm that the excess adrenalin wants to cause. I have to keep forcing myself to breathe, to calm down, to remember why I'm doing this.

Robyn and Aidan have been arguing all the way over here about how to get in the house, what to do if he's not home and what they're actually going to do when they get there. It's so odd because it sounds like they haven't actually thought about what they would do when they finally found him. Having said that, it's not completely odd because Aidan was clearly hoping the searching phase would go on and on. That he could kill and kill and kill again, in plain sight.

I do not know how long he would have kept Robyn alive, because she has a conscience and she would have grown very sick of people dying and her being blamed. And when she worked out that he was enjoying it all a little too much, she would have challenged him. People like him do not like being challenged, not even by the person they are actually capable of having feelings for.

'Look, the only solution is to let me go to the door,' I say as we approach the housing estate, a new-build that is so different from the original family home that it's hard to believe that Robyn's father could stand to live here.

'Shut up,' Aidan snaps. He has not enjoyed Robyn arguing with him, at all. People like him very rarely do.

'Don't talk to me like that, Big Bad Aidan. Or was it Luke? Or Fred? It's not very polite to speak to me like that.'

He takes his eyes off the road to glare at me.

'What are you saying?' Robyn says, calmly. 'Why should you go to the door?'

'Because I can pretty much guarantee that they will have at least one person in the house for protection. They will have put them there the second they realised what you were doing. They will be looking out for you. They will not be looking for me. I can talk my way into the place and then let you in.'

'And warn them? Yeah, right,' Aidan scoffs.

'If I wanted to warn them, I would have sent Dennis my location, I would have told the police what we were doing, I would have turned your raggedy arse in by now. But I haven't. Because I want to help Robyn. I want to help her talk to her father. And then I want her to do the right thing and turn herself in. I just want to help her.' I leave the accusation: *Do you want the same?* hanging silently and damningly in the air.

'She's right, you know,' Robyn says. 'They won't be looking out for her. They'll be thrown cos she doesn't look like a threat or an assassin, or anything but a middle-aged woman, really.'

'You cheeky mare,' I declare, outraged.

'True though, isn't it?'

'Didn't say it wasn't true, just that you're a cheeky mare for pointing it out.'

Robyn smirks, laughs a little. Connection made, finally. *Finally.* I just need to make a few more to sow seeds of doubt about what she plans to do. 'If she goes to the door, then we can get an idea of who and what we're dealing with,' she says.

'I suppose,' Aidan grudgingly agrees.

We pull up round the corner and agree that I am going to the door first. Aidan says, just as I'm about to go round the corner, not to get any funny ideas about calling the police. 'How about unfunny ones?' I respond and it makes Robyn smile, despite her nerves. Another connection. I haven't got enough time to make any more, but I can build on what I do have. I have to.

I can hear my breath, not ragged but definitely loud. I have to calm down. I have to arrive at the door with a calm aura and a smile. I have to not look as absolutely terrified as I feel. I am trying so hard not to think of what happened with Brian. How I walked in there knowing I was most likely not walking out of there alive. How I tried to reach him. How it was impossible. I almost managed it but not quite. Not quite.

'*Pick up the gun, Kez,*' Brian's ghostly voice from my dreams whispers in my head right now. '*Pick up the gun, Kez.*'

No. No. It's not going to end like that. It's not going to end like that this time. It's going to work out. Everyone is getting out alive. Everyone. Including me.

*

'Yes? Can I help you?' the person who opens the door to 67 Ferris Avenue says.

He is tall, about thirteen years old and the living image of Robyn. I draw back.

'May I help you?' he self-corrects. 'May I help you?'

I can't speak. I stand on the doorstep, staring at him, too shocked to say a word.

'*Give him to me.*'

I understand now. I completely understand. This is what Dennis has been truly hiding. This is what Robyn has been doing.

Robyn is not a psychopath, she is not a killer, she has only ever done things to protect other people.

Give him to me.

She wants this boy, her brother? Surely not her son.

'Give him to me' actually means 'give me this boy'.

Robyn

7 June, Near London

While Dr Lanyon is at the front, presumably talking to the police officer who is protecting my father, Tommy – sorry – Aidan and I climb over the high fence at the back of the property and make it to the maple-wood kitchen door. I am an expert lock picker. I've taught myself all sorts of things the last few years, and it doesn't take long to open it and enter the house.

We move quietly through the building, aiming for where I suspect the living room to be. We are correct – the living room is to the right of the stairs. And there he is. Sitting on the sofa, watching television.

I have built him up in my head to be more than he is. In my mind, he has always been a giant of a man, huge, monstrous, able to fill any space no matter how big. Here, he looks small, diminished. He sits in the old-fashioned armchair with his age-thinned hair, brown threadbare cardigan over a bobbled black polo shirt and creased brown chinos. He looks like the type of old man that he used to sneer at and make fun of.

My horror of a father is weak and small and puny.

'Hello, Dad,' I say with a smile. 'How are you?'

Kez

7 June, Near London

A tall blonde woman appears behind the boy – the 'him' from Robyn's notes – who answered the door.

'Honey, what have I told you about answering the door without finding out who it is?' she says with a smile so fake I'm surprised her face doesn't crack. She places a hand on his shoulder, and I spot the shiny wedding ring on her finger. The way she has placed her hand on his shoulder is awkward. She hasn't done this very often. She stands at an angle, hiding a gun, I suspect. Undercover police officer. Assigned to protect Henry Chambers since Robyn's threat became real. This woman is doing a terrible job. She hasn't trained this boy not to open the door to strangers. And she can't even act like she's his mother convincingly. She most likely resents this assignment because she was given it because she's a woman. Plus she's protecting a terrible human being. I suspect I wouldn't be happy with that, either.

But, much as I would resent the job, I would still do it to the best of my abilities, which she clearly is not. And, anyway, shouldn't there be two officers? Why isn't the other one stopping this from happening if she's not capable of it?

'Hello, I was wondering if you could help me? I'm looking for Henry Chambers?' I say. 'I need to talk to him. About his daughter.'

I said I was going to talk my way into the house. This is the quickest way. Let them know I know who he is.

Her face hardens like quick-drying cement. 'There's no one here by that name,' she says, and goes to shut the door.

As I put my hand on the door, hold it open, I flash my ridiculous badge, show that I am not just some rando off the street, as my children would say. The boy, who I have to stop myself staring at, is rapt.

'We both know who you are and the real reason why you're staying here. Who you're protecting. I'm desperately trying to stop something terrible happening. So please let me in.'

'Take your hand off my door,' she threatens.

'I wouldn't be here if it wasn't important. I don't have much time. They're going to be arriving very soon. And once that happens I can't help you. Or him. I can't help any of you. I just need to talk to him. I'm hoping his need for self-preservation will outdo his utter contempt for someone telling him what to do, so I just need him to know what to say to Robyn when she gets here. What not to say to her. It will make all the difference.

'You can search me if you want. I have no weapons. I just have a need to stop this going horribly wrong. And now knowing there is this young person in the house, I really don't want things to go the way they are likely to go.'

I don't have time to get this woman on side, to make a connection. If there is one thing I do know about her, she is pissed off at being here. Nervous, too. She feels like she's been parked here. Probably paired with someone inexperienced who is more senior than her and treats her badly. Her higher-ups don't like her. She feels she is disposable to them.

'Look, I know what they told you. But they weren't being entirely honest. She doesn't want to harm her father, but she will if I can't talk her down. I know the last thing you need is a gun fight or any other type of fight. But it would sure piss them off if you brought in the person none of them could find. They've parked you here to make a point. But if you could bring her in, then that would show them.'

'Look, I really am trying to help. You can have your partner keep his firearm on me the whole time I'm in the house but I need to speak to Henry Chambers before they arrive. Once they do, it'll be virtually impossible to stop this disaster from happening.'

She looks at my badge again, looks at the boy, glances over her shoulder briefly before she relaxes her arm, and moves the boy aside to let me in. Robyn and Aidan agreed to give me ten minutes to get into the house. In that time, I was to lay the groundwork for a constructive conversation, and then they would knock on the door and I would let them in.

I knew I'd been dreaming thinking they would wait that long. But I did think they'd come to the door. Shows how ridiculous I truly am.

Sitting in the living room, opposite an older white man I can only presume is her father, are Robyn and Aidan. Anyone looking in at that scene would think the two younger people are waiting to be served a refreshing beverage in a china tea set, not that they are there to end the life of the man sitting opposite them.

Robyn

7 June, Near London

My father's head snaps up at the sound of my voice. Do I sound the same as I did thirteen years ago? Or has my voice matured, deepened?

'Avril?' he says, squinting in my direction. 'Avril, is that you?' His voice is insubstantial, so fragile that the words may crack and fall away before they can reach my ears. Tommy stands beside me and he sees what I see: a pathetic frail man that I have spent years making a monster in my mind. To me he was all-powerful. He had people run around after him to make sure he was safe after he did the most awful thing. He had other people watch me throughout my life. And all along he is this pathetic creature.

He is not worth harming. Even if I still had access to the stable at our old house, I would not bother with him. He is not worth it.

'Avril,' he says, 'I missed you. I didn't think I would. But I couldn't stop thinking about you. Have you seen your brother? Have you seen how big he is?' Dad wheezes as he laughs. That doesn't sound good, either. Maybe it's a good thing I'm here. Maybe he hasn't been abusive to Milo all these years and I've arrived just in time to take him away. Because that's what this has all been about. I have wanted Milo. Dad kept him. Said no one was separating him from his son. He didn't care what happened to me, because I am a girl. All he cared about was his male child. The child whose mother he took away when he was eleven months old.

I knew Uncle Dennis and Dad would know what I meant when I wrote 'GIVE HIM TO ME'. I knew they would realise that I wanted my brother, that I wanted to take him away from the life he would be enduring with a man like my father. I needed him to learn what being a man was really like, not emulate it from seeing how my father treated people. It was Milo I wanted, not my father. In the end, my love for my brother was stronger than my hatred for my father.

That was why I had to do anything I could to get him back. I know Mum would have wanted me to take care of him, to save him from my father. And that was why I will always be grateful to Dr Mac. He gave me the space and the time to work out what I had to do. I mean, I don't think he'd be very pleased that I used him and his address to put my plan into action, but he helped me in ways he will probably never know. When Holly died, I realised I had to start the process properly. I had to do whatever it took to find Milo.

'Sit down, Avril,' Dad says. 'Tell me about yourself. Is this your young man?' He squints at Tommy.

431

For some reason, Tommy and I do as he asks and sit down on the sofa opposite his armchair. Dad grins at us, looking genuinely happy.

This isn't going how I expected. I thought . . . I'm so confused. I thought he would be raging, that he'd be angrily indignant that what I was doing had made him move to this small place. I would love to live in a place like this, but Dad would hate it because he always liked to live surrounded by luxury. This would be hell to him. Well, it would be to the old Dad, but I'm not so sure about the new version of him. This version of him seems perfectly at home.

'Thank you for coming to see me, Avril,' he says. I hate that he is using that name. That name died with my mother years ago. And I became Robyn. I love that Dad doesn't know that about me, but I hate that him not knowing means I have to listen to him use that other name.

'I didn't come to see you,' I explain. 'I came to see Milo.'

Dad's finger flies to his lips and he shhhhushes me. 'You mustn't call him that. You'll get in trouble. There's people after us and you can't call him that. He's called Bobby now.'

I nod. He doesn't seem to understand things, either. Living like this must have taken its toll on him. The guilt about what he did probably contributed to his worsening mental health as well. I remember learning in one of Dr Mac's classes as well as in the long talks I had with him, that emotions such as guilt can take their toll on you physically. I don't wish this upon him, but I'm glad he's feeling something. Has felt something.

I am about to say something to that effect when Dr Lanyon arrives with the policewoman and Milo.

Milo.

A visceral pull comes from the centre of my being and I stand up, ready to rush towards him and gather him in my arms. Milo.

'When you were a baby,' I say to him, 'I used to hold you all the time.' He obviously has no idea who I am. And I probably should have said something else like hello, but I can't. I have to let him know. 'You were my favourite person in the whole world. I would hold you and rock you. Mum would be always telling me off because I would sit and watch you sleep. I wanted to feed you all the time. And carried you everywhere. I just . . . I just loved you so much.'

Milo stares at me. But he isn't scared. He's a little confused but he isn't scared. Probably because I must look familiar – he looks exactly how I looked at his age. He must recognise me on some level.

I physically restrain myself from running to him and throwing my arms around him. 'My name is Robyn. I'm your sister. Your big sister. I have been searching for you all these years. I've been waiting to see you again. I've done everything I can to find you.' I push my fingers onto my mouth, try to stop myself from crying. 'I can't believe you're here. Finally.

I can't believe . . .' I lose my words. Lose the ability to speak because I have so much emotion racing through my veins, unfurling all my cells.

When Mum told me she was having another baby, I was scared. Because she looked scared. She was happy but obviously terrified because – now I understand – Dad had been trying to further ground her, tie her even more tightly to him, because it's harder to leave with two children. It's hard enough with one, even harder with two. This was what Auntie Meryl was helping Mum with. It's only now I realise that as well as giving her money, Auntie Meryl was probably giving her the Pill, too. She was probably helping her to not get pregnant again. But once she was gone, Mum had no way of stopping it happening because he controlled everything. He went with her everywhere – there was no way she'd get to go to the doctor by herself and get contraception. There was no way she could stop that part of his plan. And he didn't stop doing to her what he'd been doing since that night the policeman came. But she made her peace with the pregnancy. She decided to be happy, and because she was happy or seemed happy, I was happy for her.

*

August, 2011

'Milo, this is your big sister,' Mum said. She was in a hospital bed and she was holding him in her arms. She had to stay an extra few days because there had been complications and she'd had to have something called a hysterectomy. It meant no more babies and I had seen anger cross Dad's face when they told him.

434

I couldn't stop staring at the brown face with long eyelashes, a small nose the same shape as mine and as Mum's, and pursed lips, poking out of the white bundle of blankets in Mum's arms. I couldn't stop staring at my brother. He was perfect. So perfect. 'Sweetheart, this is your brother Milo. Milo, your sister is going to look after you. She is going to always take care of you. Even if I'm not here, it won't matter because she will be.'

I smiled at Mum, at Milo. He was mine. Mum was telling me he was all mine. No matter what happened next, Milo was mine. I was going to love him, and teach him, and take care of him.

'Hello, Milo,' I said. 'Hello, baby. I am your big sister and I'm never ever going to leave you.'

7 June, Near London

Everyone is looking at Milo, wondering what he will do. How he will react.

How he reacts is to stare at me really, really hard. How he responds is to screw up his face as though a memory is coming to him. How he answers is to come across the room and throw his arms around me.

Does he remember me? I wonder as I pause for a moment, shocked still by his hold. Then I wrap my arms around him, draw him close.

'Hello, baby. Hello, Milo,' I say to him. He's nearly as tall as me. 'Hello. Hello.'

435

From Robyn's Last Will & Testament

I didn't tell you about Milo, that it was him that I was referring to in the notes because, as I said, I can't tell you everything in case this gets found before I've completed my mission. Milo has been at the forefront of my mind my whole life, since he came into my life. Everything has always been about him, protecting him.

That night, the night my mother was killed, is seared into my brain.

'Avril, go and get your books to do your homework!' Dad practically shouted, storming into the living room.

I was sitting at the dining table, feeding Milo, so I replied, 'In a minute, Dad. I'm just feeding Milo.'

Mum was in the kitchen making dinner again because the one she'd originally made was leftovers from yesterday's roast. She'd almost finished heating it up when Dad said not to insult him by asking him to eat stuff that should have gone in the rubbish bin. This was what we had every Monday after a roast, Mum replied, and Dad had gone to the stove, snatched up the saucepans and dumped everything in the bin – pans and all. Mum had apologised and had started dinner again.

She'd asked me to feed Milo while she cooked and that was what I was doing when Dad had told me to do my homework. I normally would have run to do it, so as not to upset him, but I only had a few more spoonfuls left to give him.

Without warning, Dad slapped me so hard I fell backwards off the chair. Mum heard the noise from the kitchen and came running in. She saw Dad with one hand around my throat, choking me, while the other hand was raised to hit me again. She ran at him.

'Leave her alone!' she screamed. 'Just leave her alone!'

She started to hammer on his back until he let me go and turned on her. She didn't back down, not for one second. She fought him.

I ran to Milo, who had started crying and I picked him up, I cradled him to me, hid his face so he wouldn't see what was happening. The sound joined the other noise that was lodged inside my head. The noise of what he was doing became another permanent mental resident.

I hushed Milo, tried to calm him down, but I didn't want to leave. I wasn't sure if Dad would come for Milo if I tried to carry him to safety. I wasn't sure what he would do in this state. I hadn't seen him this angry, hadn't heard so much horror in such a long time. And I didn't want to leave my mum. I didn't want her to be there afterwards all by herself.

Suddenly there was silence. Suddenly everything stopped moving, stopped being. It was like all the air and all the sound and all the darkness, the soothing, comforting darkness, had been sucked out of the room. Dad staggered back, looking down at his hands and then looking at where my mother was. I stared at him for the longest time because I didn't want to look at her. After every other time he had beaten her, he hadn't looked like that. He had never had that look of horror and triumph on his face. And, in the past, after he'd beaten her, she had come round almost straight away. She had staggered to her feet; she had shown me that she was all right. Hurt, damaged, but OK.

Today there was just silence.

There was a space. An absence where my mother had been.

When I finally turned, when I looked and finally saw her, I knew.

I knew.

And the world stopped turning. All sound and colour stopped existing. My mouth opened but there was no scream. There was no sound. I remembered the little boy in my arms. I didn't want to scare him. Mum told me that I had to look after him. That even if she wasn't here any more, I would take care of him.

Did she know? Did she know that it would come to this? Did she know and that was why she had told Milo and told me that I was meant to look after him? I carefully put him down, then walked over to my mother, holding Milo's hand. I sat down and pulled Milo onto my lap. I reached out and took Mum's hand. Milo didn't make a sound, didn't fuss or cry. He sat on my lap, put his thumb in his mouth and waited with me. I held on to Mum's hand and waited. Whatever was going to happen was going to happen.

I was just going to sit here with my little brother, holding my mum's hand.

7 June, Near London

'I remember you,' Milo says against my shoulder. 'I remember you. You used to sing to me.'

I did, I used to sing to him all the time. So he does remember me! He does! I hold him even tighter. He does.

They wouldn't let me stay with him. They made me leave him behind even though I fought and kicked and screamed. But they kept saying that it would be safer for him without me. They purposely didn't mention Milo in any of the newspaper articles because they didn't want people asking too many questions. People would always be curious to know what had happened to a baby who'd lost his parents in tragic circumstances – they would never forget that a baby had been left orphaned – so they wrote him out of our public story.

They took me away and left Milo behind because the bottom line was Dad wanted his son – he didn't care what happened to his daughter.

'I remember you,' Milo says again. 'I used to ask about you, about the girl who used to sing to me, but Dad said I was imagining you. He said you didn't exist.'

The bastard. He has gaslighted Milo his whole life. I look over at my father.

And suddenly he has shed the clueless lost look he had before – now he has a wide and deep sneer, his shoulders are square and he is getting to his feet. Suddenly he is the giant, the monster, I remembered him to be.

Without missing a beat, Dad steps forward, snatches the gun from the policewoman's hand and aims it us – Tommy, Milo and me.

The policewoman steps back, horrified. Dr Lanyon sighs with her whole body and then shakes her head like she can't believe this is happening.

'You almost had me convinced,' I say to him. 'You almost had me feeling sorry for you. You *bastard*.'

He turns the gun on me. 'Don't you dare talk to me like that!' he snarls. And there he is. There is the ogre that I know. The menace who terrorised my childhood. The bastard who killed my mother. 'I am your father! You will show me respect. You will show me respect!'

The police officer has obviously never seen this side of him. I don't know how long she has been living with him, but he will have hidden away who he is. Milo will know. Milo will have seen the real him – the quiet one who threatened you without ever raising his voice or saying the actual words and this one, who screams and scares. There he is, the horror that lives in each and every one of my nightmares.

To my left, I can feel every sinew and muscle in Tommy's body tense up, ready to fight. I know he desperately wants to get his gun out and start shooting.

Dr Lanyon looks like this is exactly the last place on earth she'd like to be. 'Can we all just calm down?' she says, her voice cool and controlled. 'Emotions are running high. We all need to calm ourselves before things get completely out of hand.'

My father sneers: 'Who the hell are you?' That moment's distraction is all Tommy needs to pull out his gun and aim it at my father.

'For God's sake, why have you all got guns?' Dr Lanyon says. 'What is wrong with you people?'

I push Milo behind me. I know my father. I know that rather than shoot me, he would shoot Milo because that would hurt me more. I hate him so much. And I hate the fact that he and I share blood. I want to be nothing like him.

I studied psychology because I wanted to know about the human mind. I wanted to know why my father was the way he was. And, most importantly, if I was going to turn out like him. If I would become an abuser who killed and who felt no remorse.

What I did to those people scared me because at certain points, it felt like I enjoyed it. I felt an unfamiliar sense of satisfaction. I did not want those feelings to grow, to take root and to flourish. That was why I only went after those who it was necessary to tap up to find Milo. I did not want to do it for too long, did not want to keep bringing that part of me out. Because if I wasn't careful I could end up like that bastard in front of me.

'Listen, all of you, listen,' Dr Lanyon says, moving into the centre of the room. 'This can't carry on. You all need to take a moment, take a breath. Mr Chambers . . .' Dad looks at her, askance, again wondering who the hell she is but also why she is using his name, which he probably hasn't heard in a lifetime. 'Mr Chambers, what do you want from this?'

He sneers again, his top lip curling right up. 'She's not taking my son. She came for my son and she is not taking him. He is mine.' Dr Lanyon has her hands up, and faces him. She faces him because she knows he is dangerous and you should not turn your back on him.

'All right, you want your son to stay with you.' Still staring at my father, she says, 'Robyn, what do you want to happen?'

'Milo is coming with me. Before he did what he did to her, my mum said I was to look after Milo. I fought them when they separated us, and I've done everything I've done to get him. I'm taking him with me and we're going to live together.' I look down at Milo. 'You want to come with me, don't you?' I ask him.

He nods. 'Yes.' No hesitation, no doubt. He wants to come with me.

'He's going nowhere,' Dad snarls.

'Aidan, what do you want to happen?' Dr Lanyon asks Tommy. Everyone is confused because he's not really a part of this, but I suppose he's here, so he is involved.

'I want him to pay for what he did to Robyn. I want him to suffer.'

'Right. OK.' Dr Lanyon sounds defeated, like she knows there's no easy solution to this. 'Police officer lady, what do you want to happen apart from getting your partner here to help and/or the chance to press the panic button and get help?'

Again everyone is a bit confused about why she's asking her. But, like the rest of us, she's in the room and she has skin in the game, I suppose.

'Everyone to put down the guns. Allow my colleagues to come in so we can all talk it out.'

'OK, yes,' Dr Lanyon says. 'So, no one is going to get exactly what they want. But let's see if we can find a middle ground. What about the three of you sitting down and working out if you can come to a living arrangement that will give you both what you want? I mean, Robyn, it doesn't matter where you are – you just want to be with Milo, don't you?'

'I suppose,' I grudgingly agree. 'But I've hurt people so they're going to want to lock me up.'

'Well, we're here because that doesn't always need to happen. And if you stay with him that's even less likely to happen.'

'Don't tell her that,' the police officer says. 'Don't make promises no one can keep.'

'Oh, shush,' Dr Lanyon says.

'Even if it is possible, I'm not living with him. Not after what he did. Do you think I could forget it? For even a minute? I watched him do it and I can't forget that. Every time I see him I feel sick. There is no way I am going to be near him for the rest of my life. No way.'

'My son isn't going anywhere. Do you think I waited all these years to have a son to let someone take him away?'

'Robyn, cover your brother's ears,' Dr Lanyon says sharply. *'Cover them, now!'* I do as I'm told, clumsily covering Milo's ears while still trying to shield his body from any stray bullets.

And just in time because my father says: 'Do you think I'm going to let her take my son away? That's what *she* was planning. She was planning to leave. She had a secret mobile phone. She'd saved up money. She even had a place to go, to hide from me. She was planning to take my son. Do you know how wrong that was? Well, I stopped her. I made sure that didn't happen. No one is going to take my son away from me. I will stop anyone who tries. I don't care who they are. What they are.'

I can't see Dr Lanyon's face, but her body language changes. It becomes stiffer, less suppliant. She is pissed off. Completely pissed off.

'Mr Chambers, I can see why you're saying that. But you need to understand something; you need to watch what you say. You asked before who I am. Well, I am the person who makes monsters scared. I am the only person who your biggest champion, Dennis Chambers, is petrified of. I am serious. I terrify Dennis and I can make him do whatever I want him to. Make no mistake, if I want to, I can make him rescind all of this. I honestly can. I've made him do all sorts of things over the years. So watch what you say. Watch. What. You. Say.'

I've never heard anyone use that tone with Dad before. Well, I have. Uncle Dennis. He spoke to Dad like that the night he came to the safe house. Uncle Dennis was never scared of him. Dr Lanyon is not scared of him. I wish I could say I'm not scared of him but I am. Of course I am. I know what he's capable of. I am terrified of him.

Dad looks unsure for a moment, the first time I've seen him look like that. Then he goes back to being himself. He goes back to being a monster.

'I've had enough of this,' Dad says. He swings the gun towards the police officer and pulls the trigger. No warning or anything. The bang – loud, sudden – makes me jump in fright, as it does Milo.

Tommy jumps a little. Dr Lanyon doesn't jump at all but she does look towards the police officer, who has grabbed her stomach, covering the entrance wound, dark red blood seeping through her fingers. 'Once she's dead, I am going to kill all of you,' Dad promises. 'All of—'

Another BANG! that makes me jump. This time, Tommy. Tommy has shot Dad. Another BANG! Before he falls, Dad has fired back and hit Tommy in the shoulder, which sends him staggering backwards. The policewoman, despite her wounds, launches herself at Dad and manages to bring him down. Tommy is recovering, righting himself, and is so angry his whole body seems to be on fire.

445

I grab Milo and run for the door, leaving them to fight it out. We need to get out of here now. *Now.* Milo doesn't resist; he moves when I pull him and we run out through the front door. I need to get him to safety – I need to get us both to safety. It's only as we hit the gravel path outside that I realise Dr Lanyon is right behind us.

'Robyn, Robyn, stop. Please, stop.'

Against my better judgement, I do as she asks, bringing Milo to a standstill next to me. I turn to face her and she looks full of regret. Like she doesn't want to do what she's about to do.

'I can't let you go,' she says.

'You've got no choice in the matter.'

'Ro—'

When I produce the black gun that Tommy pressed into my hands earlier, I swear she rolls her eyes. I'm the one holding the gun and yet she's managed to make me feel incredibly foolish. How does that work?

I strengthen my stance. I will shoot her if necessary. I like her. I like her so much, but she is not going to stand in the way of us escaping. I'm pretty sure I can hear sirens. We can't be here when they arrive. We need to get out of here. NOW!

Kez

7 June, Near London

I come running out of the house, chasing Robyn and her brother. I thought her brother would need convincing to go with her, but he seems relieved more than anything. Relieved to be getting away from his father. I can't imagine what he must have lived with. Lived through. Survived. I can't imagine what would be so awful in your life that when a perfect stranger rocks up and says she is your sister, you go with her.

'Robyn, stop. Stop. You need to turn yourself in. They'll understand what you went through. What your brother has been going through.'

She looks incredulous. 'No,' she says, horrified that I would suggest such a thing.

'You're going to be running for the rest of your life. You'll never stop looking over your shoulder. That's no life for a child.'

'No, that's *exactly* the life for a child of my father. Children who have been through what we have, we never put down roots. We're always waiting for someone to kick off, to kick our heads in because the day ends in a *y*. Running and not letting anyone know where we are is exactly what I plan to do.'

From nowhere, it seems, she has produced a gun. What is it with people and guns? Why are these people so comfortable with them? I have hated every second of being forced to hold one. Every second.

'Milo, I mean, Bobby, go round the side of the house. Out the back, there's a blue Mercedes.' She hands him some car keys. 'Go and get in it and wait for me.'

Without question, he does as he's told. And, again, I have to think how awful his life must be to just willingly do whatever a stranger tells him to. Or maybe she isn't a stranger. He said he remembered her singing to him, that his dad said he was mistaken. But maybe he does remember her. On a cellular level, he does remember her and how she protected him. He might remember her scent and her face. He might dream about her. There are so many theories about how bonds are formed in the early years, how we acquire and retain information. I wrote a whole thesis on how our sense of smell was one of our biggest receptors of information on an unconscious, subliminal level – that could be at play here.

'Put your hands up where I can see them,' she orders as soon as Milo rounds the corner. I do as I'm told. I'm sure in the distance I can hear sirens. I should keep her talking. I should keep her here for as long as possible. I'll be reminded by the police, by Dennis, that she may not have killed those people, but she did harm them. She did put them in Aidan's way.

'What about Aidan?' I say to her. 'You can't just leave him here to take the blame.'

'Aidan? The same Aidan who killed people? No one was meant to die. He was just meant to put them back in their homes and leave the notes. They were all alive when I finished with them. All of them. And Aidan killed them. And he let me believe that I had done it. I thought

I had gone too far with Ted Hartley and that he'd ended up dead. And he killed those other men. He used me to get revenge on the social worker, and he killed the policeman just for kicks.

'And don't forget he told me that Uncle Dennis had sent you to kill me. You were his special assassin, apparently, and you had to be taken out. He was planning on killing you, once I kidnapped you. I hope you realise that.

'I was *relieved* when you found that board because it had become his list of people to murder. I couldn't stand the thought of him killing them and I was so pleased when it was gone and the police were keeping an eye on those listed.' She shakes her head. 'I love him like a brother, but I want him stopped. He enjoyed the torture; I didn't, and I want nothing to do with all of that. I'm not sorry that my father shot him. He needs to be stopped.'

What a time to find out that she's seen through him. What a time!

'Robyn, I can't let you go,' I tell her. 'I'm sorry, I can't.'

I can hear the sounds of the fight going on inside the house.

'Robyn, I can't let you go,' I say to her again.

'You're not letting me do anything,' she says. 'I'm going.'

'You're not going to shoot me,' I tell her.

She stares at me as though I am right. She is not going to shoot me.

'We can explain everything to the police. I will help you in any way that I can. I'll even get Dennis to help you. I will make sure that everyone knows it was Aidan who killed those people. I'll do what I can to make sure you and Milo stay together. And that Milo is kept away from your father. I will do whatever it takes to help you.'

She nods at me. She's still holding the gun, but she nods at me. I'm getting through to her.

'I believe you,' she says. 'I believe you'll do whatever it takes to help me.' She nods again, wipes at a tear that has escaped her eye. 'I believe you,' she says.

Then pulls the trigger.

Part 14

Kez

9 June, Brighton

'Welcome back,' Jeb says to me when I open my eyes. He is sitting beside my bed, looking quite chilled, actually. Maybe now his greatest fear – me being hurt – has been realised, he can relax. He can accept that I might be hurt but it'll be OK.

One look at his face and I know that is not the case. He is simply restraining himself until I'm stronger. Oh joy.

'Out of interest, on a scale of one to ten, how much trouble am I in?' I ask with a croaky voice.

'You remember how Jonah, when he was younger, kept insisting that infinity wasn't the largest number because you could always add one? No matter what I said or explained, he was always on about the fact you could always add one to it to make it bigger?'

'Yeah.'

'On the scale of one to ten of how much trouble you're in, infinity plus one.'

'Cool,' I reply. *Really, really cool.*

*

453

Robyn shot me in the chest. Right side, not that close to my heart, but enough to hurt like hell. Enough for me to fall backwards, just like Brian did when . . . when I did what I did all those years ago. Enough for me to think I wasn't going to make it.

Before she ran away, Robyn came over to me, to check I wasn't dead, I presumed. She leant over me as I reached up to her. 'I'm sorry, I'm sorry,' she said. She clasped my hand, squeezed it like she was comforting me, then got up and ran away.

I tried to get up, tried to follow, but I was only moving in my imagination. I was only rising from the ground, running after Robyn within the confines of my own head. In reality, I was lying on the ground, silently screaming.

'*Pick up the gun, Kez*,' Brian said, suddenly appearing beside me. The pain was making me hallucinate. '*Pick up the gun, Kez*,' he mocked. '*Pick it up. Pick it up, Kez. Pick it up.*' He kept saying that to me, kept taunting me until the world became blank.

15 June, Brighton

'You could have told me about Topher, Kezuma,' Dennis says by way of a hello. 'It might have saved you from a bullet.'

I do not feel like talking to Dennis today. I am leaving hospital tomorrow and I do not want to speak to him. He is the reason why I am here. I thought I hated him before, but there are in fact levels of my hatred, and we have reached a new one. He has stayed away these past few days but has come here today because he knows I will not tolerate him being anywhere near my home. Not that I'm tolerating him especially well here.

454

'Topher has recovered from his injuries and has been taken into custody. He won't be seeing the light of day. I take it personally, people using my unit and my largess to commit multiple murders.'

He's made in your fucking image, though, Dennis. I would have thought you'd love him for it, I want to say. But I won't say that because I do not feel like talking to Dennis today.

'The police officer is fine, still in hospital but fine. She has been promoted. I'm sure you would want to know that since you care about people.' He makes caring about people sound like a fatal flaw instead of being the normal default setting of most humans.

'Robyn's father is still recovering from his injuries, but once he has he will face criminal charges for shooting the policewoman. He's likely to face a custodial sentence.'

Oh right, doesn't get put away for killing his wife but does get done for injuring a police officer. I can't even with that.

'I can't help him this time,' Dennis continues. 'I'm not sure I would even if I could. I probably shouldn't have helped him all that time ago. But what's done is done.'

I *still* do not feel like talking to Dennis. I stop glaring at the wall with the TV at the end of my bed and instead stare out of the window, watching the light play on the horizon. Wondering when he'll stop torturing me with his presence and just go away. Far, far away from me.

'There is no sign of Robyn and her brother. It's like they disappeared into thin air.'

I'm sure they have, I think but do not say.

'I've watched the CCTV footage of your shooting several times.'

Of course you have, I'm sure you got off on seeing me shot, just like you used to get off on sexually harassing me as part of my training. You would have loved seeing the moment the bullet hit me. You

probably smiled, imagining the red-hot searing pain ripping through
my chest, tearing apart tendons and blood vessels and muscle.

'It was very brave of you to confront her like that. To keep talking
to her even when she had a gun on you. Last time I thought it was just
because it was your husband's child pointing a gun at you. Now I find
it's anyone. You really will try to talk anyone into doing the right
thing – even if you're in grave danger. You can't assuage your guilt by
putting yourself in harm's way, Kezuma.'

What would you know about guilt?

'You have to speak to me at some point. You do know that, don't you?'

Some point isn't now, so no thank you.

'If it's any consolation, this is why I wanted you back with me, why
I knew I needed you to be a part of Insight. Those others, well, you've
seen them, every one of them obsessed with their careers and advance-
ment. They could never have solved this in the way you did. They don't
care about anything that isn't about a promotion to do things the way
you do. And I knew I could trust you to solve it without Robyn or
Henry losing their life.'

Never mind I nearly lost my life.

'I'm grateful.' He has managed to push so many notes of sincerity
into his voice that I have to turn to face him. He *looks* genuinely grateful. I know on so many levels that he's not capable of such emotions,
and, yes, I've been fooled by him – many times – before. But his face
is set in a way that seems authentically appreciative. 'They are, for
want of a better term, my family and I'm grateful to you for keeping
them alive. And for your part in helping Milo to be with who he should
be with.' Again, that sounds like genuine sincerity in his words and
voice, on his face and in his eyes. He might actually be grateful. *Might.*
Before I completely swallow the gullible pills and open myself up to

being manipulated and used by this disgrace of a man again, I go back to watching the world beyond the window.

'I'll expect you back at work next week, then.'

I scoff loudly. *Good luck with that.*

'Fine. Two weeks.' I hear him stand. 'I'll see you in two weeks.'

Whatever, Dennis. Whatever.

16 June, Brighton

'MAMA!' Zoey and Jonah screech as soon as I walk through the door with my arm in a sling. They come barrelling into me without a care in the world or even considering the nature of my wound.

'Gentle, gentle,' Jeb says to our children.

But, 'It's all right,' I say. 'Leave them. It's all right for them to do this.'

Yes, it hurts. Yes, there is pain, but right now, holding these two, being reminded of my real life, my real world, that is far away from all that I've been dealing with these past few months, is divine. Yes, even though there is pain, I have no place I'd rather be. No place.

'So, Mum, about the capital of Colombia?' Zoey asks as they lead me into the kitchen.

'Don't start this again,' I reply. 'Cos you lot, you're gonna lose. Big time. It's Bogotá, babies, Bogotá. When it comes to the capitals, I have three words for you: Bring. It. On.'

Kez

17 July, Brighton

'I almost couldn't believe it when I saw your name on the list,' Mac says to me when I settle in the comfy chair opposite him. Yellow, like the ones I had in my private practice office. His set-up is very much like mine used to be, too. Not that I should read too much into that. Not a lot you can do with four walls, a large window, desk, couch and three comfy chairs.

'Almost couldn't believe it?' I reply. It feels odd to be sitting on this side of the therapeutic relationship; humbling, too. When I used to speak to my supervising therapist, it was always on an equal footing: we were colleagues; she was trying to be my anchor. I could tell her as little or as much as I wanted. When I sat opposite her, I wasn't completely opening myself up, I wasn't being totally vulnerable. I could never tell her the whole truth about what had happened with Brian, what I'd been forced to do, so I was never being a hundred per cent honest in that chair. When you can't be honest in therapy, there is always a little element of control that you have that will make your status in that room on the same level as the therapist's. For therapy to work, you have to trust the therapist enough to be vulnerable and honest with them.

458

That is why I've always tried to make the person I am talking to as comfortable as possible so they can be as honest as possible and get the most out of our relationship. And if I sense they are holding back, then I know I either have to get them to be honest or I have to end the relationship. It does neither of us any good to keep talking when there is a lie, an unacknowledged truth between us – that will crack, shake and then eventually disintegrate any foundations for change and wellness we construct.

Sitting here, I know I have to be totally honest. And that is actually terrifying to me.

'Yes, almost couldn't believe it because I fooled myself into thinking you wouldn't torture me by coming here.'

'Sorry for ending your delusion.'

'I know why you're here,' he says to me while holding his notepad across his body like a shield, protecting himself from me. 'And you know that I'm enough of a profiler to know why you're here.'

'Why am I here?' I reply. I look down at my hands, trying to calm myself.

He waits, sits in silence until I lift my head to face him.

'You know I've fallen for you. That I think about you all day, every day. That I think you're my soul mate, and I fantasise constantly about us being together. And you also know my therapist ethics will stop me even thinking about making a move if you become a client.'

'I married one of my clients,' I state.

'I'm pretty sure you were in love with him. And I'm equally sure that you have, at best, only a passing interest in me.'

Our eyes lock together. 'I wouldn't be here if it was only a passing interest,' I state. 'You know that.'

This is what he needs to hear, and this is what I need to do. I need to help him move on from thinking something could happen with us, and I need to make sure I don't threaten my marriage in any way.

Mac relaxes suddenly, his whole body sagging as though a heavy weight has been lifted from him. He smiles to himself, then becomes serious – he's obviously filed the potential of what could have been between us away and is moving on. That is what I'm doing here, making sure we both move on.

He lays his notebook flat on his lap, produces a pen and writes my name at the top of the sheet. 'Hello, Kez, nice to see you. What can I do for you?'

I close my eyes, exhale. *I can do this. I know I can.*

'I killed someone,' I say when I open my eyes. 'My friend. Someone I cared about. I killed my friend. And he's haunting me. He has been haunting me for twenty years. I . . . I need help.' I haven't said I need help out loud about anything in so long. Jeb always seems to know, always seems to be right there when I need it, so I've rarely had to articulate it. This is different. This is difficult. 'I need help because I killed my friend.'

'Kez,' he says to me. 'Kez,' he repeats so I will look at him.

When I do, he stares directly at me. 'I can help you with that,' he says. 'I can help you with that.'

And it feels like he just might.

Epilogue

Kez

17 August, Brighton

'I think this is one of the best ideas you've ever had,' Jeb tells me.

'Oh, but my dear husband, haven't you always said I'm full of it? I always took that to mean I was full of the best ideas. And as such, they couldn't be narrowed down to just one "best idea".'

'What you talking about, woman?'

'No idea. No. Idea.'

We've checked into a hotel in Worthing, like we used to. But now we can afford a more pricey place and this one has an iron clawfoot tub in front of the huge picture window overlooking the sea, and a huge bed that is smothered in pillows. After a long bath together, we've been curled up in bed for hours and neither of us is planning on moving any time soon.

I love doing this with this man, pretending I don't have a care in the world. And even though I'm super relaxed, even though I feel unburdened right now, my mind keeps going to the brown window envelope I received yesterday that was addressed to 'The Homeowner'. It looked like a circular letter, and I was sure everyone on the street got a version of one, but I still waited until Jeb and the children were out to open it.

461

It *was* a circular letter. And it made me smile. I burnt it over the stove and flushed away the crumbled-up ashes in the downstairs toilet before anyone got back.

Two months earlier . . .

'Put your hands up where I can see them,' Robyn orders as soon as Milo rounds the corner. I do as I'm told. I'm sure in the distance I can hear sirens. And I can still hear the sounds of the fight going on inside the house.

'Robyn, I can't let you go,' I say to her again.

'You're not letting me do anything,' she says. 'I'm going.'

'You're not going to shoot me,' I tell her.

I'm aware of the CCTV cameras on us, that there is one positioned so it shows the front of Robyn and the back of me. And I'm aware that she's not going to get away if I keep her here much longer. Those are definitely sirens. Someone in the house must have hit the panic button.

Robyn stares at me as though I am right. She is not going to shoot me . . . *And she has to.* If she's going to get away, she has to shoot me.

'We can explain everything to the police,' I say. 'I will help you in any way that I can.' I uncurl a couple of fingers of my left hand, show her the small black flip mobile phone I am hiding there.

Shoot me, I mouth at her. It's the only way to get her out of here. 'I'll even get Dennis to help you,' I say out loud for the cameras, even though I know they don't have sound. I need her to react to me like I am saying all the right things. 'I will make sure that everyone knows it was Aidan who killed those people.'

Shoot me, I mouth at her again.

462

'I'll do what I can to make sure you and Milo stay together. And that Milo is kept away from your father. I will do whatever it takes to help you.' *Shoot me*, I mouth again. *You have to.*

She nods at me. She's still holding the gun and she nods at me. I'm getting through to her.

'I believe you,' she says. 'I believe you'll do whatever it takes to help me.'

I take a deep breath. *Do it now*, I mouth.

She nods again, wipes at a tear that has escaped her eye. 'I believe you,' she says.

Then she pulls the trigger.

The pain is indescribable. It lights up a path of agony through me as I'm knocked off my feet. It feels like the right side of my body is on fire. I scream silently as she runs to me, 'I'm sorry, I'm sorry,' she says, leaning over me.

'Sumaira Wilson,' I manage to whisper, reaching out my hand. She takes my hand, squeezes it to cover taking the phone. 'Call her.'

'I'm sorry,' she says again, and then runs off to join her brother.

'I'm wondering,' I asked Sumaira as she escorted me downstairs to be debriefed about the Russell Trufton interview from months earlier, 'if I wanted to help someone who's in a bit of a bad spot to "vanish", how would I possibly go about doing that?' She stopped in the stairwell landing between the seventh and eighth floors and said, 'I don't know how you would go about it, but how I would go about it is, I'd find someone who liked me. Someone whose job it was to make people dis-appear, and would be willing to help me. And then I'd do exactly as they said when the time is right.' I'd nodded and said thank you for the advice. Hours later, when she escorted me back to my desk, she'd

shaken my hand and slipped me a small black flip phone with only one number – her number – saved. 'When it's time, call.'

17 August, Brighton

Jeb runs his finger over the 'healed' scar on my right side just below the collarbone. I have ongoing physiotherapy because of the damage that one bullet did to the ligaments and muscles in that area of my body. And I have ongoing issues with my husband because every time he sees it, he has to swallow his words, force himself not to demand I leave Insight. We both know I can't. We both know why I can't.

Thank you, we're fine. We're away. And we're fine. I hope it didn't hurt too much when I shot you. I'm so grateful. She's gone, that girl. That's why I wrote her last will and testament. The person she was had come to an end. She's reborn. With a brother. With a happy brother. And we're lucky because we can start again, together. Your friend found my aunt M. We're with her. She's taking care of us, like she always tried to do. She has some photos of that girl from before with her mother. I finally have some photos. Aunt M says thank you, too. We're all together, just like Mum would have wanted. And that's thanks to you.

One last thing. Please be careful around Uncle Dennis. He is the most dangerous man I know after my father. Please take care of yourself.

You won't hear from me again. But know that we're doing so well. And we'll never forget you. x

Jeb kisses my neck and moves his hand lower down my body, away from the scar, causing the familiar tingling all over my body.

'*Was it worth it, Kez?*' Ghost Brian, who still visits me in my dreams but only screams at me sometimes now, asked me the other day. '*When you got shot and you may never get back full use of your arm again, was it worth it?*'

And what can I say to Brian but this: For them to be free? For them to get the chance of a better life? Yes, it was worth it. It was so, so worth it.

THE END

Acknowledgements

To...

my wonderful family

my agent, Ant

my publishers

my fabulous friends

my beloved MK2

my girls J & F

you, the reader for buying my book

Thank you for everything.

And, to G & E all my love always and forever.

Credits

These are the people who helped me make
Give Him to Me *happen:*

Excellent Editing
Jennifer Doyle

Other Great Editorial
Jessie Goetzinger-Hall

Copy-editing
Helen Parham

Proofreading
Sam Stanton Stewart

Audio
Ellie Wheeldon

Cover Design
Caroline Young

Production
Tina Paul

Marketing
Katrina Smedley
Jessica Tackie

Publicity
Emma Draude
Katey Pugh

Sales
Becky Bader
Frances Doyle
Izzy Smith

Amazing agenting
Antony Harwood

Expert advice
Dr Chris Merritt
Graham Bartlett

What Can You Give After Reading *Give Him To Me?*

When I write my books and stories, I often have a real-life trigger that inspires the tale I tell. With *Give Him to Me*, the inspiration was very much rooted in the reality of domestic abuse, a subject I've covered before in *The Ice Cream Girls* and its sequel – *All My Lies Are True.*

However, this time, I wrote about it from the perspective of the child in the abuse situation. How a young girl grows up watching her father, who everyone outside of the home thinks is a good guy, subjugate and destroy her mother. And for Robyn, my main character, not only is her father abusive, when his crimes are discovered, excuse after excuse is made for him to avoid taking real responsibility for his actions.

In *Give Him to Me*, there are a whole group of people who are directly and indirectly responsible for what happens to Robyn's mother. From the police officer who doesn't help her mother when she calls for help to the journalist who finds a way to downplay violence against women and girls, what I wrote in my book is the stark and horrifying reality for a lot of women across the globe when they try to get help to deal with an abusive situation.

For many, many women, 'just leave' is not an option, especially when trying to get traditional methods of help can be lacklustre at best and deadly at worst. And for a child growing up in that situation, seeing the abuse and being powerless to do anything, it must be devastating and life-changing.

It's the life-changing trauma of growing up in that situation that I explored in this book. I wanted to give some insight into the effects of being raised in a household where abuse is ever-present, I also wanted to reveal how our society, despite having all the right words, and public messaging, still makes it difficult – if not impossible – for those in abusive situations to break free.

It was tough-going telling parts of this story. Writing about how people mistreat those they're meant to love is always difficult, and it felt like I lived with the pain of these characters for the duration of telling the story. As always, writing the book had a fundamental effect on me. It made me realise that there is more that we can do to help others in terrible situations. That we can open our eyes to the circumstances of those around us. We can allow ourselves to be open to offering a listening ear to those in need. We can call out the lurid headlines that constantly seek to downplay domestic violence while tacitly blaming victims.

And we can demand better from those who are meant to protect and help those of us in these situations. It's not easy, no. And it's not as simple as it may seem I'm trying to make it sound. But we can try. We can try to forge strong links in our communities so that those going through difficult times know they can ask for help.

We can be a safe space, a listening ear for someone who might need it. Sometimes, just being there, being someone who is open to offering a kind word is all someone going living hell might need.

I hope you enjoyed the book and I hope it will inspire you to start to build a strong, supportive community wherever you are.

Dorothy Koomson
September, 2024